THESE RUINED DREAMS

THESE RUINED DREAMS

THE COLD AS IRON TRILOGY
BOOK TWO

KAYLA MCGRATH

CONTENT WARNINGS

This book includes content that may be disturbing to some readers, discretion is advised. Content includes graphic violence (blood, gore, body mutilation, decapitation, murder, death, death of family), sexually explicit scenes, vague mentions of sexual assault/sex trafficking, substance abuse (drugs and alcohol), and alcoholism. Content will shift to slightly darker themes throughout the trilogy, future warnings will be outlined in each installment.

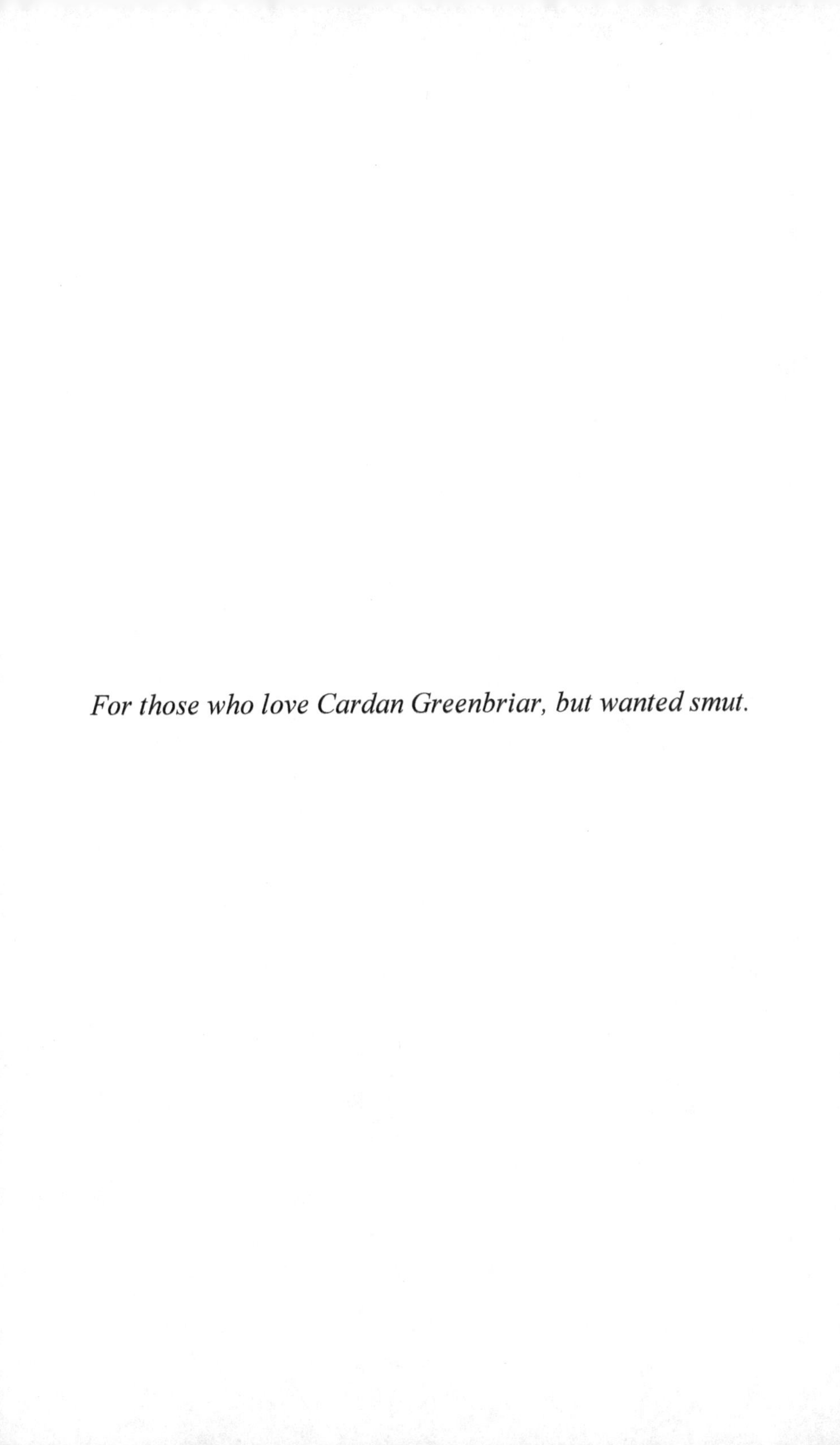

For those who love Cardan Greenbriar, but wanted smut.

CHAPTER

It has been said that a game of chess can be won in two moves. If only Lady Fate's game were as simple as that.

I pore over the verse of the prophecy-lullaby I've sketched down from the Prophet Witches, Bambalina and Sybella, rereading the same lines, hoping for enlightenment. I replace names with titles, and characteristics with personalities, circling around the point.

> *Rooks are crown and scorn,*
> *She is deceit, hers was apart*
> *Knights are murder and mourn,*

She is failure, her grief is heart
Bishops are sacrifice and cost,
She is three, his was death
Royals are found and lost,
She is true, his lies are breath
Pawn—

On the opposite page I have possible names listed for the nine pieces, yet the only two I am confident in are my Knights—Wisteria and Julia. "Mourn and heart" are a little obvious and "murder and failure" are as equally on the nose.

The Prophet Witches had defied their goddess by gifting me this prophecy, and they—at least Bambalina—were punished by Lady Fate for doing so. It was only given after the goddess had refused me a prophecy that I should have been rightfully entitled to.

My eyes flicker to a certain name on the page and guilt surges through me, making me reach for my glass water bottle.

The gin has a touch of a burn as it goes down my throat, hard and cheap. My preferred goldwine—smooth and rich— would bring into question my emotional state if I was caught drinking while training. So, I sit, watching Maelona train Julia, Wisteria, and Violante, who will in turn train the Crows. It is a circle of repeat and repeat until we die. I drink to that. The gin doesn't burn this time.

Maelona is a goddess-blessed gift in battle, her obsidian hair flashes in color with every sword stroke: in violet pride and burgundy wrath, sunny happiness, and blue melancholy. Her mood ring hair belies her emotions despite the blank canvas of her face. The refracted light from the sconces catches the metallic gleam in Maelona's bronze catsuit. The titanium overlay of deepest ebony is wrought in a skeletal corset of a ribcage and an anatomically correct—albeit highly flexible— spine, studded with black diamonds encasing her torso.

"If you don't know where their blade is, it will find *you* and you will pay dearly for it. Do not lose sight of it and be prepared for where it will fall," Maelona tells them patiently. I've never seen the warrior princess teach, but it seems quite natural to her.

Sighing, I drop my pen and bottle, and pick up Oath-Sworn, spinning it experimentally. The gold of the blade is a symbolic match to the false golden sky above us, the same one that matches the throne room and the very same one that terrified Violante.

"I can't go in there," Violante had protested, skittering to the edges of the wall after I'd rescued her from the depths of Unseelie territory and from the unrelenting weather of the Yukon. She'd panicked as she watched the shafts of false sun filter through the canopy of ivy, her ruby eyes wide.

"It's an enchantment. A false sky," I told her, sober but heartily wishing I wasn't, especially after the encounter with Emrys. My very skin had still burned with his touch, the arousal as abhorrent as my words. "The light is warm but not real. It's Seelie magic. Feel it."

Haltingly, eyes overflowing with trepidation she heeded my words, and that terror morphed into delight. It was a spot of pure goodness in a world of so much malevolence.

I remember this moment as I paste the hollowest smile on my face, filling it with smug satisfaction and letting the soft blur of liquor into the spots I miss. I take breaths saturated with the scent of home, of deep, overturned earth and low-priced juniper.

"Perhaps they'd like to see an example of true battle prowess?" I ask, serene and teasing. "It may entertain them to see you fight for your life."

Maelona sends me a scathing glance, humor on her face. "You are merciless, Evelyn."

I shrug, letting the slight jab roll off me. "It is war, darling. I can't go soft on you now."

She presses her glossed lips in a thin line. I smirk, seeing the small battle play out in her mind, before she unsheathes her dual moon scythes.

"Best two of three?" she suggests.

"Agreed."

Wisteria, Violante, and Julia take their seats along the edge of the training room, the wooden benches lined with their water bottles and sweat rags. Julia drains half her water, rivulets sliding down her neck and between her cleavage. Wisteria fans herself with her faded band tee, exposing the curvaceous swell of her midriff and jewel-pierced navel. Violante sits beside her, all anxious energy and slight touches, as if proving to herself that she's truly here and no longer alone, bound to Caethes's every beck and call.

I feel for the vampire girl, having been turned only as a teen, and forever frozen between the changing of fifteen and sixteen.

I hold Oath-Sworn aloft, ready. Maelona flashes with excitement a moment before she launches forward, coming at me in a whirl of blades and a desire to prove herself. I tip backwards beneath the cyclone of her scythes, twirl, and send a booted kick to the center of her false spine. It is a testament to its craftmanship that it does not break as Maelona buckles. I laugh, but before I can celebrate my little victory, she has regained her footing and raises her blades. I'm in her guard before she can bring them down.

"One," I tell her, my sword across her throat. I grin, remembering the last time I had her in this position—the impulsive kiss.

Maelona's nostrils flare, sniffing, and she turns aghast. "Are you drunk?"

"No," I say quickly. Because I'm not, but I wish I was.

She stares at me hard, backing away, and lowering her blades. Her hair flickers a motley riot of blue, red, and white. "I'm not fighting you when you're drunk,"

"I'm not drunk."

"You smell like liquor." Maelona looks to my glass water bottle sitting beside my notebook and pen, scribbles of the Prophet Witches' words an unintelligible scrawl across the pages. "Tell me that bottle over there doesn't contain any gin."

I thin my full lips, unable to lie, the simplest of fae curses. As a faerie, Seelie or Unseelie alike, we are bound by the inability to lie, forced to twist the truth or pass off untruths as we believe them.

Powered by my lack of response, Maelona stomps over to my belongings, her hair wholly the dark berry red of rage. Embarrassment burns through me and I race after her, overtaking the furious Lady of the Seelie Court, snatching up the bottle before she can. Keeping my eyes trained on my best friend and sometimes lover, I gather up my bottle, notebook, and pen, pointedly refusing her.

"Give me the bottle, Evelyn," Maelona says flatly. The demand in her voice is that of royalty—someone who will not be questioned. But she reserves a low volume, as a courtesy to our friendship so we are not overheard.

I adopt the same level. "I don't appreciate not being taken at my word. I said I wasn't drunk. That should be enough."

Anger flares on Maelona's face for a fraction of a second before she reins it in but, her dark eyes—normally warm like decadent chocolate cake—are sharp and cutting. "You've just returned to us; I do not wish for you to drown your sorrows in a bottle." Maelona's voice softens. "I can't see my best friend destroy herself. I refuse to watch it and I will have no part in it."

Maelona's words strike a nerve and I grit my teeth to hide the shame, and force myself to not look away like I want to. Drinking has been my escape since I returned from the Unseelie Court three weeks ago. Since I abandoned Gideon. Since I came onto Maelona. Since I told Emrys to die.

"If you're struggling you can talk to me," she murmurs.

And that does it. Because I can't. I cannot talk to my best friend about my sorrow and struggles because I am not just Evelyn Vanora, Lady of the Seelie Court, or the *Ceidwad Cudd,* spy and Keeper of Secrets, but also, the legendary Harbinger, an unbeatable warrior. I cannot be weak. My weakness is my queen's vulnerability and I refuse to speak those shortcomings into existence. I cannot speak of my abduction, the butchering of my wings, the lonely years of broken memory, the loss of Gideon, the deal I made with Lady Fate, Corvina's death, or of anything else I still don't remember.

"I think I just need to be alone."

"Right," she says, clipped. "You do that. I'll continue training."

I nod to the current company and stride from the training room, slamming the doors behind me with a satisfying crash.

I shutter my eyes and exhale sharply, hurrying to my suite. Several flights of stairs and many hallways later I find myself opening my door, revealing the chaos of my rooms.

Everything is the emerald of the Seelie Court, and if it isn't, it's live-edged wood, gilt-edged glamour, or wrought iron sadism. My bed, a mess of velvet and down, is littered with empty bottles and full notebooks, the chaise lounge that Gideon slept on—the one Emrys pinned me to and kissed down my throat and between my breasts—is brutally slashed from a drunken rampage three nights ago, stuffing puking from it like a sad cloud. The stairs that lead down to the obnoxious center-sunken level of my sleeping area are sticky with spilled wine and the stoic victim of one too many kicks of fury. I don't even want to look at all the jewelry thrown around the room, every piece reminding me of Corvina, the twin sister I buried like she was *nothing*.

This time when the grief strikes me, it strikes me down and I drop to the floor, lying against the stone with no will to move ever again. Cheek placed to the cool stone, I stare at the bathing chamber door and the jewel-hilted blade deeply wedged in it. I turn to the armchair by my face, and with my new view of its underside, I discover a half-drunk bottle of goldwine. I grab it and drink lazily, letting the wine dribble out the side of my mouth and onto the floor—banishing the lingering taste of juniper gin out of my mouth.

Desolation settles in me as I remain prone, drinking and spilling on the floor, feeling like I've hit absolute rock bottom yet I'm certain there's still a trench yawning below me. The expectations that I shoulder and the reputation I've created strain against me. Against every step, every word and every lash against my tortured soul and monstrous spirit.

I am not a good person. I am selfish. I am cruel. I am morally depraved.

I used Gideon. I used Maelona. I used Emrys.

I clench my eyes shut against the shame and take another drink, waiting for that haze. For that softened blur. For the oblivion that I so crave. It doesn't come. Apparently three weeks of binge drinking has triggered my body into thinking alcohol is my next attempt at mithridatism.

Memories surge at my decades of mithridatism. Of the deadly practice of creating poison immunity by ingesting small quantities over time. Emrys and I, during our false hundred years of Century Training, dosed ourselves with arsenic, belladonna, cyanide, hemlock, wolfsbane, and more, including iron. I remember the first time we were given the poisons by our mentors, guided on how to distribute it, how much to take of the exact measurement, how long between doses, and what to expect. They believed in us because years before they *were* us—training Centurions.

I try to ward off the painful thoughts by will alone, shaking my head. When I open my eyes again, I gape, startled to find an Unseelie blade strapped beneath the armchair I've made my view.

Scrambling to release it from its bindings, I look down at the silver athame, at the Unseelie Court sigil etched into the pommel. A full moon cupped by antlers and crowned by anemone flowers. The hilt is worked with feather wings, the grip a twisting spiral.

Emrys and I had traded matching blades during Century Training, an ancient formal practice between Centurions. By imbuing the blades with our blood, a tether between the two athames was created letting us use a limited line of communication when letters would not or could not suffice—since modern technology does not work in the courts. All it takes is a prick of blood and intent, and we can signal to the other a time. We always know the place.

Three years ago, I made Emrys promise to never contact me unless I called for him first. He swore and I've never summoned him. Had I not forced him to swear over something so insignificant I wouldn't have been trapped in the Yukon.

I place my middle finger to the still sharp tip, watching crimson slide down my finger, and whisper, *"Afon* Emrys."

Willing the magic into existence, the blade glows gold. I command one flash—to get his attention. Three breaths pause. Twelve flashes to indicate the time. I wait with bated breath, thrumming with anticipation, wanting him to refuse, wanting him to accept.

One silver flash at my vision—attention.

I wait; one for no, two for yes.

One silver flash.

Another silver flash.

The woods bordering the edge of the Seelie realm carry a chill while a carpet of fog lines the infinitely tall barrier. As with the Unseelie Court, the Seelie Court resides in a pocket realm, the very edge of which is an eternally looping forest compared to the cliffside drop encircling the bubble of the Unseelie territory. Each court is only accessible through the Faerie Roads and while the realms only exist in the pockets, the territories in the regular world span across the human lands.

Here, beneath the midnight sky—not golden, as it's not within the palace—I wait, dressed in slate-blue leathers, the

Unseelie athame strapped to my thigh. My hair, in elaborate braids is disheveled from sleeping on my floor, and the buzz I'd been working on hours before is long gone. I tap my fingers anxiously, itching for something.

The night air has a bite, the chill creeping along my skin with fingers of ice. Needles on the pines are covered in dew drops, iridescent in the lunar shine. I watch as one drop slides down, distending and then plummeting. It's foolish, but for a moment I feel it reflects the emotional turmoil raging inside me. The tension and the separation from the whole.

In the darkness, under the waxing moon and a sky full of diamond stars, I watch the fog, waiting for a new shadow to appear. The palace glows in the distance, beckoning with corrupt comforts. I ignore it and pace. Watching and waiting, anxiety trilling, hope and fear mingling like a nauseating cocktail.

While the fae can't lie, they can deceive, and despite Emrys agreeing to come, he never spoke the words. For all I know I'm waiting stupidly in the dark, getting colder by the minute while he's sleeping soundly between his sheets or hooking up with any amount of gorgeous besotted bedmates.

I ignore the roil in my gut and clasp my hands behind my back.

At exactly midnight, when the clocktower from the highest point of the palace tolls mournfully into the night, I feel awareness from my unique fae ability, before Emrys strides out of the fog, the mist curling around him like a caress. He's wearing a white blousy shirt, thin gold chains, and black leather pants. The dark and light contrast of his clothing brings out the stark brightness of his unnaturally red hair, some strands dark as garnet and others bloody as ruby.

I breathe slowly, relief coursing through me, the heat from my lungs clouding the cool air.

"You're here."

"You asked," he says softly, his gold eyes guarded.

Something soft and fragile comes to life within me, like a tentative wing emerging from a chrysalis. I feel it touching the air, and sensing the wind, wondering if it's time to appear. It brushes across my face, touching the corners of my lips, the light in my eyes. It makes my heart flutter as it grows in confidence. Rather than set it free, I squash it down.

Instead, a dead thing crawls across my face—contempt, disdain, and a haughty mask that feels as flimsy as tissue paper. I let the façade sit on my features, knowing that the smallest ripple will tear it; the wind of words, the rain of tears, the flame of emotion.

I must be silent a beat too long because Emrys groans.

"Why do you beckon me now? To gloat? You want the satisfaction that you single-handedly manipulated the monarchs into a war?"

"I want to trade information."

"You want to work with me now? Vanna, you literally told me to die three weeks ago."

An uneven thump wobbles in my chest at the use of my nickname. "Glad to see you didn't."

Sighing Emrys looks skyward, the golden coins of his eyes flicking to the heavens, very likely praying for strength to suffer me. "Just tell me what you want so we can get this over with."

Something about his dismissal and urge to be away from me bothers me deeply. The feeling vibrates like a plucked string, but I settle it with a firm hand and swallow, leveling my gaze at him.

"I want to know if Gideon is okay."

Emrys's nose twitches like he smells something vile and he looks to the side, gritting his teeth, the slightly pointed incisors lightly denting his lip. "What do I get in return if I tell you his current state?"

"I'll tell you about how I met with the Prophet Witches."

Emrys's burning gaze whips to mine and for a moment he is defenseless, his concern laid bare. The sharp angles of his face soften, desperation touching its planes. "Vanna, you wasted your prophecy? And you're willing to trade it for a word of him?"

"Yes."

Pain blooms across his face and suddenly everything in me wants to eat the words I've spoken tonight, to chew every syllable just so I don't have to see that sorrow again.

Emrys is many things, but he is also my mirror. He knows me better than Gideon ever dreamed, than Maelona imagined, than Corvina thought. For everything my twin was, she was not my opposite, my true equal. That title belongs to Emrys, and try as I might, that will never change. I had twenty years with Corvina, I've had more than a hundred with him.

"He's alive," Emrys begins, voice hard. "He's healing from that sword in his chest and at this point it won't kill him. Thanks to his vampire blood."

Because Gideon is a halfling. Half his blood is vampire, the other half all too human.

"Is he being kept well?"

"No. Now I need information from you."

"The Prophet Witch was named Sybella, but I also spoke to another, Bambalina," I pause. "Your turn."

Emrys twists his mouth in amusement. It wasn't exactly what he wanted but a trade is a trade. He must believe he has the upper hand. Prophet Witches are more valuable than an ex-protector reject of a halfling.

"He's being held in Caethes's chamber for now."

My heart sinks. "Is she—?"

"No," he's quick to reassure. "She doesn't touch him like that. She has Arawn for her personal matters."

"I killed Arawn."

"Did you?" He raises his brow. "Interesting."

"How so?"

"Uh-uh, now you tell me what Sybella said."

"Oh, she told me that it wasn't time I received my prophecy and Lady Fate refused to give more. I was sent on my way, just like you are now." I turn on my heel. "Thank you for your time, Lord Emrys."

I get two steps before I hear Emrys's softly uttered "fuck" and then a stride of his long legs carries him across the distance.

"Vanna," he pleads, grabbing my arm, the heat of his hand burning through my leathers. He pulls me to him and— goddess dammit—I allow it, stumbling into him. The scent of lemon and vetiver engulfs me, captivating me in his presence. I feel his chest beneath my captured arm, knowing beneath is the wound that gave him his name.

"What?" I hiss, but it has no venom.

Our eyes meet, silver and gold, Seelie and Unseelie. Between us burns a fire, held in precarious tension, our wills paper, and should a stray spark leap…

"What about the other, Bambalina?"

The moment dissolves and I scowl. "She defied the goddess."

Emrys's brows slowly draw together. "Tell me what she said, and I'll tell you Caethes's plans for Gideon."

I recite to him the verse from memory, knowing every word after three weeks of analyzing it.

Rooks are crown and scorn,
She is deceit, hers was apart

Knights are murder and mourn,
She is failure, her grief is heart
Bishops are sacrifice and cost,
She is three, his was death
Royals are found and lost,
She is true, his lies are breath
Pawn—

"She's sending him to the Winter Carnaval," Emrys responds after Bambalina's words.

"When?"

"You didn't pay for that."

"Oh, fuck you, Emrys," I growl, wresting my arm free of his restraint. "When is he going?"

"What is that worth to you?"

Silence. I stare at this fae male, feeling stirrings, flutters, and questions. I debate, quietly. I have no other information I'm willing to offer.

"Whatever you want from me," I say softly.

"Don't," Emrys whispers, pained. "Don't even hint at that."

"Why?"

"Because I want you to mean it."

My heart leaps and suddenly the small distance between us is even smaller. "Even after what I said?"

"Even after."

"That sounds toxic."

"We weren't."

My treacherous heart races, eager and terrified. "Tell me."

"Tell you what?"

"About us."

Emrys inhales sharply, words frozen on his tongue. I see the gears moving in his head before he decides to speak. "I know you don't remember, but I do. I think about it every day and every night. It kills me that there is this wall between us. I've waited for years, hoping you'll break the bind on your memories, but for years I've only watched you grow more distant. Every day that passes I die a little more inside, knowing it's more time I've lost with you."

"Ryss," I whisper, hurt and yearning bleeding through me.

"We had decades together and you remember only pieces of it."

"Were we…were we together that entire time?" I ask him, suddenly vulnerable, feeling like that frightened human stranded in the Yukon once again. I remember encounters, purely physical.

Emrys's eyes soften, his hand coming up to brush a lock of hair behind my pointed ear. I freeze, but the soothing heat melts my hesitation. "No, we couldn't be. I don't know if you remember, but Centurions are forbidden from intimate relationships during Century Training. We worked around that."

The forgetting elixir is gone from my system now, my memories restored by my reunion with Oath-Sworn, however there are deliberate chunks of my past completely removed. As if surgery were done on my psyche with hollows left behind as a scar to the procedure. The elixir is not responsible for my lapse now; the missing pieces are from Lady Fate. From what she took from me.

"Lady Fate did more than take my memories, didn't she?"

Emrys nods, unable to speak through the goddess's binding.

"What did she *do*?"

"She took…more in exchange to bring me back."

"Why?"

He pauses. His hand is still resting on my brow, but I let it stay there. "Because you begged her to."

I know the truth of it, I can feel it sink in, but to me it is a distant acceptance. I believe it, I know it, but when I try to recall it, nothing comes forth. I dig deep, as far into the portent depths of my soul as I dare venture, but all I find is more of those vacancies, the memories slipping through my fingers like smoke.

Slowly, I lift my hand and it glides over Emrys's smooth fingers, electricity pulsing between us. His breath hitches in response. My eyes hold his. "Do you want me to get those memories back?"

"More than anything. I just hate how it has to be done."

I startle. "You know how?"

"I do, but I made an oath to the goddess, and I cannot tell you. All I can say is that I think you're on the right path."

"I wish I knew what else she took."

Emrys curls his hand around mine. "I wish I could tell you."

We stand there, in an air of intimacy. For a breath we are just present, longing reaching between us, a wall dividing us. I feel loss but I do not feel love and that hurts because all I see in Emrys is love. Devotion. Absolute adoration.

And then I remember Gideon and shame rushes through me.

Gideon is currently captured by Caethes, locked or chained in her chamber, having goddess knows what done to him while I pine over an ex-lover. Here I am hungering for another male when the one I declared war for is suffering in confines. I relive pasts I cannot remember while Gideon, infuriating creature he is, claims a place in my heart that I am determined to get back.

The icy shock of my guilt shatters the moment and I recoil from myself in disgust.

"I have to go," I whisper, breaking the silence between us. When I pull away it feels like losing a limb. Leaving him feels so utterly wrong, and yet again I am awash with shame for feeling that way when I should be concerned solely for Gideon.

"Okay," Emrys murmurs to the valley between us. "Goodnight, Vanna."

"Sweet dreams, Ryss."

I leave, walking carefully back to my chambers, chancing a single look behind me. Emrys is still rooted to the spot, staring at my retreating back forlornly, pain written across his features. I turn my gaze away, guilt galloping through me as I return to my room and pick up the wine I ache for.

CHAPTER 3

CENTURY TRAINING

We are weighed and measured, and then our first mentor, Enydd, gives us seven milligrams less than a human's lethal dose of ricin. The white powder sits ineffectually in our cupped palms, feeling as unthreatening as snow—but we know better.

"Swallow everything in your hand and take care of each other," Enydd says in her low brogue, her tapered brows furrowed in a permanent frown. Her violet hair is sleek down her back, obscuring her gossamer wings. Her nut-brown complexion is unmarred by age lines, but spotted with a constellation of cinnamon freckles. "I will return at sundown to assess your survival. May the goddess be with you."

With that she departs, walking through an archway in the overgrown stone hall and disappearing while Emrys and I stare at each other with poison in our palms.

Century Training exists in a bubble realm, like the ones that the Seelie and Unseelie Courts occupy. Only this one is significantly smaller and the doorway only allows entry once a millennium, holding for a period of a false hundred years while simultaneously one mortal year. Within this temporary world, access to the Faerie Roads is completely cut off and aside from each other and our readily vanishing mentors we are utterly alone.

The space is a crumbling cathedral-esque structure, with arched ceilings that are broken in places, allowing dangling lichen and sunlight to filter through. Moss coats everything in varying degrees, speckling some places while blanketing others. Statues are decaying, flagstones are cracked. The staircases are in an alarming state of disrepair, entire flights broken off and lying prone on the floor below. Beyond, the structure is an endless sprawling green of moss, hills and gray sky for miles and nothing else.

It's falling apart and we are trapped for ten decades.

Today is only our second day, having re-met yesterday after years of passing between our courts. We know *of* each other in passing, but I don't particularly engage with many of the Unseelie Court, even when I spy as the *Ceidwad Cudd*. Especially not the Heart-Eater Queen's infamous pet lord. Of course, he likely has biased preconceptions about me too, about one of the Light Queen's sixteen-year-old adopted twin daughters. I am not the approachable one. I am the cold, frosty one, the difficult one, the vicious one.

When we'd arrived, entering through two separate doorways, facing a third—our exit after one hundred years—we glanced at each other with quiet approval and a fleeting look of familiarity.

"Evelyn Vanora?" he'd asked.

I nodded. "Emrys Gorlassar?"

His lips twisted in a mockery of a smile but he nodded.

"Well met," I told him.

"Well met," he returned in a low voice.

Now, we look at each other, the golden-eyed warrior looking wary for the first time.

"May the goddess be with us," I announce and tip my hand to my mouth. It's instantly bitter and burning and every instinct within me screams for me to spit it out. I do not. It's my first indoctrination into mithridatism.

"May the fucking goddess be with us," Emrys mutters and does the same.

Hours later we're on the floor, crimson leaking from our orifices, stomachs cramping. I vomit blood into a cracked, empty fountain and Emrys pisses blood behind a decapitated statue. Full of regret, we try to wash the taste out of our mouths, scrubbing our hands free of the white toxin. We collapse together at the lip of the stone fountain, eyes bleary and breaths wheezing. My wings, usually lightweight and flexible, drag limply behind me.

A second mentor, Osian, stops in every so often and looks on with pity. He monitors us for a few minutes at a time, opening a notebook and scrawling in it before watching again. Wary. He leaves. I think he arrives on every hour mark, but I'm not sure and he is my only way of knowing a sure passage of time.

We're alone again and I moan.

"Enydd said to take care of each other," Emrys rasps, choking on blood. "What do you need?"

"I need to not fucking die," I hiss, coughing up blood.

Emrys laughs, a pained sound. "I won't let you," he reaches for my hand and squeezes it weakly, but it bolsters me. I squeeze back, using his strength and support to drag myself to a sitting position against the fountain.

"Tell me how you're feeling," I say, trying to focus on anything but the incredible pain.

"Fuck Vanora, I feel like my body is boiling from the inside out." He coughs and blood trickles from between his lips, their color turning a deathly shade of white.

"Yeah. That sounds about right."

That brief amount of conversation drains me, and we settle into silence, intermittently squeezing each other's hands, so we know we're still alive. It could be hours more before we move beyond any sort of painful writhing. Our hands cool as our bodies threaten death and despite the weakened squeezes we give, we do not stop. I don't let his hand go when I throw up a third time, he doesn't disengage when he vomits for the first. It is disgusting and base, but without him tethering me I feel as if I might drift away.

Sundown must arrive because Enydd returns, her expression unimpressed. That disdain fuels a fiery anger in me enough to look up at her with venom.

"Congratulations on surviving the day. The ricin should not kill you at this point. But this—" her eyes narrow and her long pointer finger wags between us, "is unacceptable and romantic relations between Centurions are forbidden."

Something within me snaps, and wrath surges, my wings flaring. "Do you really think I'm planning to suck his dick right after you just dosed us with ricin?"

The slap comes and my head turns with it. A splatter of blood paints the fountain ledge and for a moment I stare at it like an art piece, reeling. I suppose I should have expected that.

"Insolent little bitch," she hisses in grand fury, looking like an exquisite, vengeful god. Her emerald dragonfly wings extend behind her. "Watch your vile tongue before I cut it from your mouth."

I grin, a bloody baring of teeth, smiling through the pain of the slap and poison. I squeeze Emrys's hand. "I don't think the goddess would be too thrilled to hear of you mutilating her chosen Centurions, do you?"

Because we *were* chosen. Lady Fate sent word through the Prophet Witches. Our names were on their lips.

Enydd's nostrils flare, but she does not answer.

"Why?" Emrys croaks.

"Why what?" Enydd asks, voice still hard but not nearly as harsh.

"Why is it forbidden?"

Enydd pauses, as if not comprehending, and then her eyes flicker down once and her mouth sets firmly. "We are given only what the goddess deems essential for Century Training and contraceptives aren't one of them. This realm is not equipped to handle a babe."

"And if we were two males? Or two females?" I demand. "What then? If procreation is the problem, you could have said that." It's not even the point of wanting to fuck Emrys—I don't…I think—it's the point that this fae has rubbed me the wrong way and I'm clearly delivering myself on the side of the line where she isn't.

Enydd's lip curls in disgust. "It is not simply procreation, but the sanctity of the realm. Century Training exists as the highest privilege the goddess can gift the fae and I'll not see you bastardize it so you can fulfill your teenage hormones. Romance is a distraction and should it go awry I do not want to see revenge. You are goddess-chosen warriors and you will act as such."

I wheeze a laugh and blood bubbles up. Emrys softly tightens his grip on my hand. I look over at him and he's already staring at me, eyes gold and bloodshot, and I immediately understand everything is wrong.

"Emrys?" I ask, concern turning my husky voice high. I manage to pull myself to my knees, and press both hands to his cheeks. My vision swims but I stay steady. He's cold and fear splices through me. I am not spending one hundred years in this fucking prison alone with *them*. "Ryss!"

His eyes flicker briefly and relief floods me. I search through my muddled sights for anything to help and I notice Enydd did not come empty handed. She has a basket and I plead with my eyes, while she is stone.

"What's in the basket?"

Enydd's expression remains flat. "What you need."

Hope and dread fill me simultaneously, and I sway. "Please give it to me."

There is silence, but Enydd hands it over without argument.

"If he dies it is your fault, I told you to take care of each other. See you both at sunrise…or not."

Enydd leaves, and the crushing weight of rage and fear burn the grasping effects of ricin from my blood. I banish the worst of it, forcing myself to health like I force myself into sobriety when I've overindulged at one of Corvina's parties.

Rummaging through the basket I find water with a healing tonic infused into it and dig no further. I open the canteen and sniff its contents—clean—and take a swig. Cool, fresh water and healing medicine. No added poison, no tricks, just water and help. I swallow down three gulps before I take it to Emrys's lips. As I tilt it, I watch his throat work, accepting the fluid. It's several minutes of this before Emrys returns to a passable level of cognition. He rouses long enough to thank me before slumping against my shoulder into a healthier sleep.

Through the night I force myself to monitor his breathing and pulse, squeezing his hand out of habit and seething in unfathomable anger.

CHAPTER 4

I sift through documents about previous encounters with Lady Fate, sipping on a cup of spiked tea in the library of the Seelie Court. It's a cavernous space, yawning upwards in pillaring levels until it settles above in the false gold sky. The magic writhes like an ocean, the waves sometimes breaking upon the cornices, or lapping gently against the crown molding. The levels are each barred by elaborate balustrades of ancient tree boughs, ivy draping down each floor in patterns of its natural verdant green as well as its gilded cousin.

The tea is an orange spiced blend with a splash of whiskey, just enough to take the edge of stress off. Next to me, Maelona sips daintily from her own copper-rimmed cup, hers, unlike mine, isn't spiked. She's perusing the archaic tomes with careful hands.

In the morning light, gemstone fractals from the opulent stained glass land on Maelona's long hair—black in its normal, contented state. The free flow of her tresses is hindered only by two small braids, weaving from her temples, over her pointed ears. The braids brush the book she's reading, bringing with it the scent of orchid and cherry along with the musk of parchment.

Flipping through poorly detailed accounts, I find a short paragraph hinting that Lady Fate enjoys making bargains as a form of amusement. For her entertainment. There is a brief warning that nothing is worth the return from death and my stomach recoils, the whiskey sitting uncomfortably.

"What was I willing to give up for Emrys's life?" I ponder aloud, pressing my fingers into my brows.

Maelona, not even looking up, turns the page and speaks nonchalantly. "Your firstborn child?"

"That's not funny, Mae," I growl, slamming the useless book closed. I pick up a new journal, one detailing an infiltration into the Sugar Ring—one of the adjacent chapters to the Winter Carnaval, the one *I'd* meant to infiltrate—and realize with horror that it's all done in Corvina's handwriting.

I inhale sharply and it does not escape Maelona's notice. When she catches sight of the blue ink she pales, her hair flickering white and blue.

"She did very well on that mission," she reveals softly, like I'm a startled animal and she doesn't want to scare me off. "But I don't think you're ready to read that yet. I can go over that account for you instead. I was there. What she said might trigger a memory of mine."

I hesitate but slowly pick up the periwinkle leather, closing the book with the white ribbon tucked between the pages. I hand it over like it's something precious. Maelona takes it as reverently as I offer it. Solemnity enters her eyes and she gazes down.

"I'll give it to you one day, but for now I'm going to keep it. It does not do to dwell on what if's when nothing can be changed."

While Maelona and Corvina never crossed the boundary of romance in their friendship, they were close and very much friends—the sexual barrier mainly due to Corvina preferring the company of males while Maelona only tried one every so often, regretfully each time. The three of us grew up together in court, all similar ages, Corvina and I the adopted daughters of the queen, Lady Maelona her ward. Her parents were killed in some battle that Aneira has yet to give details on and she was too young to remember much beyond her father's warm laugh and her mother's scent of orchids—which is why she wears the fragrance now.

"Okay," I manage carefully, selecting a new book from the Winter Carnaval stack—the Gideon stack—rather than the Lady Fate stack—the Emrys stack.

The Winter Carnaval is the supernatural world's most infamous black market, specializing in sex trafficking and pit fights, along with auctioning of relics and stolen artifacts.

While simultaneously researching the two tragedies involving the males in my life, I've taken on the responsibility of assisting Maelona with the training of the Crows, in addition to my regular spy network duties as the *Ceidwad Cudd*—which is likely due for a retirement. Also, we've yet to address the Harbinger fiasco that is, even now, considered a missing person's case. Bounty hunters like Jacob Dugal continue to search for me, unknowing that I am already found. If all that isn't enough, I'm also heavily involved in the strategy surrounding the beginnings of a court war.

"I miss her, too," Maelona whispers, raw. I look at her and for a moment I don't know how to respond. She stares hard at Corvina's journal, not reading her words, just seeing the imprint of the girl left behind.

"I know," I whisper back, reaching for the bottle of whiskey and taking a shameless swig. I can't be buckled by this grief. I must move past it. I need to find Gideon and bring him back like I swore to.

So why am I looking into bargains and not the Carnaval?

Furiously, I flip through a short text regarding entrance and patron selection for the Carnaval, depicting various states of debauchery and violations. There are tests and events that precede any admittance, which is unsurprising as the black market is illustrious and abhorrent. They of course, would have layers of contingencies to protect their deplorable interests.

I set aside the Gideon book, sip my spiked tea, and peruse a new tome. It's a documentation of bargains. I go to sip again but pause in my reading, slowly drawing the cup from my lips.

I've never come across these eldritch words before.

It's poorly translated, hailing from a language older than Latin, older than Welsh. In the margins are runes from the primordial fae—sharp slashes, and long, languid strokes. Question marks dot the ancient words with lines indicating the translated word—or possible translated word.

Lady Fate has been known to favor (desire?) individuals—particularly warriors, priestesses, and true (?) lovers (partially translated word, unclear definition)—and with that favor (desire?) comes an unprecedented willingness to bestow gifts (bargains? punishments?) when pleased (jealous?) by divining (dividing from?) her cosmic plan.

I blink the stupor from my brain, baffled by the steady influx of contradictory information. I read it over several times trying to process. Either Lady Fate jealously desires certain people and punishes them for it, or she favors those who follow her divine interventions and blesses them for it.

Note: The bargains (Gifts? Punishments?) are rare. Theorizing leads one to believe King Maven or Queen Theadora had successfully made one. What was traded for a crown is uncertain, but both reigns hold questions of succession.

"Are you researching for Gideon or Emrys?" Maelona challenges, peering down at my text.

Before I can rebuke her, the sound of clinking armor and weapons touches my awareness, the same time I sense five approaching fae. I tuck the bottle of whiskey between my feet and turn, finding Queen Aneira Gwyndolyn of the Seelie Court striding down the hall with four guards flanking her. For all intents and purposes Aneira is my mother in everything, but her arrival here in the library spells something wrong.

She arrives in a swell of soft pink, her gown fluttering around her like a diaphanous tulip, the sleeves coming to a point over the back of her hand. A golden crown of branches circles her brow, framing the sharp, dragonesque horns that curve back from her head as if pushed by a breeze. She stands, tall and formidable, utterly regal as she offers us a small smile.

Maelona and I both rise, doing away with the curtseys that Aneira refused to allow us—in her words she didn't want her "children" bowing before her. She may be queen, yes, but not a tyrant. We rise to give her respect and reverence and I ensure that I do not kick over the bottle as I get to my feet. I assess Aneira and the guards—Bleddyn, Folant, Cadoc, and Drysi. They are a few of the handful that know of my Harbinger identity, bound by the same oath that Emrys and I swore to each other.

"I care not to dawdle," Aneira says in her musical soprano, "so I will speak frankly about it. Caethes has demanded a meeting, as is her right when the opposite court declares war. Tonight, she requests our presence in the throne room of the Unseelie Court. Worry not. We are all bound by fae law. No attacks may precede, occur during, or follow a meeting for a period of a day and a night."

"Are you sure that's a good idea?" I say challenging, and for a moment regret filters through me for contesting the queen. I prepare to backpedal but Aneira shrugs.

"It is her right in war. We cannot refuse."

"Of course, my Queen. I assume you wish for us to join you in this meeting?"

"Yes, we are due to arrive at seven tonight. Please meet me in our throne room at six to prepare our best verbal defense and offense."

"We will arrive on time."

"Excellent. Please dress in finery. I dare not threaten Caethes by bringing warriors in leathers and armor." Aneira sighs. "I do hate dictating what you wear as I respect your individuality, but we are at war and these little sacrifices must be made in the name of politics and courtly intrigue."

"Understood, My Queen," Maelona says obediently. "A dress is as much a weapon as a sword may be."

Aneira smiles warmly, cupping Maelona's cheek and brushing a thumb across her cheekbone. "Exactly right, my darling. Intelligent and beautiful, and yet so much more, you are." Maelona blushes and her hair flares several shades of pink quickly before fading to black once again. "Follow my lead at the meeting," Aneira says, addressing both of us, "and do not speak out of turn. I fear provoking Caethes. She is unpredictable."

"Of course," I acquiesce, "do you wish to speak of anything else while we have a moment?"

Aneira's eyes flicker, but she keeps her expression cool. "No, please continue as you were."

We nod and Aneira turns with her guards. I pointedly ignore Drysi. She may have wanted to help, and she may have given birth to me, but she does not get the title of mother for two good deeds. Once the royal guard fades from view and my sense of awareness of them dissipates I release a breath and duck down to collect the bottle from the floor.

"Have you ever noticed how subservient she is to you?" Maelona says wonderingly. "It's almost like she defers to you as queen."

A mixture of alarm and horror flood through me and it must show plainly on my face because Maelona shakes her head.

"Don't be ridiculous, we all know that *you* are heir apparent. I have no ambitions for the crown." I start to say '*I am content as I am,*' but the lie won't come so I clamp my mouth and switch directions. "Why would you ever think she would select me for the crown?"

"I do not mean it like that. I understand the mutual respect, as she raised you and..." Maelona sighs. "It just feels like she's lost that spark within her. She's tired, and I worry. You did not see her for the two years you were gone, Ev. She was a wreck. Corvina and I held her together."

But now Corvina is gone.

A lancing pang of guilt and grief surge in my chest, my heart aching. I sip the spiked tea before I respond. "It could not be helped that I was gone."

"No," Maelona says, not defensively. "I was not blaming you. I was stating a fact unknown to you." She pauses and it's weighed. "We never did address what happens if Aneira hasn't named an heir."

"You could just touch her crown and see if it burns you. If it does, we know for certain you are heir apparent and we can put this to rest."

"Ev."

I trace the rim of my copper teacup, contemplating. "Then it would go to her closest blood relative, that's the way the crown understands the transference of power. If Aneira had a child it would go to them, but as she doesn't become intimate with men, she never had children. So, it would likely go to a distant cousin."

"That's not entirely true, she did try a man once just to see what the fuss is about. Just as I do from time to time." She side-eyes me. "Unlike someone else I know."

"Oh hush," I chastise jokingly. "We are not humans, we do not slut-shame."

Maelona smirks and there is a pause before she speaks again. "Not you?"

"What, not I?"

"Why would the crown not transfer to you?"

"I am not blood."

Maelona stops for a moment. "And this does not bother you?"

I shrug and take a sip of my tea. "I do not desire a crown. Do you?"

Maelona raises a brow in contest. "I do. But I love Aneira more than I prize the crown and if she never dies, I would celebrate. I just worry about her abdicating. How long do you think she's been ruling, Ev?"

I blink in surprise, realizing I don't know the exact number. It is something Aneira has always avoided. "Perhaps three hundred years?"

Maelona shakes her head pityingly. "Ev, she's been on that throne for a thousand years. She ruled during the bout of Century Training before yours."

"Are you certain?"

"I am."

Terror at the prospect of another loss fills me. I imagine Aneira staring up at the false Seelie sky vacantly, I think of her drowned in the sea—every horrid method by which she could be taken from me. It hits me like a gut punch and I lurch up from my seat.

"I can't—I just—I'm sorry, I have to go, I'll see you tonight."

Without a further word, I rush from the room, fighting off the tears burning my eyes.

CHAPTER 5

The night falls and my anxiety rises.

Typically, I would have asked Maelona or Corvina to join me in getting ready for a political meeting of this magnitude, but Corvina is dead and I cannot face Maelona just yet. It isn't just from our conversation in the library. The shame I feel makes me struggle not to drink.

I put my hair up, twisted into braids and spiked with diamonds, and I wear a dress of pearl white, the back bare but for a decorative chain that dangles from between the shoulder blades to the small of my back.

When I'd finished pulling up my hair, my fingers twitched for the bottle. When I'd pulled on the dress, my hands ached for the bottle. When I slashed black liner across my lids and a deep shade of berry across my mouth I itched for the bottle. It taunts me from its perch on my table, next to an empty crystal goblet, laughing at me with tears leaking down its side.

I arrive in the Seelie throne room, immediately catching sight of Maelona. Dressed in a long silver dress with a thigh slit, her shoulders are bare save for delicate scales, shelled and layered, and a neckline and hip line of chain mail—purely decorative. Her hair also is wrapped up in braids, silver rings lining her pointed ears and fingers, winking in the light as she flexes her hands. Next to her is Drysi, dressed in dark gray spidersilk, bronze chains the only thing holding it together at the waist. The straps too, are bronze chains. Everything about the dress flexible and delicate.

"This feels like a trick," Drysi says, pacing. Her long black hair whips around her like a sheet of darkness, her eyes— *my* eyes—flicker with tension while her pinned wings twitch in discomfort. Jealousy strikes me.

"Caethes enjoys taunting her prey," Maelona responds gravely. "I don't expect her to try to subvert the law, but—"

"I do," I interrupt. Both Maelona and Drysi turn, expressions open with confusion. "When Gideon and I entered her court for the first time, we were promised we would not be killed, maimed, or injured, and yet she tried to poison us anyway." I don't mention the poisonous sting Gideon's name leaves in my mouth. "My theory is that it was a paralytic, but I have no way of knowing aside from asking her."

"Perhaps your Unseelie contact can supply that information," Maelona says dryly.

I flip her off.

"Is it possible for her to attack without repercussions?" Drysi inquires.

I answer. "No, unless she wants to stoke the wrath of Lady Fate and be smote on the spot, she cannot. The entirety of both Unseelie and Seelie Courts are bound by the word of war and its laws. We are not humans with their blatant betrayals, ours kill. We are safe in their proximity for a day and a night."

"And if we are trapped or kidnapped?" Drysi presses.

Fear skitters down my spine, but I hide it with a malicious grin that bares my teeth. "She can try, but she will not succeed, I assure you of that."

"Even in your state?" Maelona jabs judgmentally.

"Yes," I bite out.

"Even with *him*?"

She doesn't have to clarify which *him*; I know. And regardless, both elicit dangerous responses in me. Knowing it could come down to Emrys and I battling it out after the clock strikes, and knowing Gideon is locked up somewhere in that court, alone…both prospects make me ill.

"*Yes*," I snap, harshly this time.

Drysi quirks a brow but intelligently enough, says nothing.

I prickle, the provocation bringing to the surface a rage that I generally try to quell. As my feelings begin to spiral, I sense a new presence and turn to find Aneira entering the throne room, resplendently dressed in a gown of hazelnut spidersilk, the lines of which give the illusion of branches, golden leaves sewn onto the skirt. Her queen's crown is on her brow, golden chains drape her shoulders like an ornate shawl, reaching in various lengths down her back.

"Shall we discuss what we expect from this meeting?" Aneira asks, ale eyes flittering between the three of us.

We delve into conversation regarding potential tactics Caethes may employ. Drysi and Aneira seem to have inner knowledge and understanding of the Unseelie Queen and both Maelona and I share a concerned look. I know many eons ago Caethes and Aneira had an alliance but more and more I find myself curious as to what that relationship truly entailed. Aneira prefers females while Caethes prefers both sexes, not caring about gender, only how they can satisfy her.

Nearly an hour of discussion passes before Bleddyn arrives to inform us it's time to leave for the Unseelie Court and all its horrors. We are guided through the curtain of gilded ivy to slip into the Faerie Roads with a thought. Once we arrive inside the earthen caverns, the sound of the Wild Hunt is particularly boisterous, and threatening.

"Slip the knife between her breasts and lick the sweet nectar of her blood."

"Wrap them in chains and set them free, chase them down and fuck them raw."

"Oh, to destroy the virtuous horned, whore."

I'm stepping in front of Aneira without thinking, blocking whatever depraved beings may crawl from the depths of the tunnel yawning above us. "It's nearly a full moon," I say, clipped. "The Hunt is wide awake and thirsty. They cannot touch us, but do not falter and do not wander."

Maelona peers around the space, a lace of unease playing across her face, hair flashing an indistinct color. "I've never heard them like this before. It's vile."

"I'll show you vile, Chameleon Girl," a tempestuous voice hisses. I can practically hear it licking its lips. *"Does your cunt change color too?"*

"Get fucked," Maelona growls, fingers itching for a blade she is not armed with.

"Oh, I'm trying to. Let me have a taste."

"Get away from us or I'll kill you," I threaten, voice flat with rage.

The voice chuckles. *"You cannot kill what is already dead, Harbinger."*

Ice slides down my spine. Horror fills me and flows over, crashing in ichor waves around my feet, splashing on the hem of my white gown. It stains it, crawling up my legs and up my bodice, twisting around my throat and tightening its vicious vines. It spreads and festers, like a disease it consumes me.

"Leave us," Aneira commands with unimaginable force—with the power of the Seelie Court and the might of the crown.

The voices hiss with indignation but slowly they slither away with feral taunts and final words, promising pain and luxuriating in it.

"Ev." A hand lands on my shoulder and without hesitation I flash around and lock its owner in an iron hold.

"Ow! Fuck, you're grinding my bones."

I realize with horror that the wrist I'm crushing into powder is Maelona's and I quickly release her, stepping away and shaking my head in shame and clarity. I look again at Maelona and find her rubbing her wrist, impressions of my fingers already blooming upon her fair skin.

"Mae, I'm so sorry. I don't know what came over me, I was distracted by that voice, it—it knew who I was." I swallow the revulsion seeping through my soul.

"I heard it. How is that possible? Everyone who knows your identity is sworn to secrecy."

Revulsion roils through me and I meet Maelona's dark eyes. "Everyone but Gideon."

Maelona, Aneira, Drysi, and Bleddyn are completely silent, their breaths paused in unison at the incredible problem we're suddenly faced with.

"You don't think…?" Maelona trails off, unwilling to speak the words into existence.

"That he told Caethes?" Terror squirms in me and it takes everything in me to keep it at bay. "I don't know. We—we didn't part on good terms and he…" I breathe deeply and avert my gaze, shame and guilt turning my cheeks red. I clamp my jaw. "He knows my heart's desire."

I hear a sharp inhale but I'm unsure who it belongs to.

Knowing a faerie's heart's desire is the key to holding a command over them. Each revealed desire is a separate command, and Gideon has up to three held against me. He could force me to do anything.

"Evelyn, you didn't—"

I cut Drysi off, whirling in fury. "I did, Drysi! I fucking did because I thought I was human and we were having a moment and I didn't fucking know what it meant. I am *sorry*," I spit at her, dishonor burning as I look at her face and see Corvina's. I turn to Aneira and soften. "I am sorry," I repeat, this time gentled.

Aneira inclines her head. "Then we have no choice. The halfling must die."

A wild and vicious thing takes me. "*No.*"

My queen's eyes widen. "You defy me?"

I squash the fear taking root inside me. "Give me some time to figure it out, see if I can trick him into using the command for something meaningless."

Aneira stares me down, eyes turning to gems. "You have until the timeline Caethes has already given you, but if he attempts to use that command against you, my soldiers have absolute authority to take him out and I expect you to act in accordance."

I bow my head. "Yes, My Queen."

Aneira backs off and Bleddyn clears his throat. "May we continue?"

"As you were," Aneira replies nonchalantly, waving off with an elegant hand.

The roots dangle and try to tease our hair, bioluminescent mushrooms guide the way, speckled upon the walls and curve of the floor. Bleddyn whispers *golau* to his blade and it alights, revealing brightness towards the Unseelie Court. Discomfiture threads through our group, not nearly as confident as we were upon entry.

The walk is short and then we're at the base of the gabbro staircase flanked by the statues of Emrys and I, my butchered wings a sick reminder of what I've endured, Emrys's lost sword a taunt to the memories I've forgotten. I avert my gaze as we climb, Bleddyn remaining at the foot with his lighted blade, nodding once to each of us in support. I steel myself and walk.

I am the Harbinger.

I am the *Ceidwad Cudd.*

I am Evelyn Corianne Vanora.

And I will not fail.

CHAPTER 6

The throne room has been transformed since the last time I laid eyes on it. The ceiling is still glass, revealing the scattered starlight and midnight sky through silver filigree. The fourth wall is still a vast expanse of air, exposing the wild winds of the mountaintops. Snow caps the peaks, a brisk air swirling in the space and infusing the meeting with icy tension.

As opposed to last time, where courtiers were milling about in their cruel beauty and vicious finery, the room is empty. In their place is a long table draped in a shimmering white tablecloth with four silver chairs evenly spaced to each side. Silver candelabras line the center of the table along with anemones and pine boughs, while white berries intersperse the deep green. Fae light—like the one emitted by Oath-Sworn—hovers above the table.

On the far side of the table are four faeries. My breath catches in my throat but I do not let it show. Seated and posing primly on the far left, her gasoline spill hair coiling like serpents about her face, is Tegwyn. Beside her I recognize flaming red hair and white-petal lashes, moth wings and orange eyes. One of the fae who flayed and murdered Jacob—I'm tempted to thank her. Next, in all her antlered, royal glory, is Caethes. Her moon-white hair is a sleek fall down her back, while liquid black eyes stare with leveled rage. And then beside her, golden-eyed with hair redder and deeper than blood is the Revenant. Emrys.

My heart stutters. I keep thinking back to the sour note the Revenant and I left off on, the void of missing memories between us. The anger that lashed me. I hide it and don a placid guise of indifference and casual perusal. Today, I am Evelyn Vanora and the *Ceidwad Cudd*, having torn down the wall between those two identities in weeks past. I'd be lying if I said the stress of keeping the two separate wasn't relieved.

"Welcome to the Unseelie Court, representatives of the Seelie Court," Caethes greets with a voice like frost.

Our group crosses the space, slowly. I feel a slight crackle to the air, ancient fae magic solidifying in the space, locking us into parlay. Drysi takes the seat across from Tegwyn, Maelona across from the Moth-Fae, Aneira opposite Caethes, and myself opposite Emrys.

I have never revealed Emrys's identity to my queen; not in a slip of phrase, nor in allowing thorough observation of our relationship. Upon that same coin, Emrys has not let Caethes discover who the Harbinger is, even under threat and blackmail. In fact, aside from the two of us, the only one wiser to the fact that they sit in the presence of both the Harbinger and the Revenant is Maelona.

Unless Gideon has told all.

While I was away in Century Training, Aneira had glamoured a human to impersonate me. Her name was Raina, and she was given every provision needed and paid handsomely for the service. During the year, her glamour was altered to mimic rapid aging, as I would not look eighteen upon my return. After the term ended, her memory was wiped with the same tonic that stole my memories in the Yukon and returned to the human world.

It is my understanding Caethes did the same for Emrys.

As I sink slowly into the chair across from Emrys, I hold his heavy gaze as he sits on the side aligned with a night of massacre—of Aberth's slaughter. He is dressed in a white blouse like he wore the night before, black pants and a pair of suspenders. He sips from a tumbler of whiskey, seemingly unbothered.

"Lady Vanora." His voice lingers on my title like a taunt.

"Lord Emrys," I reply tartly.

"Plotted any more coups?"

"Groveled for any other lovers?"

Emrys smirks, his eyes dark. "I don't need to."

"Funny, I seem to recall differently."

"I wouldn't be so sure."

The words leave me unnerved and I turn my attention elsewhere.

A human servant, wearing an antlered deer mask, and his neck marked with the Unseelie crest carries in a tray laden with goblets of water. I pluck one up as it passes, realizing the human is likely a remnant of one of Aberth's lotteries and my face screws up in disgust. He appears hardly thirty and already his life is over, forced into the equivalent of slavery.

I tilt my chin imperiously, turning my attention towards the Heart-Eater Queen and completely ignoring my opposite. Caethes selects a goblet at random and sips daintily, as if I haven't once witnessed her with an aorta in her teeth. She smooths invisible lines from her obsidian gown, the fabric like that of scales, reptilian and repulsive and utterly captivating.

"I called this meeting for one reason and one reason only," Caethes says, low, staring at Aneira across the table. The two queens level stares at one another and the tension rises, the air so thick you could cut it with a knife. Between them a fire burns and I'm startled to recognize the power dynamic between them. The relationship that reflects parts I've seen within myself and Emrys.

A thought strikes me still.

Were the queens once lovers?

"Well, on with it then," Aneira prods, unamused. "You've always liked to hear yourself speak and the attention that comes from it, but truly Caethes, have you not grown out of that?"

Twin points of fury bloom on the Unseelie Queen's face, the color high on her cheekbones as she curls her claws around the stem of her glass. "You once enjoyed the sound of my voice."

Aneira waves off the remark. "That was then, this is now. We are no longer allied."

The Unseelie Queen scoffs. "Allies? Is that what we were?"

Caethes gives Aneira a challenging expression before she decides against pursuing that tangent. She composes herself before snapping her fingers loudly.

A door adjacent to the throne room squeals open and an azure-haired faerie emerges from it, dragging a stumbling form into the meeting. He is slow and unsteady on his feet, bound by chains, wrists cuffed and ankles shackled. His face is sallow and beneath his eyes are bruises, as if he has not slept in all the weeks he's been gone. Crusts of blood line his mouth and his tattered shirt. His hair is unkempt and his nails are broken.

My heart lunges into my throat and then falls through my stomach at the sight of Gideon.

Yearning and desolation flood through me, filling me with the loss I've been so adamant to keep at bay. This is the result of my selfishness. Of my short-temper. Of my lack of care. Because I left him in the Roads, he is subjected to this; toted around in chains by the fae—a people he is fearful of—and held against his will in the chambers of the Dark Queen.

It takes everything in me not to leap to my feet and run, blades swinging to take Gideon, and make a mad dash for the Seelie Court. Instead, I clutch the armrests of my chair and focus on not pulverizing it. Emrys does not miss my deathly stillness—a tell I could never quite master—and his jaw sets, a muscle feathering in his cheek.

Gideon is hauled between Caethes and Emrys, the tension surrounding the room a piano wire tuned to fatal precision. He finally lifts his gaze from his feet, and as if it were fate, he meets my eyes. And I fall victim to his hollow stare, a painful gasp slipping from my throat.

Those always amber eyes are dim with lost hope, flat with betrayal, and muted with apathy. He sees me, but he sees through me. Not in the way he once did, when he saw my emotions rotting from the inside out when I'd failed to rescue all of the Aberth residents. This is the detached way a person sees through another when they've lost it all.

He is not gagged, but he does not speak either.

"I request a trade," Caethes says coolly, interrupting my internal panic. "In exchange for your halfling emissary, I would like Evelyn Vanora. Also known as the *Ceidwad Cudd.*"

Gideon's eyes come alive for a moment, fear and hope intermingling. Maelona sends Aneira a stricken look, a hand reaching, a message on her lips. Emrys's hands curl beneath the table, refusal written across every line of his body. The rest do not deign a response.

Aneira barks a laugh, full of mirth. "You are out of your goddess-damned mind if you think I would submit my child to you. Are you truly so delusional?"

Emrys snorts and Aneira shoots him a hurt look, as if by that response he was doubting her love for me.

"No, I really am quite sane," Caethes retorts. "But do you not see the way the girl pines for the boy? She is talented at hiding it—I will give her that credit—but it is there and if you watch long enough you will see the pain she carries every moment she is forced to look at Gideon Zhao, knowing she can do nothing." As if to punctuate her point, Caethes reaches behind her with a white hand and clasps Gideon's bicep, sliding her fingers down his forearm and holding him possessively while she stares at me.

I want to leap across the fucking table and throttle her.

"Do you see?" Caethes crows, stroking up Gideon's caramel skin. "Do you think if I offer her the trade she will have the same response as you, Aneira?" Without looking she continues her casual caressing, fingertips trailing Gideon's chest, over and through his chains, taking a link and tugging him closer.

Sickness roils in my gut and I grind my teeth to keep from acting rashly.

"You know, Vanna," Emrys whispers, leaning across the table. I catch the scent of vetiver, lemon, and whiskey.

"This is one of those chances I was talking about. If you're willing to take it, perhaps I can ensure you're kept well. Kept close to me."

My heart thunders in my chest for a multitude of reasons but I keep my face blank. "You would like that, wouldn't you?"

"Oh, I'd be lying if I said I wouldn't. But of course, we both know I cannot lie, so I shall just confirm. Yes, I would enjoy nothing more than to abscond with you in my chambers." He lowers his voice even more and glances out of the corner of his eye. "Just like old times."

I'm reminded of when I'd once told Gideon that faeries cannot lie. I squash the reminiscence that rises with the thought.

Emrys sips his whiskey while my cheeks burn. Flashes of Century Training come to me. Heat, skin, breath, touch. Something stirs in me and wakens between my legs. Memory hacks at the cobwebs of what is forgotten. But even though the past rises to haunt me, I do not recall anything more than glimpses and brushes of what was.

"The past is in the past," I say firmly.

"And is Gideon part of that past now? You don't seem all that devastated."

"You think you know me well enough for that?"

Emrys pins me meaningfully with his golden eyes. "I know I do."

Weight settles in my chest, spreading deep in to my heart. Into my soul. I meet him with my own silver eyes, penetrating just as hard, staring devoid of emotion. I give him nothing but intense absence.

"If you'd like, I'll add in a few of my servants to sweeten the deal," Caethes offers, waving her hand at the human with the antlered mask.

"I cannot speak for Evelyn. I leave that answer to her," Aneira decides tactfully, ignoring Caethes's *sweetened deal*.

If it were solely up to me and were I unattached to the Seelie Court, there is no doubt in my mind that I would foolishly give myself up for Gideon. That if I were only the Evelyn of a month ago, I would've ruined it all. I would have ultimately traded the Harbinger for a halfling, with it, all of the Seelie Court secrets. But I am not just her and my life is dedicated to Aneira's.

So, in response, I parse my words carefully. Schooling my features and reigning in my emotions. I hate myself before the words even come out of my mouth, but the Unseelie Queen needs to see that her bargaining chip is made of paper.

"He was a good lay but not enough for me to forsake my court."

Emrys practically chokes on his drink and other voices titter laughs.

Gideon sways like my words delivered a physical blow, hurt flares in his eyes, crushing his hope. He doesn't know the price I've paid to speak those words. He does not know that I am coming back for him. That I swore to return him to me.

Caethes's mouth twitches in rage while a couple surprised sounds come from the guests around the table. The Moth-Fae peals a laugh, the sound like bells, an unhinged tinkling. I hear the slap a fraction of a second after I realize it's about to happen. The queen has backhanded the Moth-Fae, slicing delicate lines across her pale cheek. Blood surges to the surface of her flesh and without a look of shame she reaches up to her own injured cheek, touches the blood, and then tests it with her tongue.

"Thank you, My Queen," she says beatifically and I wonder how Caethes has created such a cult-like following.

Despite the laws restricting harm against the opponent, nothing covers friendly fire nor royal discipline.

"Mind your tongue, Cariad," Caethes hisses. Then she turns to me. "So, it is true you claim the identity of the *Ceidwad Cudd*?"

Blood drains from my face and I pray she doesn't try to pry into other identities of mine. Anxiety knots in my belly while I keep my breathing level and even. "It is," I confirm, measured and flat.

"Yet you thrashed about my court and territory as a pitiful human for two years."

"When you play both courts, you make enemies who want to dispose of you."

"Did you ever encounter a Jacob Dugal?"

Ice shoots through my veins. "I did."

"Would you care to elaborate?" Caethes presses.

My eyes flicker to Aneira but my queen nods, bound by the law of war and faerie parlay.

"He was an informant for me once upon a time," I begin, giving her information I've already revealed, suddenly smiling and tipping this in my favor. I cock my head at Cariad, a feral grin slicing across my cheeks. "I appreciate you murdering him for me."

Cariad brightens, her orange eyes flaring wide. "Oh! That *is* you! You have changed so much. Goddess, you clean up well."

"I had just survived a plane crash."

Cariad touches fingers to her lips, swallowing in memory. "He was a halfling like your Gideon too, if I recall correctly. You like them mixed, I see." She waggles her brows and suddenly, by an invisible force, she is flung across the room.

Cariad's silver chair clatters to the ground and she lands by the throne. Pulling herself and her red gossamer gown together, she gets to all fours.

Slowly, Caethes has been collecting this meeting's chaos, funneling it into herself to use into a weapon. I am furious, but the only consolation is knowing she could not use it against the Seelie Court. Not tonight. Only the day after tomorrow.

"You care too much for theatrics," Aneira snaps at Caethes. "Please state your requests and intentions. This meeting has become far too derailed for my tastes."

"I have made myself clear. The boy for the girl. I want Evelyn in exchange for Gideon. She is responsible for unprovoked attacks upon my people, the destruction of my small town, and the murder of my lover, Arawn. I seek vengeance. Those are my terms."

Aneira is quiet, assessing. "I refuse."

"Then why do you linger here? Leave if you will not bargain," Caethes practically growls.

"I have one request in mind myself," Aneira begins. "I would ask that you return to us Gideon Zhao and we call off this war."

Caethes grins. "That is where you misunderstand. I *crave* a war. And just so you are aware, your declining of my offer does not spare your precious girl. I vow to destroy her now, regardless of this outcome." She licks her teeth. "I hope to eat your heart, soon. And yours," she adds, baring her teeth at me.

"That will not happen," I say through my own teeth.

"Oh, but I could sic any warrior upon you, Revenant included, and you would have no hope to fight back."

I ignore the urge to glance at Emrys and reveal his identity. Even though I do not give him away, I catch him stiffening in my peripheral vision.

"So, why don't you?"

"Perhaps I will," she hisses. "Perhaps I will let you live in suspense."

Cold dread slithers through me, but I keep it at bay.

Caethes pointedly dismisses me and snaps her fingers. "Return the halfling to my chambers. He will not be leaving there for the foreseeable future. And bring me the servant."

Gideon comes alive, thrashing in his bindings, reaching towards us. Desperation tinges the air.

"Evelyn, *please*," Gideon begs and I feel each word strike my heart. I keep my body still, held together by the monster inside, apathy bleeding from my pores. I avert my gaze and tilt my head in the direction of Emrys.

The other Centurion has his gold eyes fixed on me, face unreadable to all but mine. He watches, waiting for my tell, waiting for my falsehoods to ring out.

"No last desperate act or vow of true love to save your protector-reject?" Emrys taunts.

I do not speak.

The escort hauls Gideon away, eyes burning as he pleads silently with me. I remain aloof, staring while part of my heart is torn out and dragged across the Unseelie Court. When the door slams closed, I want to crumple with grief, but I am being watched so I pick up my water and sip.

"I have nothing more to say. Exit my court immediately," Caethes commands, cold fury settling in her gaze.

The servant in the antlered mask is brought before Caethes and almost boredly, she plunges her hand inside his chest. The sound of cracking ribs fills the massive space as she carves out his heart with her talon-sharp nails. Her fingers come out bloody with the servant's heart still pulsing in her hand. The Heart-Eater Queen grins before sinking her teeth in. Blood cascades down her face and pools on her gown, painting her chest in crimson tracks.

My own heart stutters, horror ramping up my throat. I know I fail to hide the shock from my eyes, but I'll be damned if I react further.

We do not argue and without another comment we depart, leaving Caethes bloody and seething at our turned backs. I do not think deeper on Gideon's look of betrayal, his desperation as he was ushered away.

Back in my quarters I tear off my dress and all my finery along with it, half wondering how I dissociated long enough to mist through the trek home. I find an open goldwine and drink it straight from the source, the neck in my grasp. I stand there, swallowing deeply, standing in the center of my catastrophe of a room, hair a mess, clad only in a backless silk shift. Tears stream silently down my face as the haze of alcohol permeates my blood.

There, alone, ignoring the several knocks on my door, I drink myself into oblivion.

CHAPTER 7

CENTURY TRAINING

Emrys and I are face to face, holding swords to each other's throats. My hand burns, my arm screams in agony, my shoulder cries out, my elbow threatens to buckle. We keep our expressions impassive, our arms straight, feet steady as we watch for wavers and tells. For the past hour we've been at this, holding our blades aloft. A lesson in scrutiny and endurance.

"Emrys," Enydd begins. "How is she showing her fatigue?"

Emrys inhales slowly and a bead of sweat rolls down his temple. "She's clenching her jaw, her breaths are tighter, she flexes a finger every minute, she shifts from foot to foot."

Fuck, I am doing all of that.

Enydd nods.

We've been locked into Century Training for a year now, practicing mithridatism and swordplay, hand-to-hand combat and archery, body language and outdoor survival skills. We have years stretching beyond us and we've hardly made a mark in the time we've already dedicated here.

The second mentor, Osian, circles me as I grit my teeth harder. "Evelyn," he says in his rumbling brogue, "how is Emrys showing his tells?"

"He's sweating, his arm shakes, he licks and bites his lips, his elbow dips, his eyes glaze over."

"Very good." Osian comes to my side, in my eyeline, his white hair unbound behind him, green eyes the color of oak leaves. "Would you say that these tells only show physical discomfort, or would they translate to emotional unease?"

I narrow my brows in pain and confusion. "Some would, others would not."

"Okay, I would like to try an experiment." Osian looks to Emrys. "Put your sword down, boy."

Emrys does with a groan of relief, dropping the black blade to the floor. Blissful pain scattering across his face, eyes luminous with a rush of adrenaline. He shakes out his arm, curling and uncurling his hand.

Jealousy cascades through me, and I inhale sharply, air hissing through my teeth and nose.

"Evelyn, how did you know he was relieved to drop that sword?"

I list my observations.

"Emrys, did you notice her reaction to the gift I gave you and not her?"

A muscle feathers in his jaw. "I did not."

"Why?"

"I was focused on myself."

Enydd slaps him upside the head. "That is not the goal of this exercise. Pay attention."

Emrys does this time, lifting his golden eyes to mine, holding still. I notice the subtle signs of time passing on him—his hair curling at the collar of his shirt.

"Evelyn," Osian purrs and I feel his hand slip around my waist. Unease laces through me like a toxic dart into my bloodstream. "Does my touching you make you uncomfortable?"

I cannot lie. "It does."

"Good." For the first time, Osian's voice strikes panic in me. He's always been the gentlest of our mentors, writing poetry by the fountain when we dose ourselves with a new poison, observing us rather than abandoning us as per Enydd's style. "I am going to continue touching you, but I need you not to react. I do not want Emrys to pinpoint how my hands are unwelcome. It is a test and I will see it through."

I grit my teeth. Refusal on the tip of my tongue.

"I don't think she wants—" Emrys receives another upside slap for rebelling against our mentor's practices.

"Emrys, tell me when you spot a new sign. Evelyn, put your sword down and do not react. Your exhaustion will be a hindrance to your ability to hide your reaction, remember that."

I drop the sword with a clatter, the obsidian blade refracting sunlight. A cramp immediately develops and sprawls through my arm and I bite my lip hard enough to draw blood to keep from crying out. Tingles race through my muscles, my fingers twitching.

Before I can think further, I feel Osian's pale fingers on my ribs, the ones on his other hand on my wrist. I fight a recoil and find Emrys's face. Osian's hand travels over my stomach and I fight a gag, furious at being objectified.

"She swallowed her pride or nausea," Emrys counts.

Osian's face moves closer, the white of his hair tangles with the silver of mine, his breath brushes my ear. My wings tense. Emrys notices it and calls it out. Osian's hands plant firmly on my hips. My nostrils flare. Emrys adds it to the list and I notice a small fury grow in his eyes. I focus on that as Osian's fingers continue to glide across my skin and clothes.

"Are you enjoying this?" he whispers in my ear.

Something sick slithers down my spine. "No."

"Why?" His peppermint breath brushes my cheek.

"Because I am being forced."

Aside from the few slaps, pinches and bruises they've given us, the mentors have never touched us. Not like *this*. However, I am newly eighteen and now considered an adult.

"How can you see it makes her uncomfortable?" He directs this to Emrys.

"Because she told you," Emrys bites out, that small fury has erupted into an inferno.

"No, I said how do you *see*. How can you tell these are unwanted touches, that these are shivers of revulsion rather than arousal?"

"Because she *told* you," Emrys repeats, brusquely.

Osian tsks. "That may be the case but you are still not listening. What physical responses tell you this?"

Emrys seethes, his eyes alight, agitation shaping him. "Because she curls inward every time you touch her, she leans away from you, her breathing turns quick, she swallows with disgust, she stares over my shoulder and tries to disassociate, there's panic all over her face, she jumps whenever you reach for her, she shifts her hips from you, her wings want to push you back, she—"

"Very good, now it is your turn," Osian commends, releasing me.

I skip several steps away, moving closer to Emrys—within arm's reach. I do not touch him, but I know if I wished to I could. Already he has a hand extended to his side, his pinky out in case I need it. Warmth and admiration rush through me.

"No," Emrys replies flatly.

Enydd reaches to smack him again but Osian's raised hand stills her.

"I beg your pardon?"

"I refuse this test."

"You do not get to refuse us, this." Osian's green eyes are poisonous, alight with power.

"I don't give a fuck, argue with the goddess, and ask her if this is what she dreamed when she made this place. I am tired and sickened. You will not touch me today." Emrys gravitates towards me. "Not like that."

For all our teachings about body language, Emrys's rage has clouded his ability to control his own actions and right now he is revealing a massive tell. Osian and Enydd do not miss it.

"Would you prefer it if she touched you?"

"What?" Emrys's startle is violent and my blood rushes through me. I can feel the heat of him radiating, reaching, while wild thoughts begin to uncurl within me.

"I asked you if you would prefer her conducting this experiment," Osian prods. "Perhaps you'd like that? Too much, I think. Hmm. Should we see if you can resist your attraction to the girl?"

"That is against—" Enydd begins.

"Oh, hush. It is an experiment and I quite like this change. Yes, if you will, please attempt to regulate responses, we will watch for signs of arousal or discomfort and we will call it out should we see it. For testing their self-control. In fact…" Osian grins. "I'd like you to touch each other, keep away from genitals, but other erogenous zones are quite fine. But the rules still apply. Begin."

Emrys and I gape at each other. Our touches have been regulated to what necessitated those during training—fighting and blocking and our hand-holding when we fought off poison—but beyond that, we've kept our distance.

"I'm okay with it if you are. It's just a test, after all. And should we have a response, our bodies are only reacting to stimuli," I reassure him.

"Right, just a test. I trust you."

The words slither through me, seeping into my heart. "Okay."

Emrys reaches first, his pinky touching mine, slowly moving his finger along my palm, tracing the lines there. With my opposite hand, I stretch my fingers outward, pressing them into his abdomen, feeling his hot skin through the buttoned blouse he wears, his ridged muscles hard lines. I trace them and he fails to suppress a shiver. Enydd knocks him lightly in the head. He continues his careful perusal of me, sliding up my forearm, the gentle caress erasing Osian's unwanted advances. He swirls along my inner elbow, following the bluish lines of my veins. My hand skirts to his side, nails lightly scratching against his ribs. He licks his lips. Another knock. His hand continues moving up and his knuckles graze the side of my breast. I gasp softly before I can contain it. Osian whacks me in the back of the head.

"You two are pathetic," Osian scoffs. "Hardly touching and you're panting after one another. Goddess help me."

"Maybe they've already fucked," Enydd comments, hand itching for another excuse.

"We haven't," Emrys answers, though there is another word hanging at the edge of that sentence that could change it all. My breath hitches. Osian thumps me again.

"This is your one sanctioned excuse to touch each other—do it properly."

I meet Emrys's eyes and nod once, giving my consent. He breathes quickly, tightens his jaw and nods in answer.

"Push me away if you need to," he whispers.

"I trust you."

He does not hesitate.

One hand fists at the nape of my neck, the other at the small of my back, pressing us together, fingers dipping beneath my shirt and up my spine. I let out an embarrassing sound and am rewarded with a pleased chuckle from Emrys and punished with a flick from Osian. Enydd hits Emrys for his sound.

How is one not supposed to react to this?

Emrys traces every knob of my spine and I force myself to feel but not sink into it. My hands finally connect to my brain and they move, one hand skimming between us, going to his throat. The other is beneath his shirt, touching those ripped muscles, my fingertips dancing against them. His mouth is near my throat, and I smell vetiver and lemon and leather, the scent of him consuming me. He groans into my ear and wetness pools between my legs. Enydd and Osian hit us. My hand slips down, tucking the tips of my fingers into his waistband—he freezes and I feel hardness digging into my hip. His own hands move against me, lips brushing my collarbones as I slip that hand that was on his throat, into his hair. We both make sounds inappropriate for rivals and Enydd and Osian whack us and sigh.

"Okay enough, enough!" Osian pushes us apart and our flushed faces are comically bright. "This was an absolute failure. I expected better of you." Osian sighs again and looks up to the broken ceiling, at the gray sunlight through the moss. "This will be a yearly trial and I expect you two to be able to complete it by centuries end. If not, you will not pass and Lady Fate will not let you return."

"That's a possibility?" I ask, shocked.

"Of course, it is. Should you fail, you are released from the realm and not into your courts, but into Wild Hunt's lands and chased through the woods by them and this century's mentors."

"You will kill us?" Emrys questions.

"It is Lady Fate's law, not ours."

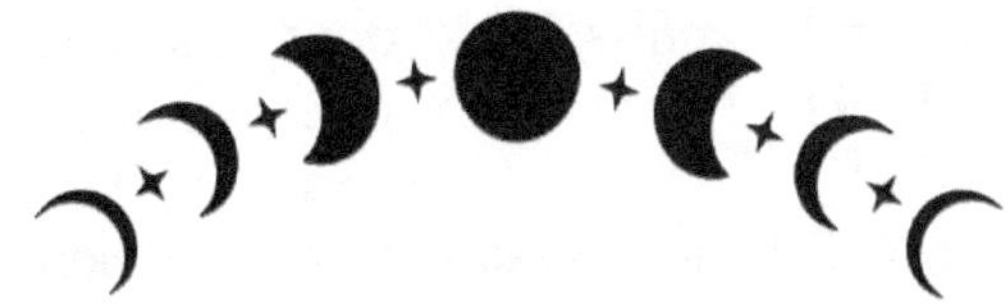

I stand behind Emrys as he sits on a broken edge of column, evening descending on us, the gray light turning dusky. He stares ahead while I hold antique shears in my hands, clipping the errant waves that cling to his shirt collar.

After the disastrous trial we both failed, Emrys asked not to be parted from me, but rather for my assistance. He hates his hair overly long, so now I'm snipping until the longest waves touch his cheekbones. I watch the ruby strands fall to the stone while he hums to himself, fingers twisting around each other, nearly every finger holding a ring—the only ones without are the ring fingers on both hands and the right middle.

The trial should have brought some semblance of embarrassment, but rather than the illness that Osian evoked, I feel closer to Emrys. Comforted. Despite the touches being inherently sexual, there was something emotionally intimate about it—about our exchanged *I trust you's*.

"Are you okay?" Emrys asks.

"I am."

"I just mean, I know that you didn't want Osian touching you and I should have done more, and then immediately after that I had to touch you and I—" he cuts himself off. "I just want to make sure you didn't feel…"

I come around to Emrys's front, stepping into the cradle of his thighs, tapping under his chin with the handle of the scissors. He looks up and I watch the shame burn away. I snip a couple more strands before I respond.

"You made me feel safe. I'm glad it was you."

Emrys smiles and it's a slow spread, his left side curls first before the right pulls back over his slightly pointed incisors. "Good." His hands come to rest on my hips. "Is this okay?"

I swallow, feeling heat coil below my belly. "Yes."

"Good."

Sensually, his thumbs stroke small circles on my hipbones and I bite my lip to stifle a sound. Emrys continues humming, closing his eyes while I continue working on his hair. I don't know what this means, but for now I am content not putting a name to it, not questioning it, and certainly not rushing it.

We have another ninety-nine years to figure it out.

CHAPTER 8

I wake to another nightmare of Gideon and Caethes having sex.

Rolling away from the reflective puddle of spilled wine next to me, I groan and scrub my cheeks, staring up at the ceiling. I can't remember the last time I slept in my bed, but I'm sure it's been more than a week. I push myself up from the cold stone and drag my alcohol-laden body to the bathing room, running myself a scalding bath. I don't bother discriminating against the labels and throw in an alarming number of oils. It's not even half full when I climb in and sink into the heat, coils of steam rising on the surface.

I close my eyes and try to banish the third nightmare from my psyche. I'm already horrified. The first time the dream came over me I puked into a vase. The second time I retched. The third time has sent me to the bath. I press my fingertips to my eyes, but still the nightmare loops over and over and I'm cursed with a replay of what I presume to be Caethes's bedchamber. A room of glass and diamond and silver and violet, a bed of curling metal, lines of fauns and filigree. Upon that monstrosity of a sleep space, Caethes rides Gideon, the globes of her full breasts bouncing while his hands crest up and down her ribs, moaning with a sound all too familiar to my ears.

Nausea strikes me and I slip beneath the water, submerging myself and dreaming of death. I ponder beneath the water if I should re-emerge, if I have the strength to resume my mess of a life. Already I've shirked countless responsibilities, many of which Maelona has picked up on my behalf, others Julia has attempted to shoulder.

Wisteria came to me four days ago, furious and brimming with resolve.

"You need therapy," she practically shouted at me.

I paused, turning toward her and away from the maneuver I was showing Julia with a dirk. "What for?"

"*What for?*" Wisteria scoffed. "Faerie, you're grieving and you're in denial."

"About?"

"Everything! All the shit in Aberth, losing Gideon, your missing years, your friend's death, your sister's death, your sense of failure and misplaced self, the romances that you can't seem to handle, your wings—"

"Who told you about my wings?"

Wisteria clamped her jaw shut.

"Who. Told. You."

Wisteria's eyes unfaithfully wavered over my shoulder. I furiously wheeled on Maelona.

"You had *no* right!" I snapped.

Maelona's hair shimmered maroon. "You're a fucking mess, Evelyn, we all see it. You're jeopardizing all of us with your flagrant substance abuse, so yes, actually, I had *every* right."

"Fuck you, Maelona."

"Oh, go dry up."

And so, I had, storming off to my room and knocking a bottle of wine to the floor and another, and another. Planning to empty every last drop into the drain and forget about my budding alcoholism. But before I could do that, a wave of grief so visceral took me out and I laid on the floor in the mess of liquor and cried. At some point I'd passed out and that was when the first nightmare plagued me.

I emerge once again from the water, choosing not to drown today. I sit there, inhaling the fumes and then I realize the scents I'd selected. Courtesy of my fae senses I can distinguish orchid and cherry, pine and lime, vetiver and lemon. I groan and cover my eyes. Because of course I did. Of course, I added the strongest notes of Maelona, Gideon, and Emrys to my bath. Because I'm a fucking sadist.

Closing my eyes I lean forward, dip my face in the water and scream. Bubbles erupt around me, the tightening and burning in my chest serving as an anchor. Once all the oxygen leaves me and I have nothing left to give I remain there, crystallized in my scalding bath, existing in the aftermath. I let the tightening in my chest turn extreme, to an unbearable point, before I resurface with a wild gasp.

Water streams off me in burning rivulets, dripping from my lashes and nose. I stare at the faucet, wishing I didn't exist. To not have to worry about the world's problems.

Out of the bath, I resolve not to leave my room for the rest of the day and figure out the lullaby. Armed with a bottle of goldwine, my overdrawn notebook, and dressed only in a green silk robe, I sit at my desk.

I jot down the lullaby one more time and run a line through the lines of "murder" and "mourn", "failure" and "heart" and then label it—Julia and Wisteria. I feel victorious and then return to the top in defeat as I pace through the lines. I sigh and take a swig of wine, crack my neck, and delve into the lullaby-prophecy-rhyme thing. I circle "crown" and place arrows and question marks with the names Aneira and Caethes—am I collecting pieces of both sides of the board, or just mine? I slip further down the lines noticing only two male pronouns indicated. I sketch down Gideon and Emrys.

His lies are breath.

Gideon is the only one of them that can lie.

I cross the verse and put "Gideon" next to it. Without thinking further, I add Emrys's name to "cost" and "death"— his Revenant title was purchased with his dying. I reread that line and my gut sinks.

Bishops are sacrifice…

She is three…

I take another gulp of wine and write my name beside Emrys's. I am "three"—the Harbinger, the *Ceidwad Cudd*, and Evelyn Corianne Vanora.

The other half of "royals" stares at me, taunting me. I bite my lip and circle it, adding arrows, questioning Aneira, Caethes, or Maelona. The first line evades me. Is the other half the heir apparent? My eyes flicker to the names I'd guessed first, flicking between the two fae monarchs. Surely Aneira is not "deceit", so does that indicate that I'm collecting Caethes's pieces too? Or is Caethes simply a piece on the board? Or am I reading this entirely wrong?

I groan. The wine is loosening my bones, putting me in a pleasant haze. To the side of the lullaby, I write down the remaining names of my suspected players and cross out the ones I'm certain of.

~~Evelyn~~, ~~Gideon~~, Maelona, ~~Wisteria~~, ~~Julia~~, ~~Emrys~~, Aneira, Caethes, Violante, Drysi, Tegwyn, Cariad, Callahan (?), Bambalina, Sybella.

The names scold me for my cowardice to write the final name I suspect. With an unsteady hand, I write out the letters: C-O-R-V-I-N-A

My sister's name blinks at me with innocent eyes, uncertain where she is meant to go. Because she is gone and no longer has a place. Was she a pawn? Was she The Pawn?

Tears slip unfettered down my face, tracing silver solemnity over my cheekbones.

"I miss you," I whisper to the faint name.

Hours later I stop working on the verse, a pounding headache in my temples from stress and booze, an entire bottle of goldwine empty at my feet, my robe parted over my flushed chest. I drape myself backwards over my chair, mind spinning. I have declared the lullaby for one side of the board and matched five names. But I wonder if there is supposed to be one pawn, two like the rest of the verses implies, or eight as a game dictates?

I create a separate list of pawns, question marks dotting their columns, moving players around my paper board.

A subtle knock raps on my door.

Tying the belt on my robe, I cross the threshold of my quarters, and open the door to find Maelona there. I slouch against the frame and cock a brow.

"Hello, Lady Maelona."

Maelona narrows her eyes at me. "Ev, I haven't seen you in days."

I shrug. "I haven't left my room in days."

"Ev, what's going on? I haven't wanted to push you because you've been through so much, but I'm worried. I've never seen you like this and if you want to tell me what's wrong, I'd like to help you."

I bark a laugh, leave the door open, and saunter in. "No one can help me now."

"That cannot be true." Maelona sweeps in and shuts the door.

"Why?" I challenge, skirting my furniture, watching the other faerie in front of me.

"Because you're not beyond saving."

"You're wrong."

"I refuse to accept that."

"Fuck Mae, do you think I would be saying it if I didn't believe it?" I shout, wheeling on her. "Of course, it's true. I have been mutilated beyond repair, my fucking wings are gone and I have no idea what has been done with them. My goddess-damned twin sister is dead and if I had remembered I'm fae just days before, then maybe I could've saved her. I left Gideon— a non-fae—in the Roads, alone. I made a deal with Lady Fate that I cannot remember and I've pissed her off aside from that. My identities, reputation, and entire life are in shambles.

"So, no, Mae. You can't help me."

"Let me try. I want to be there for you," she whispers, reaching for me.

I scoff at her, pulling away. Her fingers brush the back of my hand and I feel the lingering touch after I've pulled back. "You want to be there for me, do you? You want to be the person I come to after I've fucked someone else? You want to be a second choice? Or fuck, at this point a third choice? You want to question your place in my priorities? You want to be a repeated notch in the proverbial belt?"

Maelona thins her lips, her hair not even betraying her emotions. "Now you're just being cruel."

"I am being realistic in the crudest of ways."

"You're hurting and want to hurt me back."

"Oh, give it up, Mae."

"Don't," she says darkly and my nerves fray. She advances on me, slowly and without fear. "Don't ruin a good thing because you're in a foul mood. I have stood by you through all your bullshit, Evelyn," Maelona sneers, finally showing some emotion, strands of her hair turning burgundy with wrath. She clutches my jaw, forcing me to look in her furious dark eyes. "But this is going too far. You're drifting so far out of my reach and you're refusing to accept help, it's like you *want* to punish yourself."

My heart races, enveloped with the fragrance of cherries and orchids with the slightest hint of freesia and silk. Maelona's scent is heady, intoxicating and all too familiar, unraveling old thoughts and memories. Like feeling her satiny skin beneath my fingers, the taste of her on my tongue. I remember the way she smells at the base of her throat and how she reacts when I kiss her there.

I forcefully shove myself out of the deluge of the past.

"*A good thing*," I scoff. "Did you really come here just to berate me and my life choices? I might have a problem with that."

"Oh, you want to talk problems? You know what *your* problem is?"

"Oh, do enlighten me."

She leans in, close enough to kiss. "You're a sad, vicious bitch with barely a shred of empathy."

She practically tosses my head away while the words lodge in my heart. The sting of her nails scratching is nothing compared to the barb of her insult.

"You're not the first person to call me a bitch, don't feel special about it. Besides, those have always been my most dominant traits, it's on you if you didn't realize it sooner."

"Oh, it's not just me, it's your precious Revenant, too."

This time the blow hits differently and I flounder for a response.

Maelona bulldozes on. "You think I haven't spoken to him over the years? That we didn't know about each other? We both searched for you and he kept going even when I gave up. Goddess only knows why he still pines for you when you constantly treat him like shit. He wears his heart on his whole person and it's like you pick it up to look at it and then walk all over it. It's cruel and manipulative. Fuck, you're just like Caethes. You might not eat the hearts, but you destroy them."

I feel a spike impale the stone in my chest. The iron of it bleeding into me and sickening me, the mithridatism I'd built up dissolved in that one true strike. It thumps unevenly, paining me.

I've fucked up. I've hurt two people—more—dear to me. I am monstrous. Not because I am the Harbinger and I have been tasked with such dirty deeds, but monstrous for my utter disregard for everyone around me. My destructive behavior hasn't just been hurting me, it's been injuring everyone I touch.

But despite the epiphany, the rage and drink have me and I cannot claw myself to the surface. I am helpless, a passenger while the monster takes the reins and I watch, restrained to the back seat as it takes me away from the little good left in my life.

"You take that back," I growl.

"I'll take it back when you deserve it."

"How dare you?"

"*How dare I*? How dare *you*!" Maelona's hair is deep, seething claret at this point. "You expect us to all faun over you because you're the precious Harbinger? You may be a warrior but in every other area you're a fucking coward." Maelona strides for the door. "Enjoy your drink, Lady Vanora, I won't bother you beyond what our job requires."

She's at the door when I finally manage to swallow my pride.

"Mae…wait."

Maelona pauses, a hand on the door, her silver painted nails shimmering. She doesn't turn, but I know she's listening. "What?" It's hardly a question.

I open my mouth. Nothing comes out.

The other faerie sighs. "I can't deal with you when you're like this, maybe someone who cares more can."

She slams the door with that parting jab, and I'm left staring at the finality of her departure. I stand there for, I don't know how long, staring like an idiot. At some point a bottle of goldwine finds its way into my hand.

CHAPTER 9

The sensation of fingers stroking my hair brings me to. My internal alarm pings a familiar tune, and I open my eyes slowly, taking in the figure crouching next to me. Black leather and golden hands, with golden eyes and a concerned frown. We lock gazes and I do not move. I do not say anything; I just watch him while he continues brushing my silver hair back from my brow. Tears burn, bright and sharp, suddenly carving salty tracks down my face.

"Hi," I croak.

"Hi Vanna," Emrys Gorlassar whispers. Still running his beringed hand through my tresses.

Tears continue cutting lines over the planes of my cheeks, my throat thickens with emotion and intoxication. Emrys says nothing and lets me set boundaries, and I can see very clearly in those topaz eyes that if I asked him to "*fuck off and leave*" he'd do it; however, in this moment nothing in me wants to be alone and nothing in me wants *him* specifically to abandon me. He's known me the longest and there'd be something so imaginably painful if he also gave up on me. The reminder of Maelona's desertion sends a fresh wave of sorrow through me.

"How are you here?" I manage, ignoring the tears slipping over my mouth.

Emrys cannot kill me in my court as I cannot kill him in his—we decided this Centurion law. Therefore, my wards protecting against threat do not prevent the Revenant.

"The window," he responds. "Maelona sent me a message."

"I didn't realize you two were friends."

Emrys's mouth twists. "I wouldn't go as far to say that, but we have common ground."

I can't help the words that slip from my mouth. "Did you have sex with her?" Something about the prospect of Emrys and Maelona sleeping together twists a blade in my stomach and as soon as I pose the question, I want to revoke it, not wanting to know the answer if it's yes. Despite Maelona preferring females exclusively, she has been known to sample the odd male.

"Would that bother you?"

I can't respond.

He shakes his head. "Never." He pauses, seeming to wage an internal battle. Color blooms on his cheeks. "I haven't been with anyone like that for more than six years."

The exhale I release is embarrassingly large and Emrys quirks a smile at my reaction. He skims his thumb beneath my eye, swiping away the tears, smoothing back stray strands of hair. I stare at him—this male whom I know so very well, whom I'm fairly certain hasn't slept with anyone since me.

I pull myself up to sitting, leaning against the stairs—which I presumably passed out next to—and bring my knees to my chest. I'm still wearing the green satin robe and nothing else, yet Emrys hasn't remarked on it. He takes a seat on the cold edge, stretching out his long legs. I rest my cheek on my knees, turning my face to my true opposite. I draw in breath, resolving myself to ask a question and not let my fear stop me.

"How did you manage to carry on when your wings were severed?"

He tips his head back against the stairs, staring at the glass ceiling and the midnight sky above. The mutilation of his wings has always been one of his best kept secrets. I am one of the only people aware he'd ever had them, and I feel guilty for bringing it up. He licks his lips and closes his eyes.

"I think it was easier for me because I was a child, but there are days that I feel their loss so vividly it takes my breath away."

The loss of one's wings is an egregious insult and typically assigned to brutal torment or severe punishment, and for some reason it happened to both of us. I don't know exactly why Jacob Dugal removed my wings and what his purpose was for them—evidence of the Harbinger's capture? —and what has been done with them—where did he hide them? On the plane?

"My mother lost hers before I was conceived," Emrys continues, tapping his fingers on his knees. "She was in a battle and during the fight she was taken captive and enemy forces tore them from her. At some point she was able to escape into the woods and was found by a witch who nursed her back to health."

"I've never heard you talk about your mother."

"That's because I never have. There isn't much to tell. She abandoned me to Caethes when I was only days old." He shakes his head and I'm startled by our mirrored upbringings, my own mother depositing me at the rival queen's doorstep. Has Lady Fate been intervening this long? Did she really design my true opposite from birth? From before that? "I don't know if my wings were a reminder that she'd lost hers and she couldn't bear it. I don't know if she never wanted me but didn't have the heart to abort me. I don't know why I was surrendered, just that I was."

"What were they like?" I ask timidly.

Emrys smiles fondly, eyes distant. "Black, feathered. Stereotypical dark angel wings. The opposite of yours."

And there it is again. Opposite. My mirror.

My heart flips thinking about the insinuations of the matter, the coincidences that are a little too convenient to be dismissed. I would be lying if I said my thoughts weren't heading into a panic-inducing direction, wondering about Lady Fate's motivations.

"Did Caethes ever treat you like a sexual object? Or were you like a child to her?" I press, curious about the state of my opposite's upbringing—parentage was something Emrys has always refused to discuss with me over the years, and if he's willing to give up information now, I'm all too willing to take it.

"More like a pet," he says after a brief consideration. "I think though, that if I ever gave her the opportunity to sleep with me, she would take it. But only if I wanted it. She is many terrible things, but she has a complex when it comes to sexual consent."

That makes my heart sicken and twist, acutely volatile in our intimate environment. Caethes does not belong between us, in our small bubble of a realm, a throwback to Century Training where we were everything to each other and for that time nothing to everyone else. It's this train of thought that lets slip my next sentence.

"I've been having nightmares of Caethes and Gideon fucking."

I've imbibed far too deeply and now I'm suffering the effects of an alcohol-induced emotional breakdown with an added dose of trauma dumping.

Emrys whips his head in my direction, brows raised comically high. "For how long?"

I shrug, wanting the bottle, but also not wanting to break the space of contented intimacy we've created here. "Only the past few days and it's been a couple times, but it's been terrible."

He taps my thigh with his boot. "Your anxieties are manifesting in your dreams, Vanna."

"What else can I do? I'm trying to figure out how to get him back without sacrificing myself. The fact that Caethes used him as a bartering chip doesn't help matters, no thanks to you."

"I won't apologize for that. I gave you a possibility. I did not bar you from trying to save him."

"No, you just made it very difficult."

"I made it so you had a chance, Vanna," Emrys sighs. "Please, I don't want to fight with you. I think you misunderstand the amount of influence I hold over Caethes. You seem to think it's quite a lot."

"It isn't?"

"Clearly not as much as you have on Aneira." He says her name so bitterly.

"Why do you have such hate for my mother?"

Emrys laughs darkly, throwing back his head in mocking, horrible humor. "Your mother? Your mother is a faerie you hardly care for. I have no qualms with Drysi."

"You know exactly who I mean."

"Goddess, you have Aneira on this fucking pedestal. It's like you think she can do no wrong. As someone who serves in the opposite court, believe me when I say that I have seen the worst of her."

He sets unease in me, but rather than inquire deeper, I lash out, my alcoholic stupor allowing the monster inside to break free of the confines I barely keep it in. "But you think that Caethes is the better monarch worth serving, do you?"

"I never said that. I did not choose Caethes, nor would I." He curses under his breath. "Vanna, please. I don't want to fight."

I pull myself up, inebriation blurring my vision as I move far too quickly for my physical state to properly allow. "Then why do you continue to serve the Dark Court? Why don't you defect to the Seelie Court?"

It's not unheard of, just rare. Most fae are raised within the court of their birth, learning the customs and morals of either. I've met few who have converted—one being the pale faerie who killed Callahan, and a handful of others. It's not a perfect system, the defecting faerie not quite fitting in to either court any longer, either forced to carve their own niche, or fit in by force or tactic. Most are shunned due to the heritage they bring and the inherent Seelie or Unseelie gift they possess—if they do. I possess neither and so does Emrys, both of us displaying latent talents that have no bearing on the norm of fae inheritance. Though Seelie's having the influence of karma has been dying out for eons, while the Unseelie typically continue to retain their internal chaos detector.

The influence of karma is minimal. Those who have the ability detect the domino effect of someone else's choices and can tell if they'll get what they deserve or not. It's a finicky thing, hindered by the butterfly effect, but it exists, nonetheless. The ability is similar to a Hazelhurst witch's ability to see patterns.

Even then, I know only two Seelies to possess the karma gift—Folant and the Admiral.

Emrys sighs and gets to his feet. "It's not that simple. If I defect, it's over for me. I am the Revenant, Vanna. The things I know…that I can do…I could bring the Unseelie Court to its knees, but Caethes would have me killed the moment I thought about it. I would hardly be an asset any longer, I'd be a burden."

Our meetings have always been a secret to our monarchs, but now the possible consequences hit. A brief glimmer of all-encompassing terror races through me, like an injection of ice, arrowing for a place between my ribs, before it melts away with no trace. Within the cage of my ribs, a quiver vibrates through me, a firm *NO* resounding. Within me it quakes, trying to open the locked box that Lady Fate put a part of me in. In a starlight burst, I scramble to my feet, swaying drunkenly. I put a hand out to steady myself.

"Then I'll protect you."

Emrys raises a brow and I watch emotion he tries to repress burn in his eyes. It's a flicker, but it's there. It's hope and something even warmer than that. "You don't know what you're saying, you're beyond intoxicated."

Lifting my chin, I summon every ounce of confidence and power, despite wearing nothing but a poorly tied robe. "I know exactly what I'm saying. You are my opposite, designed specifically to mirror me, you are the other half of our Centurion. I do not care that we have been enemies, I do not care that we are in a stasis I cannot name right now, I do not wish for a world without you in it. I will fight for you with every ounce of my will. I will fight with my dying breath."

That unlocks the gates on his emotion. The dam bursts free and the wave of devotion that pours from him threatens to level me. I stay my ground, watching his floodgates rush around me—the adoration and love and desire. I step towards him, slow to remain balanced, and place my hand over his chest. Over the scar. His heart is thundering.

There is a slight crack within me, a sliver of light within my psyche.

"I refuse to let it happen," I continue, obstinate, the scent of vetiver in my lungs. "I have the might of the Seelie Court behind me. I have the knowledge of the *Ceidwad Cudd* over them. I have the power of the Harbinger in me. I will use it all to keep you alive."

Emrys carefully covers my hand with his. There is an ache in his eyes when he looks at me. "Why? Why do you care so much what happens to me? You were willing to die for Gideon, you're willing to risk it all for him, so how can you say this to me?"

This brings me up short and I flounder for a moment, my own pulse racing in tandem to Emrys's. His heart belies his emotion, passion, fear, hope, love, all shattering with every pound beneath my palm. It's a begging rhythm, pleading for me to give him the words he needs to hear. But some of the worse words I've uttered creep into my consciousness.

You are my reason for living.

Then die.
It festers and rots within me.
May we be as cold as iron, right Evelyn?
Fuck you, Gideon Zhao.
Like a guillotine I let those words cut Gideon, walking away, not caring to witness the carnage it drew.

Shame burns through me, the alcohol turning sour in my gut. I meet Emrys's face, guarded, but the door open with a security chain strung across his gaze. I know enough of a blow could break it wide open.

"Do you love him?" Emrys whispers.

Words dry up on my tongue. "I don't know."

He shutters his eyes, the door closing. "Do you love me?"

Mine close too.

It feels like a cycle, this question and my repeated response, this sick masochistic game of Do You Love Me? and I Never Loved You. This circle of insanity that always leads to his heart being broken. It's always the same and it always hurts. Dread sinks through me as I must tear him apart again. I begin to summon the words then stop, feeling that sliver that escaped, piercing my heart and bringing a revelation.

"I don't know."

When I open my eyes, I find his flared wide, a riot of feeling flashing through like a kaleidoscope.

"Okay," he finally says.

"*Okay?*"

"It's enough. For now." He cups my jaw in both hands, caressing my every feature with his eyes. I watch as he strokes over the slope of my nose, the high rise of my cheekbones, the supple fullness of my lips. There, he lingers a long time and I see—I *know*—he wants to kiss me, but I know—I *see*—just as clearly that he won't.

"For now," he whispers, more to himself.

"I don't know what I'm supposed to do now, Ryss." My voice cracks. "I'm so confused, I'm lost...I don't know who I'm supposed to be anymore." Tears fall once again, slipping over Emrys's fingers.

"Save Gideon and we'll go from there," he tells me, leaning forward to kiss the tears from my cheek. The scent of lemon drop candies, vetiver, and leather slips into me. He hovers there, his mouth soft before slowly gliding over the bridge of my nose to the other side. My skin heats at the brush of his lips, the warmth on the left and then the right. My tears shine on his lips when he pulls back.

"Wh-What? Why...? You said you lo—" I stumble out of his cupped hands.

"Because it's the right thing to do and you can never give me your heart while he still holds a piece of it. I will never have a chance if he doesn't return."

My mouth hangs open, my heart thundering the truth he's revealed. It hits me like a physical blow and I sway, but Emrys catches me around the middle—steadying me. Like he always has. His hands burn through the thin satin and I can't help it when my nipples peak beneath.

Emrys doesn't miss it.

Heat lights his gaze before he shakes himself free of it. "You need to sleep, and not on the floor like an animal."

With that, Emrys ensures my balance and strides over to the bed. He clears it and turns the covers to find a bottle on one side, lying there like a lazy bedmate, waiting for another joining. He says nothing as he removes it and I wonder if he's planning to take its place. An undeniable thrill goes through me at the prospect.

By the hand, he leads me to my bed, helping me in and taking a seat before massaging some warmth into my ice-cold feet. I squirm slightly, insecure.

"They might smell," I whine softly.

Emrys chuckles. "I've seen you in the throes of poisoning, Vanna, and all the unpleasantness that goes with it. A slight scent is nothing." He continues working the blood back into my feet, his thumbs circling into the soles, causing me to elicit a moan I cannot contain. Emrys startles and I hear the distinct hitch in his breath. My cheeks flare red.

I huff, embarrassment burning. "That doesn't make me feel any better."

He tucks my feet beneath the covers and rolls the blankets over me. He stands to leave and a bolt of fear strikes me. I shiver, realizing how much the alcohol was truly keeping me warm and how much it was keeping me afloat without him.

"Can you stay?" I say before I can take it back, and then think of an excuse. "I'm cold."

Emrys pauses but nods. He bends down to remove his boots and I turn on my side to better see him, admiring his very well-formed backside in the process. It's as I'm distracted, looking at the lovely curve of his ass that I hear a chuckle and tear my gaze away to find I'm caught and he's laughing at me.

"Enjoying the view?" he teases.

"Very much so."

Emrys searches the sky for willpower. "You can't say that kind of stuff to me."

"Why?" I ask, feeling an ache and heat pool between my legs, a taunt that is turning into dangerously explicit territory.

Emrys's nose flares, his eyes shooting straight to my core and I realize with a tinge of horror and excitement that he can smell my arousal. I drag my eyes down his form, over the black blouse he wears unbuttoned, showing off his chest and the scar and part of his chiseled abdomen. My eyes continue lower and find a significant pressure pushing against his leather pants. I lick my lips. He watches me with utter devastation.

"You're drunk and as long as you continue to be, I will not touch you and you shall not touch me. Not like that."

"Even if I ask?"

"Especially if you ask."

I shift beneath the covers, opening and closing my legs, eager for some friction. It's been so long since I've tended to myself and weeks since I've had sex, the last time being with Gideon in the Faerie Roads.

The thought of Gideon is like a bucket of ice dumped over my head and guilt replaces it all.

I sigh. "I'm still cold, though."

Emrys sighs too and climbs into the bed next to me. Facing the ceiling. "Because you said you were cold."

"Is that the only reason?" I tease, reaching for him. He acquiesces, sliding closer, the left side of his body flush against the front of mine. His heat is like an open flame and I shiver in pleasure, squirrelling closer into the cozy warmth he brings.

He doesn't answer, but I know he heard me.

We lie there, listening to the other's breathing patterns, viscerally aware of our presence. Emrys is tense, containing himself to keep from moving—from touching me. Emotion uncoils within me and sleep begins to descend. With the pull of slumber, words escape me.

"I'm sorry about your wings."

He's quiet before he reaches for my hand, pulling it to his chest, over his heart.

"I'm sorry about yours, too."

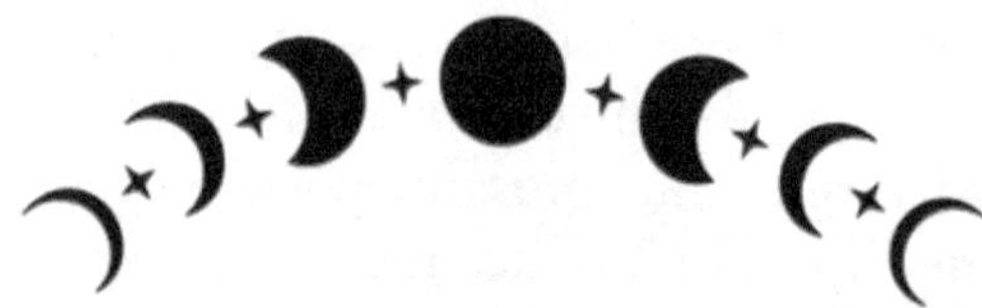

I wake at some point to find my legs tangled with Emrys's, his arm over my waist, the other beneath my head. My own hands are tucked into his shirt, seeking the warmth. The blankets have shifted down in the night, pooling around our hips. I look down at myself and find my robe parted, one white breast has slipped out of the robe, the pink nipple peaked with the chill. His face is tucked into the hollow of my throat, the soft brush of his breath against my skin heating me. That intoxicating scent of vetiver lingering.

A feeling of peace, contentment, and a tingle of excitement flare through me, but all of it is touched with sleep and I have the dizzying lack of reality that comes with it. I question the truth of what I'm seeing but my lids are so heavy.

Too tired to move, I simply settle in, burying my face into his dark red waves, ready to blame the alcohol in the morning.

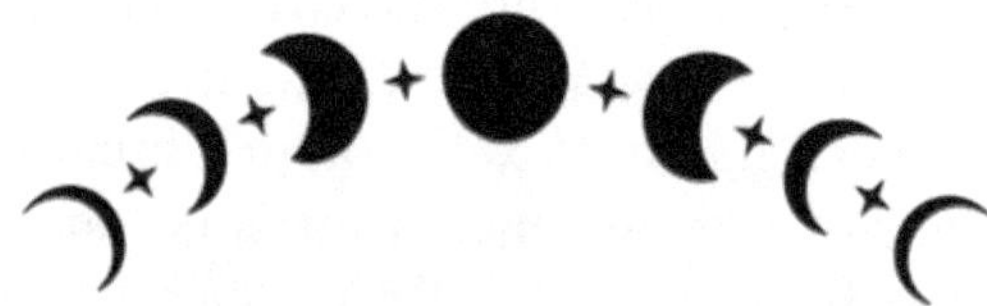

Morning comes and I wake in my bed alone, sunlight filtering in through the glass ceiling. I don't move, realizing my arms are out, reaching for a bedmate that is no longer there and notice that my robe has been rearranged to cover my chest more securely. Both breasts tucked back into the satin.

On the pillow is a note, written in Emrys's smooth, familiar script.

I left at dawn. I'm sorry I could not stay longer but my absence would be noted. I didn't want to leave, especially since I wanted to ask you; would you be opposed to me being able to signal to you once again?

One flash for no, two for yes.

Yours Always,

Ryss

On the bedside table is the Unseelie athame. I reach for it and signal for yes.

CHAPTER 10

CENTURY TRAINING

We've been failing our test every year. We're five years older and still our bodies react to each other despite overwhelming exhaustion. Days are filled with exercises, either training our bodies or minds, everything from sprints to meditation to holding planks to boxing. Nights are wrought with whispers and a tired body next to mine.

Emrys has proved more proficient with shorter blades wielded dually, while I lean towards a preference of a longer sword. I'm sure there's an innuendo in there somewhere. It's not just blades where we display opposing skills; I take better to poisons but he takes better to iron, his punches are heavy, but my kicks are high.

Our mentors work us so hard that most nights we bathe and then crash to our bedrolls on the thin mattress next to each other. Some nights we don't even manage the washing. Though, without fail, Emrys and I wake every morning wrapped in each other, seeking out the warm body.

Osian raps me on the knuckles when they curl against Emrys's shirt, his mouth at my throat making me react in the ways the mentors don't want to see. It became evident quite quickly that we could not be assessed when touching each other at the same time so now, as of year three, we are commanded to stillness while the other attempts their worst—or best, whichever way you look at it. Our self-control when it comes to each other leaves something to be desired.

One would think our inadvertent cuddling would render us immune to the other's touch but that idea proves very false.

"Failure," Osian proclaims and with the snub that it is, says nothing further and leaves us in the training room.

The door slamming behind him is a final note to the disdain he exudes as Emrys and I stand with flushed faces and frustrating arousals. We never talk about it post-test, but we both know that it leaves us painfully desiring the other every time. We talk about little despite how well we know each other. We aren't permitted the time to.

Sighing, Emrys runs a hand through his hair—it's getting long again—and paces the floor. His test was first and he received more demerits than last year. Even though we have more than ninety years to overcome it, I can see the backslide wearing at him.

I take a seat on the edge of the fountain, the dry stone cracked, details lost to moss and time. Palming the edge, I feel the rough rim to dispel the soft feel of Emrys's skin that still burns my fingers. Tiny electric pulses tingle against my hand and I do my best to ignore them.

"What's your mother like?" I ask frankly.

This brings Emrys up short and he stiffens, his crossed arms pulling tighter. "Why do you ask?"

I shrug. "Making conversation. I figured we knew *of* each other, but we've never talked about anything that deep."

"I don't talk about my mother."

"Any particular reason?"

"She abandoned me and that's all I care to know."

I pinch my lips together, my goal of getting to know my opposite failing as rapidly as our annual tests "And your father?"

"No idea."

"Hmm, you're not providing very scintillating conversation."

Emrys snorts a laugh. "I'm not trying to."

"Humor me."

He sighs. "What's *your* father like?"

"I don't know, never met the guy."

Emrys rolls his eyes but I can see he's charmed. "And your mother?"

A mix of pride and bitterness well within me. For all intents and purposes Aneira is my mother. She raised me, clothed me, fed me, loved me. She encouraged me to train when I displayed a knack for it, young as I was. She discouraged me from overdressing at events when she knew it made me uncomfortable. Meanwhile, Drysi Vanora, a faerie I met only three months before I departed for Century Training can go fuck herself. She left me and my twin sister on Aneira's doorstep as newborns and vanished for sixteen years.

"Which one?" My tone holds a sardonic lilt.

"How about the one you don't like?"

I tell him.

He thins his lips and shakes his head. "And the one you do like?"

Fondness surges within me. "She's the loveliest. I am not hers biologically but she treats me as such. I owe her everything. She raised me when I was abandoned by the one person who is supposed to love me unconditionally. Without Aneira, I—"

"*Aneira*?" he asks, as if the name is a curse.

I furrow my brow, the frown painting itself across my face in the most genuine of confusions. "Yes, I thought you knew that I was raised by the Seelie Queen?"

"I knew you grew up in the Seelie Court, I didn't know you considered the queen your mother. I can't believe you think she actually cares about anyone but herself."

Defensiveness flares inside me and I stand from my perch on the fountain, tingles forgotten. "Watch what you say. She does indeed love me."

"Does she say it?" he challenges.

I lean forward, teeth bared. "Yes."

The word seems to fall like a gut punch and he steps back. "What a stupid thing for a queen to do. She really mixed feelings with her tool, that's sad."

"I am no tool."

"Yes, you are, so am I. That's exactly what we're being designed for here. Why else would we be picked if not for becoming the best asset to our preferred courts?"

I bristle. That has not been my perspective on this opportunity. "I was afforded this because I showed innate talent for it."

"What you showed your precious queen means nothing. Do you really think she didn't know you were predestined for this?"

"What do you mean?"

"Forget it," he scoffs. "I'm in a foul mood and I'm taking it out on you, I need…I need to take a walk. I'll be back later."

Emrys goes for his walk, effectively nixing our conversation, leaving me with cut threads and questions. How did my attempts at learning him run go so awry? I resolve to ask him—gently—when he returns. But when he returns, I know something is amiss. He's closed off and shut in, as if in my absence he was able to erect a wall between us. One so high and far I cannot see the edges.

He is reserved, aloof, and utterly untouchable that night, and every night after he sleeps as far away from me as he can, across our shared room. We no longer wake twisted together and my slumbers are fitful and cold.

I attempt to reach him but he brushes me off politely and declines any attempts at broaching the topic.

Another year passes and our yearly test comes upon us again. We both fail it again, only this year it is not like previous ones. It is worse.

We are practically flogged this time, our mentors cursing us out, screaming we're sullying their names, that their hopes for us are dashed. There's a final spitting remark that claims they figured we'd be better while on the outs but clearly that proves the very opposite.

The door slams again, just as it has every year.

We are left alone, my face burning, angry tears pooling in my eyes. I stomp over to Emrys. "I've had enough of this. You need to fucking talk to me."

"I'd rather not."

His hair is significantly longer, cut jaggedly, uneven strands from his attempts lending an air of chaos. It's not a good look with his emotional state.

"Fine, you don't want to talk? At least listen while I fix this catastrophe you call a haircut." I pull up a three-legged stool. "Sit."

I leave him for a moment to collect the shears and when I do, I find him perched as I told him to, head tilted forward. I tap his chin with the cold handle and he lifts his face in acquiescence. With careful maneuvers I begin snipping the locks into the style he prefers. I work quietly, reorganizing my thoughts.

"This distance between us is terrible," I begin dispassionately, cutting by his left ear. "Neither one of us is enjoying the solitude and as evidenced by our test today it does not make us perform better. I've tried to respect your wishes but quite honestly, I am feeling awfully lonely and I don't know how much more quiet I can handle." I hesitate before saying the next part, my heart hammering as I debate. "I miss you."

"I'm sorry," he whispers, his voice like ash. Soft and burnt out. "I wasn't trying to hurt you."

"Then what were you doing?"

He closes his eyes. "I was dealing with my own trauma and emotions, but I did not handle it appropriately."

"Perhaps I can shoulder the burden with you, I cannot go anywhere so you may as well utilize me for supremely underqualified therapy."

He coughs a laugh, caught off guard. "I was jealous you had a mother who stepped up and I didn't. Our stories are quite similar. Did you ever notice that?" He opens an eye and I nod in affirmation.

"I busied myself with training because it was what I was good at and it was one of the only times Caethes took notice of me. It was also a good outlet for my rage." He licks his lips. "I didn't have parents and I suppose it felt—after hearing your upbringing—like I wasn't good enough. That I never will be…for anyone."

"Hey," I say softly, delicately placing a knuckle beneath his chin. His eyes open and I open my hand, cradling his cheek—I missed the silky feel of his skin, his golden warmth. "You *are* good enough. You're good enough for me."

Affection blooms in his eyes and he captures my hand in his, pressing it more into him. As if he's trying to absorb it and tuck me close. "Just stay here a moment."

I tuck the scissors into my back pocket and keep my hand on his face, wrapping the other around his shoulders, resting my head on top of his. We stay like that for a while, wrapped together, the unspoken words forming between us, relinking our bond. Eventually we pull apart and I continue his haircut.

That night, we sleep next to each other and wake intertwined. It's as if the past year had never happened.

We fail the next test.

CHAPTER 11

Once I get ready, I resolve to apologize to Maelona. Gathering up my pride and squashing it into a box within me, I dress in a tunic and bring no blades. I do not wish to come across as confrontational or threatening—even though I am plenty lethal without my knives.

The trek to her room has me internally dragging my feet. I am not good at apologies, I am a proud vicious creature and admitting to my faults goes against my nature. My prideful, heinous nature.

Tapping on Maelona's door is a tandem knock on my heart. I care what she thinks of me and having her disdain will only send me further into a spiral. A few moments pass and she does not answer. I knock again, knowing she is still within her chambers—I sense it as surely as I sensed the lack of Emrys this morning. I do wait though, as the lady is not known for her early mornings and a noon-time sparring session is equivalent to a five or six a.m. alarm. I'm hoping she is not refusing to answer on the grounds of ignoring me, so I remain.

Eventually, I sense her presence shifting and eventually it pings just behind the door.

Maelona opens her suite with a sigh, crossing her arms over her silk nightgown, floor length and baby pink, lined with snowy lace. She wears an equally lacy kimono hastily thrown on, which slips down one shoulder. The soft coral and peach glow of her suite wraps around her, limning her in gentle light.

"You were right," I blurt.

Maelona arches a perfectly shaped brow. "About what?"

"Everything. I am a coward."

The faerie is silent, assessing me with her dark, liquid eyes. "And?"

"And I was hoping you'd forgive me."

"You haven't apologized."

I bristle, rolling my tongue in my mouth. "I am sorry."

Maelona arches that brow higher.

"I'm sorry for taking my anger out on you. You did not deserve it."

"I did not." She pauses. "I cannot be your punching bag, Ev. You cannot use me as you so often do. I am a person. I am supposed to be your best friend. You can't just lash out at me or fuck me when you please so you can get something out of your system. You can't just *use* me to forget you hate yourself."

I hang my head, embarrassment and anger mingling. I feel the monster within salivating, screaming to be let out. Wanting to hurt Maelona again, to tell her the power it has over her and it can do what it likes. But I do not allow it and I refuse to let any more alcohol feed it. "I know," I say instead, swallowing my vanity and drowning the monster in self-loathing and starving it of its desires.

"What do you want me to say, Ev?" Maelona asks, her voice huffy and tired. "I know things have shifted cataclysmically. I know things can't be back to the way they were before. Not when you are pulled in so many directions, but I cannot subject myself to this vitriol. Especially when you're wavering on borderline alcoholism. When was the last time you drank anyway? This morning?"

I try to rebuke it, stiffening. I curl my lip over my teeth. "Last night."

"So, you're probably still drunk."

"I'm not." I'm not even hungover.

Maelona scrutinizes me and sniffs daintily, leaning in. "What is that I smell on you...? Is that...?" Her eyes grow fiery. "Did you fuck Emrys last night?"

My stomach roils. Because of course I would still smell like the other Centurion. Of course, the Revenant's scent would saturate my hair, linger on my skin. After spending the night tangled up with him and not bathing this morning, it's obvious that Emrys's scent would attach itself.

"How do you know what he smells like?"

Maelona tosses her hands up. "Because he was one of the only people who gave a fuck about you when you went missing and we went over everything together! I was near him for days, weeks. I know what he likes in his fucking tea, Ev." She scoffs, sickened by me. "And even after I told you how devoted he is to you and how you continue to treat him like shit, you still used him again! Don't you know what fucking him would do to his head? Not to mention his heart?"

"I didn't fuck him last night," I tell her softly, hurt. "Did no one else care that I was gone all those years?"

I'm no stranger to being disliked, but knowing that no one cared when I was gone…that is something I hadn't thought of and it strikes an unexpected blow.

Maelona's mood lowers ever so slightly, not enough to soften her, but enough for her hair to flicker navy blue. "Aside from Aneira and Corvina, yeah. We were the only ones to give a damn."

"Oh."

I don't know what I expected, but it wasn't that truth.

"Look Ev, I can't enable this behavior any longer. If you want to drink yourself into oblivion then leave me alone, I want no part in your self-imposed destruction. But if you want to sober yourself the fuck up and treat me like an actual person—and hopefully your best friend again—then let me know. But I don't want to see you until three days have eclipsed and not a single drop of alcohol has passed your lips. Until then…" She begins closing the door and pauses. "Just know that Corvina would not have wanted this for you and at the very least she would have asked for revenge."

And with that Maelona shuts the door, leaving me alone in the hall with my mortification stripping me bare.

I want a drink but I refuse the monster's call. Instead, I go down to the training area, there I find Bleddyn, Folant, and Drysi going through maneuvers, practicing with moon scythes—Maelona's favorites—and I balk for a moment.

"Care for a fourth?" I call out to the other warriors.

They pause but smile warmly, even invitingly—save for Drysi.

Folant tosses me a matching pair of moon scythes, his sharp grin full of predator's teeth, his gray hair like that of a shark's flesh. His pupils are slit and eerie white, colorless but seeing and penetrating all the same. He has always been the kindest of Aneira's guard, despite his threatening appearance.

Could any of Aneira's guards be pieces from the lullaby? I hadn't begun to consider them, but perhaps that has been my mistake.

I catch them while Bleddyn steps into the ring with Drysi, his scarlet wings flaring out behind him, the feathers opening like a peacock's fringe, taunting and glaring with a bloody shine. Across from him Drysi grins, baring her teeth and flashes her leathery wings—like the ones I once had—flicking them out with an intimidating flap.

Jealousy and grief surge up within me, the loss a physical ache, phantom pain spreading through me. I almost feel the weight of my wings behind me, standing proud and flaring with the threat of reprisal. I can almost feel the wind beneath them as I swoop through the sky. The wind biting at my skin, my hair like a silver banner behind me. But the daydream fades and I'm left with nerves misfiring and lacking part of my body once again.

Shaking myself free of my inner turmoil, I watch Drysi and Bleddyn spar. The two of them are innately talented, as Aneira would not allow any less. The two power through the match with a motley of strategy and pure power, the brute force of Bleddyn curated by centuries of precise honing against Drysi's deft evasion and ability to slip beneath blocks and blows creating an interesting atmosphere. And it is *fast*. So fast.

Wings propel quickly in directions of subversion and action, offense arrowed on by the hurl of leather or feather, defense aided with enhanced rolling, dives, and upward propulsions. A scythe cuts across the space where Drysi was breaths before, but the force of her wings and quick steps have her gliding back. She launches at Bleddyn from the air, coming down with a powerful kick he dodges by pinning his wings and rolling across the dirt floor. In return he flaps his wings with a hurricane strike and Drysi loses her footing. The two of them clash, Bleddyn pinning Drysi to the floor, his black hair hanging about his face, her onyx locks splayed to the ground. Both hold their curved blades on either side of the other's throats, inches from decapitation.

"Stalemate," Bleddyn says to her, just loud enough for us to hear.

"Stalemate," Drysi agrees with a teasing glint in her eyes.

I realize with horror I recognize the look in my birth mother's eyes. Desire and arousal. Goddess no. I recoil as Folant strides into the space, separating them.

"Evelyn, care for a round?" Folant asks.

"Oh, certainly."

We begin without ceremony and within seconds we are a blur of silver, gray, and white, violent in our movements, vicious in our strikes. It is only pure control and practice that we do not actually kill the other. Going through the motions like second-nature, I find myself exhilarated, pulsing with life through this routine that my body knows. Craves.

Two moves later I have Folant disarmed and pinned beneath my hips, both scythes poised over his chest and ready to go in either lobe of his lungs to spear him to the floor like a butterfly in a display case. Of course, I won't, and of course that is not how moon scythes are meant to be wielded.

"Fuck, I hate sparring with you sometimes," Folant gripes, flopping against the ground in defeat. "How am I supposed to beat the Harbinger?"

"You're not," I cackle and climb off him, offering a hand to help him stand.

"Good match, Evelyn."

"Good match," I respond in kind.

I turn to face Bleddyn and Drysi and find them—horrifically—much too close to one another. I swear to fuck, if they were dirty talking, I will have to bleach my brain.

Before I have a chance to say anything I sense the presence of approaching fae. I face the door before the others register a sound. A minute later Aneira and her remaining guards, Andras, Elyan, and Cadoc, step into the room. She is regal despite the concern on her face, dressed in hunter green, her gown velvet and heavy with a golden decolletage.

"Is everything all right?" I press, forgetting to abide by courtly manners or policies. It doesn't escape my notice that Bleddyn, Folant, and Drysi are all on a single knee behind me.

Aneira waves for the other three to rise and meets my gaze. "No, everything is not. Caethes has requested another meeting, this one within our very own throne room tonight."

"Why? And how can she request that?"

"Because we began the war and wartime laws dictate that she may call for a meeting but the setting of which must always alternate courts. It was declared by the first reigning monarchs."

It sounds like bullshit.

"Is that not setting ourselves up for possible infiltration?" I ask hotly.

"No, the earlier rules still apply, we are safe from harm for a day and night preceding and following the encounter. I just do not understand why she is beckoning us; we have nothing more to give, no further information or willingness to trade. I will not give you up, you know that." The unspoken *'not for Gideon'* hangs in the air between us.

I do not comment on the unsaid, but contemplate. "Do you think she has a trick?"

"No, I think she holds something new and wants to threaten us with it. Wants us to fear her power." Aneira twists her lips in a very unqueenly way. "I do not begin to guess what she is planning, but I for one am not looking forward to her childish games."

"You know war is as much politicking nonsense and showing off one's might as battles are," I tell her, unimpressed about tonight's meeting. I put the moon scythes away and wipe my hand with a damp cloth. "She luxuriates in attention. She created a whole damn town to be her playground. I wouldn't put much past her."

"Could she ask him to use—"

"I hope not, but I do not know for certain."

Aneira narrows her yellow eyes at me. "You know what I will have to do if it comes down to it."

The order.

She will order Gideon to be killed, should he try to use the commands over me, against her. We cannot risk someone so integral to Aneira's security being compromised and I already toe the line of that sanctity. Truly, if I were anyone else, I'm certain that Aneira would have brought the hammer down on that concern already. However, I am in a word, her daughter, and she cares for my well-being even if it's foolhardy. She is giving me a chance, an opportunity she would give to no one else and I am very aware of it.

I wonder if Gideon understands the kindness of the Seelie Queen. She—being the monarch of the court he is inadvertently sworn to—could call for his death and it would not violate the terms of fae war. I wonder if he has an inkling that my feelings for him have been the only thing staying her hand and prolonging the possibility of saving his life.

"I understand, my Queen. I have not forgotten."

"Good. Please be ready at twilight tonight. The meeting is set for the seventh hour and she has requested only you and me."

"Who is she bringing?"

"I do not know. She did not say."

The four of them depart, leaving the four of us to stand in the training room, with the tension in the air building ahead of what the future holds in store.

CHAPTER

I don't drink before the meeting even though I want to. I've decided to choose the path that keeps Maelona in my life and I will not jeopardize it. Especially when I've found a new, effective outlet that is much healthier in nearly every way. As I feel the glittery black gown swish around my feet, I wonder what Caethes's angle is. It has only been days since the last meeting and I cannot imagine what must have altered in that timeframe to warrant another call.

Meeting Aneira in the throne room—guards just outside the doors—I stand at her side, my queen still in her hunter-green velvet, now crowned by those golden branches. We do not offer a grand table nor seats as Caethes did. We have no interest in entertaining the Dark Queen; we are eager to have this meeting done and over with.

In my hair are large jeweled combs, set with diamonds and obsidian, shaped like roses and skulls. Inset in each eye is a black pearl and each tooth is a shimmering white freshwater pearl. My makeup is severe, dark and bold. It had crossed my mind to arrive bare-faced, in a loose shirt and pants, but that would reflect more poorly on Aneira than anything else. So, I donned a berry lip and black shadow, a cat eye sharp enough to cut glass and highlight bright enough to blind my enemies.

When Caethes arrives alone, the surprise that floods through me is immense.

The Unseelie Queen crosses the space in a black gown, eerily similar to mine, with a neckline that dips just as low. The dress displays her cleavage and the long column of her throat, as well as the patchwork of love bites that mark it all. Her arms are covered by the gown, save her shoulders, and even they have bruises on them. Her hair is long and sleek down her back, pushed from her shoulders, her diadem sitting primly atop her head. She smiles, silver lips pulling back over sharp teeth, dark doe-eyes sparkling with crushed pearl.

"Did you forget about me?" Caethes asks with a false pout.

"Did you forget your entourage?" I counter acidly.

Caethes tilts her antlered head, the jewels strung between the hoary points tinkling like chips of glass in a wind chime. "No, I arrived with all I wished to bring."

I narrow my eyes at her, taking her in a second time. She meets my eyes, her face placid with gentle ease and a low-level contentment. But hidden beneath is always that malicious gleam. I keep watching her for signs of change and then I begin feeling a sense of dread work through me. My face must have shifted, belying my realization because a wicked smile begins curving over those Unseelie silver painted lips. She licks her lower lip with a seductive tongue. My stomach sinks.

The dreams.

No.

No.

No.

No, I refuse.

No.

No.

NO.

No, I refuse to believe Gideon has—No, he cannot have. No, she must have forced him. No, they cannot be—

No.

The dread solidifies into a sickening weight in my throat, slipping into my stomach to grow like bacteria, like mold, like rot. It continues souring within me until I feel like I will vomit. The horror explodes like a decayed, bloated corpse.

I say nothing. My face has said it all. I try to keep most of it concealed but the devastation grows, spreading like a plague.

"What do you want?" Aneira says, oblivious to the bomb dropped on my life. On my heart. She is utterly unknowing of the tides that have turned and now the command that could surely be wielded against me the moment Gideon is within hearing range.

By this time, I'm certain that the Seelie emissary sigil I'd had Ghislain tattoo on Gideon is broken. It is what had started this war, and now it is for naught.

Internally, I stretch out my ability in panic, searching in case Gideon is hiding just behind that curtain of golden ivy, ready to force me to kill Aneira. My killing her would not go against the wartime rules, because she is of my court and the laws of parlay only protect from our enemies. We would be utterly at their mercy with no chance to retaliate.

Something touches at the edge of my consciousness and it is not fae.

I react, grabbing Aneira and steering her away with panicked force. "Go," I hiss beneath my breath, ushering her away. Aneira does not question me, instead she flees to the opposite entry, the one curtained in verdant green ivy. I sense when she reaches Drysi.

Whirling to face Caethes, I realize what this meeting is really about. Who it's really for. I storm over to her, furious, wanting to kill. I hiss, putting in every ounce of malice and venom. "This meeting is fucking *over*."

Caethes titters a laugh. "Yes, it is quite over, isn't it?" She waves with her fingers. "Farewell, Lady Vanora. Sleep well, I know *I* will."

The Unseelie Queen cackles a laugh, and bound by laws but controlled by fury I flick the fucking diadem off her brow with a well-placed knock. The cool metal against my fingers is one of the most egregious insults a monarch can endure.

Rage colors her face and I leave. Rushing through the curtain of ivy, I bowl into Aneira, like a small child needing their mother. I wrap her up in an embrace to keep from falling apart.

"I'm so sorry, I'm so sorry, I fucked up," I whisper over and other.

Aneira says nothing, just holds my head to her chest, stroking my hair. She lowers her voice and brings it to my ear. "Those marks all over her…are they from…?"

"I think so." Anguish rushes through me, tears lurking in the perimeters of my eyes. I force it back; I will not break in front of everyone.

The prospect is abhorrent and undeniable—my dreams truly portents. Gideon has been fucking Caethes and I've seen it. My gorge rises and I feel as if I'm going to be sick all over my queen-mother.

"I will have to give the order," she says like a death-knell.

"I need to go."

"I know," she says, but I am already gone and I hardly hear her.

I do not waste my moments with goodbyes and instead run past Drysi, Bleddyn, Folant, Andras, and Elyan. Maelona is nowhere to be found and it's probably for the best because I don't trust myself around her right now. I sprint to my room and reach it faster than I thought possible. Slamming the door closed and locking it, I make it to the bathing chamber, crouch before the toilet and vomit.

I've seen Gideon fucking the Unseelie Queen.

I've watched him fuck Caethes.

Heartbreak strikes through me, splitting my heart, ripping me apart and spilling everything I am on the goddess-damned floor. I am ruined and eviscerated, grief spilling from me like an open faucet. Tears are painting tracks of black down my face. I wasn't prepared and the power that Caethes brought was a fucking pestilence of locusts.

This meeting wasn't to intimidate Aneira.

It was to break me.

And it did.

I fall to the bathroom floor and sob in the aftermath of my flaying, crying silent sobs against the cold stone, leeching what little warmth I still have. My heart is breaking.

Tearing off my shoes and yanking the combs from my hair, I rejoice in the clatter they make against the floor and wall.

How the jewels break from the metal on impact. How the skulls crack in two.

I don't know how much time passes as I languish on the floor next to the toilet, but at some point, I notice the bottle hidden behind the tank and cry harder. This time the sobs are no longer silent. They are ugly wracking things, like the ones that left me when Gideon and I arrived in the Seelie Court and I wept for my wings and Corvina. Only that time I had the water of the filling tub to drown out the sounds, but now there is nothing keeping the ruin of my heart from being heard.

Caethes is probably reveling in my pain right now, the sick fucking queen that she is.

The Heart-Eater Queen.

I scream against the floor at the double meaning of the title. At the devouring she has done to the useless organ in my chest. I was supposed to be stone-cold, unfeeling. A monster. But with Caethes's manipulations she has proved in one fell swoop that I am not and I am more vulnerable for it.

The Heart-Eater Queen has chewed up my heart and spat it out, leaving it on the floor and calling around for everyone to see and point, *"Look, look what I did! Here is Evelyn Vanora's heart! I did this, celebrate my victory!"* and all she has to do is parade around with that necklace of bruises like a medal of honor and they know. *They know.* And they will judge me for it, they will be repulsed and pitying.

I grab the bottle, but rather than break my silent word to Maelona on the wandering of Gideon's stupid dick, I smash it against the wall and scream with the shattering of glass. The fucking cognac the color of Gideon's annoying fucking eyes paints the wall.

"I hate you!" I scream. *"I fucking hate you!"*

I drop to the floor, emotionally levelled, and pull into myself, tucking my face into my knees and rock. I wish I had another bottle to throw. I wish I hadn't given up the drink. I wish…

In this moment I need it, I need the oblivion.

My resolve begins to fade and I get up, like an automaton; voiceless, faceless, bodiless. As if I handed over the controls to the monster and let it take a drive. In my room there is a cart of various alcohols and liquors I haven't yet disposed of. I walk over to it and make my selection. I pick up a bottle of cheap juniper gin and catch my reflection in it.

I am a mess. Black tracks down my face, berry lipstick smeared across my mouth, that iridescent highlighter nowhere to be found.

Setting it down, I go over to the washbasin and take a cloth. I peer in the water and suddenly in the reflection there is a vision of Caethes and Gideon, fucking again. This time, it's him rutting behind her. Taking her, a hand in her hair, pulling her back to him while he whispers filthy things in her ear.

I scream in heartbreak and horror.

Shoving the basin away from me, the bowl wobbles, and crashes, spilling the vision across my floor where in fractals of the water it continues. Confusion fuels my fear induced rage and I throw the cloth over the image. It continues and I shriek. I grab the juniper liquor and throw it into the mess, the glass shattering. It continues moving—on the water, on the liquor, on the reflective shards of glass.

I must continue screaming and shattering bottles because soon enough the cart is empty and my floor is littered with glass and alcohol. The horrible picture is ongoing in pieces across the stone floor, in every sharp bit of glass and puddle.

Some emotion I cannot name takes me and I cover the mess with a blanket that was thrown over the ruined chaise lounge, stepping on glass in my haste. Blood joins the reflective liquids on the ground and I cover it all.

The floor is suddenly beneath my bottom, rushing up under me and I am planted. Reeling. Lost. Broken.

Suddenly, at the edge of my vision I catch silver. I lift my gaze. One for attention. Eight flashes follow.

I swallow the roiling within me, but I go to my athame, spill my blood and signal two for yes. Rather than leave it at that though, I add three additional flashes of gold. It is a little used code of ours, but it means, *"come to me"* and we imbued our blades to give the coordinates with that command. How convenient would that have been when I was trapped in the fucking Yukon?

Two silver flashes follow for yes.

Minutes later Emrys arrives, unaffected by my wards, and I'm startled to realize how close to eight o'clock it is and how short that meeting truly was. It wasn't even a meeting; it was a flagrant display.

I haven't moved from my spot on the floor and Emrys comes to my side, avoiding the discarded blanket. His steps are slow and measured. His arrival steeped in trepidation, as if he's approaching a predator.

"Vanna…I don't know how to tell you this…" Emrys's voice is pained, his throat thick with emotion.

I look at him, the makeup running down my face, the tears that have rimmed my eyes in red. It brings him up short, but I see very clearly such a haunted look in his eyes.

"You already know," he whispers with finality. He stretches a hand forward and lowers it, unsure what to do. I want to cry from his kindness, a feat hardly ever gentled by the fae. By nature, fae are cruel, but Emrys…he is capable of both.

I nod, new tears cutting charcoal lines down my cheeks. "I suspected, but I suppose you're here to confirm it."

Emrys comes to my side, sitting next to me on the floor, beside my mess of glass and liquor. He glances at the overturned washbasin but says nothing. He keeps a careful gap between us.

"I saw it…I walked in on it, I'm—I'm so sorry, Vanna." Emrys swallows back emotion and I realize I'm surprised to discover he's not reveling in it.

"Why are you sorry? Shouldn't you be rejoicing? He's out of the picture now, right?"

"I will not celebrate when you are sad. Aside from that, does he really feel gone from your life?"

I scoff. "Why should I try to rescue him when he's clearly happy fucking the Unseelie Queen?" I say this with such bitterness I'm surprised it doesn't burn.

Emrys tilts his head to the side, pondering. "I do not think he is happy, but I also do not think he has been coerced. I think it's revenge."

"How so?"

"You very publicly scorned him during that first meeting, and I've heard that you abandoned him in the Faerie Roads after you two…" he hesitates briefly. "After you two had sex. So, it's no question he feels injured. Wouldn't you want to revenge-fuck someone in response?"

I close my eyes, hypocrisy rolling over me. I attempted just that. Goddess I am a horrible creature. How dare I have double-standards. Nearly immediately after screwing Gideon I'd left him, bathed, drank, and then arrived on Maelona's doorstep to get the taste of Gideon off of my skin. I wanted her to replace him, and yet again I'd used her. Fucking hell, I'm just as bad. *Worse.*

"You're right."

Emrys nods, swallowing thickly, and looks away. His eyes shutter and I watch him try to regain some form of composure. He breathes out then looks at me.

"I'm certain it feels so painful because of what he means to you. The connection you two share. I'm going to try to make this right."

"What are you talking about?" I sniffle, swiping my hand below my nose.

"I've realized I need to step back, step away from this situation. From us."

"What?" I cry out, panic loosing through me. "No, no, what are you saying? Are you leaving me? Ryss, please you can't abandon me." I'm not above begging. Not now, I can't bear it.

Emrys closes those golden eyes that have always felt like home. "I can't come between you two any longer."

"No." Desperation colors my tone. I shift towards him, coming to my knees. "No, please, Ryss, I need you. Please, don't leave me, I'll…I'll do anything in my power, please."

"This is bigger than us, please don't ask me for more."

New, hot tears flood through me and I come to my feet. "Please, I—fuck!"

I slip back onto my ass, clutching the bottom of my foot where several pieces of glass have dug in. Blood slips through my fingers, the shards embedding deeper into my foot. Some are small enough to lodge fully in, others stick out at sickening angles. I hiss through the pain, examining before I pluck out the longest bit with a muttered, "Holy fucking fuck!"

"Vanna, stop. Let me do it." Emrys comes to my rescue, taking my foot in his lap and using gentle, probing fingers extricates the first piece of glass. "Is there glass everywhere for the reason I think?"

I recline back, gritting my teeth. "In a way. I was angry about Gideon and Caethes, yes, but it's also because I kept seeing the vision of them over and over."

"Seeing them as in clairvoyance or a hallucination?"

"I'm not sure, I—shit!" I stop myself as he plucks another piece. "It could be either or, I'm not sure, I feel somewhat crazy right now."

"Do you think it could be something else? Like a link of some sort?" he asks, deliberately not looking at my face, staring concretely at my foot.

Scrutinizing my opposite, my mirror, my other half, I begin to analyze. "Like what?" I do not curse when he removes the next piece.

"Perhaps soulmates."

"Soulmates? You really believe in that myth? Like actual destined soulmates determined by the cosmos?"

"Soulmates, Mates, True Loves, Soul-Bound, Heart-Threads? Yes. And not manufactured from the cosmos, but by Lady Fate."

"You think Lady Fate gives enough of a fuck to pair up people for fun?"

"She brought me back for her entertainment, surely it is within her power to create your perfect match."

"And what about you? Do you believe you have a soulmate?"

He pauses, staring deeply, burning a hole in the floor. "I don't know."

"So, you think Gideon is my soulmate?" I ponder the term, the concept, feeling it on my lips. It doesn't fit. "Why?"

"You're having visions of him, typically that's a sign of a deep connection."

"What if I was a Prophet Witch in my past life and I retained some of my power?"

"You believe in past lives but not soulmates?"

I shrug. Another piece of glass is removed. "Perhaps. What other theories do you have?"

Emrys is silent while digging out a particularly embedded shard. My foot flexes and I hiss in pain, but he continues.

"Do you know who your father is yet?"

This gives me pause. I stare at his long golden fingers, working over my foot, blood staining the tips. "I do not."

"Hmm. Maybe he has something to do with it?"

"Like?"

"Depends on who he is, I suppose. Now hold still, this piece is deep." He angles my foot to better see in the light and I watch those tapered, bloody fingertips attempt to squeeze out the tiny shard.

Blood flecks his rings and I count them. He has eight. Every one of them is spotted with my blood.

We lapse into silence as he applies excruciating pressure into my foot, gouging out the glass. The quiet is only broken by my muttered *fuck's* and hisses of pain in addition to the tinkling of each new piece of glass added to the growing pile. Eventually all the glass is removed and Emrys leaves me momentarily to get a roll of bandages, medicinal ointment, cloth, fresh water and soap. The soap he selects is one of my favorites—ginseng—and he wipes away the scarlet on my foot and his hands. After cleaning the blood, he pastes a minty smelling cream over the wounds and wraps it carefully with the bandage. As he winds the fabric around my foot and ankle, I'm hyperaware of his fingertips. His touch is warmth and it seeps into my bones, turning me golden inside, as if I were sitting beside a lit hearth.

"Do you know who *your* father is, yet?" I ask hesitantly.

Emrys shakes his head. "No, but I still can't imagine I would have much to say to him. He abandoned me just like my mother did."

He finishes with the bandage and then backs away and I have the distinct feeling of my heart being pulled from my chest. With every step Emrys takes further the pain stretches.

"What's going to happen now?" I ask, understanding that a substantial shift is coming from his end of our relationship.

Emrys looks away, breathing deeply. "I don't know. But I'll make this right."

"Please don't."

"Why not? You might love him, so if I remove myself, it should be easier. So, again, why?"

"Because…" I trail off, uncertain and unwilling. "You're important to me."

"That's not the same."

"Please."

"I'm sorry, Vanna. I—Goodnight, and I'm sorry again. About everything. I wish you all the best."

"No, Ryss…" I plead, limping onto my bandaged foot.

"Goodbye Vanna."

CHAPTER 13

CENTURY TRAINING

It's been twenty-five years and we haven't so much as kissed. Nothing more has passed than our snarled slumber and the touches on the annual test we forever fail. The sexual attraction between us is unspoken but horribly, tangibly there, and the only thing that stops us from discussing it or acting upon it is the clearcut law.

Even so, he has become my dearest and closest friend, the person who sees me like no one else does.

Our swords clash as we come together, ringing steel and a shower of sparks. Our battle is unparalleled; full of viciousness and strategy. Never have I had an equal with whom I can match strike for strike, blow for blow, slash for slash.

Emrys bares his teeth as he pushes into the blade, forcing me to buckle from my shorter vantage point. The shriek of steel is piercing as I roll away, wings folded, the sword tucked protectively as I come upon my feet again. Emrys laughs darkly, his pointed teeth making divots in his plush lip as he advances on me. I rush him, coming in for a high swipe that I fake out with a jab towards his abdomen. He catches it, elbowing my wrist. Sharp pain vibrates up my arm, almost causing me to drop my blade.

"You're tired, Vanora," Emrys teases.

"Shut up, Gorlassar," I hiss in return. It doesn't matter he's right.

For whatever reason, sleep did not claim me last night. Instead, I was awake to sense the shift of our night, the moment when Emrys rolled towards me and tossed an arm over my stomach. How he later pulled me against him, sliding a thigh between mine. I'd held my breath, feeling his whisper across my throat. His fingers had clutched possessively, curling and uncurling before relaxing against my shape.

None of that was truly out of the ordinary, what was though, was the presence of one of our mentors lurking outside our sleep chamber. All night I felt the oppressive weight of Osian's gaze on us, seething silently. Fear had submitted me to silence.

When the hours of our training are over, we are free from the watchful eyes of our mentors. They've never spied on us—until last night.

So, it's while I train with Emrys that exhaustion catches up with me.

On the sidelines, our mentors, Enydd, Osian, Urian, and Cothi watch us. Each face is a blank canvas, dispassionate and unwavering. Except Osian. His hunter green gaze conceals something malignant, a cloying, choking aura of envy emanating from him. My spine stiffens in response, but I keep training, my eyes on Emrys.

Renewed by my aversion to the mentor who has favored me, I rush Emrys, slide within his guard and effectively disarm him with two quick elbows. I'm flush against him, too close to get my sword—turned with the flat of the blade running across my stomach—to do any real damage. He twists my wrists and I'm forced to drop the sword with a cry. It clatters to the ground with an eerie ring of metal on stone.

Emrys wraps his arms around me and drives me to the floor. Had it not been for his hand cradling the back of my skull, I would have cracked it in this crumbling cathedral. He pins me down using arms and legs, thighs, and chest. Manacling my wrists, he locks me against the ground, while I buck my hips to dislodge him—which only turns me on.

I bite my lip rather than reveal the effect Emrys's weight has on me. But I notice his breathing has become thready—not short as it should be when we train, but laced with anxiety. Concern propels me to notify the mentors before I clock in on the answer.

"*Vanna,*" he whispers, the new nickname on his tongue sounding divine. Not *Vanora*, something softer. Something *his*.

Oh.

Oh, he's turned on, too.

Shifting his hips uncomfortably, I feel the slightest nudge in his pants and I flush. I've felt it before, here and there—on my thigh, the curve of my ass, digging into my hip, on my stomach—but it has always been the result of the morning. Not our waking encounters.

I will never admit aloud he is who I think about when I touch myself at night. When I have a spare moment alone to explore that nub between my legs that hasn't felt another's touch in more than twenty years. I will never admit that I imagine it's his fingers replacing mine, nor would I ever describe the vivid fantasies that drive me to completion. These private moments are few and far between, but at least once a week Emrys walks the grounds to "clear his head" which I'm certain is an innuendo and where he goes to pleasure himself as well.

I dispel the thoughts as I remember where I am and just whose pelvis is pressed against mine.

In response, I hook my ankles beneath his and force him over, his distraction lending me opportunity. He rolls beneath me, our positions reversed and I reach for a sword. The stretch has placed my breasts directly in Emrys's face. I flash up with the blade crosswise beneath his throat the same moment he reaches my former sword, the flat of it against my neck.

We hold this tie with heaving chests, sweat dampened temples, and sheer determination.

"Match!" Urian calls, his locs swinging as he shakes his head. A gruesome scar bisects his face, halving it from the smooth brown of his complexion.

As point is called, five of our seven mentors enter. Una tucks her rose-gold waves behind her ears while her white feathered wings ripple—betraying her distress. Quickly, she communicates to the group, fast hand motions describing something I can't make out, but what is immediately clear is that it's about us when five pairs of eyes suddenly lock on us.

Emrys and I are too stunned to move.

Una leaves, taking Cothi and Osian with her, the latter throwing a heavy look over his shoulder.

Closing the gap between us, Urian stands overhead, arms crossed, straining the seams on his blue tunic. Emrys and I get to our feet, helping the other up. When we look towards the mentor before us, his face is hard and unimpressed.

"That is all for tonight, please take the rest of the evening off."

I raise my brows in surprise and glance at Emrys, his look of disbelief is similar.

"That isn't typical," Emrys retorts, distrust furrowing his brows. "We've never had an evening off."

It's true. We have trained every day for two and a half decades. If it isn't swords, it's poisons and if it's not that it's hand to hand, and so forth. We haven't had any time to recover aside from the essential when we have a new bout of mithridatism starting. This is odd.

"Well, now you do," Urian responds, throwing his hands up in a helpless gesture. "Off with you both, the rest of us need to discuss."

We're shooed away and after dropping off our swords we go to the small bathing chamber and wash our hands and faces with the icy water from the spitting tap. It smells heavily of iron, but luckily, we've been regularly ingesting the toxin. Emrys peels off his sweaty shirt. I avert my gaze and splash water on my chest, ignoring how he does the same, scrubbing with a sponge. My eyes strain from peering out of the corners for so long.

He stares blankly into the sink, half full of water, hands tightening on the lip. I watch his back muscles work, seeing the two parallel scars shift beside his spine and the knobs that bisect it before curving into the valley just above his pants. Two dimples like thumbprints dip above the waistband and I find myself idly wondering if my fingers would fit in them.

"Any guesses what they're talking about back there?" Emrys asks, 'back there' meaning the door we've never passed through, the one where the mentors always appear from.

I roll my eyes. "Us, obviously."

"Thank you, that *was* obvious," he replies, flicking ice water at me. "I meant what *specifically* about us? They've never cut training short."

I shrug and push myself up onto the vanity, swinging my legs below. An Unseelie blade is tucked into my boot, gifted and sealed in blood from Emrys to communicate post Century Training. I realize my boots are in dire need of repair—the goddess will deliver a new pair very soon, as she always does.

"Maybe they think we're planning their assassination," I joke, muffling a laugh with my wrist. "Goddess, that would be stupid."

"Or maybe they think we're being intimate and are trying to catch us in the act?"

My swinging legs stop. "You can say 'fucking', you know? They should be aware of how this partnership works, they were Centurions too, once upon a time."

"Exactly." Emrys leans against the opposite vanity, shirt still discarded. "What if there's something coming that they expect? Does something change between Centurions at this mark? What if there's a—I don't know—a trial or something?"

"Between us?"

"Or them, I don't know. Century Training has always been so secretive, shrouded in so much mystery. All we know is that it is a privilege and we should be honored to come here. I just…I think something is changing."

I try not to get distracted, even when Emrys clears his throat and I watch it move. Mixed with the confusing arousal and his ominous tones, my mind is conflicted. I reach over and place a hand on his forearm. I give him a small smile and he hesitantly lets one slip into place on his face.

"Whatever it is, we'll get through it together," I reassure him, squeezing once.

"I hope so."

"Ryss, don't you trust me?"

"I do." He pauses. "I just don't trust *them.*"

It's something usually unspoken, how we feel about our mentors, but speaking it into existence now feels dangerous. The mentors are on edge, watching us predatorially and due to their constant hovering, I haven't had a chance to tell Emrys about Osian's watch over us.

"Ryss, I need to tell you something. Last night—"

The door to the bathing chamber slams open and we jump apart, the hand that was on his arm scorching in its guilt. As if it were direct evidence to a crime. Osian stands in the doorway, one palm flat against the wood, nostrils flared in annoyance.

"Evelyn, I need to speak with you," Osian intones portentously.

I send panicked eyes to Emrys and he clenches his teeth. I slip off the counter and take one step forward.

"What about?"

"That is a private matter for you and me."

Osian's words send fear skittering down my spine and I bite my lip, eyes seeking comfort from my equal. Emrys is closed off, holding still, twisting his shirt in his fist.

"Okay…I'll be right back, I guess."

As I walk past Osian, he comments to Emrys, "Don't count on it."

I stiffen, about to turn, but Osian shuts the door and steers me by the shoulder. His grip is firm, near painful as he guides me past an alcove in an unused hallway leading to nothing but ruins.

Suddenly, he pushes me against the stone wall, pinching my wings. A flash of fright ripples through me with the deadly heat in his gaze. All the discomfiting looks, the way he watched us, sends all my worst nightmares skittering through my mind. The stone is unforgivingly cold against my back and instinctually I try to break from his hold. He readjusts it.

"Do you love him?" The juxtaposition between his words and the heat of his fury is startling. I gape. His brogue is heavy on his tongue as he seethes. "Well? I'm waiting."

"Why are you asking me this?" Hysteria begins creeping into my voice. "Let go, you're hurting me."

He tightens his grip and the pain sharpens. "Answer the fucking question, Evelyn. Do you love Emrys?"

I inhale sharply through my nose, tilting my chin defiantly. He smells like ink and parchment and lanolin. I hate it.

"And what if I do?"

He slams my shoulders and wings into the wall, my skull cracking against it hard enough to see stars. I think I bite my tongue because the taste of rust fills my mouth.

"I am your superior, if I ask you a question, you damn well answer it. So, I'm going to ask you once more—do you love Emrys?"

I grind my teeth together and meet his eyes. I do not look away as I spit blood.

"Yes."

Osian's hands shake and fury rolls off him in waves. "Does he know?"

"No."

"Then here's what we're going to do. You're going to imply to Emrys we are lovers and you are going to falsely attempt to kill him tomorrow."

Disbelief courses through me and I laugh, a sharp, frenetic sound. "Absolutely not."

"Oh, see you don't have a choice," Osian counters, suddenly releasing one of my arms and producing two vials from his pocket. "Do you know what these are?"

Heat rushes into my cheeks. "They're contraceptive tonics."

"Correct. So, do you have any idea why the goddess would deliver these this month?"

I stay silent, my heart thundering.

"Right, you don't have an answer, either. Luckily, I came up with one. This one—" he selects one and holds it up. The name *Evelyn* is inked onto a tag. "Is yours." He tucks it into my breast pocket—I shiver in revulsion. "And this one—" he holds up the second where Emrys's name has been scrubbed out, replaced by Osian's. "Well, this one is mine."

Osian pulls out the cork and drains it to the dregs. For the first time in my years at Century Training absolute terror crashes through me, the deepest rooted fear in all females threading into my bones. Sweat borne of anxiety beads on my skin and a true shot of dread is injected into my blood.

I can take on a regular attacker, I cannot take on a fully trained Centurion. Not yet. Not alone.

"You will tell Emrys that you and I were given contraceptive tonics together."

"No." The need to be away from Osian is overpowering and I struggle against him. "Get your hands off of me."

"We're not finished here yet," he growls. "Do you have any idea how long I have craved you? I am taking this opportunity and it will not slip through my fingers."

Then suddenly, quick as a viper he strikes forward pressing his lips to mine in a feverish, punishing kiss. I struggle against him but it's like pushing against a brick wall. He shifts his mouth, trying to pry mine open and instead I sink my teeth into his tongue. He bites back, drawing blood. I yelp and he growls. Osian shoves me harder against the wall and the taste of blood is overwhelming.

I realize he is not letting me free, that he likely means to carry this out. So, in a final act of desperation, I reach down to my boot, slip out my blade and plunge it into Osian's heart.

He recoils with a roar and stumbles back. Osian stares down at the blade buried to its winged hilt in his chest and then to me in betrayal before wrapping his fingers around the knife. He pulls it out.

Shock ripples through me when I see the blade come away clean, not a speck of blood on it. The hole in his shirt shows a stab-wound rapidly healing, the only evidence of my attack is the tear.

I press myself against the wall, fear coursing through me like the most potent of poisons. It steals all reason, all control, all ability.

Osian brandishes the blade like a conductor's wand. "You will sell this ruse, or I will kill him."

"How-how are you alive?"

"Haven't you figured it out?" He cackles. "The Centurions who train you sacrificed their eternal rest to be the keepers of this realm. So long as we reside within it, we are undying." He pauses, a wicked smile curving his lips. "You and Emrys on the other hand…well, you do not possess that perk. If I cut you, let's say here—" he rests the tip of my knife against my jugular, "well, you'd just bleed out."

My pulse thrums alarmingly against that knife's edge.

"So, are you ready for this deception? Or shall I cut Emrys here, myself?"

CHAPTER 14

Caethes calls another meeting immediately after the next—which, accounting for the day after and day before rule, is three days. This time, it isn't exactly in her court, it's in her territory. Directly outside the charred husk of the cabin I'd shared with Gideon. She's a sick and sadistic fucking creature.

I put on a pair of black leather leggings with a gray tunic beneath. Overtop I add a long gray coat that doubles as another shirt. It is double-breasted with silver buttons and swooping chains between each one. Leather gloves cover my hands, matching my boots. My hair is free flowing, a sheet of silvery white tucked behind my pointed ears.

Unlike the previous meeting—blatant flaunting—Caethes has requested several witnesses. I don't know what she has planned next, but frankly I'd like to strangle the Unseelie Monarch and wash my hands of her. Aneira, Maelona, Drysi, Bleddyn, Folant, Andras, Elyan, and Cadoc all wait in the throne room, all of them cloaked in various winter garb, everything from wool to leather to fur.

My fae nature is likely the only reason I did not perish in the Yukon when I thought I was human.

After a simple nod we are on our way. Aneira, draped in long woolen cloak, lined with pearl silk, is ushered through the Roads. She is flanked by the rest of her guard.

Before I arrived, Aneira informed the others that should things go awry, her and I must be separated. It was not explained further but they understood the dire circumstances from her tone alone. They were further directed to apprehend me if I began acting unlike myself, and to eliminate Gideon.

The Faerie Roads are quiet today. With the full moon hidden, the Hunt is resting before the revelry and chase that the phase provides them. I wonder how exactly the lunar cycle affects them, how it leads them at different times in the phases to corporeal and less corporeal forms.

When Folant takes the first turn, dressed in a woolen cape and chocolate leathers, my stomach roils. We ascend to the surface of the Roads and find ourselves on the outskirts of the tree line, and memories suffuse me.

The trees. The clearing. The gray sky. The once-was-cabin. The moan of wind. The chirp of birds. The rustle of woods. The distant howls of predators.

This was my home for two long years. The remains of the cabin hardly stand, blackened and ruined. A hollow reminder of what once saved me in those cold winters. A light layer of snow sprinkles the husk, the roof completely toppled down, the basement blown apart by the stale gasoline explosion. Shrapnel rings the space, the water barrels all but ash. The stone steps remain.

The scent of the wintry pines is all encompassing, but there's more. The slight tinge of soil, the hint of rain in the atmosphere, the simple freshness of the forest. The wind shivers through me, bowing the treetops with its untamable force.

I can't help it, but my eyes wander. Over to the edge where I know the wards lie is Corvina's grave. I can still see the disturbed earth, the soil that hasn't quite yet settled even with the breath of snow. The truth of my sister's death lingers over me, settling into my bones and ripping me apart.

Internally, I am destroyed, groveling to the goddess and sobbing horrible hitching breaths, but externally I don a façade, cold, unfeeling, uncaring. It is a guise of smooth rock and heartlessness. But for how seamless it appears; it feels so very fragile.

Caethes appears at the other side of the clearing with her own entourage. I recognize Tegwyn and Cariad as well as the blue-skinned faerie that had accompanied Cariad in murdering Jacob Dugal all those years ago. And of course, Emrys. My heart pitters in nervousness at his presence, the cold bringing an alluring flush to his sharp cheekbones. Surrounding my opposite are five other fae, most humanoid, none beast, and within the circle of all the fae is Caethes, draped in a long fur pelt of pure, untainted white.

Gideon is nowhere to be seen.

Anxiety curdles within me and I search out with my unorthodox gift, feeling for the halfling's presence. I'm surprised when I don't find it. Curiously and with confusion, I risk a glance at Emrys and find that haunted look still painted on him, along with a new layer of solemnity.

The Unseelie group crosses the clearing in unison. When she is before us, Caethes is grinning wickedly with a malice-infused gleam touching her pit-black eyes. Her lipstick is black and her lids are violet glitter.

"Hello Caethes," Aneira finally greets.

The Dark Court Queen tilts her head, keeping that eerie grin plastered. "Hello Aneira, welcome. I thank you and your warriors for joining us. I'm sure you have many questions."

"Indeed."

"I wished to personally inform you that Gideon Zhao has been delivered to the Winter Carnaval."

"You did what?" I gasp, horror striking me dumb.

Caethes gives me an inside look with a conspiratorial wink. "He served his purpose, and he did it well. You should know."

Rage erupts within me, burning a violent, hot red. My sight is eclipsed by it, and it takes everything within me to stay my hand. My heart hammers, the wrath turning it into a raging drum, beating at the cage of my ribs.

"Though I must admit that isn't the only reason I have summoned you here, *specifically* here," Caethes announces, and a cruel curl touches her lips. "There is a reason I requested the meeting within my territory. Lady Vanora, you surely recognize it, do you not?"

The rage still colors my vision but I bite out. "Yes."

"I imagine it looks quite different from the last time you viewed it."

"It does."

"Well, with that established I'd like to divulge something of note our darling Gideon revealed to us many weeks ago. Do you recall?"

Fury rampages inside me at her casual and deliberate use of "our" and I grit my teeth. "You'll have to elaborate, Heart-Eater."

Caethes has steered this conversation to frame me as the voice of the Seelie Court rather than my queen. It irks me.

"Of course," Caethes says as if she was just being silly and forgot. She strides from her entourage, fanning her white cloak around her in a snowy display. The jewels twisted in her hair tinkle like icicles and glass shards. "See, he told me that he knew where the Harbinger was, do you remember?"

My heart sinks and then it races. "I do."

Aneira shifts, anxiety rolling off her in waves.

"And as you are fae, I asked you to confirm this, as you cannot lie." She doesn't wait for me to respond this time. "You know, it seems quite obvious now, looking back. The very nature of the Harbinger stared in our face every single day, hiding in plain sight."

Dread mixes in tandem with my anxiety. He told her. He fucking told her I'm the Harbinger and now the stupid fucking idiot has ruined it all. I brace myself for the impact of her words. Waiting for the final shoe to drop. For the guillotine to plummet.

"With you being the *Ceidwad Cudd*, too, it feels almost insulting."

I swallow, keeping my eyes level but letting apathy mask into them.

"Aneira liked keeping the *Ceidwad Cudd* and Harbinger close, didn't she?" Caethes cackles, an unkind sound. I'm not sure who she's addressing in the moment; if it's still me individually or the gathering at large. "But she lost one of her pretty toys. Not to worry though; I found it."

Caethes raises a hand and four of her warriors part from the group to surround the disturbed earth at the edge of the wards—digging.

Horror dawns as I realize what Caethes thinks she's discovered.

"*NO!*" I roar, taking off for Corvina's grave. "*No, don't fucking touch her!*"

I make it only four steps before Bleddyn tries to trap me—I evade him, rolling. Three more steps take me past Folant's reaching—I elbow him neatly in the jaw. Two more and there is Andras—I kick his ankle. I'm crossing the space, drawing closer to Corvina's grave, watching the dirt pile beside it. Too fast. Too much. Too soon.

The grass is slick beneath my boots but I have practiced, I know how to maneuver difficult terrain. I was lost to this land for two years and I trained for it for a hundred more.

So close, I'm passing the line of Unseelie delegates when suddenly one steps out and wraps me in a warm, familiar cage. I feel Emrys's hard, familiar body behind mine, his muscles pressing into me. His arms banded around me, his breath smelling of lemon drop candies.

"Stop, Vanna, please. You'll get yourself killed," he whispers.

"The fuck do you care about that?" I hiss. "You were all too ready to remove me from your life just the other night." I punctuate this by driving the heel of my boot into the top of Emrys's foot.

It doesn't make contact and he doesn't let go.

Because wartime laws dictate no harm. And he is only holding me.

"Let me go, they can't bring her out. Please you don't understand what—"

I'm too late.

I watch in horror as one of the Unseelie guards makes a sound of triumph and the edge of a dirty white sheet is revealed. Seconds later, they're hauling out my sister's body.

I sag against Emrys, a soft cry croaking from my mouth, breaking against this fae male, everything in me pouring from my eyes. Saltwater tracks down my face, warmth switching to ice once it touches the biting air. Emrys is the only thing supporting me right now. The only thing keeping me afloat.

The Unseelie Queen grins at me, caught in the Revenant's hold, but it passes over, the Dark Monarch not realizing that *this* is the Harbinger. The grieving, living twin; not the dead one wrapped in a funeral shroud.

The four Unseelies each take an edge of the blanket and pull. I'm not ready for it. I'm not ready to see my twin's decayed, rotted body. To see the bugs and maggots writhe in her flesh, burrowing in those night sky eyes. Her luscious black hair dried and flat. The blood that has turned brown on her lace and leather. I can't bear it; I can't bear to see my sister's features so utterly desecrated.

I cry silently, bowing over Emrys's arms, and all he does is continue to hold me, mumbling soft sounds in my ear that my grief cannot hear. All I can hear is Corvina's last words lapping over me and cutting my soul with every lost syllable.

I thought I'd never find you. I thought I'd never find you. I thought I'd never find you.

The edge of a leathery wing is exposed and a broken sound slips from me. Emrys holds me tighter. Desperation and desolation war in my chest. I see black leather and lace and my throat grows tight. And then I see perfectly white, unmarred skin. Silken black locks. Night sky eyes closed with pearly, lids and thick onyx lashes.

Confusion mingles within me as I stare at the perfectly preserved corpse of my sister. Of the presumed Harbinger. I blink, tears curving down my cheeks.

Caethes cackles darkly. "Oh Aneira, you couldn't bear for them to see the truth of her, could you?"

And then I realize.

Aneira cast a Queen's Glamour over Corvina. This is not what Corvina truly looks like right now. This is a magical shroud tossed over a rotting body. This is Corvina as Aneira remembered her. The slight frost of life casting her features in a bluish tint. Not enough to presume life, but still questioning death. It is eerie and heartbreaking, because Aneira was as unprepared to see the truth as I was.

I stare at my queen-mother, a grateful shine in my eyes, tears finishing their descent. I see the raw pain there and I realize my folly. A Queen's Glamour does not work on the queen. She is seeing Corvina as she really is; death, decay, rot and all. This guise is for me, to save me, to salvage what little tenacity I have. It is a mask for all those gathered here. It is nothing for the two queens. Caethes can sense it, but she cannot see it.

"Would you like me to describe it to you?" Caethes smirks at me, drawing nearer. She's suddenly so close, crouching in front of me, trapped by Emrys. By the Revenant. "Would you like me to tell you what I see, little Secret Keeper? I see desiccated flesh and worms. I see pits for eyes, and bloated, mottled skin. Lips pulled back over teeth filled with dirt. Maggots crawling, blood staining."

I let out a cracking sound. A whimper, my guard shattering.

The fae cannot lie.

"*Enough*," Aneira says, tears she does not try to hide sliding down her face. She steps forward, all her regal disposition clear. "Leave my child be."

"You're right," Caethes says, startling us. She turns from me with a whisper of her obsidian claws against my cheek before grandly throwing out her arms to the awaiting masses. "Behold! The body of the Harbinger! Corvina Vanora!"

I choke down my pain, writhing against Emrys, aching to go to my sister and cover her. To throw myself atop her and sob and take her away. I thrash harder but Emrys holds tighter. The scent of vetiver and lemon getting stronger, the touch of leather warmer.

The warriors carry Corvina in the sheet, cradled between them all like a hammock, swaying in the frozen air, stiff limbs not hidden from the glamour. Corvina is set down at the Unseelie Queen's feet, only bare meters from me.

I want to scream.

"The Unseelie Court rejoices today in the funeral rite of the vicious Centurion, the fabled Harbinger rumored to have murdered my Revenant, only for the true goddess to rectify the actions of a single hateful soul." *Rumors and lies*. Caethes throws her head back to the gray sun. "Let the light of day expose the Harbinger for what she is and let the flame of darkness purify the vessel."

The warriors back away several steps and abruptly the familiar snick of lighters sounds in the air. Caethes produces a potent smelling chemical, something I cannot immediately name, but something I know is absolutely and completely combustible.

"*No!*" I scream, turning my throat raw. Reaching towards her, towards one of the things I fear most.

But it is too late and she has poured the accelerant on my sister and the four lighters follow.

Corvina goes up in a wild inferno. Her beautiful, magically altered body curling at the edges, turning black. Her clothes and hair burn first to char, her skin blackening and cracking and I watch, in pain, as the Queen's Glamour flickers and the decay of my twin ripples through the magic. Aneira quickly repairs it, but it was enough. I saw it.

"Witness the destruction of a pillar of the Seelie Court!" Caethes intones loudly, whirling around to our faces of horror

I scream.

It's a wordless sound.

It is grief and aching and pain and sorrow.

It is everything that empties me.

I watch Corvina burn and then I see no more.

CHAPTER 15

I wake somewhere in the Seelie Court. At some point someone pried me from Emrys, announcing that he was flouting the boundary of Fae War Laws and that it would be wise to release the *Ceidwad Cudd* back into their custody. I believe it was Drysi.

My eyes open, heavy and tear-swollen, but I assess my surroundings and find myself in one of Aneira's private receiving rooms. Everything is brushed gold and deep emerald. There are partitions in the room that are tangles of vines and thorns, wrought in plated or karat gold, rugs woven with care in shades of hunter, viridian, and forest. Heavy and ornate furniture is placed deliberately about the room, forming a U for conversation, and a quiet nook with towering bookcases filled with ancient tomes. Chandeliers dangle above, forming crescent medallions and chrysanthemum-shaped bowls, sconces of climbing ivy, and candles pressed with the Seelie Court sigil.

A roaring fire burns on the hearth, warming the room to a cozy degree that does little for the ice inside my soul. My coat is quickly overheating me and my growing rage rivals the conflagration that swallowed my sister.

Rising from the couch I'd been laid upon, I tear off the coat. I am not alone in the room, Aneira, Maelona, Drysi, Bleddyn, Folant, Andras, Elyan, and Cadoc are all present, and staring at me.

"Do we have an in at the Winter Carnaval?" I ask, a manic edge to my tone. I throw down the useless layer and stand in my tunic and leggings—someone removed my boots as well. I'm now desperate to get to the supernatural black market. "Well?"

Aneira raises a brow at my outburst.

Cadoc clears his throat, carding his hand through his hay-colored hair. "Why is that necessary, Lady Vanora? The halfling will be disposed of there soon enough."

"No," I say, continuing with my lunatic stream. "No, you see, he's still on our side."

I meet the blank stares of eight faces.

"Don't you understand? Can't you see the bigger picture? He lied to protect us."

"Sweetie," Maelona says, stepping forward tentatively, her voice deceptively soft. "He turned on us. He's with Caethes."

"No, he lied about the Harbinger's identity! Don't you get it? He told her Corvina was the Harbinger, not me. Which means he's protecting me still. We need to save him."

Silence answers me.

"Come on! Aneira, do you have a way to infiltrate the Winter Carnaval or not?"

Aneira's lips thin. "At this time, I do not."

I huff a sound, cross between a laugh and a scoff. "Right, of course. Well, we have all the resources here, I'm sure we can figure it out."

"No, we cannot," Aneira articulates.

I turn to her, startled. "What do you mean?"

"I am devoting our efforts to the war between the courts, not the war of your heart. If you decide to take on this passion independently, that is your prerogative, but you may not take from me to do so. We are already stretched too thin while we prepare for attack and you have shirked too many responsibilities to make anyone shoulder any more."

"I can't leave him."

"You can, and you did. I am sorry, but you must let him go. I will not risk my own for a halfling that holds commands over you."

My heart trips as gasps sound in the room, the remaining fae who hadn't known about my faux pas, reeling. This is Aneira's form of punishment, inducing this mortification. It's not just to shame me, but to show who is in control and to keep me in line. She is kind for a fae, but she also has a cruel side.

"You said—"

"I said many things, but many things have changed. I am thankful Gideon afforded us this respite; Corvina's death is tragic but it has given us an out. We can finally withdraw the bounty for the Harbinger without suspicion. He did well, but that is all that is left."

I turn the tables, rage brewing, the monster cackling inside. "So, what if he decides to tell the truth at the Carnaval? What if he tells the wrong person who the Harbinger really is?"

"Then in that case, I will send an assassin to eliminate him." She glances about the room. "Drysi."

My birth mother nods to my chosen mother.

"You can't do that!"

"I just did."

My nostrils flare and before I can take the words back, they spill out of me unbidden.

"In that case, enjoy the fact that Caethes thinks the Harbinger is dead, because she isn't coming back to you."

And with that I stride from the room, leaving shock in my wake.

In a haze, I make it to my chambers. I sit, looking at the mess that is splayed around the room like a storm blasted through it. Glass is still shattered, chaise lounge still sliced, the scent of booze permeating the air with the lighter smell of parchment, oiled blades, and my various perfumes. I stare at the mess of my life, told by this suite, and I sit against the door, head in my hands.

There's something flat living in me. Something broad and ironclad pushing down my emotions. Everything related to Corvina is locked away behind an intricate vault I have no code for.

A knock sounds at my door and I jolt in surprise. When I get to my feet and open it, I'm startled to find Maelona there, concern painted across her radiant features.

"I thought you could use some company," Maelona murmurs softly, chocolate eyes on the floor. This visit isn't just on my behalf, it's on hers too. She watched the same scene I did; she witnessed the burning of someone she loved just as I did. "If you're sober, that is."

I crack a short laugh. "I have not consumed any alcohol since you gave me the ultimatum."

"I wouldn't call it—"

"It was an ultimatum."

She sighs. "It was. I'm sorry."

"Don't be," I reassure her, shifting uncomfortably from foot to foot. I miss Mae, but I don't want her to see the disaster of my room. It was bad enough Emrys saw it. "If it isn't much trouble though, could we go to your chambers? I'm afraid mine are in no state to entertain guests."

Maelona curls a wry smile. "Of course."

Mae turns from my doorway and I lock the chamber behind me, keeping pace with the Lady. I am acutely aware of the space, how it electrifies when she shifts closer, when my hands move. We arrive in her rooms quickly and Maelona sweeps into the space, doffing the thick black coat she wore to the meeting, plucking the golden buttons one by one.

There are so many of them.

Desire shoots through me and a sudden wanting overtakes me, heedless of the abandonment from Emrys and the betrayal from Gideon. The yearning takes my breath away, thoughts of the fae male and halfling protector fleeing my mind, saving space only for Maelona. For comfort. For escape.

"Here," I say, crossing the room, "let me."

Before her I stand, only bare inches taller, her petite chin inclined towards me as her decadent eyes take me in. Her lids are heavy as they watch my fingers work, memories hazing her eyes. Her lips part and her breaths quicken.

"I missed you," I whisper as I work a third button through its hole.

"In what way?" Her hair flickers red, pink.

I undo the final button and push the coat gently from her shoulders, palms grazing the bare skin of her arms, feeling gooseflesh ripple beneath my touch. Her breath hitches as I glide the fabric from her arms and let the coat drop to the floor. The black shirt she wears beneath is torturous. It rises around her neck in a high collar, but the sides expose the supple curves of her breasts and the lack of bra is evident from her peaked nipples. I graze my thumb over one and she tilts her head back with a moan.

"This isn't what I invited you in here for," she says huskily, breath hitching as I brush against that peak once more. Her hand clutches for my hip, fingertips digging in; grasping, needing.

My other hand finds the nape of her neck, fusing my fingers in those rapidly changing locks, the black flickering with crimson and rose. I brush my lips along the edge of her jaw, breathy kisses just shy of her lips. She digs her hands into me harder. I grin against her cheek, placing an open-mouthed kiss against it. She tastes like cherries.

I've felt so disconnected and overwhelmed by everything, but in this moment, I feel grounded—safe. This is familiar, this is Mae. I want to keep this thing between us, to let it bloom and wrap us in its tender embrace. I don't want the divide that has been so tangible of late. I want what we used to have. The ease of friendship and romance. One set aside for the other.

I want her.

"I can't handle this distance between us. I want you," I whisper in her ear, my teeth catching her lobe and pulling slightly. Her hips roll once in response, a sound sticks in her throat.

She moans and suddenly her lips are on mine. Her kiss is desperation and seeking, feeling for that connection to tether us back to the earthly plane from the nightmare of the day. Her mouth moves in a sinuous dance, her tongue slipping into my mouth while I let my own twine around hers, tasting Maelona and everything about her I've missed. I angle her head to the side to deepen the kiss, plundering her mouth with a sweep of my tongue that she returns in battle.

My hands find the snap at the back of her neck and peel the shirt off her, revealing Maelona in all her glory. Smooth white flesh, and generous breasts tipped with pert, pink peaks. I palm one, catching a nipple between my forefinger and thumb, rolling gently. She lets out a mewl and writhes against me, tearing off my shirt and then reaching for my pants.

She slips her hand beneath the band and moans when she finds me bare beneath her touch. My core aches, wetness blooming there as I feel her fingers dip, touching the damp heat. She slips two fingers low, finding my sex soaked, and plunges inside. I groan, thrusting my hips as she brings those two fingers out and circles my clit, once, twice. Dipping her head to my breasts, she pulls a nipple into her mouth, suckling gently before flicking her tongue rapidly against it.

"*Fuck, Mae,*" I groan, my hand working her tips to hardened points.

She pulls free of my pants and I let out a sound of indignation. She chuckles low and pushes my pants down.

I let her, and moments later I'm stepping out of my leather leggings and backing her into the bed, utterly naked. I guide her down onto the coral sheets, kissing her mouth, lingering as her fingers trace the knobs of my spine. I trail kisses lower, down her throat and between her breasts, my tongue swirling around the edges of her navel before finding the edge of her pants. I roll them down her thighs, finding a thin pair of soaked, white silk panties.

Freeing her strong legs, I spread her thighs wide, kneeling on the bed between them. Lace edges the top of the underwear, cutting high on the bikini line to tiny strings on either side. It would take so little to snap them.

"Mm, is all this for me?" I ask, nuzzling my nose against her wetness, so clear on her undergarments. I smell her innately female fragrance, the warmth, the sweetness of her skin. I lay the flat of my tongue firmly against her core and travel upward once in a measured stroke.

Her hips buck. "*Yes*," she gasps.

"Good," I purr against her thigh. I kiss the left one, nipping once, then doing the same to the right.

With one finger, I hook the material and pull it, revealing her glistening sex. Delicate folds and that tiny, powerful bud. Leaning forward I lick once, a stroke through her center and flicking over her clit, tasting her, and humming my pleasure. She gasps, but suddenly she pulls from me, grabbing me instead, and dragging me over her body.

"No," she commands. "You first."

Pushing me down onto the bed, onto the pink-orange blankets that smell of cherries and orchids, Maelona hovers over me, a hand going to my throat. My thighs drop open as she dips her hand to my breast. Bringing it to her mouth, she begins licking and teasing the nipple while her free hand goes between my legs, two fingers parting me and dragging through my soaked folds. She circles my clit with her fingers while her tongue flicks against my nipple. I moan and mewl, bucking against her ministrations. I feel a climax building, but Maelona can sense it and she stops her fingers.

Parting my thighs wider, she brings her mouth down to my core, looking up at me with sultry, dark eyes. She's lust-soaked and addled, hair cerise with passion. Still looking up at me, she licks up my pussy once, jolting me. Her tongue finds my clit and she swirls it rapidly, sending delicate bolts of pleasure through me. One arm bands over my hips to keep me from moving, from reaching the friction I seek. While the other is between my thighs, her fingers dipping into me over and over and then curling inward, driving me to the precipice. I fist my hands in her hair, pushing her harder into my sex, feeling the subtle graze of her teeth. A bolt goes up my spine and I feel my climax building.

"Fuck, I'm so close," I breathe, hips thrusting upwards against her arm.

Maelona continues flicking and sucking on my clit, her fingers still pumping into me. I feel the orgasm build low in my belly, feel it begin to explode, and then it consumes me. I let out a breathy shriek as the climax takes me over the edge, hands still in her scarlet locks, pulling and pushing as she continues her feast between my legs.

When it's over, I collapse, sated and boneless, sweat glistening over my skin. Maelona pulls back and sits on her haunches, delicately licking my wetness from her lips.

I grin, blissfully infused, and reach for her. "Now it's your turn." Rather than pin her to the bed, I pull her over me, hovering her hips over my face. With two fingers, I snap the fragile band of her panties and tear them from her, seeing her center bare and glistening. I look up at her from between her pretty thighs, feeling the heat of her sex only a breath from my mouth. She looks down at me, incredibly turned on, and clearly aching for me.

"Grab the headboard," I tell her.

And with that I pull her down to me and lave up her center, tasting her and plunging my tongue into her very core. She mewls against the ministrations of my tongue, flicking against that little pearl, pulling it into my mouth. I bury my face in the apex of her thighs, tongue moving, aching as it coils her higher and tighter. I hear her breathy moans growing messier, her rhythm breaking as she closes in on her climax.

"Don't stop," she begs, riding my face, hips rolling as she steadies herself on the headboard. "Please."

I continue, and moments later she shatters above me, her orgasm powering through her as I work her, letting the waves crash and settle. I give her a final lick and a kiss to that sated pussy as she climbs off me.

She lies next to me, fingers trailing between my breasts, one circling my nipple and I feel a new wave of wetness between my thighs. I twitch, suppressing a moan, and then I feel an emotion surge. I shutter my eyes and realize that fucking Maelona has broken that hold on my feelings. That someone has finally flipped the breaker in me and all the sorrow and rage and guilt surges through me.

Maelona senses the change immediately. She assesses me carefully, peering down at me from a perch on her elbow. Her face hardens. "You regret this, already, don't you?" She flops down, covering herself. "Of course, you fucking do."

"Mae…" I trail off uncertainly, realizing I don't have an answer for her.

She gets up, pulling the bottom sheet from the bed and wraps it around her like a misshapen toga. She covers herself as if I hadn't just seen, touched, and tasted everything.

I sit up in response, folding my arms over myself.

"Are you just using me so you don't have to think about Gideon and Emrys? When are you going to admit you love both of them, already?"

A gasp catches in my throat and I flounder for a response, sitting naked in her bed. I hesitate for a moment too long. "I-I…"

"This," she circles one hand between us, dark hair mussed. "Is done. You are far too fucked up in every aspect of your life. I will always be your friend but I am through being anything more. I refuse to be the person you fuck to get the taste of someone else from your mouth."

Guilt barrels through me. She's not wrong, I've used her, and I keep using her.

"I can't lose you." My heart breaks on my words.

"You're not, but these dreams you may have had of us are no more. I will not give my heart to you and I will not take yours. We will no longer share bodies. You are my dearest friend, but that is all."

I nod once, gaze askance at the peachy pink and coral shades of her bedchamber. I breathe again and exhale slowly. "Okay."

I gather up my things in silence, dressing quietly while Maelona departs to her bathing chamber. The sound of running water is a definitive barrier between us, thwarting any further conversation. In my room once again, I'm left alone with the destruction I alone wrought.

I stare at a bottle.

CHAPTER 16

CENTURY TRAINING

With a heavy heart and new boots, I return to Emrys, contraceptive tonic still tucked into my pocket. I shiver in disgust over the entire encounter. Osian's hands on me, his mouth on mine. My body trembles with aftershocks of repugnance.

I find him in the room we share, the one that is in less need of repair than others, but wind still whistles through the cracks and shattered panes of stained glass—even with the sheets tacked up. Emrys is lounging on the mattress Lady Fate finally gave us, an arm tucked beneath his head, staring at the ceiling.

"So," he begins, not looking at me. "I was thinking—" he breaks off, hearing something unspoken. Whether it be the energy I give off or the shuffle of my feet, Emrys is instantly at attention. He snaps up and takes me in. It's less than a second before he's on his feet and racing to me.

His arms are warm on my biceps, so comforting and familiar. So much like home that I want to cry. A sob builds in my chest, but I stifle it. Dipping my fingers in my pocket, I produce the vial and wrongness bleeds out of me.

Wrong. Wrong. This is so wrong. This is not what the goddess wants. I know it. It's not what I want.

"What is that?" Emrys asks alarmed, seeing my name attached.

"It's a contraceptive tonic. One is for me and Osian took the other."

Emrys stumbles back as if burned. Pain flares in his eyes and I feel it penetrate deep within my heart. I want so badly to take the words back, to tell the truth, but Osian made me swear an oath. If I reveal it, he will kill him, and I will lose Emrys forever.

"Why? Why would the goddess give you two those?" the heartbreak in his voice is palpable.

"Osian has admitted to his attraction to me."

"Oh, so that means that you should fuck him? Are you serious right now, Vanna?" He's practically spitting, but I flinch from the use of the nickname. "Do you even like him?"

"I have very strong feelings for him." It remains unspoken that they are adamantly negative ones. Murderous ones. "We were kissing, just now actually."

It hits him like a physical blow. Words fall from my mouth like embers. He sees the lips that are bitten and swollen, the hair that is mussed. But if he looked harder, he'd see the defensive wounds for what they are and that the bruises that ring my arms are not from lust and desire.

"So, that's it? You're going to start fucking our mentor?"

"Who says I haven't already?" The words taste bitter.

"Is that what you were going to tell me last night? That you had a tryst with Osian?"

I twist the truth. "I was going to tell you about him, yes."

He nods and looks away. "Do you think it'll make you a better warrior? That somehow you'll gain some experience through this? You're already great, Vanna."

I laugh but the sound is broken. Emrys is gracing me with cruel kindness, but it would be so much easier if he were angry. If he were spouting insults, and calling me a bitch or a whore this would be so much simpler. But instead, he's giving me fucking praise.

I hate myself for having to break Emrys's heart, and I vow to one day kill Osian.

"My personal relationships are none of your concern."

"But what if they were?"

I freeze. "What are you talking about?"

"Is the relationship with you and Osian just physical? Is it just a means for release?"

I don't answer, fearing what my words will give away.

Emrys steps closer and spreads his arms, as if trying to encompass the room. "What about us? What if this wasn't here? What if it was just you and I?"

My heart thunders, hope blossoming to life in my chest. "I suppose we'd be in enemy courts serving our queens."

"But what if we felt about each other as we do now?"

"Like how?"

"Can you keep a secret?"

My mouth goes dry as his hand goes to my jaw, tilting it up.

"Yes," I finally manage.

"I am absolutely captivated by you and I have been for years."

My heart shatters in its cage.

Emrys just professed *captivation* to me, and I am locked in a fucking oath to deceive him. And due to that fucking oath, I can't admit to him that I feel the same. I cannot tell him that I'm wild about him, that I think about him all the time. That he is the first thing I think about when I wake and the last thing I dream of. He is what I imagine when my fingers stray between my legs. He is my best friend and my very equal.

I so desperately want to reach out to him, to accept his confession, but if I do, it's his life on the line.

"Do you feel the same? Do you really want Osian?"

"I have a situation with Osian and I am not calling it off to be with you. I have no interest in two lovers."

Only you. Only you. Only you.

Emrys recoils. "I'm so sorry, I thought—Evelyn, I'm so sorry that was my mistake."

Evelyn. Not Vanna. Not his.

"It's all right—"

"No, I made you uncomfortable. I apologize. I should give you a moment anyway to wash up after—" He hesitates. "If you're happy that's all that matters. I'm going to go for a walk."

And with that he leaves the room. I curl up on the floor and sob.

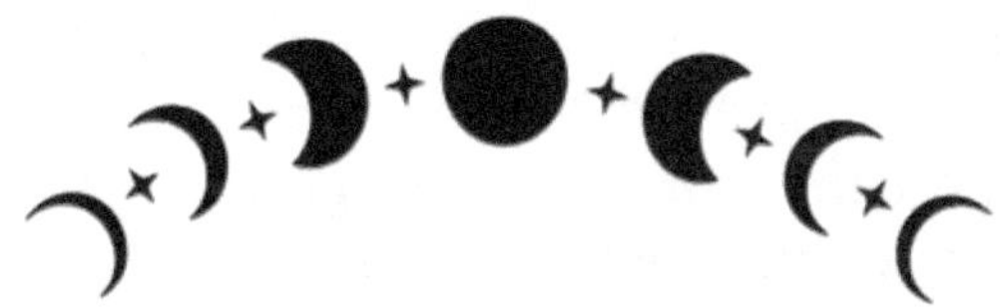

I dread the morning. I'm chilled with Emrys across the room, sleeping on a patch of moss that grows by the window. My heart feels heavy, aching with the pain I've caused. Of all the pain I'm about to cause.

I get ready alone, changing and braiding my hair into a severe crown about my head. When I leave our room Emrys is curled on his side, covered by a ripped blanket, his back to me.

Early in the training room, hazy gray light filters in, not yet touching the stunning stained glass that reminds me so much of the Seelie Court. I sigh and take up a staff, twirling it between my hands. I imagine jabbing Osian's face with every spin.

"I figured you'd be up early, so I brought you breakfast."

The parasite in question arrives, a bowl of oatmeal and berries held in one hand. My stomach growls even though I want to reject his offer, but hunger wins out over pride. I set aside my staff and walk over to him, fury in every line of my body.

I reach out for the meal but he pulls it away quickly. "Nope, this first." He taps the side of his cheek with a finger.

I slap him across the face.

His head turns, but despite the power behind the blow, he laughs. "Now that doesn't sell it, honey."

"I'm not your fucking honey and you won't touch me again."

"Ah, I see the boy took it well."

"Go eat shit."

Osian tsks but hands me the bowl. "You haven't forgotten already, have you?"

My nostrils flare. "I've forgotten nothing and I'll remind you I'm doing this for Emrys, only."

"Oh, I know, that's why it's so effective." He stops and ponders for a moment. "I wonder what it'll be like when he hates you? Will you still continue to fail your tests every year?"

Fear plunges through me, but I refuse to answer, the thoughts in my mind spinning and devolving into violent tangents. Worst case scenarios flitter through my brain, crushing dreams and hopes. What if I fail? What if I actually kill him? Anxiety rises in me like a tidal wave.

My breakfast sits like a lead weight in my stomach when Emrys finally arrives. He looks disheveled, hair unbrushed, bags beneath his eyes. He returned late last night, after I'd already gone to sleep.

Emrys skips breakfast and takes up two stilettos—small, thin blades.

I take up a matching set, my stomach heaving. The plan is memorized in my mind. Every scenario running through my head; everything from where I have to stop, and where I need to get as close to lying as possible.

It's not often all seven of our mentors gather at once, typically it's one or two—one for mithridatism, two for weaponry—almost never more than three. But I know why. They're here to witness the event that will cleave the relationship between Emrys and I apart and fortify speculation on mine and Osian's. It will break my heart.

I send Osian a look so full of vitriol that Enydd tightens her jaw, as if bracing herself. Urian, Una, Cothi, Desmond, and Reagan all hold unreadable masks.

I stand still, knives grasped at my sides as Urian steps forward explaining the day's maneuvers, but I hear none of it.

I already know. From the sides Enydd and Osian step toward us, and my hackles rise when his hunter-green gaze spears me.

Osian trails his fingers over my shoulder and I shudder—I'd put my hair up as high and tight as I could to dissuade him from using my long locks as an excuse to touch me. My eyes are murderous as I track him, but he continues smiling placidly.

"I hate you," I whisper.

His smile only gets bigger. "Save that passion for our private moments, honey."

I've never hated a by-product of bees more.

Osian walks away and I chance a look at Emrys. My stomach sinks when I find his eyes already on me, having seen all that transpired between us and reading it completely wrong.

I hate myself. I hate myself. I hate myself.

Urian directs us to begin and we do with fervor, battling with an unprecedented heat. Fire burns between us, adding another layer of power. Our strikes are brutal, our advances feral, the sounds animalistic. Emrys draws first blood, but the small burst of pain is nothing to the anguish in my heart. We come together and apart, shoving, clawing, disarming, slicing—wounds we hardly feel.

I wait for an opportunity to do the very thing I never want to do. I hate this. I want out. I begin to move but falter back, earning a new slash to my ribs. I hiss out a breath but continue our dance.

It continues like this until I sense the antsy energy of Osian on the sidelines, the raised tension from the rest of the mentors. Their stress is palpable and soon enough Emrys will feel it.

Finally, I create my own opening and in a burst of protective instinct I rush Emrys with all the self-loathing and hatred for Osian I can muster. I tackle him to the ground in a messy maneuver and disarm him by forcing his wrists inward. He's forced to drop the knives or cut himself, and by choosing the former I'm given my opportunity.

Tears well in my eyes as I lift my knives high. "I'm sorry."

And then drive them down—slowing just enough to be stopped.

With only an inch left to spare, Enydd knocks me from astride Emrys, rolling across the floor. One of my knives nicks me under the eye and I lose it in the tumult. Several rolls later I splay on the ground, flattened to my stomach, regret barreling through me with the force of a battering ram.

I lie there, heart breaking and thickness in my throat. When I get to my hands and knees, I scrub at the blood and tears that course down my cheeks.

Emrys's eyes fill with despair and it makes me feel like the most monstrous creature. He's still down, one knee propped, raised on his elbows. Disbelief and misery written across every line of him.

"You tried to kill me," he whispers brokenly.

The obnoxious sound of slow clapping fills the room and I instantly want to murder Osian. The clapping echoes about the space, mocking me as the white-haired mentor approaches, a vicious grin on his face. He pulls my unwilling body to its feet.

"Very well done, honey," he murmurs just loud enough for Emrys to hear.

I seethe and my equal flinches.

Osian crosses the space, practically strutting in his black leathers and velvet tunic. He crouches down to Emrys, his unbound white hair so like that of the Unseelie Queen's.

"Do you understand what just happened here?" Osian asks Emrys contemptuously.

My hands curl.

"No, I don't understand any of it."

Osian smiles and leans in, preparing to spin a tale. "Evelyn admitted her feelings to me the other day." Twisting the truth, turning it into a weapon. "I told her she must inform you about our new situation and the presence of the contraceptive tonics. Has she done so?"

"Yes," Emrys replies bitterly.

"We struck a deal. She had to prove her commitment to me by making an attempt on your life. She had to supply evidence that our agreement meant more than the bond between you two."

Of course, Emrys's life means more than any feelings!

But of course, he doesn't understand that's what I'm fighting for, because Osian has bastardized the context and ripped this thing into something wholly unrecognizable.

Emrys gazes at me wretchedly, as if he doesn't recognize me, and I feel like the worst scum of the earth.

"Is this true?" he whispers.

Bloody tears track down my face. "Ryss…"

"Is. It. True?" he bites out in a savage tone I've never heard from him before.

Pink, salty lines burn on my cheeks as I look away.

"Fucking answer me, Evelyn!"

I hitch a sob. "Yes."

The silence is deafening but I keep my eyes trained on the wall, not willing to watch Emrys strip away the layers of what he used to think of me. I don't want to see that love and reverence and loyalty torn down to scorn and distaste and loathing.

"I hope he's fucking worth it."

And then Emrys storms out of the room without a look back.

The sobs come in earnest now and I break in front of all seven mentors, all of them watching me impassively. Not caring that they've witnessed my most hated moment.

Osian comes to me—gloating—and I stab him through the eye.

CHAPTER 17

To prove a point to Maelona—and more importantly, myself—I throw myself into training Wisteria and Julia. It's been six days without a sip of liquor and only two since Maelona completely rejected me post lovemaking. It should hurt more than it does, however, our relationship has always been fluid and variable. We fell into bed as often as we didn't, and never had friendship been sabotaged by the mixture of sex.

It's a little different now, knowing that physical release will no longer involve Lady Maelona. That loss, missing out on a facet of our dynamic bond, is odd. But it is also reminiscent of my recent abandonment.

The past few days have been consumed with teaching Julia new knifework and swordplay—that I then entrust her to pass onto the rest of the Crows under Maelona's supervision. Today though, Julia is a guinea pig for Wisteria's witchy learning. Each day Maelona has hired a specific witch—with permission from the Seelie Monarch—to assist Wisteria in mimicking their magic and exploring the extent of the replication. Thus far, she has successfully and without impediment copied the gifts of a Blackthorn witch—summoning weaponized vines of ebony briars—as well as a Greenleaf witch's talent of advanced botany, and a Blueblood's inherent poison immunity—with the added effect of her blood temporarily turning into poison like that of the original witch. Truly, Wisteria is displaying untold feats of power, the limits of her Greyvale magic uninhibited by constraints I'm used to seeing.

Always on standby is a healing Fairwalker witch, for the express purpose of adjusting any ails that Julia develops from this experimentation.

I watch, slowly sharpening a golden blade as a Hazelhurst witch with the ability to predict patterns displays her magic. While observing, I sense, rather than hear or see, Violante's arrival beside me. My internal alarm hums as she plops next to me, elegantly crossing her legs. She's comically out of place in a pair of blue jeans and a fuzzy pink sweater.

"I hear Lady Maelona has brought on a Frostsinger witch for Wisty tomorrow," Violante comments idly, her purring accent rolling off her tongue.

I lift a brow in interest, a slight thrill going through me.

Frostsingers are wildly powerful and incredibly rare, hunted to near extinction for their dangerous possession of two talents. They can kill with an icy kiss, freezing the internal mechanics of the body with their breath, as well as lull into a catatonic haze with their voice.

"That shall be interesting. Will Julia be the victim of tomorrow's lesson?"

"Mm, I believe Lady Maelona actually volunteered to test that one."

I blink, my only show of surprise while I continue sharpening and buffing the blade. "Interesting." I pause. A smile curls the edge of my lips. "You know, I was once accused of being a Frostsinger."

Violante gasps, turning her attention to me. Her crimson eyes are wide. "How so?"

"I was on a mission that required mild seduction and I possess the physical appearance of such a witch. Frostsingers are exclusively fair of hair and skin with eyes just as colorless."

Violante leans in, keen interest painted on the lines on her oval face. "Did you successfully complete that mission?"

"I did, and it was the beginning of a business relationship." My smile begins to falter when I recall Jacob Dugal and how our agreement devolved so hellishly that I was left in a wasteland and he was murdered. "He was one of the first and only people to discover I was the *Ceidwad Cudd* before I revealed it. Instead of killing him as I was recommended to do, he became an informant to me and his contribution to that identity helped in the infiltration of a faction of the Winter Carnaval." The reminder of the Sugar Ring only makes me think of Corvina. "He's dead now."

"Oh," Violante says blinking rapidly, "that is so sad."

"Not really. He was a traitorous bastard who deserved everything he got."

"Oh…well, in that case, I am happy for you."

"Are you?"

"I…why wouldn't I be?"

I shrug. "That's just my side of the story, perhaps I am not the hero of it."

Violante purses her glossed lips, considering this. Her eyes flicker to Wisteria, weaving prediction magic under the watchful gaze of the healer. "Wisty wouldn't have trusted you if you were all that bad."

"Desperate times make for desperate calls. I was her only choice to get out." I don't add, *and look where it got her*.

"Maybe that's true, but you forget that I saw you all those years ago and I know what you ran from."

She's wrong though. I have not forgotten. I still remember the sight of those scarlet eyes peering at me from the entrance to the cave, sheets of rain coming down from the heavens. I thought for so long I imagined it.

Maelona meets my eyes from across the room and nods as she circles the makeshift arena, prowling in a high-necked catsuit, so shiny black it appears lacquered. She has that stunningly ornate ribcage corset over it. Her hair is pulled up in a high tail, with a single thick braid going through it.

Julia stands attempting to circumvent any of the predicted outcomes of her future attacks. Wisteria's eyes are blank, courtesy of the pattern/outcome witch, flickering as she runs through the variables. Julia begins with a punch and is immediately stopped by a simple block. The battle is attempts and then blocks, over and over.

Despite the late hour, the false golden sky above us undulates, like a living thing. Beyond the rooms and beyond the court, it is impossibly dark. I yawn once, fatigue drawing on me, especially as I've given up the drink and the waning addiction has sapped so much of my energy. I envy Maelona's tendency towards nocturnal inclinations.

"Very good!" the Hazelhurst witch compliments Wisteria. Her eyes are glowing the same jewel green as the other witch.

When Wisteria borrows a gift from someone, her eyes temporarily change to match them. It's eerie, watching Wisteria's eyes transform from brown to blue to green to gray to hazel. It's eerier still to see them transform into Caethes's obsidian orbs.

"Now, let's try—"

But Wisteria is unable to try anything as an arrow protrudes from the throat of the Hazelhurst witch.

"Get down!" I shout.

Wisteria screams as the witch's mouth floods over with blood, her eyes widening, before she collapses to her knees and falls heavily to the floor. Julia has already darted towards Maelona, a splatter of blood on her face. I'm on my feet before the witch hits the ground, unsheathing my blades, and stretching out my innate talent, seeking a source for alarm.

There isn't one.

Uneasily, I focus harder. A witch was just murdered from the shadows and there is a very real arrow sticking out of her. I narrow my gaze, zeroing in on spaces and alcoves where darkness is the deepest. I can't see anything. But then suddenly, I realize *something* is there.

Wisteria is on the ground, crouching in a ball, arms covering her coppery curls. With ragged breathing, rushed words fall from her mouth. I curse when I understand. I've seen enough post-traumatic-stress to know Wisteria is being triggered by the attack. And now she's an easy target.

"Go to Maelona," I bark at Violante, shoving her. She doesn't question me and is behind the warrior princess in a flash.

I run towards Wisteria, eyes watching the shadows for unnatural movement. I grasp Wisteria's shoulders, knives still clutched in my hands. "Hey, I'm right here. Listen to my voice, you need to follow my instruction."

Wisteria rocks harder, tugging on the roots of her spiral curls. "It's happening again. I can't stop it. I keep seeing it."

"I know," I say softly, eyeing the shadows. "You need to get to Maelona. You need to get out of here. She will protect you."

Something gets through to her and she looks up with hollow eyes.

"Go," I urge. And she does.

In a daze, she manages to get to Maelona, huddling with the healer, Julia, and Violante. The Lady has outfitted them with weapons, ones she deemed them most proficient in during training. I stand in the center of the room, turning in circles, trying to find that presence again. I slow my breaths and wait. On an exhale I catch it, and without hesitation I throw a blade straight for my target.

And then through it.

The shadows dissipate, parting around the strike of the blade, only to coalesce together after the blade sticks into the earthen wall. An unearthly chuckle reverberates through the room and my mouth drops.

"The Wild Hunt."

It has been millennia since the Wild Hunt attacked a court. Beneath the full moon the Hunt can take on the form of tangible shadows or smoke in order to play their vicious game of chase and capture. But the prey has always been fair game. It has always been lost humans or punished fae—not an outright rebellion against a court. They are supposed to be a neutral party, but it's clear now they have picked a side.

"*Hello Harbinger*," the voice croons, approaching me. The shadows take shape, slowly collecting into a man. "Do you remember me?"

The shadow takes clearer form and a face is revealed. "Arawn."

The voice of Arawn rumbles in the shadow's chest, the lost soul of the fae warrior materializing only because of the shifting of the moon. "Indeed."

I'd killed Arawn, run him through with Oath-Sworn a breath after he discovered I was the Harbinger. He was the living leader of the Wild Hunt, but by not ensuring decimation, the Hunt was able to resurrect him for his second shadow life. The Hunt's members are both living and unliving, the latter, starving creatures, only half lucid with a pounding desire to destroy and take. As the newfound dead leader, Arawn has succumbed to a beast's fate of lost souls and reprehensible hunts.

Once the tamer of the beasts, now becomes one of them.

"Who will you choose, Little Warrior? Your queen or—?"

I hear a gasp and whirl, finding Maelona held tight by two shadowy figures. The things have caged her in their invincible smoke, holding a jagged blade to her throat. At the back of the room, each of my huddled allies are clutched in the arms of more shadow things.

My stomach drops out from under me, staring at the fear-filled eyes of Lady Maelona. Her hair has gone white, but her teeth are gritted in determination.

"Save them, or save Aneira, but you cannot choose both."

"Go!" Maelona hisses, eyes wild. "Go save our queen! What are you doing?"

The shadows hiss at Maelona, applying pressure to the blade. A bead of blood slips down her throat. "Shut up! Speak again and we will kill one of your friends to prove a point."

I hesitate, wavering between the love for my best friend and the love for my mother. For my loyalty to the court, and the loyalty to myself. My guilt flickers to Violante, Wisteria, Julia, and the healer. Is my queen-mother worth five lives? As a member of the Seelie Court, it shouldn't be a question. My queen is supposed to be my highest priority. As my mother, I shouldn't even consider not saving her. But…

"GO!" Maelona hisses.

One of the shadows slices the throat of the healer without another word. It drops the witch while Violante and Julia make sounds of disbelief and Wisteria's eyes flare wide with revulsion. It was seconds.

Arawn chuckles. "It seems the Lady has made the choice for you."

And with that, the thing that was Arawn draws its sick blade across Maelona's throat.

Horror and devastation rip through me, tearing unbidden through my heart and soul. I watch the fount of blood flood over that stupidly high neckline of her catsuit, through the gory slit. Her eyes glaze and her skin turns colorless.

"NO!" I scream, slashing uselessly at the shadows. He laughs. My grief and rage block out everything. I am focused in my one singular goal of destroying Arawn.

Suddenly, a figure knocks me aside. I stumble, and see Wisteria, eyes blazing a brilliant cobalt. A glow hovers over her fingers as she presses them to Maelona's ruined throat. The healing magic slowly sews up the slash in my best friend's throat, and I witness the witch replenish the faerie's blood supply.

All the shadows filter out of the room.

"What are you still doing here?" Wisteria demands, voice high, every inch of her feral and desperate. "GO! Go save Aneira!"

I don't hesitate. Rushing, I gather Oath-Sworn from its resting place on a bench and dive through a curtain of golden ivy. I race through the halls, finding guards and servants massacred on the way. My gorge rises with so much carnage wrought, so much blood spilled. I'm slipping on it, dodging fallen bodies and reaching hands, ignoring gasping breaths and pleas for help. I am single-minded in my pursuit of the throne room.

Breaking through the ivy, I find myself staring at my worst fear.

Folant, Elyan, Cadoc, and Andras lie dead on the floor surrounding the throne. Aneira is held against Arawn's shadowy chest. She does not struggle and her face is painted with a mask of resolve. I realize with terror she has submitted to her fate.

"No, please," I plead hoarsely, stumbling as close as I dare, watching countless shadows writhe against the walls. The force that had overtaken my fellow warriors was immense. "Not like this, please. Mother, please no."

Aneira smiles at me sadly, her golden eyes filled with solemnity and acceptance. "I am sorry. It is my time, daughter."

"No, no, it's not," I croak. My throat is thick with burning tears, my heart heavy with their weight. "We can bargain."

She shakes her head slowly, aware of the blade resting only millimeters from her jugular. "I love you very much."

Then Arawn plunges the blade deep into my mother's heart.

CHAPTER 18

In fits and bursts, I see blood and Aneira's snowy gown turn claret. The graceful fall of the Seelie Monarch. The spill of her dark hair across the floor. The tumble of her crown, rolling haplessly away from her.

Arawn evaporates in a gust of smoke, his substance slipping away to nothing as he begins melding into the moving golden ceiling of the throne room.

Rushing to my queen's side, I cradle her head in my lap, brushing the waves back from her brow. Her lips are parted and chalky, the slight points of her incisors so unthreateningly sharp now. The light still left in her eyes glimmers as she tries to take me in.

"I'm so sorry, I love you," I rasp, feeling tears plummet onto her chest. It makes no difference against the scene of scarlet. The words feel familiar in the worst way. "I've failed you."

"You have not failed me." Her hand reaches for mine and squeezes. "I love you, too, and I am so sorry for everything you're about to go through."

"Don't leave me then, I-I can get the healer," I say, panicked. Her warm blood pumps over my hands. I don't mention how the healer on hand has been killed by the same shadows that took her, but Wisteria was borrowing the witch's magic when she died. Maybe she still has enough left over to save my queen after healing Maelona.

"No, it's too late. And I…I've ruined so many things. There are so many things I've selfishly kept from you."

She is deceit…

No. I push the thought away.

"No, no you haven't."

"I have, daughter, and you won't see until I'm gone."

I sob, my heart wrenching from my mouth with every labored breath.

"I wasn't always a good mother, but you have made me so proud," Aneira rasps, voice paper thin. "I'll give Corvina your love."

"Please don't go," I beg.

I watch the light slip from her eyes and her chest still.

"Mother?" I shake her. "Mama? Mama please! *Please!*"

She's gone.

I let out a keening sound, something animalistic and pained. The loss bowls me over, stripping me raw as I wallow in my failure to protect my court, my queen, my mother.

Suddenly, Arawn appears from the golden ceiling, standing over me in all his newly gilded glory, dripping liquid gold Seelie magic on the floor. His shark black eyes burn me even through the smoke and melted gold. I watch his tangible apparition grin, pulling lips over sharp teeth. He picks up Aneira's tumbled crown, grinning maniacally.

The crown of gold branches transforms in his hands, defaulting to its original shape. It is spired with fleur-de-lis, filigree and rubies wrought over the brow. No longer does it bear the symbol of Aneira's reign. I can feel the magic of the Seelie Crown untethered, reaching for its new successor that it cannot see or feel.

The court cannot be ruled by anyone but the one it is destined for. So, until the rightful heir claims the crown, it will remain in the state chosen by old human hands, waiting to alter to the new monarch's power. If a new ruler fails to be crowned, Seelie magic will be erratic at best and catastrophic at worst.

Untamable vengeance floods through me and I stand, bathed in Aneira's blood, sword raised. I hold Arawn's vicious gaze with the furious one of my own. A horrible curl of my lip takes over my mouth.

"Give. That. Back," I demand, parsing the words carefully through my teeth, the cauldron of my fury boiling over.

Arawn smirks. "No, I don't think I will." He twirls the crown on a golden finger. "I'll give Caethes your regards."

As I lunge with Oath-Sworn, Arawn chuckles and vanishes through the air, escaping my attack and taking with it the soul of Seelie magic.

The moment the crown unwillingly leaves the Seelie realm, tricked by Arawn's coating of gilded magic, I feel the shift in the court. The air snaps with a ferocious current, the unequitable aura of wrongness. The very nature of the Seelie

Court is torn off its axis, the symbol of its power wrenched from the very heart of it. The earth rocks beneath my feet, and cracks snake the wall, seeping and disappearing, while swaths of golden and green ivy shake free.

I race for the throne, seeking the vial in the carved pocket of its side to signal an SOS alarm to every trusted warrior of the Seelie court. It will direct them to the training room. I smash it on the quaking floor and shout the summons, the words flooding out from instinct alone.

Speeding for the training room, I take out a blade I'd tucked into my boot, slicing my arm with the Unseelie blade from Emrys and flash the code we devised. One we'd hoped we'd never need to use.

Three rapid golden flashes, meaning; *emergency, come now.*

I leap over the remains of Seelie comrades and servants, of courtiers and friends. I run so fast the world is a blur around me. Tearing through the entrance of the training room, I stutter-step. There, I find Drysi, Bleddyn, Violante, Julia, Wisteria, and Maelona, all living. Maelona bears a thin white scar across her throat, a permanent reminder of the death she so scarcely evaded. Relief surges in me just as potent as my misery.

I take two steps into the room and falter, dropping my sword as tears cut pink lines down my bloody cheeks.

"I was too late."

Falling to my knees, I bow over and haul heaving breaths into my hardly functioning body. My sense of smell is overcome by my blood-soaked clothes, the copper tang suffusing my nostrils and threading down my throat. My arms wrap around my middle, trying to keep in the tearing anguish that threatens to rip me apart.

"The queen is dead. She's dead, she's *dead*, she's *dead*!" I howl.

I feel a hand on my shoulder and look up into silver eyes that hold pools of starlight, those constellations falling down her cheeks like comets. Drysi hitches a breath and licks her lips. "You did everything you could."

Then I break, and as I do I realize Emrys never answered my call.

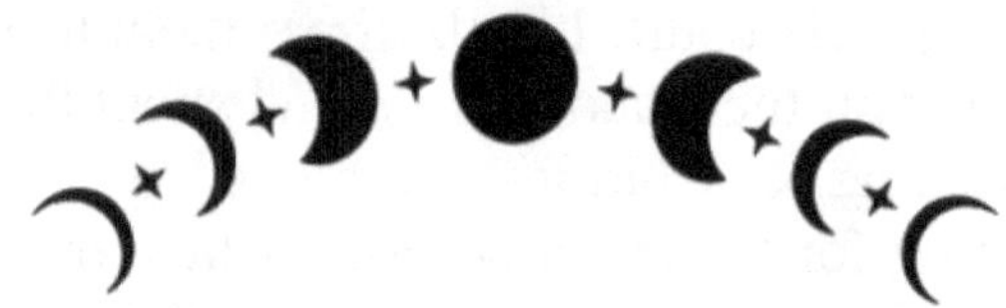

The next day is a mass funeral for all of those lost to the Wild Hunt's attack. We lost most of the Aberth forces and many great warriors, including several of those in Aneira's inner circle. Loyal servants are gone, courtiers have passed. All burn together.

In the courtyard, pyres are set up with bodies wrapped in cloth. I stand between Maelona and Drysi, dressed in black, my hair unbound with no artistry done to it. I stare at the result of the night's carnage with puffy, red eyes. The scent of burning hair and flesh pollutes the air, and the crackle of flames eats away at our losses.

I have no more tears left to cry.

Apathy coats me in a comfortable blanket, the morning's chill numb against my skin. I hardly feel, I hardly think. I am an automaton, and although the monster is in the driver's seat, it too, is quiet.

Is this what Lady Fate wanted? Is this part of her destined lullaby? I want to tear up her prophecy and damn it all to the afterlife.

I barely hear it when the priestess announces Aneira's funeral tomorrow night.

Moving through the motions, Drysi and Maelona guide me back to my chambers, slipping me a sleeping draught. I don't fight it. After being up all night, helping haul the bodies into the courtyard, I am exhausted.

When I wake next, it is late afternoon. Maelona is in my room, silently bringing an onyx gown and a wakeful tincture infused with caffeine and sugar. I take the items to the bathing chamber, attend to my body's needs, don the dress, and down the drink. Maelona guides me to the throne room where the funeral is held, an affair not nearly as grand as it should be. However, things are more unorthodox than ever.

Aneira looks perfectly at peace upon her bed of blue mourning chrysanthemums, her gown a golden-dipped thing. Her crown is a fabrication, the branches nearly a perfect replica for her true adornment, but I saw the theft myself and I know the falsehood for what it is. Her makeup is simple, elegant, enough to highlight her natural, severe beauty. Her obsidian horns are polished to a perfect shine. She looks ethereal and lovely. Something that no longer belongs to this earth.

I again stand beside Maelona and Drysi. Again, dressed in black. Again, the body burns.

This time I cry.

Emrys still hasn't answered my call.

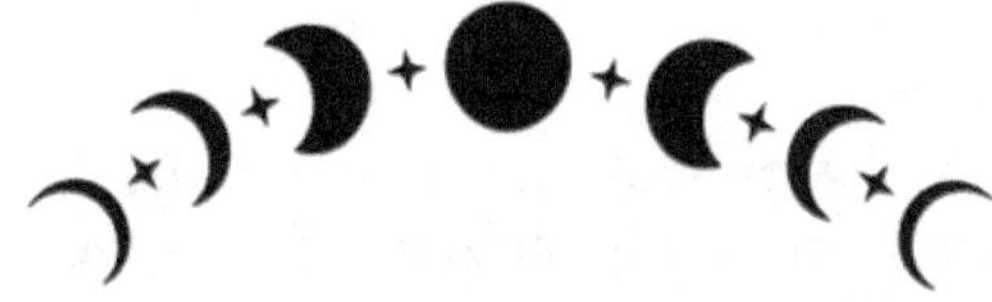

That night, alone in my chambers, the silence wages on and the monster still has the power. I have not wrested control back from it yet, content to let it drive my automated body through the motions.

I participate in a staring contest of iron wills with my last remaining liquor bottle, despite its lack of a single eye. The monster, however, has eyes only for it. Maybe it's because the amber matches Gideon's gaze.

It goads me and laughs at me and eventually, I relent, giving in to it and letting the brandy take me. And that one bottle leads me to calling servants to summon more. So, one turns into three, turns into five, turns into seven, and suddenly it is three days later and I am obliterated drunk on my bedroom floor.

Without an invitation, Emrys arrives in my room on the evening of the third day, climbing in the window as he usually does. I had caught flashes of silver over the past few hours, but chose to ignore them. Although, it did seem petty after the requests came a bit more frantically.

"Vanna, I didn't know," Emrys says in a rush. "I swear, I didn't know. Caethes sent me away on a mission, I think she suspects…" he trails off once he catches sight of me.

"Suspects what?" I ask hoarsely, dangling an empty bottle of brandy between my fingers, watching light catch the facets and distorting the walls and furniture of the room. I tilt my head towards him lazily, letting the sleek panels of my hair slip from my shoulder.

I may have elected to drop sobriety, but I have not forgotten hygiene. What did it matter that I chose to drink in my tub as I do so? What difference does that make from my current perch on a ruined lounge? I am less drunk than I want to be, the mithridatism kicking in after a three-day bender. As of this moment I am simply buzzed and very, very tired.

"Vanna…"

"Yeah, I know," I say dismissively. "I look terrible. Please continue what you were saying. What has her Regal Heart-Eatingness discovered now?"

"I think she suspects my loyalty has shifted."

Surprise flares in me, the first emotion to puncture my fog. I drop the bottle and rise on bare feet, the hems of the black silk pajama set brushing my toes.

"What are you talking about?"

"I found an in at the Winter Carnaval and then I disowned the Unseelie Court."

"Caethes will kill you."

"I don't care. I cannot abide by her actions any longer and this half-life with you is better than all the freedom Caethes can dream of offering me. I would battle every warrior she sends after me just so you know that I am on your side. That I am *always* on your side." He speaks so passionately, fisting his hands together. "If I had my wings still, I would sacrifice them just so you'd remember it all."

What of his theory of soulmates? Does he no longer care?

His knuckles turn white with the intensity of his feelings, his golden skin starching beneath the rings. I watch him play with the plain gold band and a thought strikes me dumb.

"Is that a fucking wedding ring?"

Emrys freezes, his forefinger and thumb pinching the object in question. I cross the space between us and take his left hand, examining the simple band. It is just that. Simple, plain, gold. All of his other rings are so much more detailed or ornate.

I lift my startled gaze to Emrys's timid, guarded one. The apprehension darkening those topaz eyes.

"Yes," he finally answers.

I let go of his hand, stepping back in disbelief. Betrayal and dismay rage through me. I feel so deceived.

That's why he no longer cares about his theory of Gideon and I being soulmates.

"Where is your spouse, then?" I gather my wits and turn my vulnerability into anger. How dare he pine after me when he has a significant other waiting for him, surely unaware of our twisted, sexually charged relationship. I feel ill.

Emrys softens his features, looking at me meaningfully. "Vanna…"

It clicks, horror driving through me as fast as the truth settles in me. Familiarity and rightness fall on me like a comfortably warm blanket, while the gravity of the situation slams against my soul like the locked doors of Century Training.

"*I'm* your wife."

CHAPTER 19

Bound hands beneath the goddess's sky, exchanged rings, and a sealing kiss. Gold eyes of devotion. Silver of adoration. Deepest crimson hair adorned with chrysanthemum petals. Platinum locks twisted with blooms of anemones. Late summer heat, chill night air, a swollen moon. A smile touched by pointed teeth. A thumb brushing a lower lip. Hot hands on a slim waist. A smile against a mouth.

The marriage returns to me in flashes. A half-remembered dream at the tail end of July, a wonderland of hills and stars and us. Just us. The imposing, broken cathedral of

Century Training at the far end of the field. The two of us at the edge of the realm, taking our moment.

I step back, watching Emrys, eyes flickering between his face and his hand. To that golden band that sits plainly on his finger. I put a hand to my racing heart, stilling it through the silk and flesh and blood and booze. It hammers, pounding against my palm like an angry drumbeat.

"Why didn't you tell me?" I ask hoarsely, heart in my throat. I wonder distantly—stupidly—where *my* ring is.

The look he gives me is aching. "I couldn't. I was bound."

Because Lady Fate did more than just take my memories.

I swallow once and nod rapidly, trying to regain a semblance of normalcy, but my life has been turned upside down, chewed up, and spit out. In such a short period of time I have lost so many people in so many ways and now here I am, presented with my *husband*.

Somehow, I find myself sitting on the ruined chaise lounge. Emrys approaches tentatively, sitting on the opposite end. He stares at his hands, at the multitude of rings and the one that means the most of all.

"How can you bear it?" I don't have to clarify. He knows I mean everything; how he kept our marriage secret, how he dealt with me having no recollection of it.

He swallows and stares at the gold mirror across from my bed—I had thrown a sheet over it, unable to stand looking at myself, but it has slipped, the curlicue edges gripping it with the last vestiges of strength—and I can see him reflected in it. Solemn. Lost. And I can see him barely holding himself together.

"With much difficulty," he finally manages.

I put a hand on his, pulling it toward me and brushing a breath across his knuckles and the golden band I put there. He shivers, warm pleasure dancing between us.

"We will figure it out." And I say it because I believe it.

"We will. We always do."

It's nice, this moment. Sharing our connection and pain and bond. It is easier, this grief, when I am not so alone, even though we are not discussing the source of it. Just having Emrys nearby banishes the worst of the agony Aneira's death has left.

Still holding Emrys's hand I recall what he'd begun to say when he arrived. "How do you plan to get us into the Winter Carnaval?"

"There's a private sex club in Prague that exclusively hosts supernaturals and their guests. It has connections to the Carnaval. If you're witnessed behaving a certain way, you're invited into an exclusive venue with more connections or to the actual Carnaval itself. I've secured three invitations."

"Three?" I ask, raising a brow. I don't recall all of my memories, but I'm quite certain Emrys and I never engaged in polyamory, nor entertained threesomes. Not that they're uncommon in the courts, but I've never enjoyed sharing my partner. Of course, during Century Training we had access to no one else but ourselves and our mentors.

"The idea is that Lady Maelona would be willing to help us."

There it is, the acknowledgement of their odd friendship. It's enough of a relationship that he's considering her for this plan, likely thinking of no other. Not to mention, brought up in the context of a sexual nature.

"How so?" I inquire, crossing my legs.

This time Emrys blushes. "It would be a simulation."

"Of?" I think I see where this is going.

"Depravity, licentiousness, recklessness, extravagance. The organizers enjoy when there is a third involved."

"I see."

"And I considered options but I thought of the one we'd be most comfortable with, should you decide to go through with the plan."

"Why wouldn't I go through with it?"

"Because you would have to touch us."

"I've touched both of you many times before."

Emrys quirks a smile and I'm sure if its nervous or endearing. "Vanna, it would be a public sexual display."

"I understand."

Emrys seems relieved and continues apologetically. "This is all I could manage in the short time and I know Caethes's deadline is quickly approaching."

Because Caethes gave us until the Summer Solstice to rescue Gideon before she executed him and it is already May. I feel a pang of guilt over dismissing Gideon so hastily, casting him aside in pursuit of Lady Fate's bargains and newly seeking the return of the crown.

"Why do you care about Gideon so much?"

Emrys leans towards me, putting both hands on my knees. "It's not just Gideon anymore. Caethes has given Aneira's crown to the Winter Carnaval."

I jump to my feet, scribble a message, and seal it with emerald wax with a stamp of the Seelie crest. Stepping out into the corridor, I summon a passing servant which I inform the letter must be delivered promptly. He scurries off with the envelope held carefully between his hands.

Minutes later, Maelona appears in my chambers, eyes wide at the sight of Emrys lounging on my ruined chaise.

Immediately, she picks up on the gravity of the situation and sighs.

"Why do I have the feeling I'm about to be roped into some scheme?"

As soon we fill her in, she volunteers so enthusiastically I wonder if she even needed the details. It crosses my mind, however that she might just be involved in order to be crowned the new Seelie Queen. But I banish the thought immediately with guilt.

"When do we leave?" Maelona presses, pacing the floor on the most sunken level of my room. Emrys is still sprawled on the lounge, while I lean against my bedpost, not having changed out of my silk pajamas.

"In exactly one week." Emrys says, tilting his water glass between his fingers. The wedding band sitting boldly on his finger—how did I ever miss it? "The first event is elite but not exclusive, the second is invite only, so we must ensure we receive that invitation or our opportunity closes. Unless we receive a key."

"But you can figure out another, can you not?" Maelona inquires in a swirl of charcoal satin. "Using contacts and resource, I'm sure you can ascertain another opening."

Emrys grimaces. "This was hard enough to come by and now that I've forsaken the Unseelie Court, I doubt I will be welcomed warmly. Especially if I'm prodding into the machinations of the Carnaval."

"You did *what*?" Maelona asks, threads of white appearing throughout her onyx locks.

Ah, so it seems we did leave out a detail or two.

Aside from the revelation of our marriage and everything pertaining to our relationship, we hold back no more secrets. As Emrys talks, I am enraptured, staring at this fae male, my opposite, my mirror, my *husband*. Emrys truly is stunningly attractive. All angles and severe beauty, sharp lines, and jewel tones. His eyes are heavy lidded, sultry, his lips built for pouting and kissing. I remember the feel of his sculpted nose skimming my throat, my breasts, my thighs…

He notices me watching him and his lip curls in a secret smile, eyes twinkling with delight and teasing. My heart flutters and the empty space between my legs throbs.

We wrap up the rest of the conversation and Maelona retires to her chambers, swearing to secrecy on all matters discussed. As the door's hinges keen behind her, I lock it firmly and turn to find Emrys collecting bottles from around the room. I watch him for a moment, staring unabashedly, considering that he *is* my husband and I have every right to look. He bends down and I watch the muscles beneath his shirt ripple, the curve of his spine, the shape of his ass in those leather pants.

"You always did stare so boldly," Emrys says while he plucks up a ninth bottle and shuffles his armload over to an empty wicker bin. He doesn't even look up at me.

I twist my lips in a wry smirk and cross the floor, carefully descending the stairs.

"What are you still doing here?"

Emrys straightens and rubs the back of his neck with a hand, ruffling his hair. "I have nowhere else to go and you are the only person I trust."

"There is no one else?"

"I only trust you. Caethes is putting a bounty on my head any moment now, and no one is going to be loyal to the Revenant for any boon from her. The Seelie Court is the one place she can't attack right now due to negotiations. I would have glamoured myself, but nothing is powerful enough should the wrong person see, except for a Queen's Glamour. But…" he trails off uncomfortably.

"But Aneira is dead and the crown is gone."

"Yes, that."

"But you thought I would not give you up for the same reasons?"

"I trust you. I also counted on you hating Caethes."

I choke on an unexpected laugh. Emrys smiles softly and for a moment we lapse into silence, while he distractedly cleans and organizes.

I close my eyes, imagining what it'll be like, living with Emrys again. Back during Century Training, near the end, we did not have plush beds and luxurious sheets as we do now. We had lumpy bedrolls and a decaying mattress, moth-eaten blankets, and threadbare pillows. We found it easier to share body heat than stave off the chill with the mildewy supplies we'd been given. Though there were many years where we refused to unless it was the coldest of nights, when we spent foolish years as enemies until, evidently, we transformed into spouses.

"Do you want me to leave?" he asks insecurely when my silence lasts too long.

I open my eyes to find his trained on me.

"No, I don't."

"Okay."

"I do have a question though," I begin, approaching him. "Why did you push me away a few nights ago, but now you come crawling back? Telling me we're married and you cannot live anywhere else?"

Emrys flushes and straightens some haphazardly strewn papers. "That isn't why I came here."

"Isn't it? Ryss, why are you evading the question?"

"I thought I should give you the choice, not take it from you."

"Meaning?"

"Meaning Gideon possibly being your soulmate shouldn't dictate who you decide to be with if you decide anyone at all. And I regretted leaving you the second I was gone, you practically begged—"

"Don't remind me."

"And yet I abandoned you when you specifically needed not to be abandoned, so, I am sorry for hurting you."

I raise a brow at his response. "You're apologizing to me?"

"Yes."

"Ryss, you were doing the honorable thing and now you're apologizing for what—? Not being selfish? For thinking of my feelings?"

Emrys steps forward, closing the gap between us. "I'm apologizing," he says slowly, "for giving up on you for the right reasons and not letting you go for the wrong ones."

"That doesn't make sense," I breathe as he comes directly to me, our chests flush with the other. Any further words get stuck in my throat at the intensity that burns off him.

"I am a selfish, greedy creature," he whispers to me, "and you possess me of everything in my soul. I am happy to let you take all of me and I will thank you for decimating my life."

He places a hand to my throat, cuffing me just below my jaw, his other hand going to the small of my back. All those rings dig into my flesh and it does something to me. I fist my hands in his partially buttoned shirt.

"I think of you every waking moment, desiring you and cursing you," he continues. "You challenge me, captivate me, and utterly condemn me. I want you. I *crave* you." His lips dip down to mine, breath smelling of lemon drop candies. "If I have to pretend to be good or truly be good, to have a chance, I will do it. Just so I can tell you all the dirty things I used to do to you. Does *that* make sense?"

A flood of wetness crests at the apex of my thighs. My clit tingles from the possessiveness in his voice, and my delicate inner walls clench, seeking my *husband*.

"Yes," I breathe, feeling my lips ghost across his, softer than a butterfly's wing. Everything in me wants to lunge forward and capture his mouth with mine, take him to the floor, straddle him, and ride him through the night.

I may not be able to recall our marriage vows and the love that supposedly existed between us, but the desire is still very much there and very much potent.

Emrys pulls away before I can act on my urges and I feel a swell of disappointment.

"But I will not take advantage of you when you are drunk."

I pout. "I am *not* drunk. In fact, I have been inadvertently practicing mithridatism."

"With alcohol," Emrys deadpans.

"Yes."

"I see."

"Do you?"

"I refused to consume any alcohol while you were gone because I knew if I started, I'd never stop. I saw my future coming when I drowned my sorrows in several bottles of wine after news of your disappearance reached me."

My heart thunders. "And now?"

He pins me with those eyes. "Now I will keep from the drink in solidarity with you."

That vulnerable thing that tried to come to life when I met Emrys on the grounds of the Seelie Court creeps out of my heart, peering out of my chest and fluttering its wings. It is still within its chrysalis, but soon it'll break free.

"You'd do that…? For me?"

Emrys gives me a smile, all endearing charm and self-deprecation. "I think we've established I'll do anything for you." He makes for the bed. "Do you still prefer the left side?"

Surprise takes me and I blink. "I do."

"Lovely," he responds, stripping off his shirt. I'm left staring at him, dumbstruck.

I take in the expanse of his golden skin and the muscles beneath. The build of his chest, the cut lines of his abdomen, the enticing V disappearing into his low-slung pants.

My mouth goes dry.

In addition to the scar over his heart he received when he died, he also has two curving slashes parallel to his spine, like two crescent moons back-to-back. I can't see them without thinking of his missing wings.

He starts to get into my bed when I stop him. "Are you really going to go to sleep in leather pants?"

"You want to get me naked that bad?"

I sigh in exasperation. "You're not wearing any undergarments?"

"We both know neither of us care for them much."

Rolling my eyes, I shuffle over to my chest of drawers and pull out a pair of lounge pants and toss them at Emrys. He catches them midair with a simple stretch of one arm and raises both brows as he looks at the line of florals and arachnids down the sides.

"These are mine."

"Huh. That makes sense, I think I stole them from you."

I turn my back as he changes into them and I hear his choking laugh as his belt jingles. "When?"

"About a year after Century Training."

He's still laughing, a throaty sound that has me throbbing in all the right places. Flashes of memory intersperse with fantasy.

"Why would you do that?"

I shrug, back still turned. "Because I could. Also, it was fun to imagine you wondering which bedmate of yours was snooping and thieving."

"I don't have bedmates." The sound of fabric sliding over him has me turning. I don't miss that this is the second time he's told me he's been with no one else.

Because he has been faithful to your marriage. Unlike you.

The thought hits me like a gong and guilt tears through me. I didn't *know*.

"Regardless, it's what I thought."

Emrys climbs into my bed and I douse all the lights but one, illuminating the sheets with a soft amber glow. I approach and put my hands on my hips.

"That's the left side."

"Is it?" he asks innocently, crossing his hands under his head, looking indulgent and sultry in my bed. It has my thoughts turning explicit. "Hmm, maybe you can try to take it from me."

I huff and stubbornly get in on the right side, pulling the downy blankets over me. There is a solid foot between us as I lie on my back and stare up at the stained glass ceiling. The true night sky is scattered above.

Suddenly, I lunge for him, straddling his thighs, and tucking my arms beneath his. He expects this and laughs, full of delight and playfulness. The blankets are tossed from the bed or tangled around us. With a roar of false fury, I push us over and he lets me roll him to his predetermined right side as we come to an abrupt stop with me astride him. One hand finds the side of my hip, his thumb rubbing aimless circles over the silk of my pants, his other wrapped around the spindles of my headboard.

"Well, this feels familiar," he chortles, and his laughter does something to me as it causes me to bounce on his pelvis. I put a hand to his bare chest, steadying myself, feeling electricity flare to life between us. There's an answering hardness surging between my legs, seeking the wetness there.

"*Ryss*," I half moan.

I trail that hand down his abdomen, following the ridged lines until I come to the apex of my thighs and stroke between my legs once. I bite my lip to keep from a crying out while my clit tingles from the brush through the fabric.

Emrys freezes and an erotic sound leaves his throat while I watch the flex of his arms. He tightens his hold on both me and my headboard. I have a brief, yet vivid fantasy about tying him to it and teasing him to completion.

"Vanna," he sounds like a man in pain. "Not like this. Not when you've just given up a vice. Don't make me a new one."

We both stop immediately, the realization dawning as clear as ice water, sobering that spirited gleam. Gently, he rolls me off him and I go with the motion, ignoring the raging crave in my core as I settle on the left side.

"I will not do anything with you while you are drinking. Not until you are certain of what you want or you remember us."

This time when I lay on my back staring above, it is not to plot an attack, it's to quell my wild heart.

CHAPTER 20

CENTURY TRAINING

Ten years I've kept up the ruse with Osian and for ten years I've hated myself more every day. Emrys holds back nothing in our training, coming for me with a viciousness that is utterly unprecedented. I realize with dismay that he's always been restricting himself to some degree. I earn more scars in the recent decade than in the two and half decades preceding it. Mithridatism is horribly painful, not only for the lack of support from him, but his utter disregard. Most times I feel like I'll truly die without him, and sometimes I dream of giving up.

We continue failing our yearly test, now for a different reason. We cannot handle touching each other in any way that isn't to harm. The squirms and moans of arousal have now turned to flinches of disgust and repulsion. But I don't blame Emrys for holding the grudge. For all he understands I tried to kill him for a fling. I'd hate me too.

Funny how the goddess never sent tonics again.

The mentors have become increasingly unsettled, more often arguing amongst themselves and more than once I find them snubbing Osian. It's become all too evident that Osian overpowered the others with the ruse that is destroying my life, and I wonder how he was able to force the action that directly counters the wishes of the goddess they serve. Does he have blackmail against them? Some special power? Is there a hierarchy?

One night during my new nighttime wanderings—unable to bear the distance between me and my equal—I caught Osian and Enydd at each other's throats and it took Una and Desmond to pull them apart. I'd frozen at the threshold, seeing blood on the two mentors and I realized two things in that moment.

One: they are not as allied together as they'd like us to believe. And two: they can harm or even kill each other.

Emrys's arrow nicks my thigh and I lunge away with a gasp, thrown back into the current moment. He is absolutely lethal with the crossbow, even blindfolded as he is. The current task is for him to draw blood without maiming me, while completely sightless.

He's on point three in ten minutes. I only had one in the entire fifteen we were allotted.

The predatorial way he tracks me is insanely terrifying and simultaneously sexy. The way his lithe, built frame is focused completely on me, attuned to my every movement, every breath…it has me aroused in the worst of ways.

But of course, he hates me and nothing now will change that.

My foot kicks a stray pebble and the skittering rock betrays my position as Emrys whips to me, aiming without sight and releases an arrow. It grazes my ear. With my heart hammering and my breaths coming in rasps now, I'm all too easy of a target and I disregard my careful tiptoeing. I sprint the edge of the training room, ducking and zig-zagging, throwing myself with longer strides and skipping with smaller ones. I hide behind collapsed columns and leap over the broken staircase, all while arrows fly behind me.

"One minute!" Urian announces from the balcony overlooking the training area. Enydd and Osian are leaning over the rail watching us.

Emrys finds me behind a crumbled balustrade and leaps over, landing perfectly on the edge of the stairs. Balancing surefooted, he aims the bow and arrow directly at me. I inhale sharply and dodge to the left as he lets the arrow loose.

My ankle catches between broken stone and twists. I go down too soon and instead of the arrow grazing me, it lodges beneath my ribs.

"Fuck!" I gasp, falling to the ground, my ankle barking and my side burning. I apply pressure immediately to the area and look down.

Blood blooms freely on my gray shirt, spreading like a macabre rose. I hold the wound, my fingers turning crimson and the scent of copper fills the air.

Emrys tears off the blindfold and looks down at me, shock across his face.

"That shouldn't have hit you like that," he says angrily.

"I tripped."

The sound of Urian, Enydd, and Osian's approaching footsteps reach us and Emrys doesn't move. Ever since Osian's ruse he's made himself a stubborn ox, defiant and insubordinate. If he doesn't strictly have to do something, he won't. Every opportunity to thwart the mentors, he does.

I'd once overheard Una complaining that she attempted to seduce him and he shut her down hard, growling his disinterest while sending her from the room. She'd attempted again and whined about how she'd only been offering him comfort after my betrayal, but his clear intonation of *"fuck off"* was heard throughout the structure of Century Training. After that, Una seemed closed off and frostier towards me than usual.

"You never trip," Emrys says flatly.

"Yeah, well, this time I did," I retort sharply. He doesn't need to know how distracted I've been of late, knowing that every day he hates me is another day I love him.

Osian is first to arrive and drops down beside me, replacing my hand with his. I slap it without realizing my error. I freeze and so does Emrys, but the moment passes and he continues his fury-fueled watch, pissed at my fumble.

Enydd's hands push away Osian's and he lifts his scarlet stained fingers in surrender. Urian comes to my side, his scarred face softened as he takes me in and he probes gently as he turns me over.

"It went through—good." Urian exhales, then meets my gaze. "We're going to remove it." He looks over at Osian. "Go get the bandages, hot water, and wound cream."

Osian goes to retrieve the items without a second's hesitation and I don't miss how Emrys deliberately jostles the mentor's shoulder with an aggressive amount of force. Confusion lances through my haze of pain. I didn't think Emrys cared enough about me to react to Osian, but I appreciate it nonetheless.

"Enydd, hold the arrow steady," Urian commands, tying up his multitude of braids. She does as asked. Urian's deep green eyes find Emrys. "Emrys, I need you to apply pressure to the wound while I break off the arrowhead."

Emrys licks his lips, showing a rare sign of nervousness. "Why?"

Urian raises a scarred brow. "You did this, didn't you? Help the girl out." He pauses. "She needs you."

I blink, surprised by Urian's words. Emrys drops down beside me and presses his beringed hands against my wound, bracketing either side of the arrow.

Urian has never cared much for me either way, the most detached of our mentors, easily able to dispose of kindness for effectiveness, urging us on to the best of our abilities as well as hitting us when we do not meet expectation. But this…this softness, speaking of need? It's not him.

I'm unsettled by the rest of the encounter, Emrys's hands hot on me, Enydd and Urian's clinical and efficient. When Osian arrives, he stutter-steps when he catches sight of Emrys's hands on me and the look my equal sends him is the most malevolent silence I've ever seen.

"The bandages, Osian," Urian demands, clipped and impatient, having no time for his bullshit. He hands them over, making no secret of his staring, the possessiveness of his gaze on my body. And I realize.

Osian did this because of his own jealousy. Because he feels entitled to me and the connection between Emrys and I threatened him. He wanted me so much he decided if he couldn't have me then no one else could. But how did he convince the others?

When the arrowhead snaps off, I inhale, expecting the pain coming with the removal and I'm unsure if I imagine it or not, but I think I feel Emrys's fingers tighten on me in reassurance. Urian tells me to breathe and when I do, he yanks out the arrow. I curse profusely and Enydd succinctly cleans the wound, applies a salve, and bandages me.

After the worst of it is through, Urian dismisses Osian, telling him to inform the others of the events, and Emrys's number of points over me. He mutters and drags his feet, but does so. Enydd leaves to dispose of the ruined cloths and filthy water. Then I'm left with Emrys and Urian, the former sitting on his haunches, bloodied hands hung uselessly between his knees.

"Go wash up, boy," Urian tells him, gently pushing him. "That is all for today."

Emrys lets an unreadable look linger on me, before he nods and gets to his feet. I watch him leave, taking my heart with him. When the door creaks in closure, I turn to Urian.

"Why?" I whisper brokenly, tears in my eyes. "Why did he make me hurt him?"

I don't have to elaborate—Urian knows, just as all the other mentors do. It is an unspoken thing, but they planned it, they saw it. Though, I don't think they anticipated the damage it would cost us.

Urian clenches his jaw and looks away, sighing. "We were overruled."

"Who is we?" This is the first time I've been told anything about the inception of the ruse, or how the deception came to be and why. "Who opposed it?"

His nostrils flare and I can see him fighting against something.

"You're bound." I realize. "You were oathed not to speak of it."

He nods.

I begin to wonder how to get around it. "If I name someone, can you nod?"

"Only once," he manages. "It would serve as a warning, but anything after would be excruciating and your emotional peril is not worth that."

Thoughts rampage in my head, mentors and motivations filtering through. I compile possibilities, trying to see which would be the most likely. This goes on for several silent pauses before I take a breath.

"Did Enydd also oppose it?"

Urian clenches his teeth but nods once.

Relief floods through me with a mix of hope. She has always favored Emrys but unlike the rapacious way Osian likes me. While I don't expect love from the fae woman, knowing she cares about Emrys shines her in a positive light.

"Was she the only other?" I press.

Urian's face folds in sadness. "I could only answer once, I feel the warning prickling now. I will not risk it again."

I suck in my cheeks and inhale. "I appreciate it, nonetheless."

"Do not challenge him, Evelyn."

"Who?"

"Osian."

"Why? What hold does he have over you all?"

Urian pauses for far too long. "Everything."

CHAPTER

The week comes and goes quickly. Every night I go to sleep next to Emrys, a foot of space between us, and just like during Century Training we wake entangled. Always in different positions. I leave every day, locking Emrys in my suite, unable to risk a sighting of the Revenant in the Seelie Court. Even if that identity is unbeknownst to all.

To pass his time, he tries to glean new information from the Lady Fate lullaby and cleans my chambers, tidying the mess I've left in my devolution to alcohol. I hadn't yet cleaned the glass and liquor from my breakdown. We keep topics light, not daring to delve into anything like that first night. After my wagon falling, I've only been sober for six days, and that first one was deadly.

It becomes comfortable, this unorthodox routine, regaining Emrys just when I've lost Aneira. His familiarity enough to keep me from going over the brink. So, while Emrys busies himself in seclusion, I and Maelona take charge of the court. We complete all the tasks necessary and assign new faces to duties. With so much life lost at court things are in dire disarray, and without our monarch the court is slowly descending into chaos.

Quakes from the crown's loss are becoming all too frequent. Twice daily has become the norm and the court's anxiety has risen to troubling degrees. Bleddyn, Drysi, Maelona, and I hold a council meeting, debriefing all the details of the ongoing war and the daily court machinations. We also address the Corvina/Harbinger issue.

"Is it true that the Harbinger is dead?" a Seelie fae with black antlers and cobalt eyes asks. Her tawny skin is spotted like a fawn's. "And you've known since Lady Vanora returned?"

"Corvina Vanora has passed away," Drysi deflects the faerie's question, "but I was not made aware until later."

Some mother, I think snidely.

"Murder?" A separate voice.

"Yes," Drysi confirms.

"Who killed her?"

The casual and detached manner which the questions are spoken is like a dagger to my chest, each one a new blade. This is my sister and yet they are gathering pieces of her death like reciting a fact sheet.

"We do not know," Drysi answers reluctantly.

That troubles me more than I care to admit. How do I seek revenge if I do not who to thrust it upon? Vengeance against the Unseelie Court can only go so far.

"How?" one voice intones.

"Why didn't you use her murder as a point for announcing the war?" a commander with ram horns asks.

"We did not have proof and we cannot force them to admit to the deed." Drysi looks at me, concern rising. This is causing near physical pain. Aside from her gaze she looks so much like Corvina. I look away and steel my spine.

"Did you always know your sister was the Harbinger?" the antlered fae asks me specifically.

"I was one of the first to know the Harbinger's identity."

"What is being done about the Seelie Court's crown?"

I let Bleddyn, unknowing of the plan, take over. On and on the questions and deflections go, especially keeping the situation of the crown retrieval under wraps. The meeting draws late until a quake brings us abreast of the situation and forces everyone into action. The room empties quickly and on everyone goes to stabilize the court and keep it running as smoothly as possible.

How much of this was foretold in the lullaby? How much of this is unchangeable?

Back in my room I find Emrys ready and I stutter-step. He's dressed in a sheer black blouse, unbuttoned halfway with epaulets of iridescent wings—gold and dark. His pants are—as usual—black leather and his boots are black with gold buckles. Thin gold chains hang from his neck and ring his ears. There's even a swipe of the metallic shade on his eyelids.

"When do we leave?" I ask, anxiety thrumming.

"In an hour. The venue is nine hours ahead," he responds, and he keeps his voice level, but I've known him too long not to notice the trepidation in it.

"Has Maelona been notified?"

"I sent a letter to her recently. She should receive it any moment. Not to worry," he says when he sees my stricken face. "I used a glamour." Then he hesitates. "Vanna, I don't want to have to ask, but…"

"Yes?" I quirk a brow, admitting only to myself that I adore that he still uses that nickname he gave me almost a hundred years ago.

"I can't touch you—I *won't* touch you—if you're not sober."

"I have not had any alcohol since you came to stay here. Not even a taste." And it has been a challenge. The monster inside hates it.

"I just—"

"Don't explain yourself. It's a valid concern." I sigh. "Can we risk bringing any weapons?"

He seems grateful for the topic change. "Not really, we're searched at the door. Weapons would be near suicide."

"Right, okay." I pinch the bridge of my nose. I have not had enough sleep for this. "Give me a minute to pick something out."

"Already done," Emrys says smoothly. "It's in the bathing chamber."

I raise a brow. "If you went through my lingerie—"

"Don't worry, I didn't snoop. Though I am curious about that strappy black piece."

I throw a crystal tumbler at him as I pass. He catches it—just as I knew he would.

My makeup is quick, a cat eye and gloss, pearly shimmer, and some gel in my brows. I play with my hair, lifting it up and down, brushing it out, fluffing it up, feeling uncertain and insecure. When I see the gown Emrys picked out for me, I put it on, stare in the mirror and flush with rage. I storm out of the room, barefoot and furious.

"What the fuck is this?" I demand, standing legs apart, arms upraised.

Emrys turns and I watch him swallow once. Twice. His eyes burning pools of molten gold, desire running hot and rampant through them. That look melts some of my rage. He's staring shamelessly—as he should, the dress leaves little to the imagination.

The dress is snow white and skin-tight with two high slits on either side, stopping just above my hip bone, the hem brushing my toes. Diamonds drape on the straps, dropping from my shoulders like a fall of stars, resting provocatively on my arms.

"You look absolutely delectable," Emrys purrs, purposely eye-fucking me and letting me know it.

My core turns liquid and the rest of the ire slips from me.

He crosses the room and I notice he holds an assortment of rings, all gold and silver. Taking my right hand, he slips rings seemingly at random upon each of my fingers until my hand is as bejeweled as his. He takes my left and does the same, pausing on my empty ring finger.

"Where is my ring?" I ask softly.

I glance up and find Emrys already looking at me, hope and fear mingling on his face. Silently, he goes to the ring on his littlest finger, twists it off, and holds it up. It's a teardrop emerald flanked by diamonds.

I stare at it for a beat, watching the light play across the diamond, fractures of multi-hued rainbows shattering off it. I swallow once and I watch him do the same.

"If you are inclined to sell this charade, wearing the ring will help," he says throatily. "Only if you're okay with it."

"I am." So, I hold out my left hand and he slides it into place. It fits perfectly. Still warm from his skin, I tilt it, feeling the weight of it and flexing my hand. It feels right.

"How long did I wear this before?"

"Not long enough." I find him struggling for words and I realize what he's seeing. Me, in a white dress and a gold ring on my finger.

"Does this bring back memories?" I ask delicately.

His jaw works and he averts his eyes, nodding. His mouth parts and his tongue darts out to wet his lips. I'm captivated by the movement. Hypnotized by him and hanging on his very breath, awaiting what he'll say next.

"There's more," he announces finally, startling me out of my lusty haze. He turns to the table by his side and dips his hand into a box. He holds up a gold and silver chain garter, a crescent moon dangling from the swooping lines of it. He goes down on one knee and swallows, looking up at me with that darkened gaze. "May I?"

Lifting my foot delicately onto his knee, I rest it, feeling the heat of him seep into my toes. He takes my ankle and a riot of thoughts rush through me. With my ankle in his grasp he could do so many things to me; he could snap it in one movement, he could pull me down and tumble me to the floor. I could be at his mercy if he so chose. But instead of what I intrusively fantasize, he swirls a thumb gently, and slides the jewelry up my leg, his palm grazing my calf, the underside of my knee, my inner thigh. He settles it into place high and tight, and I feel an ache seize me between my legs at the too distant brush of his fingertips.

I know what we're doing tonight. The façade we're painting, the show we're selling, the attention we're seeking.

But I can't help but feel temptation and trepidation unfold through me. I'm also hyperaware of the ease of access afforded in this dress.

"I feel like you chose this piece on purpose," I whisper breathily.

"I chose it all on purpose."

Heat sinks into me, mellowing my bones, turning me languid and hot. I'm slipping into the sensation when he slips a shoe onto my foot and removes my step from his leg, somewhat reluctantly. I settle on that foot and then offer up the other as he adjusts the opposite one. I glance down and then grin, recognizing the onyx heels with the pearl switch.

"So, we *are* sneaking weapons in," I say jubilantly, examining the shoes I'd once threatened Emrys with. The shoes I'd dropped when he began kissing down my throat.

"Of course. But you should know we're bringing in the greatest weapon of all right under their noses…" he responds, an air of allure on his tongue as he pulls my long silvery hair over one shoulder, twisting it around his fist. "*The Harbinger.*" He tugs my hair. "Leave it down."

My core is completely molten and the violent sweep of desire that takes me is unannounced and unquenchable. I've always been attracted to Emrys. I've always found him wickedly sexy and deliciously enticing, but now I'm learning that I had all that and more—that there was love, too. I try to reach for it, to find it inside of myself, but there is no lingering trace of the feelings deeper than physical desire and a new flutter that keeps trying to be born.

There's a moment, a breath really, where I think about nothing but us and taking what I want. Saying *"fuck it all"*—but there's a knock on the door.

I snap out of my stupor, knocking something off the table, and make for the door, confident in the heels I typically despise. Maelona enters my chambers in a sweep of scarlet, and I feel a stab of envy.

"Why does she get to wear red?" I complain.

"Because I look best in it," Maelona replies simply. Her brow quirks as she takes in the room, eyes flickering between me and Emrys.

A black satin choker wraps her neck, and in the hollow of her throat a small ruby dangles like a single drop of blood. It's an acknowledgement. Remarking on the occasion of her near death, spitting in the face of it and telling it to go fuck itself.

I sigh and bend down to pick up the box my jewelry was in, resetting it on the table. Emrys went to great lengths to tidy my disaster of a suite, and who would I be if I just let calamity take it again? When I straighten, I find my husband's eyes locked on me, which he quickly averts when he's caught.

"Feeling that cabin fever yet, Baby Revenant?" Maelona teases and I can hear a smirk in her voice.

"I'm quite literally more than a hundred years older than you," Emrys retorts, shifting uncomfortably, reorganizing books on a shelf.

"Yeah, I don't care. Besides, those hundred years are fake." Her eyes flick downward. "And you have a problem."

Blood rushes into his cheeks as he whirls away from us, but not before I notice the strain in his pants.

"They're hardly false. I aged," he ripostes, completely ignoring Maelona's call out to his erection. "And I *stopped* aging there, too."

During Century Training we aged toward our natural progression and stopped when our fae bodies were meant to. For eternity we will look like this, youthful in the grace of our mid to late twenties, our bodies constantly rejuvenating themselves. Some fae stop aging as young as seventeen while others do not until their thirties. So, while our hair and nails continue to grow, everything else does not—immortalizing itself every day.

Maelona huffs. "This is boring me, are we ready to go?"

She isn't even looking at us. Instead, she's toying with the silver bracelet dangling from her delicate wrist. Her silver jewelry continues; a few rings, a thin necklace, several hoops and baubles in her ears, the longest a pair of floating butterflies.

"Yes, we're ready," Emrys confirms, and he takes my arm in his and loops his other through Maelona's crooked elbow. "Follow my lead and just remember, everything we do tonight is fake."

"We've been on missions before," Maelona tosses with a shake of her long hair.

"It's easy to get caught up in the moment," Emrys cautions.

Maelona gives him a droll look. "I'm not attracted to males." His eyes counter meaningfully to me. I blush before she continues. "And we had our last tryst already and are both quite content calling that time of our lives over. Right, Ev?"

"Right," I agree, feeling a wave of heat and embarrassment. It's one thing to talk about sex. It's another to talk about sex with two of my former partners present, especially when one of which is my *husband*.

Emrys does not react with jealousy, but rather with concern. "Are you still comfortable with this? I didn't realize—"

"It's fine, pretty boy," Maelona scoffs easily, patting his arm, warmth in her voice. "I know how to separate those feelings, and I only have to *look* like I'm doing everything. Not actually do it."

He turns to me. "I didn't ask, are you...?"

I smile at him, genuinely pleased to see the care for not just me, but my best friend too. "Truly it is okay. Maelona is lovely, but we are no longer suited for romantic or sexual pursuits."

"Are you sure?"

I sigh. "Let me make it perfectly clear—" I place my hand on his chest, the three of us still standing in my chambers. I force out the words that suddenly feel so wrong to say. Not because they're untrue, but because they're to my husband. "I will not fuck Maelona again."

Color brightens high on his cheekbones. "Okay."

"I would also like to confirm that I will not be fucking Evelyn again, either," Maelona adds.

Emrys laughs as we step onto the Faerie Roads together.

CHAPTER

22

The pulsing beat of a club hits us as we step off the Faerie Roads and out from beneath an archway that is clearly regular architecture from the look of several others on the street. The air is cold, chilled with late spring that summer has yet to grasp onto. The sound of a busy, bustling city is raucous around us, streetlights reflecting on the wet pavement, the rush of vehicles blending with the multi-storied buildings of stone. Elaborate and gothic structures all around us.

"Welcome to Prague," Emrys intones, arms still tucked into ours.

We dart across the street, past a bustling nightclub. Dolled up girls in short dresses and impossibly high heels shiver next to men reeking of department store cologne in rolled shirtsleeves and tee shirts. We bypass them, instead detouring down a side street and towards a jewelry store.

"We cannot discuss this plan further inside, there will be ears keenly listening even if there aren't cameras," Emrys whispers, meeting us levelly. "This is your last chance to back out."

"I'm still in," I announce firmly.

"As am I," Maelona adds.

"Just remember, it's all for show," he warns with finality, his gaze dropping to me. Heated. "Even if it feels differently." The words hit me, charged with electricity and it burrows directly into my chest and between my legs. It feels like he's trying to convince himself.

Emrys casts a thin glamour over himself, something just enough to discourage looking at him too long or retaining the particular shape of his features. It is something the fae can innately do and many use them for frivolous things, yet I typically choose not to, reserving it for serious situations.

I'd inquired through Aneira's spy network, speaking to the Admiral—a talented faerie with a penchant for wanting everything I have—and discovered that Caethes hasn't put a bounty on Emrys's head, yet. Nor called for his return, which is a larger concern in and of itself.

Either she hasn't realized he has forsaken her, or she is saving her wrath for something greater.

Inside the jewelry store, the lights are dimmed for closing, but a I sense a presence in the receiving area. When a halfling steps out, my breath catches in my throat.

It isn't Gideon, but their signatures are the same.

The halfling is dressed as a security guard and folds his arms over his chest as Emrys escorts me and Maelona over to him. Mae and I pretend to be absolutely enamored by him. My head tips onto Ryss's shoulder as I blink, slow and sultry.

Emrys greets him warmly and says something in Latin to the effect of "the winter is long, but the delight lingers," and with that the guard waves a hand over a wall, a small object clutched between his fingers. I'm unsure what enchanted piece of magic he holds, whether it be witch or fae in nature, but it reveals a door covered in sigils.

We are patted down and escorted silently through, and once I step past the threshold, the air changes. Deepens. The heat and anticipation are leaking from the very walls. Luxury and depravity curl up the stairs, leading into the bowels of pleasure and kinks and taboo.

There's space for the three of us to navigate the staircase downward and we do, carefully piloting into the club, speaking under our breaths. At the bottom is another door, heavy black wood, and frosted glass. As we approach it, it swings open.

A riot of sensations hits me all at once. The scents of bodies; of heat and sweat and oil and perfume. Of colognes and soaps and booze, interspersed with incense and weed, blood and cigarettes. The lighting is low, ruby red and erotic, meant to entice couples or triads or groups into shadowy alcoves of velvet boots and heavy curtains. Low tables with silver trays meant for cocaine or other substances are around the edges with cushions surrounding them—for the fall following the rush of the drug. Everything is crimson lust and dark temptation. The vampire woman crooning into a microphone with yearning, her voice made of smoke and sex only adds to the atmosphere.

Already there are people scattered about; fae, vampires, witches, humans, even a few werewolves—near extinct as they are. Everyone is early in their night, slowly slipping into drink and lingering touches, holding eyes of banked fire and fingers scalding just as hot.

I recognize faces, some high up court members of the Unseelie and vampire royals, halflings, and powerful witches. Humans, both celebrity and politician, are steeped deep in decadence and immorality. My internal alarm is pinging, picking up all the different signals of the creatures surrounding us, and even though the alarm from another halfling reminds me of Gideon, I disregard it, focusing on tonight.

Had I still been the human I thought I was two months ago, I would have been terrified of all the supernatural around. Now, I am empowered knowing that I am more lethal than all of them here—and with Emrys and Maelona at my side we're unstoppable.

Emrys leans low into my ear, his lips brushing from the pointed curve of it all the way down to the lobe. He catches it between his teeth and I make a sound low in my throat. "Are you ready for this, love?"

Butterflies dance in my belly and between my legs.

I turn to him, angling my lips up, tracing his jawline. I nip it. "Of course, darling."

He chuckles low and slips his arm to the dip of my waist before his hand trails down, holding possessively to the curve of my ass. Opposite him, he has trailed his fingers along Maelona's ribs, the lady leaning into his touch as I did, his mouth at her ear, but hardly touching.

I feel a flash of pride and possessiveness rush through me, and I have to remind myself that this is for the crown and Gideon.

Spotting an empty booth, Emrys guides us towards it, hands claiming us to any who decide to come hunting this way. We settle into the scarlet velvet, noting the slight bite of magic in the air from a recent cleaning spell. I internally thank witches for creating that particular enchantment. Goddess only knows what these walls and floors have seen.

To my surprise, Emrys urges me into the center and from where I sit, I can see the whole of the room including the even more elite section across from us, cordoned off with silky ropes. For a while we converse lowly, heads brought together in an intimate air, tentative touches bracing each other.

Eventually, a human server drops off three drinks on the extremely low table meant for coke, not asking us for orders before departing again. The scent of whiskey reaches me and the monster awakens. A bearded vampire with sycophants hanging on him in the VIP section across from us lifts a glass in toast. Maelona grabs hers and absentmindedly skims her fingers over my arms, starting the display. I turn to Emrys in astonishment, realizing the Vampire King has acknowledged us, but he has a look on his face that has all the questions and hesitations drying up on my tongue.

"Everyone is looking at you *Ceidwad Cudd*. Let's give them a show, shall we?"

I realize it is not Maelona and I fawning over Emrys tonight, it is Emrys and Maelona fawning over *me*. Because I am instantly recognizable as the figurehead of the war, Aneira's former right hand, and Keeper of Secrets. I am dressed in white because no one else is and beneath the ruby incandescence I positively glow.

Determination strikes me and a wicked smile paints itself across my face. "Yes, lets."

I lean forward and grab the tumbler of whiskey, taking a swig and Emrys nearly launches out of his seat.

"*Vanna—*" he exclaims lowly. But I stand, push him down, and briefly enjoy the look of shock on his face before I clutch him by his angled jaw. I let the liquor in my mouth pour into his.

Intense desire flares to life in his eyes as he swallows the drink, whiskey painting his lips. He stares at me, astonished and very clearly aroused.

"Thank you," he hums, a growl in his chest.

I wipe a drop off the edge of his mouth with my thumb, tucking it between his lips. He sucks on it, swirling his tongue. His teeth drag, holding my gaze with heavy lidded topaz eyes. The constant arousal is becoming near painful in its lack of relief.

I slip my thumb from his mouth.

"You've been *so* good for me," I whisper, and the effect my words take on him is immediate. I can practically see his thoughts, clear as day across his face. I can see how badly he wants to fuck me, to feel my mouth on his cock, to put his face between my legs. He wants it all and he wants it *now*.

Seated again, I lean back and let the game begin.

On my right, Emrys's hand trails across my ribs, fingers tracing every bone and curve while his mouth dips to my throat, lips and teeth pressing. My fingertips follow his jaw. On my left, Maelona cards a hand through my hair, her mouth at my ear. My other hand trails between her breasts, lightly scratching.

"This isn't real," Maelona murmurs, so low I almost don't hear her.

Her mouth graces over mine, pulling my lower lip between hers. With her teeth, she pulls delicately, flicking her tongue out once. She tastes like expensive whiskey. Her hand goes to my breast, palming it. Releasing my mouth, she slips to the opposite side of my throat, pretending to press kisses against my skin. She's hardly breathing against the erogenous zone.

It's like I'm hypersensitive to all the going's on; I sense every time eyes drop to us and hold, feeling that internal alarm ping a statelier alert when we're being actively watched. The King of Vampires is making no secret of his voyeurism. Others are being more discreet.

I can hardly think past the signals and sensations I'm receiving, utterly overwhelmed by the input. And even though this is fake, I am horribly, terribly turned on—the rush of liquid between my thighs proves it. I want to touch myself, right there in front of everyone. To let the release barrel through me.

As if he read my mind, Emrys's hand slips from my waist down to my thigh. His fingertips start just above my knee, swirling gently, circling ever higher. Mouth hot on my throat. My knees begin to drop open, and my head hits the back of the booth as I moan.

"That's right, love," Emrys breathes, his voice husky. My nipples peak in response. "Keep making those sounds and keep being such a good girl for me."

I want to fuck him right now.

Maelona reaches for my other thigh and pulls my legs apart, insistent as her hand traces the skin above my knee and fiddles with the chain garter. Not so far towards the inner thigh as Emrys is gracing, but the point is made, nonetheless. With Mae's hand busied falsely between my legs, I reach for her, unsure.

"Touch yourself, Ev. It'll drive them wild." She pauses. "It'll drive *him* wild." And with that she takes the hand that was uncertainly reaching for her, and places it on my breast. "Do it."

I feel the eyes of two humans and two halflings on us. The king hasn't stopped.

Maelona goes back to pretending, hand sliding up and down my left thigh, nails on the crescent moon. Her other hand is in my hair, her mouth near my collarbone. The hand I keep on Emrys has slid down his body and I begin to toy with his waistband, tugging on it and circling the button there. I do the same with my left hand, learning the shape of my nipple through the thin dress, and I gasp as sensation rushes through me.

Emrys nearly growls in pleasure as he sees what I'm doing, his mouth lifting away from my throat and the trail of love bites he's leaving. I meet his eyes and pinch my nipple between two fingers, hips rolling in response. His hand briefly crests higher and then stays there, pausing. I can feel all those rings on the sensitive skin of my upper thigh, and I wonder what they'd feel like in even more sensitive places.

"Touch me," I whisper. "Please."

He needs no more prompting; those fingers just a brush away from the silky heat of my core—of the slicked center of me. I tuck my fingers into his waistband and tug, Maelona's touch all but forgotten as she tugs my hair in a fist, like she's giving me rough hickeys to the unsuspecting crowd.

Thoughts of Gideon vanish, his betrayal to Caethes dissolving into nothing. Screw him and screw his screwing. He may have been abandoned by me, but he chose her. Now, he's just a tool and that crippled piece of my heart that he inhabits curls up. I close the door on it.

Something in Emrys changes. His hand cups my face and suddenly he's kissing me. His mouth is hot and passionate against mine. His slightly pointed canines rasp across my lips in a tantalizing and dangerous seduction. I moan into his mouth and part my lips wider, allowing his tongue entrance. He slips it between my teeth and I meet it with my own. He tastes of lemon-drop candies and the echo of whiskey. He groans against my lips, his fingers still so devastatingly close to where I want them.

This feels so familiar, so right, so heart-achingly perfect that I pull him to me, wanting to be—no, needing to be—closer to him. Needing *him.*

We're still being watched, by more eyes than before. Fae, halflings, witches, humans, vampires—the king still.

My palm brushes against the front of Emrys's pants and he groans such a deep rumbling sound, something so masculine and vulnerable that I purr in response. I continue to kiss him as I pinch the tip of my breast, drawing his lower lip between my teeth like Maelona had mine.

"*Emrys,*" I whisper against his mouth, pressing my lips to his again.

"*Evelyn,*" he murmurs, and a lash of heat strikes me through. He never uses my full name, but something about it in this moment is driving me absolutely feral.

Maelona returns to my ear. "Everyone is looking, I wonder what they're saying?" Which is code for, "*We have their attention; I'm going to go scope things out and find out if anyone is talking about the crown or Caethes.*"

I pull away from Emrys, and as if he can't bear for his lips to not be on me, he slides his mouth down my jaw, my throat, the juncture of my shoulder.

"Find out," I whisper, "and kiss me before you do." Which really means, "*Good luck and let's sell this charade one last time.*"

Maelona presses a lingering kiss to my lips, and like Emrys she tastes like expensive whiskey. Tongue darting along mine quickly, she amps up the erotic encounter for those viewers, ensuring their investment. Her hands are cupping my cheeks while mine are playing with Emrys and myself.

When she pulls away and slips from the booth, I realize this was all predetermined, because in the red light, and in her red dress, she is smoke in the air. She's as close to inconspicuous as she can get, blending in with the jewel brilliance of the night. Her dark eyes flash once at me, acknowledging everything unsaid—that she'll be careful and for me to enjoy this moment.

The Vampire King is still watching, so are his many vampires and one of his halflings, too. Fae and human men, also. There's a vampire blatantly sucking blood from a human's neck while she strokes his cock, using us as their pornography. I can practically hear the sounds of their urging, the desire of the theatrics we display practically tangible. And while we are not the only ones enacting erotic content, I am one of the most infamous present and therefore, a delicious commodity. Not to mention, Maelona's notoriousness, the presumed heir to the Seelie throne should she find the crown.

I can't imagine what they would think if Emrys was un-glamoured.

Suddenly, the heat in the booth rises and I turn fully to Emrys. One hand fuses in his hair and I pull at the root while he groans in pleasure. My other hand is working against his crotch, feeling the proud length I remember so fondly. He's thick in all the right ways and impossibly hard. I stroke him through his pants, feeling the clench of my delicate inner walls, thinking of him inside me. He's big, but not painfully large and flashes of memory come to me. Snapshots that have me rolling my hips and moaning.

Emrys's mouth is still all over me, as if he can't get enough of me, as if he can't fathom that this is real and happening. His hand is at the nape of my neck, gathering my loose locks in his fist, the other skimming so tantalizing between my legs.

But then the pad of his finger skims higher and I know the exact moment he encounters wetness.

He stiffens, a gasp coming to his throat against my collarbone. Biting on the fine skin there, his fingers tentatively explore a little higher, swiping once against my soaked entrance. I make a soft keening noise while he groans, a sound of absolute desperation.

"Fuck, Vanna, you're not wearing anything else."

I smirk as I roll my hips and am rewarded with another slip of his fingers. "You chose it all, don't you remember? And I don't recall any undergarments included." He makes a suffering sound into my neck. I put my mouth against his ear. "Don't you want to find out how wet I am for you?" I tilt my legs open wider for him. "Don't you want to feel how warm it is inside?"

"*Fuck*. I've missed all the filthy things you used to say to me." Emrys's fingers tighten everywhere he touches me and he makes that sound again. Fighting an internal war with himself. "You can't do this to me, I can't resist you."

"Then don't. Let this be real."

He stills and I understand the enormity of what I've just said.

At the same moment we look at each other, locking gazes, and between us flows so many emotions. Everything from fear to hope to lust to adoration. I've realized that even though I cannot access my missing memories and lost feelings, I cannot quit him. I feel for him too potently. There are moments I truly believed I hated him, only because hate is so close to passion, and it is the only intense feeling I could attribute to him. But I know, intrinsically and inherently, that I want him and without him, I cannot be complete.

The eyes on us are now burning.

"What are you saying?" he breathes, anticipation wavering his words.

I run a nail along the opening of his shirt and let my hand sprawl over the scar on his chest. "I'm saying we'll discuss the rest later, but for me this is real."

He captures my lips without another word, his mouth moving over mine, trying to fill me with all his devotion and heart. I melt into his touch, opening for him, and as his tongue touches mine, I feel his hand slip beneath the neckline of my dress. His fingers find my nipple hardened to a stimulated point, and his thumb brushes over it once, twice, three times. He circles it with firm, slow circles, sending zings of electricity directly between my thighs. His tongue sweeps my mouth the same way his fingers play on my breast, and I moan into his mouth. The hand between my legs is stilled and I ache for his touch. I am so tightly wound it is agonizing.

I need release.

Feeling the desperate urge, I skim my hand down my body and slip it between my legs, encountering Emrys's fingers so close to that heat.

"What are you doing down there, love?" Emrys asks and I can hear the smile in his voice.

I make a sound of frustration and shift my hips. "I need…" I trail off, feeling a blush stain my cheeks.

"Does the *Ceidwad Cudd* want to come?"

"Yes."

"Allow me to oblige, then."

Finally, his skillful fingers find me, and he traces the shape of me, glazing my entire sex with my desire. The sound that leaves me is embarrassing, but I do not muffle it. With wet fingertips he circles that agonized bundle of nerves at the apex of my thighs, pressing on it firmly and rubbing.

Stars explode behind my eyes, jolts of pleasure building and fraying. I thrust my hips for friction and Emrys chuckles lowly, slipping a finger into my very center. It takes everything in me to not pin him down and straddle him. He pumps that finger and I writhe. A second finger joins and I feel the divine fullness of him. My orgasm climbs while his thumb continues the ministrations on my clit, the other still toying with my nipple. I bite the underside of his jaw, a hand splayed against his cheek, the other one seeking his hardened cock. I want it out of his pants.

I can't believe the intensity building, that this is really happening with the Revenant as he circles with perfect pressure, bringing me so close to the edge of what I need. The edge comes closer and my hips move in halting rhythm, the climax within reach.

"Don't stop. Don't stop, Ryss. I'm so close," I manage, breathing and voice husky.

"Come for me, Vanna. Come on my fingers, I want to feel it."

The prospect takes me over the edge and I come, shattering into a million pieces in the middle of a fucked-up sex club with dozens of people watching—and I don't care. My breathless scream is muffled against Emrys's throat as I bite down, leaving the most aggressive of love bites. I break apart, my nerve endings shrieking because of Emrys Gorlassar. He keeps his fingers moving as I ride the waves of my orgasm, slowing as the sensation fades, my inner muscles clenching around his pumping fingers.

I drop my head against his shoulder, breathing ragged as I finish, the last dredges fading away. Desperately, I reach for his face and kiss him deeply, and it's clear to anyone that it isn't false. He returns it and I can feel the emotion swelling in his chest, tipping into me.

Pulling back, he watches me with wickedness and delight, removing his fingers from between my legs and bringing them between us. His fingers are glistening with my wetness and slowly, eyes trained on me, he licks them before slipping them into his mouth as he sucks my essence off. My pussy throbs, insanely turned on despite just orgasming. Having Emrys around, close enough to touch, yet not doing so for the past week has been excruciating. And apparently, I won't be sated until I get more.

Suddenly, Maelona materializes beside us, panic only I can see lacing her features and destroying the last vestiges of my lingering desire. If it weren't for the scarlet lighting, I'm sure I'd notice the violet hue her hair turns with the dread.

"I have good news and bad news," she tells us, voice heavy.

"What is the good?" Emrys prompts, clearly flustered.

"We're certainly getting an invitation forward." She holds up a glossy black card.

"And the bad?" I press, anxiety coiling.

"Gideon was here and he saw everything."

CHAPTER 23

CENTURY TRAINING

It's another ten years before I can get any information from Enydd. Urian remains a steel trap, with no further discussion about Osian's forced plan. For a decade I've tried to worm details out of the mentor who favors Emrys, while he continues to loathe me.

It hits a breaking point after Emrys's tact becomes less effective and I begin besting him ten times to his one. His rage is a tired thing and it has made him predictable, forming a pattern I have learned.

Resentment boils in Enydd when she decides to tell me Osian's manipulations, only because they have inadvertently led to his favored becoming the more powerful of us, and she is sick of it.

After the day's training winds down—a bout of iron mithridatism—Enydd dismisses Emrys and pulls me aside. She wraps my angry red palms in ointment and bandages, thinking very loudly.

"Penny for your thoughts?" I inquire.

Enydd stares at me in confusion. "You have no money."

"It's an expression."

"Hmm, funny you can say those."

"You can't?"

She grunts an answer but lapses into silence.

"Are you trying to decide what to tell me?"

"Yes," she says, clipped.

I bite my lip to keep quiet, joy suffusing me. I have so little to be happy for, and I cherish these small victories. Osian has remained committed to this stupid farce, pulling me aside in my few free moments so that Emrys believes we're fucking. It never happens, I either ignore him or scream at him. Sometimes I stab him. It hardly makes me feel better.

"I will say what I can, and do not think for a moment it means I care for you, girl," Enydd begins.

"Of course."

Enydd's violet eyes weigh heavily on me, but she harumphs. "Osian is the eldest of us."

I blink. That isn't what I expected to hear.

"He has personally met the goddesses."

"Goddesses? There are more than one?"

Enydd raises a brow. "Did your queen teach you anything?"

"I've never heard anyone speak of any goddess but Lady Fate."

"Yes, there's Lady Fate, but there's also Lady Chaos and Lady Karma. Karma is the oldest and Chaos the youngest. Fate has always been the mediator, therefore the most powerful. In the past she has also been referred to as Order."

"This knowledge has been lost to the courts; I assure you."

Enydd stares at me, reorienting her thoughts and sighs, setting down my bandaged hands. "I have been here too long, and I forget how quickly time passes." She suddenly looks every inch those very long years. "I was in the second round of Century Training, back then we were taught by the Wild Hunt and previous mentors. My equal…she was everything to me." Her eyes darken. "Until she wasn't."

"What happened?"

"Osian happened." Her face screws up in anger, the grudge fresh despite the thousands of years that have eclipsed. "He was fucking her. Or so I'd thought."

I say nothing.

"I loved her. Arwen was everything to me. We did everything to hide our relationship. Osian had told us love between training Centurions was not permitted, but we did not care—just as you very clearly do not either. We thought we were hiding this from Lady Fate and we may have been, but Osian caught us.

"Our relationship was cold awhile, and we decided to halt things until his suspicion died down. But of course—" Her breath hitches regardless of the years. "He took her and he claimed her. I didn't know. I thought she had forsaken me for him, and I…" she bites her lip. "When she went to kill me, I did it first."

Her eyes shut from the shame, and then those purple depths open to a chasm of pain. "I never understood the look of betrayal on her face. But I thought all these years—" She breaks off. "Now I know."

"Now you know he orchestrated it, and Arwen never abandoned you."

She nods, wings drooping. "I realized when he brought up the plan and I've never experienced such rage. It made me question every memory. I've been living in such a fog and it's taken me years to realize the damage that I've caused.

"I have stood by and watched your pain, like it was my own punishment. But it does nothing for my guilt and grief, and every day I watch you two break away from what you used to be."

"So, what does Osian hold over you and Urian and…whoever else tried to oppose this plan?"

Enydd grits her teeth. "He covered up that I fell in love with and killed my Centurion partner during training in exchange for an oath of fealty. Because of my crime, my life is bound to this place. I can never leave."

"So, if I had killed Emrys…"

"You would have been abandoned by Lady Fate. You would be stuck here too, and become a mentor like the rest of us."

Terror rips through me and I blink. "Is everyone here stuck because they killed their equals?"

"And now you know."

The silence is deafening.

"Did…did Osian manipulate all of you?"

She nods. "We all fell for his ruses and now he holds it over us."

"But…if you all fell for your opposites, why did you go along with it? Why did no one oppose him?"

Thoughts rearrange in my head. If falling for our equals is so common, why is it forbidden? And if it's forbidden like this, why aren't they taking severe measures to prevent it?

"Oh, you misunderstand. Only three of us loved our equals, everyone else very willingly killed their Centurions."

"Who was the third?" I've deduced Urian was the second.

"You realize when I answer this, I cannot say any more? This is agony enough as it is."

I remember suddenly the pain this is causing her. There is anguish in every line of her, but she's holding on much longer than Urian was willing to.

"I understand."

She steels herself and closes her eyes. "Desmond."

The moment she utters the name she groans in horrible pain, clutching her head and keeling to the side. I leave her, racing for the room I still share with Emrys. He looks at me coldly, seeing my flushed cheeks, and thinking the worst.

I begin to tell him the truth, but realize I am still bound by my oath to Osian. That this is connected to it, and if I should manage to find my way past the barrier, it's going to cause me unbearable pain. And I am not strong enough.

Not yet.

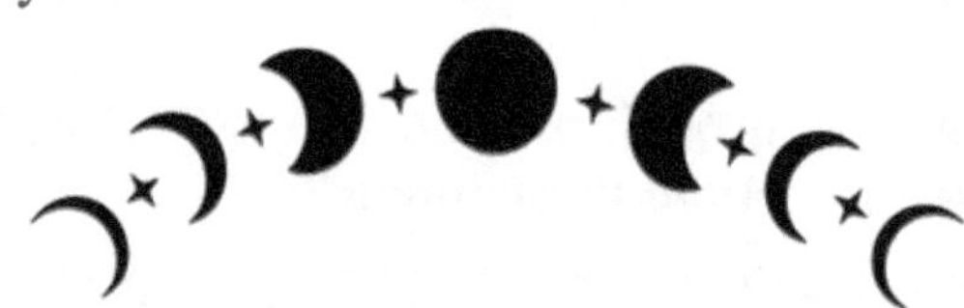

It's four years later when I finally break Desmond down. I save him the pain of having to tell me what Enydd already did, and instead figure out how he can help me reveal the truth to Emrys.

"Can you explain pieces of the ruse within earshot of Emrys? So, he knows that I never betrayed him?"

Desmond's acanthus flesh feathers as he clenches his jaw, the green and violet skin fading into a gradient of highlights and shadows. His jade, serpent's eyes flicker to the side.

"If you can assure me that Osian cannot overhear, then yes."

"Why are you scared of him?"

"He can commune with goddesses, Evelyn. At a word from him I can be annihilated for my sins."

"Lady Fate would do that?"

"Yes, she likes control. Order. If we defy her…it is one thing to do it here, in private where no one will ever learn our treachery—if we can keep it quiet—but, if it's ever announced…"

"So, it's all about blackmail."

"Partly. It's also about staying in line. Here, we're more sensitive to her whims and fluctuations. Her moods are more palpable here."

"She's aware of all that happens?"

"To a degree she knows everyone everywhere, she just has favorite toys, and Centurions are near the top of the list."

"Then can't you call on her and reveal his machinations?"

"It's not that simple," Desmond argues softly, running a clawed hand through his silver hair. "We're oathed to her first, Osian second."

"Desmond…" I start, the wheels turning in my head. "Where did the law against Centurions being romantically involved come from?"

"From the goddess."

"Are you sure?"

He narrows his eyes. "What do you mean?"

I scratch my nails against the edge of the windowsill. I play with a splinter. "What if it's Osian trying to take control of the realm? What if his Centurion spurned him, and he killed them so now he's stuck here and he's trying to bring everyone down with him? Like he's making his own rules, and passing them off as hers." I pause. "What if the sin is not love?"

"You think the goddess is punishing us by bastardizing her word and taking his?"

"Like praying to a false deity, yes. I think he's turned you all into heretics and murderers."

"Fuck," Desmond hangs his head in his hands. "Then we are well and truly doomed."

"Not if you can help me," I counter.

He laughs darkly. "Evelyn, you can't trust us."

"Why?"

Desmond looks at me, eyes solemn and dark. "Because your annual trial is a joke and the goal has always been to make one of you fall so this plan can happen. And Osian had a contingency, because he is nothing if not prepared."

"What's the contingency?"

He stares and opens his mouth, shame pouring out. "If you do not kill him during Century Training, we will be forced to hunt you both to the death the second you leave the realm."

CHAPTER 24

Dread drops through my gut, coiling with sickness, and I realize all my disregard for Gideon wasn't entirely accurate. While the shriveled piece of my heart unfurls from its protective hold, I realize the small thing that tried to flutter to life with Emrys is alive and thriving—and it has *grown*. But neither take from the other. They both currently reside in my heart.

It feels like revenge. Like this scene was meant to be me getting back at Gideon publicly since he fucked the Unseelie Queen. But I know—in my heart, in my mind—it was not revenge, it was just what I wanted. It's what I still want. This horrible feeling has not neutralized how I feel about Emrys.

About my husband.

"Are you sure?" I ask quietly, forcing a veneer of calm—but how can I be calm when I was just finger-fucked by my husband while my former lover watched and my other ex, told me of it?

"Yes," Maelona says concretely, sipping from my virtually untouched whiskey. "Now pull your shit together. Someone will be coming by to speak with us."

We do as commanded, and I avoid Emrys, not because I don't want to see him, but because I don't want him to see my inner turmoil. I meant what I said. I want us to be real, and I don't want *this*, to break it.

The sexual acts and various bouts of debauchery increase. There's a French politician sucking on the toes of a pale-skinned faerie woman with gossamer wings. She in turn is sucking the dick of a Hollywood actor, who supposedly has a squeaky-clean image. The smoke-crooning singer continues her haunting tone, while bodies writhe to her voice, patrons riding partners and offering cunnilingus and fellatio like the drinks that come around. The air becomes saturated with the scent of sex and pressed bodies to the point I'm leaning deeper into Maelona and Emrys's throats, not only to keep up the ruse, but to suffuse my lungs with the scent of cherry and orchid, or vetiver and lemon.

Servers keep blank faces, watching but revealing nothing. We continue our display in the laziest of manners; slow decadent strokes and tangling fingers in hair, lips brushing throats, jaws, and mouths.

Near the wrapping of the night, my internal alarm pings with approaching bodies. We settle into our roles again, and I settle into Maelona, resting my head on her shoulder, while twisting Emrys's garnet locks about my fingers. Emrys lifts his whiskey glass to his lips, taking a small sip—or pretending to—as he leans back and spreads his legs—his arousal mostly faded.

An unassuming halfling crosses the shining black floor, dressed in a three-piece suit with silver earrings curving up one ear. His hair is some light shade of brown and his eyes are likely just as brown. When he comes close, I balk when the King of Vampires rises from his veritable throne, the girls who'd been clinging to his legs falling away like leaves from autumn trees.

Joseph Harrow joins the halfling standing before our table. He is lean and tall with a short well-groomed beard and a narrow face, while his eyes, like all vampires are red as blood. Though, unlike all, he keeps his fangs out.

He smiles at us, those sharp teeth gleaming as he clasps his hands in a mockery of respect. The king is not well known for his polite nature, nor his aversion to human rights violations. These offenses also extend to the fae, and it is no secret that Aneira hated him with a vicious passion. More so than she despised Caethes.

The reminder of her loss tolls like a clock.

"Good evening, I assume you've been enjoying your night," the halfling begins with an oily smile. "It certainly seemed the case."

"Mm," I demure, licking my lips. "You'd be correct."

"I must ask—and forgive me for being frank—but pray tell, why is the *Ceidwad Cudd* here, when your queen has so recently passed?"

I bite back the emotion that rises, and shrug lightly. "You know as well as I do that the *Ceidwad Cudd* was known for never being fully allied with one court or another. I served my own interests." It doesn't need to be known they were synonymous with Aneira's.

"So, does that mean you are forsaking the Seelie Court?" the halfling presses. Joseph Harrow watches.

"The Seelie Court is near shambles; would you find it so odd if I were sampling my options?" I maneuver my language carefully, mixing truth and something far from it. "I was gone for two years and many things have changed."

"I'd heard about that," the halfling replies, shifting a look over his shoulder at his king. "How did that happen?"

I give him a smile that is all teeth. "A halfling betrayal. Don't worry though, he's dead now."

The halfling blanches and looks over at Joseph again. The King of Vampires steps forward clapping his hands together.

"Well, I am pleased you are sampling the delights of the night, and I would be thrilled to offer you further invitation." His voice is melodic and low, like bourbon and smoke. "It seems your presence will garner the attention of new folk and enemies. It's quite exhilarating, don't you think? Would you have any interests in visiting my section, darling? I have a suite at the Carnaval that is ripe with pleasures."

I struggle for words. He's offering the Carnaval. I should be jumping at the opportunity, but I want to reject him. Luckily, I'm saved by Emrys's throat clearing.

"That's a generous offer," Emrys interjects, putting his left hand directly between my legs, cupping me possessively. "But my wife won't be indulging in it."

And there it is.

Maelona jumps against me, shock transforming her dark hair beneath the red light. I can feel her astonishment bleed into me, but she tries to hide it behind a glass of whiskey.

I bite my lip to keep my face neutral, because the bolt of possessive pleasure that races through me from our marital status has me positively territorial.

The king raises a brow and attempts to take in Emrys's features through the glamour shrouding him. Joseph works his jaw, too stunned by the information that the *Ceidwad Cudd* is married to be slighted by the rejection.

"Is the *Ceidwad Cudd*'s husband a secret?" the king asks.

"I have been," he informs candidly.

"I see."

"Why don't you remove that mask?" the halfling asks flatly, menace gleaming in his gaze, restless fingers twitching. "You shouldn't need a glamour among us. This place is already secret. What more do you need to hide?"

"Are the *Ceidwad Cudd* and Lady Maelona not enough for you?" Emrys deflects. "Won't you let a male have some privacy in the company of such loveliness? Do you really need to know who I am or are you just wondering how I was able to pull these two and lock one down?"

He shifts, caught.

Emrys leans forward. "I'll let you know for free," he says conspiratorially. "I just *asked*. You'd be surprised how effective that can be." He winks.

Joseph Harrow laughs, delighted by the halfling being slighted. "Oh, you're good shit," he says joyously, annoyance forgotten. "I'm not sure what your angle is, but please see us tomorrow for an event you won't forget."

The King of Vampires produces a copper key with a parchment tag pinned to it. "This is how you gain entry. The address and directions are attached."

In one smooth motion the king deposits the key into Emrys's waiting palm. He taps the key to his brow and tips it like a formal gentleman's hat. The king nods, appeased, and the halfling huffs, sauntering off, another key in his hand.

Once they're out of earshot, I lean into Emrys. "Are they just handing out those fucking things like candy?" We had tried for years to gain entrance into the Winter Carnaval and now after one fingerbang we have it? "You said this was elite, but how exclusive is this event really?"

Emrys eyes me pointedly. "Very. The other even more so, and it begins in three hours, so I'm pleased we don't have to attend it."

"What did you do to—"

"Later," he interrupts, voice clipped. To assuage his tone, he leans into me. "I told you I'd do anything for you." And with that he kisses my jaw once; a token, an apology, a promise.

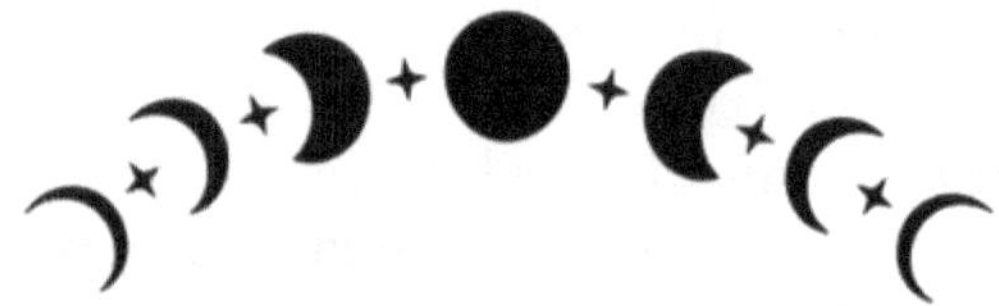

We leave the speakeasy soon after, slipping from the jewelry shop doors, and passing into the Faerie Roads via an alley. We remain silent on the Roads, not daring to breathe about the night's activity until we're safely ensconced in my chambers. In regards to eavesdroppers, the Roads are safer than public areas of court, but they're not infallible.

As soon as my chamber door shuts behind us, Maelona whirls, brows dancing toward her white hairline.

"You're married?"

Emrys calling me his wife evidently did not escape her notice, and as the fae cannot lie...

I twist the offending ring between my fingers, blood blooming on my cheeks. Emrys stands at my side, not touching, but his own wedding ring is stark against his golden skin.

A sense of pride hovers in my chest, laced with possession as I look at Emrys—at my *husband*. Something about that word turns me absolutely predatory and giddy All of that—all of him—is *mine*.

"Yes," I say finally, still not touching him. "We are."

"How long?"

"I've only known for a week. He hasn't told me exactly when it happened, though."

"Because forgetting that was part of your bargain," she replies flatly.

"That is likely correct."

"Holy fuck." She runs her hands through her hair and blinks rapidly before turning on Emrys furiously. "Why didn't *you* tell me when we were looking for her?"

"I was bound. I could only say when she discovered it herself."

"And it's real," she deadpans.

"It's real," Emrys confirms. Hesitantly, he reaches for my hand, and I give it to him.

"Holy fuck," she repeats, blinking. "So, what about Gideon?"

I hesitate, uncertain. She doesn't ask about herself, both of us know that door is very firmly closed. "I don't know, we're still discussing everything."

Maelona sucks in her cheeks, nodding distantly. "Well, I'll leave you to that. You two probably want to talk about married couple things. I'll uh, see you two tomorrow." She's at the door when she pauses. Some of her natural ebony locks have returned, and there's a small smile on her face. "I'm happy for you both, truly." And with that she slips from the room.

Emrys squeezes my hand once in the silence of Maelona's wake, and walks over to a pitcher of ice water. Pouring himself a cup, he takes a deep swallow, drains it, and then fills a second. With his other hand he's undoing the remaining buttons on his blouse, untucking it from his pants—my mouth waters. Setting down the glass, he digs through his pocket and produces the copper key and the rolled piece of parchment.

I walk up to him and read the script over his shoulder, inhaling in surprise.

"The Winter Carnaval is utilizing forgotten pocket realms," I breathe. That's why we could never infiltrate them. Why we only found events and associated clubs, but not the true source. Because it's constantly moving.

The text depicts the use of rediscovered and decaying realms found by rogue factions of fae chaining them together by their will, and directing a steady stream of traffic to keep the door moving. Each pocket realm is a tenuous link where one lapse could spell the collapse of the entire chain. The writing cautions the reader to move through these unstable environments hastily. The realms revolve, and the last one in the new order will be the location of the Carnaval, for which only one of the copper keys will open. A fae escort is essential for travel as they are inherently linked to the Roads.

It's exactly like the Century Training realm; a pocket, and a door, and only one key to open it.

"Goddess," Emrys curses, putting the key and re-rolled parchment into a jewelry box. He kicks off his boots and sinks onto an emerald pouf that I hadn't destroyed, and puts his head in his hands.

I take up Emrys's water glass and fill it for myself. "Is it true that Caethes hates the Winter Carnaval, or is that a façade?"

Emrys chuckles darkly. "No, she absolutely hates the Carnaval, but she's too prideful to join forces with anyone to take it down. She wants to be the sole hand that does it."

"Then why give Gideon and the crown to it?"

"I don't know. To trick us? To fool them? I haven't been in her good graces for some time."

"How long?" I inquire, sipping the cool water.

Emrys shakes his head. "Years? She was suspicious of me in Aberth. Especially when I went for you instead of her after Wisteria reversed the chaos on her."

The memory comes to me in a new light. I recall the failed night with the Crows, Wisteria's despair, the smell of smoke and blood and burnt sugar. The sounds of screams and pandemonium. Of the chaos Caethes hurled at the crowd, and the second wave of it. The one that sent me down the stairs and coming to with Emrys looking at me...

About to call me Vanna.

Come near me and I will kill you. I had snarled at him.

The look of hurt that crossed his face makes sense now.

"Why did you do that?"

His face opens, like it's the simplest thing in the universe. "Because I love you."

My heart increases its rhythm, beating against my ribs like a caged bird. I freeze, held by his declaration. My lips part and oxygen rushes into my lungs in short, sharp inhales.

"I have always loved you," he pronounces passionately, taking measured steps towards me. "Even when you deceived me with Osian. Even when I thought I hated you. Even now, when you can't recall returning the feeling, I still love you. You are my everything. You are my all. My reason. I have never taken another to my bed. I have never taken another in my heart." He pauses. "It's you. It's always been you."

Blood rushes through me, dizzy as my husband approaches while pouring his heart out. The room is utterly silent aside from his declaration and the only thing I can smell is him—lemon, vetiver, and leather—and the clinging scent of various smokes like a carnal veil. Everything in me goes liquid in his presence. At his words. At him. Despite orgasming by his hand only hours ago, my need returns furiously, *demanding* him.

"I want to say the words back," I whisper, placing a hand over my heart. "I *want* to, so desperately, but I *can't*. I know I feel something for you now, but it's a fraction of what is locked inside. Even so, it's fighting to grow every day. Every moment that passes I find myself more attached to you and the prospect of you leaving me is unbearable. I need you and I think you are integral to my very being. I—" I hesitate just as he did and I realize our speech patterns are similar—and why wouldn't they be? We were alone together for decades. "I want to try something."

"What?" he asks, voice soft. As if holding himself back.

"Just…trust me."

I approach him slowly, the click of my heels across the stone floor the only sound aside from our hitched breathing. Directly before him, I look up from under my lashes, lingering on his full lips.

I cup his cheek delicately and keep our gazes locked. Gently, I pull him down and press my lips to his. There are no falsehoods this time. There is no audience. It is just us as I part my lips and carefully press my tongue against his. He releases a small sound and meets me, a slow, languorous dance of decadence. Of lips moving over mouths that taste like the echo of whiskey and the permanence of lemon. I keep this up, this chaste slide and motion. Neither deepening the kiss or pulling from it. My hand is on his chest and his jaw, his gliding around my waist and cupping the side of my neck. We meld together as if designed; lips captured and claimed, hands steadying and sure.

I pull back and gaze up at him, still holding him. "Everything I am, everything I can offer…is yours. If you want to take it," I whisper, the enormity of what is between us catching its breath, waiting.

The smile that breaks over his face is brilliance. It is radiant starlight streaking across the sky. It is every diamond point in the cosmos.

"I will take all that you can offer me and treasure it as long as you are mine."

"I'm yours," I declare.

This time when Emrys catches me up, the kiss is sorrowful and full of longing. He pours devotion into every press of his mouth. He's holding it in his chest like the first sob before a breakdown. Like the release of all that's inside will break him and his breath won't put him back together. His teeth nip my bottom lip, and I let out a low sound that has him gathering me in his arms.

I'm against the wall and the next thing I know my head is cradled by one hand and the other is clutching my thigh. Hitching my knee on his hip, he rolls his pelvis against me, the hard length of him awakening as it stimulates my already greedy clit.

"What about Gideon?" he whispers raggedly in my ear, his hips pinning me as I balance on one knife shoe. "What does this mean for him?"

"I cannot lie, I do feel something for him. But that something is twisted and broken, borne of survival and proximity. I do not wish to face it, nor to feel it. He is not what I want. You are."

"And you're prepared to give him up for me?" The hope in his voice strikes me. He does not judge me for having feelings for another man. He is understanding my situation, confirming what I truly want. There is no jealousy in his voice, it is only pure love—love for me. "You want to repress or sacrifice that part of yourself?"

"I will give it all up for you."

"You'll deny him?"

"My world no longer has space for him."

He chuckles throatily and presses a light nip to my jaw. "Don't you know, darling? We could destroy and remake the world."

I press my palms to his cheeks. "*You* are my world."

His breath hitches and then everything changes.

CHAPTER 25

His mouth claims mine in a wild gasp, and he pins me to the wall with a rough, exquisite grind of his hips. Hands are everywhere, I feel his fingertips clutch and pull and grip, seeking skin and heat and everything I want to give him. I tear his lovely black blouse from his shoulders, stitches rending. I'm sad to see the sleeve rip, but not enough to stop. The shirt flutters to the ground, and I'm gifted with these sight of Emrys's lean, sculpted frame, the muscles cording his arms and ridging his abdomen. I trace the scar on his chest and my mouth slips to drop a kiss on it.

"Will you tell me about it?"

"*Later*," he growls and carries us to the bed, wrapping my legs around his hips. My shoes fall to the floor.

He deposits us on the plush blankets and urges at me with taunting thrusts of his pelvis, delivering a godly amount of friction exactly where I want it. My head drives back into the pillows as I arch, Emrys's hands going to the diamond straps of my gown and snapping them with ease.

"This dress needs to be on the floor," he growls, breaking a third row.

"Around the waist is good, too."

"Like something quick and dirty?" he asks and pulls my hair tight. I whimper in excitement.

"Whatever you want," I respond wantonly, baring myself to him.

"Do you think this is going to be fast, Vanna?" Emrys leans down by my ear, pulling the lobe and trailing hot kisses down my jaw, my throat, the swell of my breast. "No, wife. I am going to *savor* you and I want you coming until you can no longer walk." Emrys calling me wife has ravenous arousal rushing between my legs. He bites my collarbone and soothes the sharpness with a hot kiss. "I want you blind with pleasure, writhing under me and begging me not to stop, begging me to let you come. How does that sound?"

A ragged sound very much like, "*yes*," slips from me.

The final strands snap and Emrys pulls down the top of my gown with his teeth, baring my breasts to him. My nipples are tightened to points, and the slight brush of his breath has me gasping.

"You're absolutely glorious," he whispers reverently, before dipping his mouth down to my chest, his tongue laving over one of those hardened peaks. He suckles once before scraping with his slightly sharp teeth, tearing a sound from me that is decidedly not glorious.

Turning to bless the other with the same attentions, I grind my hips upward against him, eager to sate my need. His hands are firm on my waist, positioning me exactly where he wants me, which is something I'd always treasured with him.

"This body needs to be celebrated," Emrys murmurs between my breasts, hands and teeth rolling the dress down to my hips. "Fucking cherished."

"Mm, and what of my personality?" I tease.

He nips my ribcage for my insolence. "You are a vicious thing, but you are my vicious thing and I'll have you no other way." He gentles, kissing a belt across my stomach. "You have kindness that few are privileged to see and loyalty even less are permitted to experience. Your need to protect those unwilling to save themselves is something you keep hidden, but I see it. I see you. Your flaws—and do not mistake me, you have many, but I love each of them—and all. You may be stubborn, hot headed, and ruthless but I know how to soften those sharp edges."

The last of the dress comes off, tearing at one of the incredibly high slits, leaving me completely bare before him. Emrys flings the dress to the floor and takes me in. His eyes are glazed, so magnificently hazy with lust that my toes curl and my core clenches in anticipation.

I part my legs, letting him see all the wetness he has elicited. He travels down my body, breathing me in, his mouth so horribly close to where I yearn for it.

"Have you any hesitations?"

"No, I just want you."

"Good, because you need to be worshipped. Luckily, I found my temple, and I'm happy to kneel at the altar."

His eyes never leave me as he slides off the bed and pulls me to the edge, pushing my legs apart, and pressing his mouth to my core.

My back arches up with the first stroke of his tongue. A single hot line from my center that comes up to swirl my clit, applying exquisite suction. His tongue moves rapidly against me, hands cupping my breasts, fingers rolling my nipples. My own hands are fused in his hair, guiding him against me. He continues laying prayers against that bundle of nerves in the form of expert pleasure.

I'm trying to thrust against him, but his hands keep me still, and I'm utterly at the Revenant's clemency as he brings me to the edge of another orgasm. I feel it build within me, curling low in my belly as my hips lose their rhythm, railing against the coming onslaught of ecstasy.

"*Emrys*," I gasp, his mouth continuing its devouring as I teeter on the precipice. I cup the back of his head and force him urgently against me. His eyes meet me and I'm lost. "I'm going to—"

The climax bursts inside me, sudden and violent. A shriek rips from my throat at the rush of pleasure, the bliss temporarily blinding me to everything but Emrys. My husband. He doesn't stop tasting me, licking me through it, slowing his ministrations like the waves that crest over me.

But he doesn't stop.

I mewl as he picks up his tempo again, pressing the flat of his tongue to my over-sensitized clit. He thumbs my nipples, coiling me back up. I tremble and shake; the pleasure too much, the sensation too much.

"Emrys, I can't—" I gasp, my toes curling. The whimpers he condenses me to would normally have me blushing, but right now, I can't think past anything but how it feels.

"Didn't I say blind with pleasure?" He taunts, pulling away from that swollen nub to nip my thigh, watching me with voracious delight. "I want to make you feel so good, to the point you don't know when the last orgasm ends and the next one begins."

My head is thrown back against the bed, as he returns to his goal, my hands scrabbling helplessly in his hair. Too much, *more*, not enough. My thighs clench together, holding him where he is as he continues his faithful sermon, delivering on his promise.

Suddenly, one arm is banded across my hips, and a hot palm pushes my legs apart while the other trails up my thigh. A fingertip brushes my soaked sex, and then is plunged into me, curling in a come-hither motion. My nails scrape his back as I am sent arching from the bed, so close to being untethered. A second joins and I realize exactly why two fingers have no rings as he brings me to a third climax, and I scream.

I'm flying. I can feel the crystalline fractures of my nerves and bliss launching me to nirvana. The breaking wave of my orgasm is thigh-trembling, toe-curling ecstasy. My nails dig into his flesh as my hips roll with the final throes of passion. All the while Emrys is there with me, working me through it, maximizing my pleasure.

I pant as I come down to earth, my body splayed uselessly on this bed, a thin veil of sweat on my skin. Emrys slows his licks and finally travels up my body, an arm banded beneath my waist as he drags me up to the headboard.

When my muscles begin to regain control of themselves, I cup my hands on Emrys's jaw, and lock eyes with him. "I missed you," I whisper. I pull him down for a kiss and I taste myself on his lips, making me purr with greed.

"I missed you too, Vanna. So fucking much." He drops his head to my collarbone, fingers trailing over my ribs. He inhales against my throat, as if trying to brand my smell into his brain.

Slowly, I scratch my nails down his abdomen, and flick open the line of buttons on his pants. He lifts his hips just enough for me to push them down and my palms graze the strong lines of his hips and thighs.

He pauses and I sense his hesitancy. "I still take a tonic," he tells me throatily, "But I could still wear a—"

"No," I interrupt him firmly, the idea of anything separating us feels wrong. I want to feel all of him with no barrier between us. "I still take mine as well."

He exhales against my throat and shyly admits, "I haven't done this in a while. I don't know how long I'll last, but I want to make it good for you."

I grin. "Luckily for you we have all night, and you'll have many attempts to make it up to me if you feel it's anything but your best."

"Only the best for you." He brushes a silvery strand of hair behind my pointed ear. "I love you," he murmurs.

"I know."

It's not the same, but it's all I can give, and for now it's enough.

I reach between us and find his thick length, stroking it, feeling the silk of his skin. He groans, such a low, masculine thing that has my empty channel clenching. I tighten my hold and he thrusts into my hand, a slow drag that has him sucking air through his teeth. Swiping a thumb over the head of him, I wipe the bead of arousal over his shaft, painting him with his own essence.

"Goddess, fuck, Evelyn."

"Mm, do you want to be inside me, husband?"

Emrys's gasp is wild as his cock flexes in my hand. "Do that again, please. Say it again," he begs breathily.

"I want you inside me, husband."

The word turns Emrys feral.

What I thought was going to be a tender lovemaking session of reuniting our bond, rapidly devolves into a carnal act of claiming.

He lifts my hips and in one full thrust, Emrys buries himself to the hilt in me. We gasp and moan together, his cock filling me so perfectly tears spring to my eyes. I'm so wet for him and that ache is finally sated with him seated inside me. We move together, my hips rolling against his as he plunges deep, pulling out almost to the tip before slamming back into me. I cry out, the bliss radiating from me.

I've had sex many times before, but I cannot imagine anything better than feeling Emrys Gorlassar, the Revenant, my husband fucking me. Even with Lady Fate's block on my memories. The feeling nestled in my ribs is no small thing, and I can feel the mass of it spreading, cracking papier-mâché constraints that were once iron shackles. It's more than desire, it's deeper than attraction. I think it's exactly what the goddess tried to take from me.

Emrys's pelvis rolls in a heavenly motion, the friction grinding against my clit as I follow it desperately. His free hand is all over me, dragging across every curve and dip of my flesh, palming my breasts, toying with the tips, wrapping my throat. His speed is increasing, losing control.

"You're so close, husband. I can feel it," I murmur, hands going to his hair, running down his back and clawing him as I feel a fourth release climb through my belly. "Don't you want to come in me?"

He lets out a muted roar and withdraws from me. His absence is near painful and I mewl at his loss, but before I know it, he flips me on my stomach and raises my ass in the air. He enters me swiftly, pounding into me—a punishment and a present. Leaning against me, the front of him pressed against my back, he wraps an arm around my hips, while his opposite hand necklaces my throat. I'm pulled up so I'm flush against him.

"Look at how fucking wrecked you are," Emrys growls in my ear, directing my eyes to the full-length mirror across from the bed. I glance at it and I'm ruined.

In the gilt-edged frame we are captured like artwork; lust-addled eyes, sex-mussed hair, yearning-drenching bodies. I see the two of us kneeling on my bed, Emrys's golden limbs wrapped around me, his beringed hand at my throat like the sexiest of chokers, my hardened nipples, aching to be touched, my slender, smooth belly and the bare skin below where Emrys's other hand splays, his middle finger a hairsbreadth from that deliciously pleasured nub. I can see his cock buried in me, the lips of my sex parted around him, and noticing where my eyes have landed, he thrusts slowly as I watch my pussy take him with new wetness on his girth. My eyes come back to our faces, and Emrys is right—I *am* fucking wrecked.

Blood flushes my cheeks, and a bead of sweat slides down my throat, My eyes are bright and silver, reflecting like a pool of starlight, while my full lips are swollen by his kisses, and parted with the beginnings of another orgasm. Behind me Emrys is ravenous, preparing to devour and consume my every pleasure, and hoard it like a dragon. He too, is flushed, his hair damp and sticking to his brow, eyes the deepest gold I've ever seen them.

"I am ruined for anyone else." His voice is devotion. "Seeing you like this is the hottest thing I could ever imagine. You are a fucking masterpiece," he growls, staring at our reflection, biting my throat as he begins to pound into me again.

His hand slides down that littlest bit, two of his fingertips massaging my clit while he thrusts harder. In the low light his wedding band glitters against my throat.

"You've ruined me too," I moan as that fourth orgasm comes cresting from deep within me, coiling at the base of my spine. "*Ryss.*"

"That's right, wife. Come for me. I want you to watch when it happens. I want you to see what I am so blessed to."

I stare at our reflection, my hands going to my nipples as he pleasures every other inch of me. I see his fingers against that little bundle of nerves, working absolute magic to wring out another climax. It's so close, and I tell him just that.

Emrys's cock flexes inside me and his tempo falters, the last of his strength failing as his own orgasm threatens to take him over the edge. His teeth bury against my throat as I feel him pump again and again.

"Come," he commands.

And I do.

We come together, hard. The heartbeat of his cock pumps into me, spilling and throbbing. His roar is muffled by the grip of his teeth in the juncture of my shoulder, and my shriek is unmuted and breathy.

The fourth orgasm is a tidal wave, a shattering that breaks and forms again just so another wave can take me. The undertow of my climax is a vicious, pulling thing, flooding me with bliss and paradise. It's even more powerful for the view; for watching me come hard in the mirror as he pulses into me.

We collapse together, tangled and utterly sated. Emrys falls onto his back, pulling me atop him, while my breasts crush against his chest as I splay, unable to move. Twitches of my orgasm still thrill me as he trails his fingers along my spine and the scars demarcating my life—the evidence of my lost wings, the same scars as him.

"I almost thought I'd never get to experience this again," Emrys sighs.

I hum a low note, agreeing languidly. I curve against him, pressing myself to his naked body while I feel some of his essence slip between my thighs.

"Was it like you remembered?"

He groans. "Better. So much better." Pressing a kiss to my bare shoulder I watch his abdomen flex with the movement, the low V welcoming his member—which seems ready for another round.

I skim my fingers down the line of his muscles, letting a fingertip follow each groove of his body until I come to the crease of his leg, directly beside the length that just so beautifully fucked me. It twitches as I get close, the pad of my finger just brushing his head. I giggle, but before I have a chance to do more, Emrys captures me and rolls, pinning me to the bed.

"You are a menace," he growls, settling on me, his brow at my collar. "And you smell."

I gasp, smacking his shoulder. "I do not stink!"

"I said smell," he chuckles, inhaling audibly. "Like sex and sin."

"And whose fault is that?"

"Oh, I take entire fault in it, and pride, too. Shall I announce it outside your door?" he teases and the mirth in his eyes has me playing along.

"Only if you also tell them about that time that I—"

"Nope, I'm not playing this game with you. You're a fiend." He goes to the washbasin, cleaning himself with a cloth. I go up on an elbow and watch him, admiring the lines of his body before he tosses the cloth in a laundry bin, and then grabs a new one for me. "You lack many of your memories but apparently you still threaten enough."

As he says this, a few memories begin to crack through. Of him pressing me up against the mirror in the cathedral bathroom, my wings splayed, and my perched ass on the edge of the counter while he thrusts into me, pressing *I love you's* down my throat as my gasping breaths claim the same. Of the field under the stars where we dragged out a blanket where I kissed him drunk on adoration. Of reclaiming the hallway Osian had forced me to deceive Emrys, replacing it with gentle lovemaking.

I swallow and blink away the memories, realizing the hold on my psyche is breaking. I cannot feel the love I used to have, but I know for certain that it was there. That tiny thing in my heart grows bigger and a thought strikes me; could I be falling in love with him anew? *Again*?

Emrys comes to the edge of the bed and parts my legs, wiping his release from my inner thighs. Watching me with rapture, he presses a kiss to my knee and disposes of the now soiled cloth. When he returns, I entangle my body with his, twisting our legs together. I sigh and rest my head on his chest, as his fingers trail through my hair, so content as we let slumber claim us.

CHAPTER 26

CENTURY TRAINING

I've been mulling over when and how we'll reveal Osian's duplicity every spare chance I get. Emrys often catches me watching him, and he becomes confused and angry. I've been using excuses to touch him, to let my fingers linger and my hips to bump into him. His golden eyes are untrusting every time I do, and I try to be soft and welcoming, but it falls flat. Emrys remains unaware of how desperately in love with him I am.

A year after the conversation with Desmond, and I've still not managed to outwit the fucking oath and tell Emrys.

At the fifty-year mark we are given our signature swords. Both of which are quenched in our own blood so that they may never be used against us. I receive a plain, proud blade of gold and name it Oath-Sworn. I hope the mentors notice it for the jab it is. Emrys names his—a spiked silver thing—Hearts-Desire.

It was supposed to be a grander ceremony than it was.

Emrys has been taking more walks lately and I've taken advantage of those walks to pleasure myself. It starts slow, a brushing of my hands down my body, imagining Emrys's fingers toying with my nipples and circling my navel. I stifle a groan at the sensation. I picture my opposite peeling my pants down, as I do now, slipping them down my hips and baring my glistening wetness to the night air. I bite my lip.

The pants are quickly kicked off, and I push up my shirt, moonlight lining my breasts ethereally. Like I should be untouchable. The fact just turns me on more, especially when I fantasize about the forbidden acts I want Emrys to do to me.

My fingers skim down to my core and there I slowly slip a finger into myself, my toes curling at the contact. I plunge in slowly and surely, once, twice, three times before bringing up that wetness to my clit. I swirl that bundle of nerves, pressing with two fingers, gasping at the exquisite pleasure. My movements continue, circling and dipping while my other hand goes to my breast, tweaking my nipples.

An orgasm begins to build low in my belly, and I hurry it on. I'm panting, soaked, and wanton in my yearning. I continue to imagine my fingers are Emrys's—graceful, long, jeweled.

As I near my climax I hear a distinctly masculine gasp from the doorway. I look up in panic and find Emrys standing there, topaz eyes wide, shock clearing his face of every other emotion.

"Ryss," I gasp, my hands paused on my breast and between my legs.

"Do you do that every time I leave?"

A thrill goes through me at the idea of him knowing I play with myself when I'm alone. "Yes."

"Why?" he asks, eyes never leaving me. And I don't want them to.

Feeling bold, I move my fingers on my aching nub and toss my head back. "Because it's the closest I can get to being with you."

He takes a step forward, wide eyes secured on my hands. My orgasm climbs. "What are you talking about?"

I look at him as I continue my ministrations, biting my lip, because now, with him here, the fantasy has become so much more erotic. "Things here are not what they seem and though we cannot lie, no one is telling the truth."

"You have secrets?" He presses, eyes hungry and he steps forward again. Close enough that the moonlight highlights him and the arousal in his pants.

"Against my will."

"Can you tell me?"

"I can't," I pant, getting close.

Emrys's gaze is between my legs, taking in the wetness there. He licks his lips and I nearly come from that alone. The moan I let out is mortifyingly loud.

"Do you want to?" His voice is husky.

"*Yes.*"

"Stop what you're doing."

I do even though it's the last thing I want. My orgasm is so close, but he asked me to stop, and I will—this is our shared space. I clamp my teeth down on a whine as Emrys approaches me.

Emrys kneels and takes me in. He is hungry and greedy, and I draw in a shocked breath when his fingers brush the outside of my hip. He coasts along softly, his callouses rough on the silk of my skin.

The desire to feel him everywhere has me in a chokehold. His hands graze across my lower abdomen and my flesh positively quivers. A new rush of liquid heat starts between my legs.

"May I?" he asks huskily, fingers sliding over my pubic bone. "Can I touch you here?"

"*Please*," I practically beg.

Emrys's fingers replace where mine were, and it is heaven. I let my thighs fall open so he can see all of me. He runs a finger down the seam of me before sliding a finger inside. I feel my delicate inner walls clench around him and I groan. His finger begins moving, curving deep in me while his thumb presses directly on my clit. I gasp as he rubs it, the friction incredible. I buck against his hand but he pins me with the other, keeping me against the floor.

"Do you think of me when you do this?"

"Yes. Every time."

"Vanna, you keep saying things like that and I'll have to show you what I think about, too." He pauses on a ragged breath. "When I go outside and touch myself, I pretend it's you. I always have, even now."

Knowing Emrys pictures me, despite the loathing, turns me molten.

"I can't get you out of my head, Vanna."

He continues pumping me with a finger and circling with that thumb, finding a godly rhythm that has me coming in seconds. Emrys clamps his free hand over my mouth to keep my scream quiet as I come apart, my nerves splitting and electrifying. The pleasure bursts and careens from my clit straight down to my toes.

When it's over, I lose my strength and lie there, dazed and staring at Emrys.

For a moment we stare at each other, realizing what just happened.

"You never wanted to kill me, did you?"

With tears in my eyes, breasts heaving as I settle down from my orgasmic high, I shake my head.

"Was any of that real?"

"Come to training early tomorrow, but wait until I've already left. Do not enter until after you hear what Desmond and I talk about, and do not let him or I know you're there."

"Why?"

"You'll understand tomorrow."

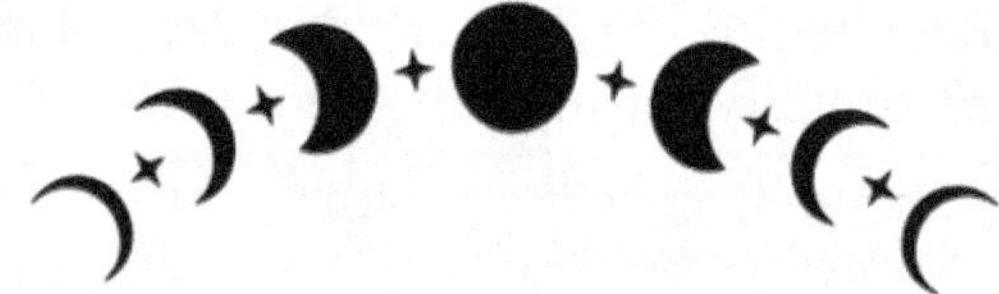

The next morning I'm still high on euphoria as I wake early for training. I manage my extremely long hair into two French braids and change into a white shirt and caramel-colored leathers. The pants are sculpted to my frame and the shoulder holsters buckle snugly beneath my breasts.

When I rush out of the room, I hear Emrys stirring behind me, and grin as I make my way to the main area. Desmond is there, as I expected, this being his regular training day—how serendipitous?

"I figured it out."

"What did you figure out?" he asks, a dainty cup of tea pressed to his lips.

"How to fix this. All you have to do is recap the ruse in a few minutes."

He quirks a brow, but knows not to question it. As he finishes his tea, I tremble with anticipation. As he places the cup on the saucer, he regales with the ruse. Of how the tonics arrived for me and Emrys, how Osian was infuriated by it, then how he pushed them into the plan—to coerce and force me to twist the truth, then threaten to kill Emrys if I don't pretend to. Then he states how the ruse must be kept up for appearances, so he doesn't turn on his word and kill Emrys. He finishes it all by saying what I've already told him—that other mentors have fallen and that all of them have killed their opposites.

At the conclusion of the tale, Emrys steps from the shadows, a terrible look of shock on his face. He takes me in, and glances back and forth between me and the mentor.

"So, you never…"

"Never," I confirm.

"I'm so sorry I believed it."

"It was quite convincing."

"Even still," he breathes. He turns to Desmond. "Does she have to keep pretending?"

He nods regretfully. "I will not say anything about this, but do not let any of us catch you. We cannot lie if we are questioned."

"Noted," I say softly. My eyes shimmer with tears. "Thank you."

"Do not thank me, girl. And remember, we cannot be trusted."

With Desmond's back turned, I reach out and squeeze Emrys's hand.

He squeezes back.

CHAPTER 27

We wake sometime in the night and couple again. It's pleasant to wake to Emrys's fingers coasting along my ribs, feather-soft against my skin. His touch is heat and comfort, and it lights a frantic desire in me.

The moment I remember everything that transpired earlier, I put my legs astride him and plunge his length into my wet core, slamming down to the hilt. He moans, topaz eyes darkening. I ride him hard as he sits up, hands fused in my hair while he plunders my mouth with his tongue. Hot kisses trace down my throat before they come to capture my nipple between his teeth. From there his tongue continues its luscious swirling and suction while my nails turn to claws on his back, dragging up and down in pleasure. The grinding of my pelvis on his stimulates my clit perfectly, and my orgasm blasts through me, careening through waves of bliss.

"You're so beautiful when you come for me, wife," Emrys murmurs, kissing me deeply.

I hum in agreement, sated. But Emrys isn't finished, and rather than continuing my furious rocking, he pushes me down, and hitches a thigh high on his hip while he drives into me. The force is as glorious as it is punishing, and I toss my head back against the pillows, whimpering. His pounding thrusts are bringing me close to the edge again, while he begins to slip in control—right at the precipice.

"Come for me, husband," I command, knowing the word will shatter his self-control.

He comes with a throaty groan against my collarbone, and his slow pumps have me clenching around him. My moan is loud and it ends with his name on my lips. I can feel his cock throb with his release as my inner walls wring every nerve of our mixed climaxes.

We collapse together, limbs soft and languorous. Filled with pleasure, I run my hands over his body, refamiliarizing myself with this body that hosts the other half of me. Even so, apparently two orgasms aren't enough for him. With his fingers between my legs and his mouth on my breasts he coaxes out a third climax that has me writhing against the sheets and almost screaming his name.

Again, we settle and I find the scar on his chest. I pause, preparing myself. "Ryss...?"

"Yes, Vanna?" he asks, tracing shapes on my arm, pressing a kiss to my shoulder.

"How exactly did you die?"

The words taste like poison on my tongue. The prospect of my husband dying is horribly painful, the idea such a brutal wound that I wonder how I suffered it once. But considering how I feel *now*, how bad was the anguish back then?

"I can't say specifics without you knowing it first," he answers softly, tightening his hold on me. He presses every curve against him, reaffirming I'm here, and real.

"Was it a sacrifice or a battle?"

His jaw works. "Both."

Suddenly, a horrible, obvious realization strikes me.

Gideon's notes.

Something about a battle of thirty against two. Of an ambush post Century Training.

Upon sixteen bodies stood Gold. Upon fourteen bodies lay Silver.

We'd fought together, till his death. Until I summoned the goddess and demanded his life, then earned our new titles directly from Lady Fate herself.

So, begins, the legend of two. Harbinger and Revenant, forever remembered, never truly known.

Did Emrys tell Gideon? Gideon told me he'd met both of us at one point so did Emrys tell him, or did someone else figure it out?

"We were overwhelmed after we left Century Training," I state.

"Yes," he confirms.

Should you fail, you are released from the realm and not into your courts, but into Wild Hunt's lands and chased through the woods by them and your mentors.

"Were we attacked by the Wild Hunt?"

He makes a sound that might be affirmation.

"What about our mentors?"

This time he looks at me in surprise. "You don't remember that?"

I shake my head.

"Oh, hell, Vanna, oh that's bad." He presses a hand to his forehead. "Fuck…uh, okay, that one—that's a big one."

"What is it? Tell me."

He tries. I see his throat working, his tongue moving. He exhales in exasperation. "I can't."

I sigh. "I wish you could just tell me everything."

Emrys pulls me closer and presses a kiss to my forehead. "So do I, love."

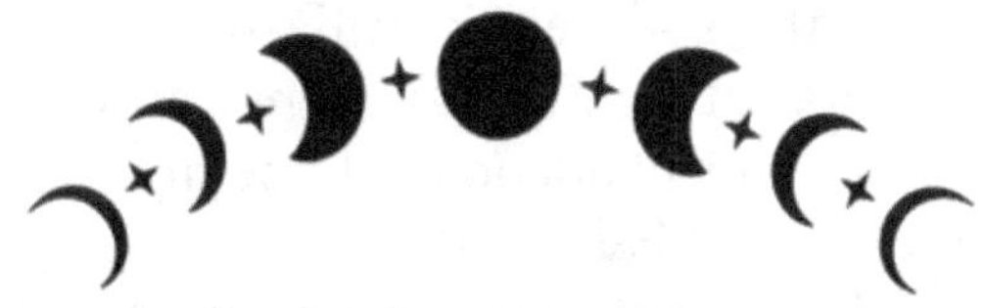

The next day I exit my chambers with a distinct pep in my step, having been taken for a third round of fucking in the bath, both of us overcome by massaging oil and soaps into each other. The kisses at the threshold lingered long and hard, neither of us wanting to part from the other, but of course, Emrys cannot be spotted.

When I arrive in the training area, Maelona gives me a lascivious grin. "Well, married life seems to suit you. How was it?"

I blush and bite my lip. "Which time?"

Mae throws her head back in a laugh, yellow gold threading through her hair. "Such a nymphomaniac you are! Did you even let the male rest?"

I cackle and she links arms with me. "He is insatiable. Mae, you would not believe his obsession with driving me to completion."

"Oh! One could dream." She leans in conspiratorially. "Should I change teams then?" She's joking but the words evoke a violent wave of jealousy.

"*No*," I bite out harshly and then backpedal in horror. "I'm sorry, I have no idea where that came from."

"Are you sure he's just your husband?"

I narrow my eyes at her. "What are you talking about?"

"Have you not wondered if he's really your soulmate?"

"You believe in soulmates, too?"

"Of course, I do. What do you mean by '*too*'?"

I lick my lips, chancing a look around the empty training room, at the solid earth walls so different from the crumbling cathedral of Century Training. "A little while ago Emrys told me he thinks Gideon could be my soulmate."

"No. No, I don't believe that."

"Why?" I ask, not because I want it to be true, but because I'm surprised by her tone.

"Because of Emrys. Because of how conflicted you were between pursuing the Winter Carnaval and bargains. Even now, the Carnaval has only taken precedence because of the crown."

I grind my teeth in guilt and pivot. "Speaking of the Carnaval, I think we need a backup plan."

"Do you have any ideas?" She doesn't point out the topic change.

"Yes, but I think we'll need to let others in on the secret."

"What do you—?"

We are interrupted by the arrival of Wisteria and Julia, their signatures alerting me at the same time as their actual presence. I was too distracted by Maelona's talk of soulmates.

The two women arrive dressed in training clothes; tee shirts, leggings, and flexible shoes. Wisteria's dark eyes are still haunted by Caethes's blatant murder of her boyfriend and now, there is an added layer from the recent attack from the Wild Hunt. It's a reminder of her stolen safety—my fault, always my fault. Beside her, Julia is wary, but her blue-gold eyes are determined. They are also too perceptive and within moments their faces transform, understanding something has changed.

"What is it now, Faerie?" Wisteria demands hotly, hands on hips. "Is there another shitstorm coming?"

I sigh and look at Mae, silent conversation passing between us. A short argument between our eyes and shaking heads ensues, her hair flickering before settling into acceptance. The witch and the leader of the Crows are waiting and staring unabashedly.

"The fuck was all that about?" Wisteria asks, gesturing between us.

"I have something to tell you. But you have to swear to secrecy."

While concerned, they do swear, and though it is not as effective as an oath from the fae, I believe them nonetheless.

"Follow us."

And with that I lead them to my chambers.

We arrive at the door and I unlock it, urging everyone into the room first before any guards or prying eyes catch us. Closing it quickly behind the four of us, I step past them.

Emrys is standing bare-chested in the center of the room, a shirt grasped in his hands. The look of shock on his face would be humorous if it weren't for the slight slip of fear in his eyes.

"Um...hello," he says to the frozen females softly before turning to me. "Vanna, what's going on?"

I cross the room—he made the bed, revealing no evidence of our sexual antics last night.

Wisteria's voice is interrogative behind me. "Uh, Faerie, is that not one of Caethes's bodyguards?"

I reach Emrys and he looks down at me questioningly, still holding his shirt. I wrap an arm around his bare waist and press the other—my left—to his equally bare chest. I've removed all rings but one.

I see very loud queries in everyone's eyes, while Maelona just smiles sympathetically, crossing her arms over her armored chest. Wisteria's pointing finger is upraised, Julia's hands are on her hips, her head cocked.

"Wisteria, Julia," I begin, swallowing. "This is my husband, Emrys."

There is silence. Blinking is the only thing to show time passing. Eventually, Wisteria nods.

"That would explain the scratches on his back and the hickeys all over your neck." I blush, but she continues. "So, okay, you're married to an Unseelie. Kinda fucked up with this whole war thing, but is that such a big deal?"

I look at Emrys, the two of us having a silent conversation. He knows exactly what I'm asking and nods.

"You sure?" he asks.

"I am."

Emrys licks his lips. "I'm also the Revenant."

The two girls gasp, eyes bulging, and I decide to drop another bomb.

"And I'm the Harbinger."

This time cacophony breaks out.

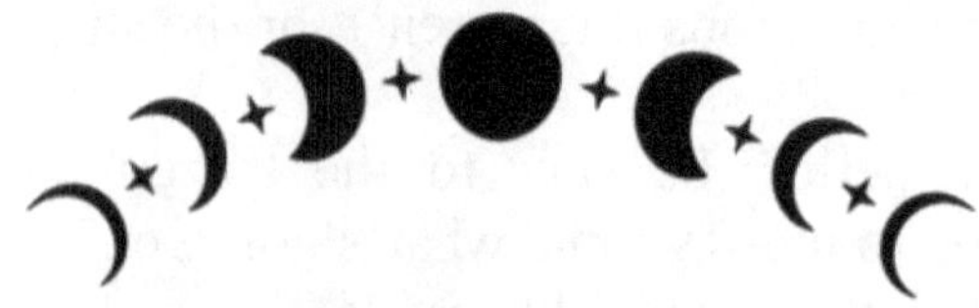

After calming the girls and explaining the mess of our identities, marriage, and what I don't remember, we continue to reveal the plan about the Winter Carnaval and how we may need them in case everything goes awry. Maelona had taken it upon herself to make a duplicate of the key—something that isn't supposed to be possible, but she has connections with the faerie, Ghislain, whose magic is life and other. We also explain the catastrophe that is Gideon's betrayal and the command that he holds over me.

"We aren't sure if it's only one or up to three." I flush with embarrassment. "I was drinking and didn't understand the significance at the time. I may have only worded it properly once, but regardless, he has at least one." At this Emrys squeezes my hand in reassurance.

"So…you are not with Gideon any longer?" Julia asks, arched brows pulled together.

"No."

"But we're still trying to rescue him?" she presses.

Guilt flashes through me. I've moved on from Gideon quickly, but I'd be lying if I said I regretted reuniting with my husband. Gideon and I had ended things, quite succinctly and clearly, and nothing—including a hate fuck against a wall— was changing that. I should logically feel the same way about things being broken off between me and Mae, but that has always been the state and flux of our friendship. Losing the romance was not the detriment to the bond that it was to mine and Gideon's.

My lips thin. "I suppose that part is complicated. I…I've already abandoned him once and I want to give him the chance to explain."

"To explain why he's banging the Unseelie Queen?"

I wince. "Perhaps not that part. He's not all bad, he assisted with the retrieval of Aberth residents and he's doing it all for his dad. And he didn't tell Caethes my identity."

"If we weren't also going for the crown, would we still try to rescue him?" Wisteria demands, arms crossed.

I scrounge for an answer. "I don't know."

"So, you want us to put our lives on the line when you don't even know if you want to save him?" Wisteria is incredulous.

"You're right, you deserve better than that."

"You're damn right I do. I went along with one of your half-baked plans before and look where that got us."

I absorb the blow and nod. "I deserve that."

Wisteria's arched brow and nod says: "*Yes, you do.*"

"Why aren't you asking the other faeries to help you?" Julia interrupts, changing the topic. "Drysi and whoever is left of the guard?"

"Because we need liars for this part. Besides, they're needed here to continue operating the court."

And then we tell them the rest of it, telling them we have only hours before we enact it.

CHAPTER 28

We travel the Faerie Roads, finding the turn for the chain of forgotten realms. Entering the first realm is unsettling, like stepping onto solid ground only to discover quicksand. As the directions said, we are to move quickly as they are unstable, held together by strength of will.

I look down at my chunky heeled boots, seeing the ground tremor beneath my feet. The three of us silently lock gazes and hastily skip through the glowing cave entrance at the base of a massive granite mountain—a copper glow indicating the path through the chain. We're then deposited into a wasteland with a concrete building. Our footing here is slightly better, crumbling rather than sinking. We enter the building within which is our next stepping stone.

The third is an island with ocean as far as the eye can see, our feet slipping into sand, lacking only a bit more substance than a regular beach. As we traverse each pocket realm it becomes more and more apparent that it's stable closer to the final link.

Our fourth stepping stone is a sprawling manor in the middle of the woods. The fifth a block of city with skyscrapers, empty streets, and abandoned shops. It isn't deserted like everyone just up and left, but more like nothing was ever here. I wonder if this is like a prison. Like a mirror of someone's former life and they were deposited here, designed to go insane with the familiarity but lacking any of the society that should come along with it.

I wonder if that was supposed to be my fate in the Yukon.

When we step into the sixth, Emrys and I both stutter-step. The crumbling cathedral, the vast greenery that sprawls the walls and the field beyond. I can see the broken stained glass, the collapsed roof, the wing half decimated on the west side.

"Holy fuck," I whisper, pure, unadulterated shock coursing through me.

Because this is Century Training. This is where Emrys and I spent a false one hundred years, training, becoming close, hating each other, falling in love…getting married. This is where we were simultaneously abused and disregarded. Where Osian forced me to deceive and betray my husband.

Century Training isn't like one of the forgotten pocket realms—it *is* one of them.

Emrys reaches for my hand instinctually. "Vanna…we shouldn't linger."

The prospect of seeing the mentors when I don't recall how training ended has me holding my breath.

"What is it? Have you seen this?" Understanding dawns on Maelona. "Is this Cen—"

"Yes," I interrupt her.

She curses and makes for the arched doors of the cathedral.

"Mae, wait!" I hurry after her, dragging Emrys. "We need to be careful. You don't want to meet the mentors."

Maelona whirls. "Ev, there's no one here. These are forgotten realms."

I blink and look at Emrys, his face flat. "Where else would they be?"

Emrys is silent, weighing his answer—no, trying to figure out if he *can* answer. "They're not here, love."

"How?" I demand, gaze flickering to the Revenant and back to the cathedral.

He shakes his head. "I cannot say."

I try to understand what I'm missing, going through everything left unsaid. Do the mentors skip to another realm during the millennia Century Training is shut? Or darker…

"Are they dead?"

That can't be possible, I'd stabbed Osian so many times and he never bled—not until Enydd attacked him.

Emrys's lips thin, unable to answer because I'm blindly guessing.

"Ev, I'm really sorry but we need to get going," Maelona informs us, hand on the door. "We don't have much time."

I give Emrys one last look and nod. "Right, okay let's go."

We enter the cathedral on a squeal of hinges, the air dusty and stale. Motes swirl about the room as we pass the threshold, Maelona's heels click on the broken stone. I gravitate towards Emrys, winding my arm around his waist as he does the same.

Everything is the same, only older. More lichen and moss have overtaken the space, but the stairs are still ruined, the columns crumbled against the floor. The hallway that Osian cornered me in is still bracketed by rubble, and the wooden doors that house the bathroom and our claimed room still stands, though splintered. The fountain is as dry as ever but still in one piece. The seven faces of our mentors stare back at us from the center of it, the goddesses hands reach up to the night from the very top of it.

This is where I fell in love with my husband for the first time. This is where he became my dearest friend, my equal, my mirror, my enemy, my everything,

"I never thought I'd see this place again,"

"Me neither," Emrys responds, tightening his grip on my waist.

The door that the mentors had come and gone from is the one that glows with coppery light. The one in which we will find the Winter Carnaval. It's kind of poetic, honestly.

Maelona observes everything as we cross the floor of our former training room, looking at the cracked stone and half ruins surrounding us. Emrys and I keep each other steady and anchored, plagued with memories—good and bad and missing.

As a safeguard, we don light glamours. Not enough to drastically change our appearances, but enough to make our faces vaguely forgettable. Like someone you'd once seen before but cannot quite recall. It's as easy as breathing, willed into existence with just a thought. Though the more complex the glamour, the more effort it takes to create and maintain.

With a simple twist of the key, Maelona opens the last door, and we step through it, feeling the familiar prickle of magic on our skin. The wards let us pass, and we step into the final pocket realm, finding ourselves standing in an underground ecosystem.

It's as if a giant has dipped their massive fist into the ground and tunneled down, their fingers leaving furrows in the earth where elevators and platforms operated by pulleys descend. Deeper into the bowels of the structure are winding staircases, and along those staircases are doors leading to open floors and rooms, as well as cages and prison cells. The well is so deep I can't see the bottom despite burning torches studding the cylindrical walls at five-foot intervals. It supplies the realm with light and heat, though neither offer much comfort.

Screams of pleasure and pain as well as music are heard from far below, the scents that rise are similar to that of the nightclub in Prague. It reeks of sex and sweat, blood and booze. All of it has my fury flaming. It is a hollow place filled with depravity and the worst the world has to offer.

I inhale sharply, wondering how I've made it here. Despite Aneira's desperate attempts to infiltrate the Carnaval for years we'd managed nothing more than a faction, but Emrys was able to secure entry alone. How? What was said and what was done for us to glean this?

A particularly piercing shriek rents the air.

We're finally at the Winter Carnaval.

Sharing a look, the three of us begin the descent to Hell.

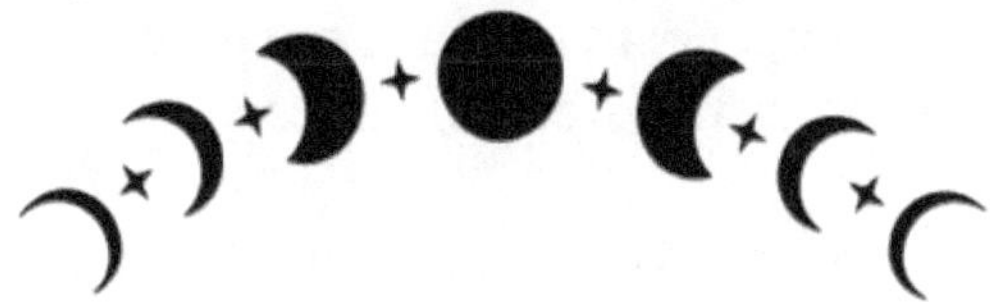

After several flights of stairs, we reach a lowering platform and ride it down to the lowest level. The lift creaks and rolls steadily, our slow lowering allowing me an opportunity to get my bearings. I think through the plan and our singular goal—find and retrieve the crown. Once secured, we can think about rescuing Gideon.

Emrys's fingers trail soothingly down the bare expanse of my spine. My shirt has a marquis-shaped cut-out in the center of my back, covering the scars that herald my missing wings. I lean into his touch.

"We'll return one day," Emrys murmurs into my hair. "One day we will end this."

I don't have the heart to tell him places like the Carnaval are like a hydra—cut off one head and another one will take its place.

Maelona taps her titanium nails on her vambraces. Upon each is an etching of rabbits and foxes, chasing each other around the cuff, roses flowing between them. Her face is impassive but I know the tell of her nerves even though she sprayed her hair black in anticipation for tonight.

The lower we get, the louder and clearer the voices become. The sounds leave no illusions about the state of this hellhole. Blood scents the air in light wafts, overwhelming the odors of everything permeating the Winter Carnaval. Around us, people mill about, every type of supernatural and human alike, the depraved and elite huddling in mutual understanding of tastes and kinks and desires. It sickens me.

Our platform shudders to a halt, and we step off, wrapped around each other as we saunter over to an imposing faerie whose skin appears to be made of stone. He confirms the guests in line possess the sleek black card as proof they were formally invited.

His heavy gray gaze assesses the group directly in front of us; two human girls with dog collars and matching heart-shaped tags that read *Vixen* and *Cosette* with a shifty looking halfling holding their leashes. He looks like a junkie, fidgeting and casting wild eyes.

"No." The stone-fae stops the halfling. "You are not welcome here."

"Come on, Carrick," the halfling says, his voice slimy. "I'm good for it this time."

"No. Your invitation has been revoked."

"I bring girls! New girls!" The halfling tugs on the leash of the one with the *Vixen* collar, bringing her up beside him. Her blonde hair is bottle-bleached and her blue eyes limpid. She licks dry lips and I notice the unnatural stretch in her cheekbones, her skin practically hanging off her.

"The last humans you brought were riddled with venereal disease and died within weeks," Carrick replies flatly.

"I somehow find that hard to believe." Carrick doesn't respond and the halfling gives him a greasy smile. "Besides, you're supposed to be gentle with them, break them in slow. Maybe they were clean before your patrons got their filthy bits on them."

Carrick silently seethes, and while the halfling hasn't realized, we certainly have.

"Leave now, or there will be consequences," Carrick warns, a final intonation. I can sense the halfling's fate teetering on a precipice.

The halfling doesn't see this.

Instead, he laughs, thinking Carrick is a good buddy, and claps him on the shoulder.

It happens in a flash. Carrick grasps the halfling's wrist in his granite fist, and wrenches his arm back, snapping it in half. The halfling shrieks in agony, but Carrick isn't through. Before our eyes, he claps those mountainous hands together, pulverizing the halfling between them.

Blood and bits of bone shower us, brain matter oozing over Carrick's fingers as the rest of the halfling mists in the space he once was. The lower half of his body collapses to the floor in a ruin of viscera, organs, and shattered spine.

Vixen and Cosette do less than bat an eye.

Sticky blood drips off my lashes as I look at Emrys, dumbfounded. A spray of blood coats his jaw and lips, and a piece of bone rests on his shoulder. Maelona received the brunt of it, the whole front of her drenched, her face a streaked mask of crimson.

Carrick himself is painted in the death and gore like a warlord, begging anyone to challenge him. He runs an offal saturated hand through his colorless hair, staining it, before rubbing the remainder on his pressed black pants.

"Apologies for that," Carrick says, lifting his unaffected gaze at us. "I'll have a witch clean that for you, post haste."

He rings a small bell on the wall and as soon as it chimes, a slight witch arrives. His brown eyes are distant as he takes in the scene of the former halfling, sparing no reaction, and I begin to wonder how common this is.

Without speaking to us, he murmurs something low in Latin and casts a hand across us, then pulls it back. With the draw of his hand, the gore of the halfling lifts from my skin and clothes. The residue congeals into a red, wet orb in his hand, writhing as if alive, while bone and sinew are manipulated into it. Once all of the halfling is removed from us—even the bits imbedded—the witch twists his wrist and whispers an incantation that has the remains transforming into glass. It gleams between his fingertips, swirls of pink flesh pressing against the globe. I'm simultaneously fascinated and nauseated.

Despite knowing nothing of him is left on us, I still feel dirty and defiled. The violation sticks to my soul like a spill of ink—not easily scrubbed away.

The witch waves another spell to quickly mend our nicked clothes. Rends in fabric reverse back to their pristine condition. A third spell cleanses and heals our already healing wounds.

"Thank you," I manage finally, glancing at Maelona and Emrys who wear similar masks of *What the Fuck?*

"Very welcome," Carrick responds affably, extending a blood encrusted hand. The witch sighs and repeats the spell, forming a matching marble from the remaining slaughter. Carrick nods once in gratitude. "Do you happen to have an invitation?"

Without shaking, Maelona silently passes over the sleek black card she was given last night—was it only last night? —and Carrick examines it closely. I do not know what the process for identifying fakes are, but frankly I don't want to find out after witnessing such a bloody destruction.

He harumphs in pacification and pockets the card. Then, he reaches out and presses a hand to Mae's and says, "Accepted patron."

Immediately, she draws a breath and an icy blue snowflake ringed by three incomplete circles appears on the back of her hand like a glittering tattoo.

It is neither Seelie nor Unseelie magic and that unsettles me deeply.

He repeats this twice more; first with Emrys, then me. The bright shock of coldness penetrates my bones before it dissipates into a watery sensation—like snow melting against flesh.

Assessing us carefully, Carrick takes in Emrys slightly longer. "What are you, boy? Seelie? Unseelie?"

"Unaffiliated," Emrys says nonchalantly.

Because he has not formally made a motion against Caethes, his nature has not recognized defecting from the Dark Court even if his heart and mind have. So, until he does, he can truly claim the status of unaffiliated. But he can also choose to represent himself as Seelie or Unseelie because all three are true.

Carrick huffs a low laugh with a crack of a smile, relaxing with Emrys's answer. "You will be assigned a guide shortly and they'll show you to your suites in addition to the common areas."

We wait only a few breaths before a striking vampire woman comes from the hallway behind Carrick, her violent red hair brighter than Emrys's. Almost painfully so. Her eyes, her lips, her dress—all of it is red. Deep, heart's blood crimson. She pulls her lips back over her teeth, baring white fangs, stark against the bold lip.

The vampire waves her hand and a servant quickly comes to search our bags. He finds nothing more than clothes.

"Welcome to the Winter Carnaval," she greets, huskily. "Enjoy your pleasures and forget your inhibitions. Follow me, please."

With that, she steps over the lower half of the deceased halfling and escorts us into the first labyrinthine hallway of the Winter Carnaval. We follow, forsaking everything we've ever known, and dive into the abyss of everything I sought to end when my freedom was last taken from me.

CHAPTER 29

The vampire woman leads us to a set of adjoining suites, three bedrooms connected by a common area with very large lounge—or bed? —clearly meant to encourage orgies. The furniture is such a juxtapose to the structure.

Everything from the floors to the walls and support beams is rough-hewn wood and stone, pillars of great granite etched with runes in the ancient fae dialect that were drawn in the translated journals. Though the bones are gargantuan and archaic, the furniture is plush and rich—silk, velvet, satin. Tapestries depicting various sexual positions with a variety of partners dress the walls, the participants wearing gowns as often as nothing, horns and antlers and wings as common as not. The lighting is low but warm amber glow that enchants guests to sprawl and luxuriate, prompting delights from languishing and lasciviousness—consent ambiguous.

A glass bar holds alcohols, perfumes, and oils, while a nearby tray has neat lines of coke and ecstasy as well as something fae I know not to mess with. And there, high up on a shelf are faerie tonics of forgetting.

The forgetting elixir, as it's known, does not have a formal name. Due to its very nature, it has become a victim of its own design. Memories of it have my stomach tripping at the three bottles. Upon closer inspection, I notice the label indicates that they are spelled only to remove human memories for whatever transpires at the Carnaval.

I shudder, my spine rolling at how fucked up all this is.

"I'll leave you all to get settled in. Please venture out to the common area any time. Parties evolve and devolve throughout the hours. You never know what tastes you're in for until you sample the menu."

The vampire leaves and the three of us are locked into a staring match of the century, wondering if we've just made the worst mistake of our lives. I swallow the bile threatening to rise and nervously pace our main room.

"Okay, are we ready for this?" I ask my two closest friends.

They both nod, and Emrys grins before he speaks. "Let's make them regret everything."

The three of us deposit our bags, exit the suites, and carouse through the hallways, an act of feigned intoxication and forgoing inhibitions carrying us. The walls seem to be made of raw clay earth, unlike the Seelie Court's dark polished earth, but it feels like it's taking from the Light Court—

bastardizing it. What was this realm used for before it was forgotten?

We arrive in the first common area, a large cavern with stalactites reaching down like sharp fingers, and fat white candles drip from hollows and crevices. Opulent rugs cover the bare dirt floor, overlapping and layering at random, a deep red Persian set atop a terracotta one with a rip on its right-side edge. Upon all the carpets are various pieces of furniture; fainting couches and poufs, sofas and daybeds. Beside them sit tables laden with bottles and trays with little bronze cards and fingernail sized spoons. It's as if various mansions were raided and the robbed goods were put into this cave.

Some patrons wear masks for anonymity, others don glamours. Others proudly display their identity, eager to flaunt their presumed power and invincibility.

A human man approaches us with a charming smile and dips in greeting. "Good evening, what would you like to begin with? Down this hall—" he directs his arm to our left, "you will find libations and recreational substances. Down this one—" he goes in a clockwise motion, "are other common areas if you wish to mingle. The next leads to the fighting pits, and the following contains the wares to be sold tonight—there are many lovely specimens available. And the last one you will find your way to the auction." The human winks. "Any tickle your fancy?"

"I wouldn't mind perusing the items for purchase. I'm intrigued."

"By all means, my lady. The live products are on either side of the hallway and at the end you will find more material objects. Should you need anything else of me, please find me promptly." He inclines his head at Emrys and Maelona in acknowledgement before he departs.

The three of us head down the hallway, ringed with rock formations before coming upon a heavy, almost medieval door. Emrys swings it open and we step through. I don't say anything when he wraps an arm around both our waists, sensing the desolate air. We walk, ignoring the whispers of patrons up ahead, keenly listening to the sounds of the people in cells while I stretch out my internal alarm.

The hopeful purchasers are fae and I extend outward, finding twelve souls in the cages—four humans, three witches, two faeries, a vampire, a werewolf, and one halfling.

I practically drag Emrys and Maelona to the halfling's cell.

I came here for the crown, to regain the court's power and magic, but if Gideon is right here within reach? Why wouldn't I *try*? Why can't I do both?

Emrys must sense what I've discovered because while he doesn't slow his steps, tension radiates from him.

The two faeries have moved on, tittering and browsing the atrium full of jewels and scrolls, and tonics and magic. My heart races as we pass every cell and find the one second from the end on the left.

Am I only doing this out of guilt? Or is it something else? Something Maelona threw at my face and Emrys asked if I was ready to repress? If it is what I dare not admit, it changes nothing. I've made my choice in all aspects with each of my lovers. I know where I stand.

Directly before the cell I grasp the bars and peer in, finding a male curled beneath a blanket, hair dark as ink spilling across a moldering pillow. He doesn't move, but I stare, trying to see the shape of him beneath the rough wool through the dim light. I push my face closer, and suddenly he leaps from his prone position, launching at the bars. He shoves his arm through, nearly grabbing me by the throat.

I stumble back, his fingers brushing my trachea, but he doesn't have time to pull away before Emrys takes hold of his wrist and wrenches it upward. Had I not been trained for as long and thoroughly as I was during Century Training, those long, scarred fingers would have crushed my windpipe. I find my hand going to my throat, not of my own volition.

The male hisses at Emrys and then all of us pause when we take in the halfling boy.

Because that is what he is.

Sixteen or seventeen, covered in a thick layer of grime and sporting bruises all over his arms and throat. Bite marks pepper his pale flesh and scratches cut the muscles of his bare torso. Tattoos cover the entirety of his right arm, elements of a shield, a tree, chains, scrolls, and flowers visible. His hair is midnight black, thick and waving over his strong brow and brushing cheekbones that will be devastating in a few years. His lips—split in more than one place—are full and his nose is strong and proud—though maybe broken once. But it's the eyes that stop us dead.

Not the slightly too orange shade of amber, but bright, burning gold topaz.

The exact same shade as Emrys's.

He has heavy lids, built for promising secrets from beneath those thick lashes just like my husband's. The shape is so alarmingly familiar that breath is stolen from my lungs.

Whoever this halfling teen is, he is somehow inexplicably related to Emrys.

"Who are you?" Emrys demands on a growl. It's clear he's come to a similar conclusion, but a familial bond is not enough for him to forget the slight against his wife. He squeezes to drive the point home.

The halfling hisses in pain, baring his teeth, fangs digging into his lower lip. "You first," he manages.

Emrys grinds his bones harder, and while the halfling grimaces he does not scream as anyone else likely would. "I asked first."

"Will you do it again? Nicely this time?" The halfling forces through a hollow smile. "The least I can ask is for some manners in here, no? If you want to be rough, you have to pay first."

Emrys sucks in his cheeks and releases the halfling's wrist. The boy strikes out through the bars again, this time meaning to harm my husband. I intervene.

Before the halfling can blink, I've pulled his arm through and pushed it against the bars, flat to the outside. I lean against the cell, wrist grasped and pinned. My flushed cheek meets the iron bars that separate us and I look at him docilely. Emrys does the same.

"Mae, stay away from the bars, they're iron," I tell her nonchalantly.

"Duly noted," she responds, examining her nails.

"You sure? Maybe she should test it. They don't seem to be bothering you much," the halfling growls.

"Hmm, perhaps," I return, and slowly I drag my tongue up the length of one bar, the sharp tang of metal biting my tongue. Iron may no longer affect me, but the taste has never been pleasant. "No, quite sure they're iron."

"What the fuck?" the halfling says in disbelief. "What the fuck are you?"

"Now, I don't think that was very nice," I tell the young halfling then face my husband. "Was it, love?"

"Quite a bad idea, truth be told." Emrys's low laugh vibrates in his chest and does funny things to me. "Would you like to try again? Your name?"

The halfling stares before he deflates. "Caspian. Caspian Lockwood."

I lift a brow. "Of the warrior witches?"

"Yes."

"But you're a halfling."

"And he's a faerie, but that doesn't seem to have stopped his mother or father from fucking a witch," Caspian fires back, plush and bloody lips peeled back from his teeth.

Shock rushes through me and it's too potent to hide. I blink at Emrys, puzzle pieces coming together. Every question about why he's the way he is coming together.

Lockwoods are unparalleled warriors, the only ones greater than them in skill have been Emrys and I. But if he *is* a Lockwood…

He's not fully fae.

And in that moment, I realize there's no way I can be either.

We both have achieved immunity from iron even though no other fae to date has—resistance, yes, but not immunity. And both of us do not retain the gifts singular to Unseelie or Seelie fae. Emrys has never displayed chaos and I've never shown karma—which is already rare—yet I possess an internal detection that Aneira had no words for and swore me to never reveal. But now that poses a new question all on its own—what sort of witch was my father?

It hits me with a comical sort of illumination.

Visions. Premonitions. Clairvoyance.

Searching for the future in your brandy? I thought only Whitecrest witches could do such a thing? Mayhap you'll change that piece of fact. Maelona had said.

The vision of Gideon and Caethes fucking, spilled by my washbasin and scattered all over my floor in flickers of glass and pools of liquor. Knowing something was innately wrong when I stared into the decanter of brandy. Seeing the cabin fire in my waterglass.

Premonitions painted upon reflective surfaces.

My father was a Whitecrest witch.

I feel my insides roil with the intense urge to vomit. Sour saliva pools in my mouth and I force it down as I take in my husband.

We are perfectly mirrored. Two half witch faeries with absent witch fathers and faerie mothers who deposited us with opposite queens.

The moment has stretched on in silence. Maelona waiting with a brow quirked while Emrys and I stare at each other, a halfling between us who has flipped our identities upside down.

I cast a thin glamour around us, temporarily blocking out sound. It's not ideal as it's very easy to infiltrate, but it'll do if no one is specifically searching for it.

"Did you know?" I inquire tautly, releasing Caspian from my slackening grip.

Emrys does the same and shakes his head slowly. "I figured it out just now, did you know? About yours?"

Emrys, my perfect equal, has come to the same unspoken conclusion I have. After cohabiting with someone for a hundred years you learn things about them even if against your will. You learn their speech patterns and habits, aversions, and quirks. Their trains of thought. After a while it feels as if nothing is secret.

"No." I pause, an epiphany coming to me, a secret that might still linger between us without Lady Fate's intervention. "Ryss...can you sense someone's presence like an internal alarm?"

My husband's eyes flare wide. "Yes." Then he realizes. "Can you?"

I nod. "I was oathed to secrecy."

"So was I."

Oaths like this weaken and fray when people already know the subject. I belatedly realize the oath is why I never told Gideon of this gift.

Horror climbs through me. It's too much of a coincidence to believe that both our queens chose to hide our gifts separately. Isn't it? What purpose did us hiding our internal detection systems serve? Propriety? Secrecy? For what?

I've ruined so many things. There are so many things I selfishly kept from you.

No, no you haven't.

I have, daughter, and you won't see until I'm gone.

The conversation replays over in my head like a sick, villainous monologue.

"You've had visions too, haven't you?" I accuse flatly, coming to the realization in that very breath. "For how long?"

He inhales slowly. "I've always had prophetic dreams, but the first waking one was during—" his eyes flicker meaningfully, "*then*, about Osian. Right before he pulled you away in the bathroom."

I remember the moment clearly. Training had been cut early due to the arrival of the contraceptive tonics from Lady Fate and Emrys and I had gone to the bathroom. There, I had perched myself on the counter while a shirtless Emrys stared down into a filling sink of water.

I inhale sharply.

"I thought I was going crazy, Vanna. So, I never said anything."

"Okay, this is much too large to speak of now, we'll discuss it later," I say in a whirl, dismissing the fading glamour dampening sound around us. "Caspian, how long have you been here?"

The halfling has retreated only a step back in his cell, taking us in and missing nothing.

"Two months. Why?"

I glance sideways, looking down the hallway towards the atrium where the non-sentient wares are housed. Anything taken down that way must be carried directly past Caspian's cell.

I lower my voice. "Have you ever seen anyone bring a crown through here to be auctioned off?"

"You're going to have to be more specific than that, there's been a few."

Hope surges within me. "A gold thing with fleur-de-lis and rubies. Almost gaudy and more masculine in shape."

Recognition alights in Caspian's face. "Yes, but it's not up for auction."

"Where is it?" I press, desperation tugging my heart. It's here. It's really here.

Caspian narrows his brows in concentration. "Last time I saw it, Gideon was wearing it."

Shock floors me, flooding like vicious mercury.

"*Gideon*? You know Gideon?"

"Yeah, I've known him for years. We were training to become protectors together."

It's as if Lady Fate has divined this exact plan and pushed us—her little pieces on her little fucking board—right where she wants us. Out of everyone we could have come across in this disgusting place, we come across someone who is not only related to Emrys, but has knowledge of Gideon. It feels like a giant, cosmic joke.

I stare at this young halfling that has clearly been through untold horrors and abuse, when all the blood drains from my face. There is no way we can continue a conversation like this here. My gaze skips up and down the hall.

"What is the price they usually ask for you?" I demand anxiously.

Caspian's lips whiten and his topaz eyes turn hard. "It depends on the service." He looks away. "I serve a dual purpose. If it's for the fighting pits it's seven thousand, if it's for fucking it's ten." Caspian swallows, disgust warring across his face with anguish. "Everyone wants to use or fuck the night's champion."

Because of course as a protector, he'd be a skilled fighter. And being one of the warrior witches…I can't imagine the hell he has endured. Then there's the forced sex.

A surge of protective instinct rushes through me and settles in my bones. I meet Caspian's heavy gaze. "We will buy you tonight, and after we achieve our goal, we're getting you the fuck out of here."

Surprise lights Caspian's face before suspicion replaces it. "What am I doing for you?"

"You're going to tell us everything about what you've seen, from Gideon to that crown, and then you're going to have a nap."

"You're serious?" Tears pool in Caspian's eyes. The silver line shimmers, but doesn't spill. He flexes his throat and his tongue works as he nods rapidly.

"I am."

"Okay."

Unfamiliar softness threads through me and I tentatively reach out a hand. Offering peace to Caspian. "I am going to do everything in my power to make sure you get out of this place."

Caspian takes my proffered hand and nods. He lets the tears fall this time.

A few hours later we're seated on plush, midnight velvet before the auction's stage several rows back. Maelona on my right, Emrys on my left, and in my lap is a black disc on a stick with the number 7 emblazoned on it. With the stick are rules outlined for the bidding process; that all must be conducted in US dollars, though other currencies are accepted if they equal the bid upon dollar amount, and that payment must be made before taking the winnings back to the suites—in addition to reparations for damages and deaths.

Arounds us greedy supernaturals and vile humans titter expectantly, anticipation threading through the room like a heady fog. The scent of bodies and incense is thick in the air. From braziers the sticks burn on a plate, licked by the flames that simultaneously heat and light the room. As per the rest of the Carnaval setting, this room is raw clay with stalactites and stubby candles. The stage is a wooden thing, rough, raw wood with intricate carpets rolled across it. A mural spans the furthest wall, a depiction of a faerie revel with angels staring down with horror and demons grinning up maniacally.

I shift, taking in the other patrons—the competition for Caspian. Nearby a pair of vampires sip from crystal goblets of blood, while goldwine is spread freely. My fingers itch for a drink, but Emrys carefully captures my fingers and squeezes— just as he did during Century Training. It says, *I am here and you are not alone.*

Maelona signals for a passing server and when he arrives, she requests three waters. Appreciation and gratefulness rush through me. They see me, they understand, and they care.

Within moments our waters arrive and the rustle from behind the stage indicates that things are about to start.

The scarlet vampire from earlier strolls across the stage and stands behind a podium of ornate scrollwork. She drums her equally red nails on the edge and sends us all a blinding smile.

"Prepare yourselves for a night you'll never forget. Tonight, we have some truly spectacular specimens lined up, in addition to some favorites. First, we will have the playthings available and then we will move onto the items. To kick off the night we shall begin with a favorite." She casts her arm out welcomingly. "Ysandre—Unseelie fae!"

A voluptuous faerie with glittering green hair and two little horns crosses the stage. Her skin is pale and plush, sparkling as if brushed by tiny diamonds, while her eyes are just as luminous. She is not hesitant as she crosses the stage, she knows what this is and she has either reluctantly accepted it or is consenting to it.

The bidding begins at five thousand and ends at twelve.

A human man with a recent hair enhancing treatment and the start of a paunch claims her for the night. I think he's involved in American politics. The thing with the supernatural world and everything that pertains to it is that federal governments know about it, but have a very uneasy relationship with it. It's not surprising though that a man in power has decided to sample the delicacies of those considered *exotic*—fuck, they treat their human women similarly and worse. These types of men believe laws do not apply to them.

Next up is a brand-new faerie female, this one bearing almost no considerable fae attributes, and I begin to wonder if any features were removed from her as they were from Emrys and I. She is startlingly beautiful and her pale eyes are glacier blue. When she's purchased for three thousand dollars her eyes flicker burgundy and I realize she is not like Emrys and I at all, but like Maelona. The Lady next to me recoils as she notices this too, her own hair flickering white and violet too—shock and anguish—beneath the spray.

A faerie male—also very humanoid in appearance—follows, then the werewolf I'd sensed in the cells, two humans—purchased together like a fucking set—and then a Blackthorn witch. I make a few low bids to avoid suspicion and luckily—though guilt strikes me—I manage none. All sell for four figures, yet nothing like Ysandre's disproportionate amount and nothing like what Caspian claims he goes for.

"Now, time for another favorite!" the vampire woman croons to the crowd. "Caspian Lockwood—halfling!"

With that, Caspian crosses the stage, full of undiluted rage. He has since been washed but still bears all his wounds, clothed only by a pair of thin linen pants that are nearly see-through—I can make out the design of a tattoo going down his leg, opposite from his arm sleeve. New on his face though, is a black eye that he sports with pride and disdain.

"With Caspian, we have the option to purchase him for the entertainment tonight at the pits, or for more you can purchase him in the bedroom." She pauses, throwing a look at him. "It is the mass's choice."

The crowd goes wild, the feral anticipation ramping up and sounds of glee stir up the room. Caspian's face is hard, but I can see the fury pouring off him in waves and I want nothing more for him than to be let loose and tear these fuckers apart. If he could get as close to me as he did, he's supremely gifted.

"First bid determines! Shall we start with nine for the pits and twelve for the bedroom?"

Anger punctures me—they're price-gouging with Caspian's life. I let the feeling cut me, but I toss up my sign. "Twelve!"

The vampire grins gleefully. "Fantastic! Do I see thirteen?"

Another bid goes up. I furiously counter with fourteen. Another counters with fifteen. I counter with sixteen. The first competitor comes back with seventeen. Rage courses through me, fire burning my veins. I bare my teeth as I continue fighting back.

"Twenty-one!" I call ferociously.

"Number seven seems positively feral for Caspian tonight. Think she's taken a liking to the boy? He *is* quite yummy," she says, stroking scarlet claws down his throat. Caspian's lip curls back from his teeth. "Twenty-two?"

Mumbles go up about the room and my apprehension trills, but no one else makes a move. The vampire searches the room, but the auction of Caspian Lockwood concludes, and then she writes down the information.

I've won.

And I've saved him for a night.

Caspian spares me barely a glance, but I see the gratitude in it before he's ushered off the stage.

The rest of the auction continues similarly, a few newer options and then a favorite. The favorites go for twelve thousand or more, each one progressively more ludicrous in amounts—does anyone here realize these are *people*? But of course, my disparaging is internal and it falls on completely deaf ears. The two girls, Vixen and Cossette that were brought by the deceased halfling go for seven and six thousand respectively, and then, the final is a wild card to end the night.

The last is a bound girl about Caspian's age with ambiguous origins, and neither the Carnaval nor mine and Emrys's detection systems can determine what she is. She appears humanoid with blonde hair and large blue doe eyes, but with a wholly *other* quality. Magic radiates off her like a hurricane, the sharp bitter taste like that of December nights and electricity.

"Annabelle Laroche—unknown. This one is quite the masterpiece; a curiosity and one of a kind. She recently came to us from a hunt in Versailles after her family could not pay their debts. Here, she is fulfilling the remainder of her indenture that their blood did not pay."

The stunning supernatural-mixed girl, Annabelle, inclines her petite chin, face fierce with hate, and I see the emotion ripple—actually ripple—off her. This urges the horde into a frenzy and the bidding takes off in earnest. It goes on for a while but eventually she is purchased for two-hundred-fifty thousand dollars by the King of Vampires.

Annabelle resists the entire way as she's led towards Joseph Harrow, her tied hands keep her from halting his pawing. He catches me staring and winks at me once before forcibly dragging Annabelle off the stage. I want to shove this bidding sign right through his fucking eye.

The night wraps up and we are escorted to an adjoining room where we reluctantly hand over the twenty-one thousand dollars for Caspian. It isn't that I'm sad about losing the money—I'm stupid rich and the court provides everything I could ask for—but it's about funding this horrible organization. After the money is exchanged, I sign the paper—an unreadable scratch of my last name—before we retrieve Caspian.

He stands off to the side and Emrys and I wrap an arm around him while Maelona leads the way. We pretend, as we have been doing with everything, to be pawing at him and murmuring in his ear sweet, sick nothings.

"What's the black eye from?" I say lowly into his ear.

He chuckles shortly. "I always put up a fight, I wasn't going to stop now." Meaning: he had to put on a show to avoid suspicion. "It'll fade within an hour or two."

"Want me to kill who did it?" I ask, only half joking.

"I wouldn't mind."

"Give me the name and I'll see it done."

Caspian laughs as we are all guided by the warrior princess to our adjoining suites. When the door is firmly closed behind us, we let go of Caspian, giving him space as the three of us stand apart from him.

"Do you need to bathe again?" Maelona inquires, taking in Caspian's form clinically.

Caspian shakes his head. "No, they cover that before we go up on auction."

"All right, well, take seat. We have questions for you," she says, gesturing to any of the seats offered.

He takes an ottoman and as he does so, Emrys grabs him a blanket, wrapping his shoulders before stepping back. Caspian stares at us unbelieving.

"You really aren't going to…use me?"

I frown. "No, we told you; questions, nap, out of here."

"Yeah, but…" he squirms. "I thought you were lying,"

"We're fae, we cannot lie."

"Right. Right. Okay, so what do you want to ask?"

I glance between my two partners in crime and affirm I'm taking the lead. I step forward and sit on the edge of the large orgy bed, crossing my legs and leaning forward.

"The crown. Why would Gideon be wearing it? Isn't he a prisoner here too?"

Caspian scoffs. "No, he sold out. He's not a member, but he's little more than a pet. He isn't used like the rest of us."

"This isn't what we were told."

"That's what I've seen. He walks around with it on and has girls practically hanging off him at every opportunity."

My stomach sours at this, but I push on. "Have you seen anyone else wear the crown?"

"Yeah, actually. A couple of the girls would take it from him and wear it for a little while before someone would bring them one of their own. Sometimes esteemed guests have it for the night."

"Wait, there are replicas of the crown?"

He nods. "Yeah, approximations, but they're all glamoured. You can tell they're fake. I guess Gideon's…it could be the real one, but it could just be a really good copy."

I think about all the crowns that could be swimming about and wonder how I'll be able to figure out which is the real one in a sea of gold. But the crown is magic. Pure Seelie magic.

"Do you know what crown it is?"

Caspian smirks darkly. "I've figured it out. Three faeries show up looking for a gold crown after the Seelie Court was just sacked? Yeah, I have an idea exactly whose crown that is. Besides, people talk and I have all the time in the world to listen to gossip when I'm in my cell. People forget you're listening when they consider you less than a person."

Swallowing, I nod and look away, catching sight of Emrys while the grief crashes over me. The implication that gossip is so regular about my mother's death peels away a healing layer of that newly healing wound.

"So, which one of you is heir apparent?" Caspian presses, tightening the blanket around his shoulders.

We all look at Maelona. She flushes prettily and her hair flickers pink beneath the fading spray.

"I see. Well, Future-Seelie-Monarch, pleased to meet your acquaintance."

Maelona inclines her head. "Likewise."

I shake my head and try to rerail the conversation. "Has Gideon recognized you?"

Caspian's face darkens. "Yeah, and he looked damn shameful about it too. Refused to talk to me and since then he usually tries to go out of his way to stay far from me."

"Was he just thrown in here?"

"No, Callista—the vampire from earlier—she brought him here. He didn't seem all that pressed about it when I saw him the first time, but I did hear that his position here is a temporary one. I have no idea what that means."

"I do," I say, realization dawning.

Caethes moved him here out of our reach, yet is still keeping the timeline of the summer solstice before she decides to kill him. It's a means to put pressure on us without having him in the court where we could feasibly infiltrate through non-fae means, and retrieve him. Placing him in the Carnaval's grasp—though despicable—affords her a certain amount of security. The Carnaval has never been breached before.

Gideon's fate is a ticking timebomb and though he betrayed me by fucking Caethes—not barring double standards—among other things, it is all my fault. His life is on the line and petty squabbles about sex are what will define his furthered existence?

I glance at Emrys and I see concern there with poorly covered pain. Whatever he sees painted across my features— the questioning, the whole of Gideon—is hurting him. Plastering on a smile for my husband, I give him a look to indicate we'll speak later.

"Okay, that's all for now. Pick any of the rooms, Maelona has her own and Emrys and I will be sharing."

Caspian stands, keeping the blanket tight around himself. "I forgot to ask and there wasn't a time in the midst of all this—what is your name?"

I smile softly. "I'm Evelyn."

CHAPTER 31

CENTURY TRAINING

"*Evelyn*," Emrys moans against my neck, hands furiously going to the ties of my corseted blouse, his teeth biting against my throat.

He has me propped against the edge of the sink, my wings splayed across the mirror. It's after midnight, our mentors long gone to bed—or whatever it is they do behind that door. My hands are untucking his shirt from his leather pants and frantically undoing the buttons. When I get them open, I shove it from his shoulders and let my hands rove over his perfectly muscled chest. My fingers are quick as they push against his abdomen and tuck into the waistband of his pants.

My shirt is forced open, the stays frustrating Emrys. But soon my torso is bare and his hands go to my breasts, kneading them before his mouth replaces one. His mouth latches onto a nipple and rolls it in his mouth, flicking his tongue and nipping lightly. I moan, trying to be as quiet as possible.

I work the buttons free of his pants and push them down, freeing his straining cock. The hot, hard length of him is pressed against my inner thigh and I reach down to palm him, stroking his silky skin. He thrusts into my hand and groans low in his throat as I continue.

Emrys becomes wild and is suddenly lifting my ass off the edge of the sink before he tears down my pants, pushing them to my ankles. He drops down to one, and releases an ankle and foot from my boots. But then he surprises me by parting my thighs, hanging my knees over his shoulders, and pressing his mouth to my core.

The first lick is bliss. He dips his tongue into my pussy and tastes me—savors me—while I throw my head back against the glass, my wings trembling. He goes to work, dragging his tongue up my very center and then sucking my clit into his mouth.

My gasp is rough and I thrust both hands into his hair, pulling those deep crimson locks. He growls pleasure against my sex and my hips buck against him. When he sucks that bundle of nerves into his mouth, I cry out. He reaches up and clamps a hand over my mouth, pulling back.

"Bite my fingers if you have to but I'm going to make you come and you're going to be quiet," Emrys commands and his words drive me closer to the edge. His mouth dips back to me and his licks are lashes of pleasure.

I'm panting, one hand in his hair and the other plastered to the wall. I'm arching, the climax so close. I tell him this on a moan and he tightens the circles he's playing with his tongue, and suddenly, I shatter. I do end up biting his fingers as I come, thrusting my hips against his mouth as he strokes me through the last shivers.

I pull him up and bring him into a harsh kiss, tasting myself on his lips. I crush his mouth, kissing deeply, holding his face tightly. I can't believe I have him. I can't believe he's mine. Mine, mine, mine. The possessiveness is potent and I reach down to his hard length, positioning it at my entrance for our first time together.

He pauses. "We don't have anything."

"I know," I say deflating, pressing my brow to his shoulder. "How good are you at pulling out?"

His breath hitches. "As good as I can be, I suppose."

"Well in that case."

And then I guide him into me and shift my hips so that I take him in full. Our mixed sounds of relief are like a symphony, and my eyes flutter closed. I am decadently full with his length, the heavy weight of him stretching me. I thrust my hips forward more and he slams himself to the hilt. For a moment we are locked like that and stare at each other.

"I love you," I whisper.

"I love you, too," he murmurs back, and suddenly he's pumping into me, his hands on my hips to steady and angle me.

His thrusts are deep and rolling, grinding my clit on every upward move, driving me to another orgasm. He sets a punishing pace and I feel him begin to throb, my climax coming.

With a gasp he withdraws and then his two fingers plunge into me as his thumb presses my clit. He moves with his hips, grinding into me and sending me over the precipice. I come as hard as he does, burying my face in his neck.

For a moment we just breathe against each other, luxuriating in the moment. Already, I miss his length inside me, and already I need him again. But we cannot, we must be cautious. After a time, we pull apart, clean ourselves up and go to sleep as we have always done.

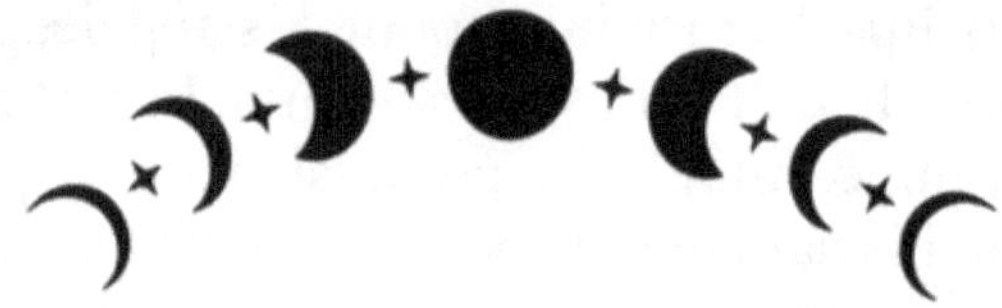

In the morning, Enydd comes to us wordlessly and hands us two contraceptive tonics. "These came in today's supplies from the goddess. Tell me nothing." And with that she surrenders responsibility and returns to the door that all the mentors use.

That night Emrys takes me again, over and over, and each time he need not remove himself from me. There's something so primal and possessive and satisfying about having him finish inside me.

We keep failing the joke of the annual test, slipping away nearly every night to fuck outside, in the bathroom, or in our sleeping area. At least twice a week, Osian takes me aside to continue our ruse even while Emrys and I laugh in secret about it. He's careful not to leave marks on me since Osian watches me so closely, and I leave marks on Emrys only easily explained away. I think about telling Osian maybe it's time to quit the act. After more than three decades anyone would be suspicious if there wasn't love, and quite the opposite of that has grown between us. I hate Osian more every day, and every day it becomes clearer which of the mentors are also sick of his controlling bullshit.

Emrys and I continue the remaining decades hopelessly in love and obsessed with each other. Every day we become more and more talented in our training and lovemaking. We study what each other likes and dislikes. I discover he's obsessed with making me come several times before we get to the main act and doesn't mind when a finger wanders to his backside. He learns that he loves when I tie him down and have my way with him and that I don't enjoy being spanked. But it's fascinating, growing and discovering together, and I love him every day more for it.

In the final month of training, I suggest something insane.

"Will you marry me?"

"What?" he asks, surprise coloring his voice as he props himself on an elbow, grass sticking to him from the field we just finished having sex in.

"I want us to get married," I repeat.

He groans and drops his head to the grass. "Fuck, Vanna. I was going to ask you when we get back. That's not fair."

I giggle and push him down, climbing atop him. "Is that a yes?"

He sighs. "Of course, it's a yes, you beautiful Seelie."

I grin and drop a kiss to his mouth, sealing the deal. "I love you."

"I love you, too," he replies tightening his hold on me.

Pulling back, I look at him squarely. "Will that be a problem?"

"Will what?"

"Being of opposite courts?"

"No, I'll just defect to the Seelie Court."

"What?" I say, eyes rounding. "Ryss, you can't be serious?"

"Why not? I hold no love for Caethes, and I can be with you if I do."

"Is it allowed?" I ask tentatively.

"I've never been told otherwise; it just hasn't been done."

I inhale quickly, filling my lungs with this moment— the scent of Emrys; vetiver and leather and sex. "So, we're really doing this? This is happening?"

"We are," he confirms.

To properly seal the deal, I seat myself over his hips and impale myself on his cock, riding him again in the open night, and luxuriating in the feeling of my future husband.

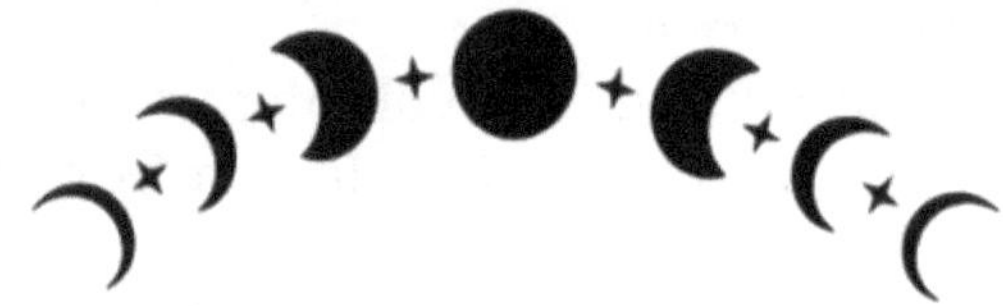

On the morning of the last day before Century Training ends, Enydd comes to us with a grave expression on her face. Silently, from within the folds of her gown she reveals a velvet-lined box and two rings nestled inside.

My breath catches. Emrys's is simple, a gold band engraved with our names and today's date, mine is more. The ring has a pear-shaped emerald the size of my nail, bracketed by two diamonds with a curve beneath the widest part of the emerald where seven diamonds drip from the lower half like an upturned crown.

Enydd's lips are thinned. "I don't know which one of you two idiots suggested this but the goddess condones it. I will officiate tonight at midnight." She pauses sadly. "I don't know how long this marriage will last, but I truly wish it is forever."

Enydd tucks the box away once more and nods.

"I'll also have you know that you two are the most talented Centurions I've ever witnessed and I'm so proud of how far you've come." Enydd swallows, her eyes lined in silver. "If anyone can win against us, it's you two."

She turns around, leaving us gaping.

That night, on the furthest edge of the field, beneath the nearly full moon Enydd officiates our wedding. Lady Fate had delivered a simple white dress with flowing sleeves and a fresh white blouse for Emrys in addition to flowers. We dress our hair with the petals, everything simple and us.

Desmond and Urian are our witnesses, presumably been made aware by Enydd. They say nothing but I can see the solemnity mixed with happiness in their eyes. We know what this means, but Emrys's continued living spells the hunt tomorrow night, and I want to spend these last few hours—if that's all we have left—married to him.

The ceremony is quiet and we exchange vows.

"With this marriage, I make a vow of everlasting love," Emrys begins, holding my hands. "With this oath, I swear to stand by your side, as your equal and other half. With this ring, I declare my heart to be wholly yours." He slips the emerald ring onto my finger. It fits perfectly. "You are my reason for living."

I swallow, overcome with emotion. "With this marriage, I make a vow of an eternal bond," I whisper. "With this oath, I swear to give you my heart and my soul, in every intangible way. With this ring, I declare my love before the goddess." I place Emrys's ring on him. "Everything I am is yours."

We seal our love with a kiss and when the three mentors wish us all the greatest, we squeeze their hands in thanks. They nod their heads and once they go inside Emrys and I consummate the marriage in the moonlight.

CHAPTER 32

I sense Caspian and Maelona's presences through the walls. At some point, Maelona disappears, but returns soon after. Before Caspian had retired to sleep, we'd given him our clothes so he'd smell like us. Everything was laid around him like a nest, with the blankets pulled up high and tight about his chin. His features never relaxed, even in slumber.

How can Lady Fate allow so much misery in life? She has the power to instill prophecies and lullabies, yet cannot prevent the Carnaval from flourishing? She orchestrated the sacrifice and cost of mine and Emrys's Bishop roles, gave us our Centurion names, and brought him back from the dead, but this all powerful goddess is content to let me flounder. Struggling to get the crown. Struggling to figure out which pieces are who in her stupid verse, wondering with every passing ally if they're someone I need to gather.

I huff, wrapped in Emrys's warm arms, hands pressed to his chest beneath silk sheets.

"Do you want to tell me how you're feeling?" my husband asks softly, lips brushing my hairline.

I inhale slowly, drawing in that reassuring and familiar scent of vetiver. "I'm not quite sure what it is I'm feeling. I think most of it is guilt."

"And the rest of it?" There is no judgement in his tone and I feel my heart swell with the outpouring of love he cups between us.

"I don't think I've admitted it to myself," I say softly.

"Do you want to?"

"No. And whatever it is, I don't want it."

"Vanna, you can trust me."

"I know." I press a kiss to his scar. "But I don't trust myself. Not with this."

"Why?"

I bite my lip. "Because I don't want it to hurt you. To hurt *us*."

"It won't."

"How do you know?"

"I just do."

We are silent for a time after, my breathing hitched, Emrys's heart racing.

"You know I—" I break off. "I choose you."

"I know," he whispers back and hooks a finger beneath my chin, tipping my mouth for a kiss. "And I love you."

My heart soars, that little thing inside breaking open a little more. A couple more memories sifting out. Playing with myself in from of him, welcoming him to watch, inviting him to participate. Blood rushes through me, pooling in my cheeks, and settling between my legs.

The screams of fucking filter through the halls—some consensual and some not—and that instantly cools the lust surging through me. I scrunch my eyes and rest my head against Emrys's bare chest.

"We should get some sleep. We're going to be busy tomorrow."

"You're right," he agrees on a sigh. "Goodnight, wife."
"Goodnight, husband."

The evening comes quickly and we dress for the occasion. Winter Carnaval patrons milling about in finery and nothing at all. Emrys wears a white silk shirt and black leather pants, festooned with gold jewelry. His shirt is left open and underneath thin chains wrap around his waist and rest against his navel—a look I find incredibly sexy. An opaque chalice of water with the tiniest splash of goldwine—for coloring purposes—poses in his hand. His hand is on my lower back, burning through the black fabric of the extremely low-cut shirt I wear tucked into rib-grazing high waisted pants.

The morning had dawned too soon, having to return Caspian with promises to retrieve him. Doubt and fear leaked into his eyes, but with a subdued nod, he let himself be taken back to his cell by Callista. After that, the rest of the day was a rush, coming at us with the force of a typhoon.

In the corner of the large "ballroom" Joseph Harrow watches us eagerly, hand gripping the bloodied neck of Annabelle. She's forced to sit on his lap, tears tracking down her cheeks as he brushes his fingers down her body from his perch on the red velvet couch that he has claimed.

How do these injustices stand? How do they exist in our world?

I swallow my nausea by forcing water down my throat. It helps little.

Discreetly, I track Maelona through the throng of people, her long bronze dress with high slits affords her comfortable movement. She also wears that black diamond skeleton corset. Socializing candidly and scoping the space, she plays her role expertly. Right now, she hangs on the word of a vampire who keeps Vixen's leash in his hand, the girl, still drugged beyond comprehension, smiles dazedly.

I realize there is a false Seelie crown on her head.

Blinking away my shock, I knock my elbow into Emrys, and tilt my head meaningfully. He follows and in response he sips his drink to hide his surprise. There are more crowns on the heads of patrons and the indentured, some less impressive than others, but all of them gold with rubies and fleur-de-lis. Why is the Carnaval flouting the Seelie crown like this?

The reasoning hits me like a blow.

The crown cannot be hidden, it wants to be seen. It is a nearly sentient thing and if it's locked away, it will use the magic of the Light Court to place itself at a point of attention. They're using decoys to subvert this, having the true one displayed, but not singularly paraded.

So, which is the real one? Was Caspian right and it's Gideon's? The obvious answer? Or is it just a random one put out in hopes that it'll be overlooked?

A faerie steps into the room and all the blood drains from my face.

Her hair is snow white. Her skin pale as an opal. Bejeweled antlers above her head.

Sensing my panic, Emrys looks in the direction of my anxiety, and he freezes. Every muscle in my husband stiffens, terror racing and linking between us like an icy chain.

She turns, and although her eyes are black, her face is not that of the Unseelie Queen. I presume the black, sclera-less eyes are contacts, and the longer I examine her, the clearer it becomes that both the wig and antlers are fake. The look is artifice, a practical costume.

"It's not her," I say.

"Thank the fucking goddess for small mercies."

It's as if the goddess herself is laughing at us, asking; *Oh, what was that?*

A fake Seelie crown is placed on Fake Caethes's head and everything in my brain empties. The hands who place it there are Gideon's.

Gideon appears untouched, his thick black hair shiny and falling just over his brow in an endearing way. A gold crown sits atop his head, tilted at a jaunty angle that makes his smiling amber eyes seem filled with mirth. His jawline is still square, his cheekbones still proud. He's dressed in slacks and a nondescript button-up. Nothing left of the marks that the Unseelie Court left on him.

My heart burns, shame lighting me up like a torch. Insidious feelings writhe through me, sickly like smoke, coiling and choking. My emotional turmoil rampages and my all too perceptive husband tightens his hold on me.

"He's here," I whisper.

Emrys's eyes flicker. "I know."

Fake Caethes twirls in the cage of Gideon's arms, a thin glamour lines her, surely upholding her guise. She skims her hands up and down him, her laugh sultry. His smile is broad but inauthentic. He touches her and I'm horribly reminded of all my visions where he fucked the real Caethes.

I track Gideon. He remains with the Caethes impersonator while chatting to another halfling, this one with Cosette on a leash. She is distinctly less muddled than Vixen, and her fear is palpable.

Nearby, Maelona continues to flit about, and Gideon notices her despite the thin glamour. His eyes widen infinitesimally, but I see it. The moment he locks onto Lady Maelona his whole demeanor changes. Immediately, he discards the aloof air and he searches the room, panic livening his frame. I inhale sharply as his eyes skitter close to us and then come to a stop on me.

Amber meets silver and for a moment an unspoken conversation flows between us, big emotions and small betrayals, bladed words, and jaded looks. Everything comes to me in a rush, all the moments from the cabin to the town, to the court and the Roads, and then the last time I saw him in Caethes's clutches.

Shame. Shame lights my bones. Nostalgia, loss, denial, and a feeling I do not wish to name flushes through me.

Gideon whispers something to Fake Caethes, and she gleefully takes the arm of the halfling, keeping an increasingly panicked Cosette close. The halfling beams at Gideon's "generosity" and with a slight tilt of his head, he indicates a hallway, his eyes saying *alone*. He leaves.

I turn to Emrys but he watched the whole exchange without expression. "Go," he whispers. "We'll be close."

I don't comment on the lack of emotion in his voice, or the dam he has built up. I see him struggling for composure because there's too much thundering inside. My hand goes to his chest, over his heart, over his scar.

"I've made my choice."

He has the barest brush of a smile. "I know."

Quickly, I pull him down for a brief kiss, letting the sweetness soak between us. I let my lips linger on his; sugar and sadness, honey and hurt. His lips move slowly, as if trying to savor the taste of me, the feel of me.

"We knew it would come to this, even though we never spoke of it," Emrys whispers against my mouth. The soft words are like a dagger to my heart. "I trust you. Now go."

With that, he takes the first step for me, and retrieves Maelona, leaving me staring as he weaves through the crowd. For a moment I am stunned, unable to make my muscles work. Through the masses, I watch the depravity around me; the quiet violence and the bold viciousness, just as terrible in equal measure. These are the worst of the worst and I want to burn it all to the fucking ground.

Swallowing my anger, I ensure Emrys has pulled Maelona from her socializing, before steeling my shoulders and walking.

In slow motion, moving through molasses, Emrys's eyes never leave me, even when his hands pretend to play up and down Maelona's spine. Music floats up, distorted, and haunting. Feeling like I'm walking upside down, with my mind flipped the wrong way, I forge ahead.

The empty hallway is like a sharper reimagining of the Faerie Roads. Instead of bioluminescent mushrooms there are tallow candles, replacing the dangling roots are spiky rocks, and rather than rich dirt this is raw, reddish clay. Even so, the similarities disquiet me.

Just ahead, Gideon stands off to the side, arms crossed over his chest. I stop several paces shy of him, watching carefully.

"Hello Evelyn."

"Hello Gideon." My heart riots beneath my ribs.

"You seem to be doing well."

"I wouldn't say that."

"No?" He quirks a brow. "I'd say better than me. You seem to have a new play toy. Did you move on from Maelona already?"

Anger weaves into my tone. "You don't get to shame me. Not when you've moved on just the same."

He ignores the jab. "I just find it odd you're messing around with one of the Unseelie Queen's bodyguards. Tell me, is he the Revenant?"

My mouth clamps.

"I figured as much," he replies taking a few steps closer—I bristle. "He seemed to truly hate me when we were together. But it makes sense now, doesn't it?"

I don't reply.

"Come on, Evelyn, you're killing me here!"

"What do you want me to say?" I bite out.

"I don't know. That you're sorry for how things turned out? For leaving me or maybe for the chain of events that led us to this moment?"

"I am truly sorry things turned out the way they did."

Gideon seems to startle, not expecting my answer. "You really mean that."

"I said it, didn't I?"

"I just didn't think you would."

I laugh darkly. "Well, aren't we both full of surprises."

"Care to elaborate?"

"This—" I say, pointing to the false crown on his head. "I can hardly say I expected to see that on your head. Why do you even wear it?"

"Caethes's idea."

"Oh, so you actually listen to Caethes and not just fuck her? Noted."

His brows draw together, anger and surprise coloring his face. "How do you know about that?"

"That's what you're upset about?" I cackle. "For fuck's sake Gideon, you weren't discreet."

"Yes, we were."

"Clearly not enough."

There's a pause between us.

"Evelyn, I command you to tell me how you know about me and Caethes."

Betrayal scorches through me seconds before the command grips me. The ripping of the words from my throat is agony and I try to fight it, but the rending gets worse, spearing every nerve ending the longer I battle it.

"I had visions of it and Emrys caught you," I say on a gasp, the words like acid.

As soon as they're released, the burning dissipates, but fury and treachery are a conflagration in me. My hands turn to claws at my side and the lengths that I could go to decimate Gideon are near infinite.

He used a command against me. And he may have two more.

How could he!? How could he use a command against me spoken in confidence?

"How fucking *dare* you?" I screech, advancing on him. I shove him, and the force is euphoric against my rage. "You *fucking* asshole, you had *no* right!"

He stumbles back one step and shoves me in return, my shoulder absorbing the impact. My lips pull back over my teeth, a growl building in my throat.

"Oh, *I'm* the asshole?" Gideon returns, rage spiking off him. "You left me to get kidnapped by faeries! You're the one who turned into a total bitch the second you were reunited with your precious fucking sword."

"You threatened me and by extension, my queen. You should be grateful for my mercy. She wanted me to kill you."

"Such a shame your reunion was so short-lived."

Anguish lances my heart, knocking the breath from my lungs. My voice is low, dangerous. *"Shut up."*

"Did that one strike a nerve?"

"Why are you doing this? I was trying to save you. I was trying to bring you back."

He scoffs. "It sure looked like it when I was begging you to help me."

"What did you expect me to do? Jump up and challenge the whole fucking table? I was trying to throw away suspicion, you idiot! Do you know how much attention we would have drawn if I didn't act like I don't care?"

His anger falters.

"You didn't think! You didn't even try to see my perspective. Goddess, Gideon, you know faeries can't lie." I exhale sharply, trying to banish the anger that steams from my ears. We could never communicate. It was him lying and me keeping secrets. It was my stubbornness and his deceit. "What were you thinking?"

"I was thinking that Caethes comforted me when you left me. That she showed me her plans and offered my dad treatment if I agreed to be given to the Carnaval."

"Why? That doesn't make sense."

He lunges, pins me against the wall, and traps me—because stupid me is taken off guard by this stupid halfling.

"Because I'm the bait."

Half a dozen faeries converge on me and a needle pierces my neck, bringing with it the scent of seven times the lethal dose of nightshade and horrible memories of Jacob Dugal abducting me.

CHAPTER 33

The poison incapacitates me for an hour, long enough for Gideon and the Unseelie fae to bind me. Across from me, Emrys is similarly bound, victim to an equal dose of nightshade. His golden eyes take me in blearily, matching my own double vision. Nausea roils in my gut and I grit my teeth to keep the sickness at bay.

Maelona is nowhere to be seen.

Small mercies, I suppose.

His lies are breath. I should've known Gideon would betray me.

"Ryss," I croak, trying to stretch toward him but he's too far and the ropes holding me are too tight.

"I'm here, Vanna."

We're alone and still in the Winter Carnaval, the architecture a dead giveaway. Our arms, ankles and torsos are tied to cold, iron chairs. The room is chill, lent no light or heat from the doused torches on the wall, illuminated only by a few squat candles.

The poison is already waning, leaving with it an uneasy air. Anxiety prickles and my thoughts begin to despair, but I try to peer around and seek out with my internal alarm.

"Do you sense anyone else?" I ask.

"No, nothing beyond the main rooms."

He's right. I can feel the echo of others as far as the general areas—which confirms we are nearby, just in an empty suite. The Carnaval is continuing as if we haven't been drugged and abducted, but of course, that sort of thing is likely commonplace. They probably didn't bat an eye.

"Where's Mae?"

"She got away. The second we caught wind something was wrong, I told her to get backup and then everything went to shit."

"Good, I'm glad." I tilt my head, resting it on the back of the chair, sighing deeply. "This is all my fault."

"You can't take all the blame, love."

"Can't I?" I counter, lifting my head to stare at him. "I scorned Gideon, he thought I was leaving him to perish with Caethes, and I gave him the commands over me. If I hadn't done everything I did…I don't know, maybe Aneira would still be alive."

"Evelyn," Emrys says sharply. "Do not go down that hole. Aneira's death is *not* your fault."

"But if I weren't here—"

"No. You can take your part of the blame in hurting Gideon – that's yours, own it. But his decisions were all his own. He's a grown adult and he chose. That is the extent of your blame."

Gratitude suffuses me. He's not eradicating my fault, but he is easing it, cutting it into pieces that are easier to swallow. They still burn, but they do not lodge and kill. And Emrys sees it. All my faults and broken pieces, the worst sides of me, the monstrous aspects. And still, he loves me.

My heart swells, burning with golden warmth. That little thing has bloomed into a vibrant flower, sprawling its petals throughout my chest. It grows with abandon, and I feel it take me, I feel myself fall. I feel the first flickers of that emotion I want to name but not yet can. I feel the first pangs of what Lady Fate took from me.

Tears prick my eyes. I want to say the words, but I can't. But I let it show in my eyes. Letting it burn out the last dredges of nightshade.

"I choose you."

"I love you, too."

I close my eyes against the influx of emotions, tears eking out. He knows how I feel and is accepting what I can give him—as limited as it is. It would be a perfect moment if we weren't bound to iron chairs about to face certain death.

My internal alarm spikes. Both Emrys and I sit up straighter as Gideon and six faeries arrive—all of them Unseelie—carrying with them an aura of danger. Cariad goes around lighting torches until the room is bright with amber light. Gideon hands off his smoke and mirrors crown to the Fake Caethes and she holds it in her hands, still wearing the one Gideon put there earlier. I clench my teeth together and stare balefully at Gideon.

He used a command on me, he forced me to speak against my will. Hatred burns through me, like an ember striking tinder. Everything wild and foul rears its ugly head, and the monster within rejoices.

"I trusted you!"

"You shouldn't have," he retorts softly. "You know how I feel about the fae."

I have equal amounts of crippling fear and morbid curiosity for faeries.

"You said I was different."

I'm the cold-hearted bitch that has your heart.

"Not anymore."

I think my heart breaks. The reality that any softness, any warmth, anything between Gideon and I is well and truly shattered. Shredding and ripping every good memory between us, discoloring with dark, ominous venom. Black ichor striates every touch and stains every word exchanged. It poisons our past and there's no antidote.

"How could you do this?" I pause. "I thought we were…friends."

"Friends?" Gideon says in disbelief. "Friends do not threaten to cut out friends' tongues. Do you really think I'd count you as a friend after you dumped me, just to immediately make out with Maelona in front of me?"

Despite everything, Emrys quirks an amused brow. My face flames.

"You put me in harm's way with no regard for my safety. You are a selfish creature, Evelyn Vanora," Gideon spits, then turns to Emrys. Almost lazily he asks, "How many times have you fucked her now?"

Embarrassment courses through me but I can't do anything—although, I'd love nothing more than to punch Gideon in the face. He knows he's dealing with the Harbinger and the Revenant, but the power trip of having both at his mercy has gone to his head.

"Do you think she was thinking of me when you were inside her?" Gideon continues.

Emrys's quiet fury seethes off him in palpable waves. "I would caution you to watch what you say about my wife."

The words hit Gideon like a physical blow and he steps back. Shock plasters itself across his face before a sick gleam of delight settles over him.

"Oh, *husband*, this should be good." Gideon grins fiendishly. "Tegwyn, can you gag him?"

I watch while Tegwyn observes Emrys warily, truly seeing him for the first time. The evidence of our marriage has unmoored her, showing in her hesitation. Were they friends? Did she respect Emrys? Surely, she doesn't know him as the Revenant, but he is considered one of her comrades, right?

Tegwyn's iridescent fingers wrap a length of silk over my husband's mouth twice, effectively muting him.

Gideon waits, watching Emrys's eyes blaze before he turns to me, ensuring he has my attention.

"Does your wife know *you* were the one sent to kill her sister?"

I thought my heart broke before, but it's nothing compared to the shattering now. Horror and rage rip through me. It burns through every remaining granule of poison, turning my blood to pure fire.

"No..." Denial saturates my voice.

I meet Emrys's eyes, staring at the golden depths that desperately plead with me.

"It's true, ask him yourself. Ask him if he was sent to kill her. He can't lie."

Fear grips me as Gideon moves behind Emrys, placing a knife below his ear. "One-word answers, pretty boy." The *or else* is implied. "Go on, ask him, Evelyn."

My tongue moves mechanically. "Were you sent to kill Corvina?"

Gideon tugs down Emrys's gag and his face is a mask of devastation.

"Yes. Bu—" Emrys doesn't get the next word out before Gideon flicks the knife against his ear and gags him once again.

My heart cracks. I feel like a stone someone has taken a hammer to, breaking down the center, never to be put back together again.

I stare at Fake Caethes, wishing she was the real one so I could tear her goddess-damned antlers from her head. But the fake queen is giving me something else to focus on and from there I see the glamour rippling over her. Was she always wearing a glamour?

Gideon crosses to me, smiling smugly, and crouches before my bound feet.

"How does it feel to be betrayed like this? Maybe it amounts to a fraction of how you fucked me over."

I shake my head, not trusting my voice.

All this, but I don't understand why he hasn't revealed Emrys and I for the Revenant and Harbinger we are. Why has he kept it secret? Why did he never tell Caethes? It never slipped out post sex? It never came about before he was sent here? Is he protecting me? If so, why?

Gideon turns his head to Emrys. "Did she tell you about that? How I fucked her in the Roads and then she left me there?"

I burn. All my faults laid bare before Gideon, these fae, and my husband. Putting my dignity on the floor and letting them laugh at it. Painting me like a whore, my exploits being revealed in the worst of ways. I want to argue it, explain there was no overlap, that while I enjoy sex, I'm not bouncing around bed to bed. But that doesn't matter. What matters is how Gideon perceives and spins it. And he's winning.

"Gideon, stop."

"Why should I?"

"Please."

A feral look crosses his face and for a moment he is unrecognizable from the man that I'd shared a bottle with. The one I'd dragged from a cabin fire. He is nothing of that person any longer.

"Then beg. I seem to remember you liked that."

The jab hits home and I feel the scraps of my dignity fall off me like paper.

"Why are you doing this?"

Gideon leans forward. "Because you are a monster. Do you even care about anyone? Have you ever? Tell me the truth."

"Yes," I say thickly. "Of course, I have." I care about so many; the residents of Aberth, the members of my court. But a deeper care? That number is so few and so many of them are gone. Corvina and Aneira, both gone. Maelona and Emrys, both in danger. I care about Wisteria, Julia, Violante, and even to some degree Drysi.

"And somehow I still think you're lying." Gideon scoffs. "I can't believe I ever loved you. Did you ever love me? Can you even admit that to yourself?"

That unspoken word rises to the surface, the very thing I keep trying to deny. I've repressed it, happy to let it rot and die, but here it surges up into the light.

"I did. I did love you."

My heart hitches with the confession, breaking open, that thing for Emrys that has grown into a full bloom pushing out. The love I held for Gideon uncurling from that ball in the corner of my heart, squirming out and digging claws into my chest.

I can't bear to look at my husband.

Surprise passes over Gideon's face before disgust replaces it. "Well suffice to say the heart you held is no longer yours. I despise you. In your own words; whatever was between us is over."

I duck my head as my heart takes another blow, the jagged edges pulling apart.

Suddenly, Emrys laughs from beneath his gag. I'm confused, but then I feel something else snap in my chest and Lady Fate's binding give way.

CHAPTER 34

CENTURY TRAINING

The doors leading out to Century Training are due to open in ten minutes. Emrys and I stand side by side, not touching and painfully aware of the distance between us. Heavy on my hand is my new wedding ring, lightly glamoured unless the person knows it's there.

Everyone here knows that the moment Emrys and I leave here the mentors will be forced to hunt us down until we either die or reach the courts. In anticipation for this, Enydd, Urian, and Desmond have dressed in oversized shoes and heavy robes, allowing us every advantage. The other four have done distinctly the opposite.

The mentors bracket either side of the door like a wide aisle, Enydd and Osian on opposite sides and closest to the door. Beside Enydd is Urian, then Desmond. On the opposite, directly beside Osian is Una, then Cothi, and Reagan. It's a clear line of allegiances.

I flex my hands, stepping side to side in my black leathers. Emrys and I wear a matching set, a final gift from the goddess.

The countdown is internal. With five minutes left I begin to sweat, anxiety rolling off me in waves. We know we must escape and we have to do it quickly.

Good thing I have wings and they do not—aside from Enydd. Flight will be the difference between our life and death. Even so…I'm jittery and nauseous.

Finally, with the last minute counting down, the locks on the door begin unwinding.

"You have completed Century Training," Osian begins, the tone of his voice dark. "If you are deposited in your respective courts, you have successfully won favor, if you have not, you will be let loose beyond the northern Unseelie Court territory where your mentors and the Wild Hunt will track you down." Osian pauses to smile sinisterly. "I wish you all the very best."

With that, Osian steps towards me and faster than I can react, he takes his blade out and slashes my wings.

I scream, feeling the wounds dig deep. Not enough to sever, but enough to make them unusable. I stare at him in shock and then turn to Emrys, fear painted across his face. My wings were the difference. And now…

Desolation strikes me deep and tears pool in my eyes. We have to run as hard and fast as we can until my wings heal.

Heartbeats later, the double doors begin to creak open.

I turn to Emrys and take his hand in mine before pulling him in for a deep, passionate kiss. "I love you, husband."

Emrys smiles against my mouth, but it is a sad, final smile. "I love you, too, wife."

When we break apart, I see three shocked faces and one violently furious one. Osian's face turns maroon with rage and I flip him the middle finger.

"Get fucked, Osian. I hope you have a terrible rest of your life."

And with that, Emrys and I step through the open doorway and take off running.

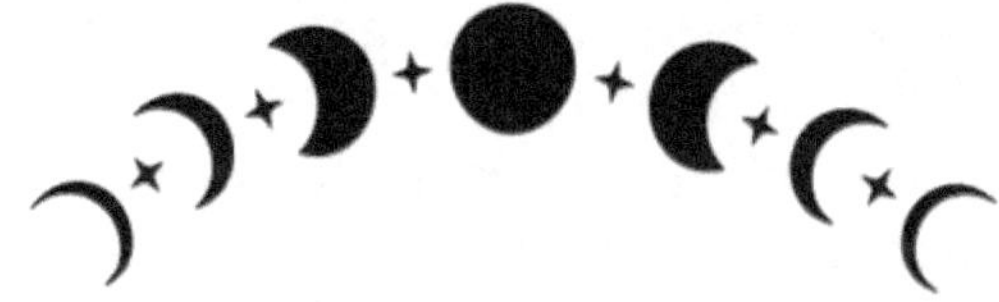

The night is punishingly cold even for the first of August. As we run, I try to deduce where we've been deposited, attempting to recognize the flora and fauna we pass. The air is scented with pine boughs and lake water. From the presence of midnight sun, it's clear we're in the northern hemisphere, from there I deduce from the growth around me that it's Russia or Canada.

Emrys and I sprint side by side, our swords holstered on our backs, keeping pace. My wings are heavy and useless as I grit my teeth against the pain, cursing as they leave a very clear blood trail.

Yet the mentors have not passed through the doorway, and I worry for what that spells. The mentors can hurt one another. Are Enydd, Urian, and Desmond, okay?

No sooner than I think it do I feel the presence of six of our mentors. I lock eyes with Emrys and he blanches, likely realizing the same thing I do. Panic spurs us on and we launch ourselves across the ground, heedless of roots and rock—we've been navigating the broken cathedral of Century Training for years, this is nothing. We pass a bear and it is too lazy to give chase. We startle rabbits and squirrels, birds launching from their nests as they pick up on the dooming vibrations. My wings are still ruined, bleeding profusely and sweat streams down my back.

I don't know exactly where we're going, just that it's south. The Wild Hunt territory stretches as far north as the arctic circle, and wherever we are it's warded against the Roads. The Unseelie Court is warded against the Light at its northern edge to its middle, while the Seelie Court is warded against them at the southernmost edge of its court to their center. It has always been this way and has served as an ideal prison or punishment for the fae.

The alarm indicating our mentors grows more frantic and soon enough their footsteps are far too close.

I look at Emrys. "We have to fight."

We stop in an upcoming clearing, spin around, and draw our blades.

Six of our mentors arrive in the clearing and I blanch when I notice Enydd missing. My heart hurts knowing that whatever she did, she staved off the chase for as long as she could. I'd like to believe that Desmond and Urian were reluctant to uphold the oath, but I know what an oath feels like when you try to act against it. It is crushing. Excruciating.

Urian and Desmond are at the furthest edges, away from the group, and it's clear they're here unwillingly.

"You little fucking cunt," Osian growls stepping from the center of the group. Blood paints his features and shows through the tears on his leather. Knife wounds cross his face and arms, and one of his eyes is gouged out. I smirk, knowing at least Enydd got in a few good marks before she went down.

"Better a cunt than a narcissist," I retort hotly.

Osian laughs. "It's a shame you turned out so devious. You could have stayed by my side. We would have had millennia together."

"I would quite literally rather die."

Osian's face screws up in rage. "So be it."

The mentors converge.

Emrys and I battle through instinct alone, feeling each other, sensing with our internal awareness, every facet of our training working in tandem. Everything from the blindfolded arrow shooting to the swordsmanship to defensive maneuvers. We attack with abandon, a new level revealed when fighting for our lives.

There are nicks and slices when we aren't quite fast enough, and each time a shot of adrenaline shoots through me. We've all managed to draw blood, but nothing so permanent has happened yet.

Reagan comes at us, and in a concerted strike I shove my sword through his chest while Emrys spins and lops of his head. It is quick and heartless, but with our dual maneuver one mentor is gone.

The battle continues, clashes of swords and knives, feet and hands dancing. Suddenly, I have an epiphany. Emrys and I have a massive advantage over the others. We have trained together every day for a century; we know how the other moves. They do not. None of them are partners, none of them understand how the other works. They are proficient yes, they have taught us everything they know, but our pairing cannot be learned without the years we were given.

As if we've become one organism, we battle against Cothi. Taking her out quicker than Reagan, each of us skewering her with our swords on either lobe of her lungs. We duck in opposite directions before pulling out our blades, missing a broadsword swing from Desmond. The attempt saddens me, but I understand it. He cannot act against the oath.

The smallest of our mentors is next. Her rose gold hair is splattered with blood and due to her slight size, she moves dangerously fast. She carries twin daggers with wicked blades, sharp and waving like a decorative athame; the tip serrated, promising damage on the way out. She fakes out a dive for Emrys, but she taught us that move, and I'm prepared when she dekes out to strike me instead. Instead of surprising me, I get her, slamming my sword through her jaw and up into her brain. I withdraw it and kick her corpse aside.

Emrys finishes off Desmond with a devastated apology. Desmond smiles in understanding before he's gone. Tears burn in my eyes and hatred for Osian grows. This is his fucking fault. If he wasn't possessed by an egotistical desire to manipulate everyone and everything around him to his wants, the mentors would never have been forced to hunt us down.

Only Urian and Osian are left.

Urian is on the waning side; a vicious sword blow has nearly severed his good arm and due to the blood loss, he's stumbling. I do not forget about him as I advance slowly.

"I am sorry," I say tearfully.

"I know," he replies sadly—in acceptance. "Be happy."

And then I plunge my sword into his chest with a sob.

Urian dies with a placid expression—at peace.

One left.

Renewed by my wrath, I seek out Osian, Emrys closely following. I intend to end Osian once and for all with my husband at my side.

Osian stands, poorly hiding his shock at the carnage Emrys and I have wrought. We advance menacingly, our swords and faces bloodied. Fatigue wars against the adrenaline permeating our blood but we hang onto that panic-inducing chemical for as long as it takes to end our final mentor.

"We can make it fast if you lay your arms down now," Emrys says roughly.

Osian cackles. "No, I don't think so."

Emrys shrugs. "Your funeral."

Twirling his sword, Osian grins. "No, I think it'll be yours, boy."

We attack. We are a flurry of gold and silver against Osian's slick black sword. The ground is soaked with blood and strewn with the bodies of our mentors. Fury strikes against the steel, sparks dancing. The sky is a violent pink against the midnight sun, bathed by the gore.

Osian strikes with a high blow and blocks with a dagger before kicking out and stumbling Emrys. He swings for Emrys's head, but I'm there to block it in time, going up against his strike with an attack, meeting him and shoving with all the force of my damaged wings. Emrys rights himself and dives for Osian, driving his blade in the direction of his chest, but he dodges it. Lunging away, Osian is forced back and I advance on him in a flurry of golden strikes.

He is waning, but we are not. We have something to live for, Osian does not. He has nothing and no one. I feel triumph rise, but I quell it, committed to not celebrating before the job is done.

Another blow falls and I dodge it, but I'm not fast enough when Osian swings with his dagger, and instead of my side like he intended, I lift my leg and take it in my thigh instead.

Sharp agony explodes through my leg, the puncture threatening to make my gorge rise. I shout in pain and Osian loses his grip on the blade, but it stays lodged in me.

Osian grasps Emrys's sword arm in an iron grip and Emrys rears back, delivering a wrath-fueled punch to Osian's face. The mentor staggers back but Emrys is forced to surrender his sword in the process.

Taking out the dagger strapped to his chest, my husband battles it out with Osian as I get my bearings. With my sword in hand, I advance once more. Prepared to finish this. This time, it is fear and hope and adrenaline that drives me, and with everything that I am, I drive my sword into Osian's chest while Emrys shoves his dagger between his vertebrae.

Osian falls, choking on blood, and then he is no more.

I stare at my husband in shock, looking around at all the death. The death that we brought. We killed all our mentors. The people who trained us, we bested. Shock is too minimal a word for what I feel. Something breaks in me, and I sob.

Falling against my husband, tears pouring down my face, I clutch him desperately, and pull his face down to mine, kissing him endlessly. I don't care that we're covered in blood, I just want him. I need him. Our lips move together, practiced after all these years, our tongues sliding against each other.

I pull away and rest my forehead against his, still crying.

"I love you so much," he rasps.

I sob. "I love you, too."

I grin, letting that triumph win.

But I'm premature as a signal of twenty-four almost-faeries rises within me.

My eyes widen just as Emrys's do and we pull apart, my husband taking up his lost sword and standing ready. Within minutes twenty-four faeries made of smoke come from the Wild Hunt and converge on us.

The battle goes on horrendously long and time loses its meaning. I am a machine, I am instinct. I am driven by the simple goal of keeping myself and my husband alive. Nothing else matters, nothing else exists. As one, Emrys and I take on the specters of the Hunt, only our goddess blessed swords working against their half-formed apparitions, our human or fae made blades doing nothing against their darkness.

The Wild Hunt can take substance on full moon nights and as a rule, Century Training always closes on a full moon in case their services are needed against failed Centurions. But never has it been accounted for the goddess to bless Centurions with blades.

I don't know how long we fight, but after a certain point it becomes clear we've brought down the Wild Hunt's forces to single digits. Bodies lay strewn over the blood-drenched ground, the grass completely crimson with it—spattered on trees and bushes, all over our faces and our clothes.

The battle ends without my conscious awareness of it, but suddenly there are no more opponents and Emrys and I stand, breaths heaving, arms trembling. Utterly spent. I drop my sword and it lands point down in the ground, inches from my fingers. Emrys does the same. It takes everything in me not to sag to the bloody earth.

"We did it," I rasp in disbelief. We did it and the entire time I had a dagger lodged in my thigh.

Emrys's golden eyes meet mine, hardly lucid. "We're alive."

I begin to laugh hysterically and rush my husband, wrapping him in my arms. I clutch him close, breathing in deeply, finding the scent of vetiver beneath the blood. We hold together, keeping the other from falling apart. So much death. So much destruction.

Suddenly, Emrys shoves me away, my natural resistance causing me to stumble. Frowning, I reach out to my husband, but he's staring at me in unending shock. Confused, I watch as his eyes lower to his chest.

Where a dagger sticks out.

Disbelief courses through me, not processing what I'm seeing. It doesn't hit me until I see Osian standing behind Emrys with a wicked smile on his face.

I scream as Emrys falls to the ground.

Without thinking I pick up Emrys's silver sword and drive the blade directly through the forefront of Osian's skull. He's pinned to the ground, half elevated by the sword that props him, his body arching.

I abandon our final mentor and rush to Emrys's side.

He's choking on blood, hands uselessly going to his chest, trying to stop the bleeding. I desperately try to do the same.

The worst fear I've ever experienced courses through my blood, turning my mind to nothing. I am a rabid animal, and I am driven by this faerie, and this one alone.

I gather my husband into my lap, cradling his face, the other hand staunching the flow of blood. It pumps freely, pouring out onto our leathers, draining away the heart I love so much.

"No, no, no, no, no, no, no," I cry like a mantra.

Emrys's hand weakly lifts to my cheek.

"I'm sorry, Vanna."

"*No*! No, you're not going anywhere! Do you hear me? You don't get to fucking leave me, not now!"

"I can't—I love you."

And then my husband is gone.

And I scream, ripping the most soul crushing sound from my body.

CHAPTER 35

POST CENTURY TRAINING

My keening heart is heard for miles, my shattered soul felt throughout time. I scream against the midnight sun and the pink sky and the red earth. I curse Century Training and Osian and every mentor. I rail against the Wild Hunt. I cuss out Lady Fate.

How dare she let a simple fae male take over an institution she created? How dare she let Osian become leader and brainwash the rest of the mentors for his personal, manipulative gain? How dare she let him take my husband from me?

I stare down at my husband, his golden skin paling beneath me, those golden eyes losing their light. We were supposed to be together. He was going to forsake the Unseelie Court for me. We were going to be forever.

I sob against his bloody chest, every breath bowing my back. My fingers grasp urgently, looking for any sign of life.

Maybe we would have had children, and maybe we would've been content to just be us. But now I'll never know, and I mourn these ruined dreams.

Suddenly, I steel my spine, refusing to give up.

No.

No, they can't take him.

She cannot have him.

Desmond's words come back to me.

Here, we're more sensitive to her whims and fluctuations, her moods are more palpable here. And then: *To a degree she knows everyone everywhere, she just has favorite toys and Centurions are near the top of the list.*

I scream up to the sky.

"YOU BRING HIM BACK! YOU BRING HIM BACK NOW!" My shriek is piercing to my ears, ripping my throat raw. *"YOU FUCKING BRING HIM BACK NOW!"*

There is silence, nothing but my words echoing in the pink night air.

"GODDESS, I KNOW YOU CAN FUCKING HEAR ME! I'M CALLING ON YOU LADY FATE TO BRING BACK EMRYS GORLASSAR. BRING BACK MY HUSBAND!"

"What is his life worth to you?"

I whirl at the melodic voice, and I'm met with the sight of a being more radiant than I could've ever imagined.

Lady Fate stands at the edge of the blood-soaked circle, her skin moonlight pale, and her hair as deep and lush as pomegranate seeds. Her face is carved marble, supple cheekbones, plush lips, a delicately sloped nose, with two different colored eyes—one sapphire blue and one emerald green.

She crosses the ground, the hem of her white gown dragging across the offal and gore, yet remaining pristine. She's tall and extremely slender, everything about her graceful and elegant. Lady Fate stops directly before us, looking down sadly at Emrys's deceased form, her long hair drifting like a curtain over her shoulder.

"He's worth everything," I manage finally, no longer paralyzed in the presence of divinity. "I will give you anything to bring him back as he was."

"Everything is quite broad, Evelyn Vanora."

"I don't care. I will pay it, just bring my husband back." I choke on the last word.

"Would you fall in love with another to bring him back?"

"Yes," I say, no hesitation. I don't care, as long as he is alive.

"Would you lose that love to bring him back?"

"Yes."

"Would you do all of that without your memories? Having him remember all your love and you recall none of it?"

I'm desperate so I say yes again.

"Would you do so even if your heart was locked from him?"

I tell her my answer again.

"Do you understand what you're asking for?"

"*Yes.*" I don't care. *Just bring him back, just bring him back, just bring him back.*

"If that is what you wish," the goddess says softly. "In exchange for your soulmate's life, you must fall in love with another and lose that love whether by death or betrayal, without your memories."

I reel from her words. "Soulmate?"

The goddess smiles. "Of course. You two are fated. I created you both myself, destined you for each other and completed the bond with a strand of my hair." She waves her hand and I see bold red thread tied around my littlest finger and Emrys's smallest one, his end graying. "There are so many bonds I created around your bloodlines. So many interconnected and apart."

"What?"

"It is not a worry for now. I just take great pleasure pulling the threads of families and seeing my meddling change the stars. Your love has made you the harbinger of this era."

I blink. "I'm a harbinger?"

"*The* Harbinger. Of many things, but the first in this cycle of soulmates." Lady Fate sighs. "Your bond will awaken once you reside in the same court." The goddess's lip curls in distaste. "Your fae magic is a stubborn barrier even my will cannot breach."

I stare uncomprehendingly. Soulmates exist and mine is dead in my lap.

"Sweet girl, did you never wonder why you shared gifts? You are unparalleled because you are fated mates with an unbreakable bond and the magic of witches in your blood."

I'm floored, but even through it all, all I can think of is getting Emrys back.

"Please, just bring him back. I want him back."

"Give me your hand." I do as commanded and the goddess slices open my palm with a nail. I do not flinch. "You will swear to me, the goddess Lady Fate, sister of the goddesses Lady Chaos and Lady Karma to uphold the bargain. In exchange for your soulmate and husband, Emrys Gorlassar's life, you will fall in love with another and lose them without any memories of this interaction or the past romance with your fated, do you swear?"

"I do."

"Then it is done."

"Not quite," says a new voice. It is just as musical as Lady Fate's.

I'm startled when the new voice takes my bleeding hand and presses it between hers. Vicious green eyes meet me, set in a face of creamy beauty, hair like spun gold glittering behind her.

"I hereby bind you to your oath to Lady Fate, but the parameters of the bargain must be completed within seven years or your soulmate's life will be forfeited." The new speaker grins maliciously. "I, Lady Chaos, decree it."

A shockwave of power blasts out from both goddesses, the two binding bargains taking effect immediately. Like starlight, it falls around us and bursts in me, taking memories, dissolving parts of my psyche as that very same star-fall sinks into my husband—my soulmate—and brings him back.

Lady Chaos vanishes, taking with her Osian's body, and Emrys's sword.

Emrys's eyes flood with light, the golden topaz bright with life and I sob in relief. He clutches his chest, feeling for the wound and finding a fully healed scar instead. Emrys stares at me in shock.

"Vanna, what did you do?" he rasps.

I let out a sob that is a mixture of a cry and a laugh. "I forced Lady Fate to bring you back."

"You did what?" he gasps. "How?"

"I made a trade."

"What was it?"

"Until she falls in love and loses another, her heart will be locked from you," the goddess intones from beside us. "She will not remember your romantic relationship and you will be bound from telling her."

Emrys startles and gazes at the goddess. His eyes are golden coins, whites showing round.

"Holy fuck," he breathes.

The goddess smiles sadly. "Unfortunately, a new addendum was added. She has seven years to complete the task or else this second life I gave you will be taken away." Something like sadness flitters across her face. "I am regretful about the last clause."

"Can you take it back?" he asks.

The goddess shakes her head. "It was bound in blood and sworn in word." Her eyes flicker to me. "Make your goodbyes, Revenant, she will forget all of this soon."

Emrys gathers me up without another word and plies me with kisses, as if trying to pour every ounce of his love into me, to replace it with the pieces that are fading from me.

"I love you so much, Vanna. So, so much. I love you, and I will do everything in my power for you to remember. I will do everything to get us back."

I cry, watching my soulmate's face haze beneath the tears. "I love you too, and I swear I will fulfil this bargain. I will fall in love with you again if I have to. You are my forever. Don't give up on me."

"I won't, you are my reason for living."

Memories begin to turn to ash and I lose my grip on reality. I kiss my husband once more and then I feel the shift. Everything between us fades, and I'm left staring into wicked and heavy-lidded eyes, wondering why Emrys Gorlassar is sitting so close to me.

And then nothing.

CHAPTER 36

I come back to reality, trapped in the Winter Carnaval, and bound to an iron chair. I stare across the space at Emrys, my husband, my *soulmate*. I stare at him with new eyes, every memory finally returning. The missing pieces of Century Training. Our wedding. The battle with the mentors and the Wild Hunt. The deal with Lady Fate and the interruption of Lady Chaos. Everything comes back to me in a tidal wave, bringing with it the intense emotion and love that was trapped by the goddesses' lock.

If my hands weren't tied, they'd go to my chest, to calm my panicked heart. That little thing—that blooming flower, that transformed winged thing—that was growing in my heart bursts from it and encompasses me in all the love that I have ever held for Emrys. The years in Century Training when he hated me for Osian's deception, those years that I was hopelessly in love with him, begging for him to see reason.

"Ryss," I breathe, disbelieving.

"You remember." Tears and hope spill from his eyes.

"I do," I whisper back, tears slipping down my cheeks as well.

"What the fuck is going on here?" Gideon says, confusion marring his features.

I pick up on two presences moving rapidly toward us when shouts go up. I grin when I recognize the faerie and witch signatures.

Maelona and Wisteria burst into the room, the Lady carving through the Unseelies with ease, Wisteria rushing over to us with a very sharp and serrated blade. She begins to saw through my bindings, working first on my wrists. The look I give her is beyond grateful.

"You have no idea how happy I am to see you, Witch."

I realize Maelona left in the middle of night to retrieve Wisteria. How she managed to hide her in or near the Carnaval is a mystery to me, though.

Wisteria gives me a beaming grin. "I'm sure you are, Faerie. But I'm starting to believe all your plans are shit."

I laugh. "Yeah, me too."

When she gets through one set of ropes, I pull my arm free and take the knife from her. "Go help Mae, I'll take care of the rest."

I make quick work of the ropes and within a minute I'm free of them all. I spring across the space, the sound of

Maelona's battle continuing behind us, and saw against Emrys's bindings. He's freed within seconds, and with the drug having burnt out of our systems, we are unstoppable.

My mind is so tangled, coming to terms with the fact that my husband—my soulmate—is mine once again. That all my memories have returned, but also that he is the one behind my sister's death. But I cannot think of that now, so I shove it into the deepest corner of my mind, into a drawer and lock it away for later.

Without consulting anyone else, I spring for Fake Caethes, plucking up the crown Gideon had placed on her head, and feel the magic thrum through my blood. The glamour only came to be the second the crown was plopped upon her. It was not to hold the guise together; it was to shield the truth of the real Seelie Queen crown. Because the crown must be seen, it must be in plain sight. So, why not place a true crown on a false queen's head?

"Wisteria!" I call loudly. When she looks up, I toss her the crown. "Take this and go! We'll follow you soon, just get the fuck out of here. Take the magic that lets you travel the Roads and get this to the court!"

She doesn't question me. I feel her mind pry into me, finding my magic, as if dipping a hand inside to quickly learn it. The sensation is odd, but because this isn't an outward gift, she must reach in to copy it and feel it. Once she senses the structure of my ability, she pulls back and I'm unsettled to see my silvery eyes reflected back at me.

"Go!" I command.

Wisteria takes off.

I turn to the havoc that Maelona and Emrys are wreaking and find Unseelie bodies on the floor. Tegwyn and Cariad are nowhere to be seen, presumably fleeing as per the nature of the former faerie. I look up just in time to see Emrys drop Gideon with a hilt blow to the head.

"We need to get out of here before they figure out what's really going on," I tell them, staring at Gideon's limp body. "Leave him, we have someone else to save."

The three of us leave the suite and find ourselves down a hallway. We make our way closer to the sound of voices and find ourselves in one of the mingling areas, recognizing the hallways the human servant pointed out.

Inconspicuously, we turn down the one with cages and find Caspian's cell quickly. The halfling is sitting on his pallet, dressed in the flimsy trousers he wore when we "purchased" him. He cocks a midnight brow.

"We're getting you the fuck out of here," I announce, and with a heavy blow of Emrys's dagger, my husband breaks the lock.

It falls to the dirt floor and Caspian stares at it uncomprehendingly. "How?"

"I'll explain later, let's just go," I tell him.

Guilt crushes me as I ignore the other cells, but almost every single one of them is empty—their residents currently rented.

The three of us usher Caspian down the hall, praying that no one heard the lock or that there was an invisible security system we activated. Everyone is drunk or high, so Caspian huddled between us draws no attention. We weave through the throng and find ourselves in the last hallway. At the end of it I can see Carrick's back, and with a wordless glance from Emrys I take his proffered blade and step forward.

I've killed a faerie before of Carrick's type. His skin is as hard as stone, but there's a juncture right below the ear that is softer, and if you plunge a blade in at the right angle you can reach the brain.

I leap up, legs straddling Carrick's shoulders from behind, and yank his head to side before doing just that. The knife slides in easily, and Carrick drops to the floor, deceased before even a sound of surprise exits him. A couple girls being brought in by a human man scream at my violence, but rather than attack, they huddle in a corner fearfully.

Caspian stares at me speechlessly and Emrys grins fiendishly—pride shining.

"Goddess, I fucking love her."

We jump on the first lift, and with brute strength we yank it to the surface, the wood groaning concerningly. At the top of the giant's fist tunnel, we run.

The four of us make it to the last exit and we begin realm hopping, the sight of Century Training and the massacre we'd caused makes me to falter. Can there be another Century Training if there are no mentors to run it? Emrys and I never told anyone about the mentor's deaths.

No.

That's not entirely true, I reflect as we pass through the city pocket realm. *Somehow Gideon knew.*

His notes…

He was singled out by six and he was one, count down from ten and they were done. None stood before him, but the corpses he slew, flaunting the dangers of which he can do.

It had taken us ten minutes to kill the six mentors—not counting Osian's comeback. He knew about the battle with the Wild Hunt as well. Emrys must have told him, but how?

A century of training eclipsed the lives of two fae, one of gold, one of silver. It was a fateful night when the two warriors ceremoniously concluded their arduous training and were ambushed. With a contingency of thirty against two, Silver and Gold threatened to be swallowed whole. Equipped with dagger and sword, the ground was soon soaked with blood.

We skip through the realms feeling the earth become less and less solid beneath us; Century Training, the city, the manor, the island, the wasteland, and then the mountain. The last exit glows, leading us to the Roads. My heart pounds in my chest. We're so close.

Did Wisteria make it back? I didn't sense her signature through any of the realms so she must have. Internally, I pray she did. I couldn't forgive myself if she didn't.

Finally, we step onto the Roads and a net of safety cascades over me. We made it. We infiltrated the Winter Carnaval and took one of their precious commodities with us.

Our Carnaval tattoos also disappear.

Caspian gazes about the Roads with wonder and I watch as the realization dawns on him. He smiles as he figures out he's free. And then he cries.

Feeling a surge of comforting instinct, I wrap him in my arms. "You're safe now, we have you." He sobs into my chest and wraps his scarred and tattooed arms around me. I stroke his hair and hold him for as long as he needs.

He pulls away seconds later and steels his spine, rubbing all traces of the tears from his face. With gentle prodding we guide him along and carefully, selecting a Road that will lead to one of the Arcana Society outposts.

The four of us come out to a stretch of woods, a black, iron fence a hundred feet from us. I can feel the wards securing the haven from here. But the society is there, within reach and Caspian is almost home.

At the edge of the forest, Caspian turns. "Is it true you're the *Ceidwad Cudd*?"

I let a small smile spread across my face. "It is."

"But that's not all you are, is it?"

That smile twists into a smirk. "No, it's not."

Caspian's eyes light with surprise at the fact I'm even admitting it. "And him?"

Emrys matches my smile. "We're equals. Let's leave it at that."

"Your secret is safe with me." Caspian opens his mouth, then closes it. "If you don't know your heritage…I'll be happy to help you discover your witch ancestry. We have Lockwood genealogy records stretching back centuries."

Emrys smiles, a genuine one full of warmth that shows off his slightly pointed canines. "I'll take you up on that offer one day."

Caspian nods and then goes for the gate, pausing. "What should I tell them?"

I shrug. "Tell them exactly what happened, but perhaps don't tell them by name."

Caspian heads to the gate and rings the bell, his scarred back glowing in the moonlight. Minutes later a figure is sprinting across the grounds, and a boy, hardly a year older than Caspian and looking alarmingly identical, rushes through the gates, wrapping Caspian in a chest crushing embrace.

It's clear as day that this tattooed and dark haired halfling is Caspian's brother. The brother cups Caspian's cheeks and looks him in the eyes. I can read his lips, him asking if he's okay, and I can see Caspian replying he's alive. The brother captures him up again and holds him, dragging him through the gates as tears pour down both their faces.

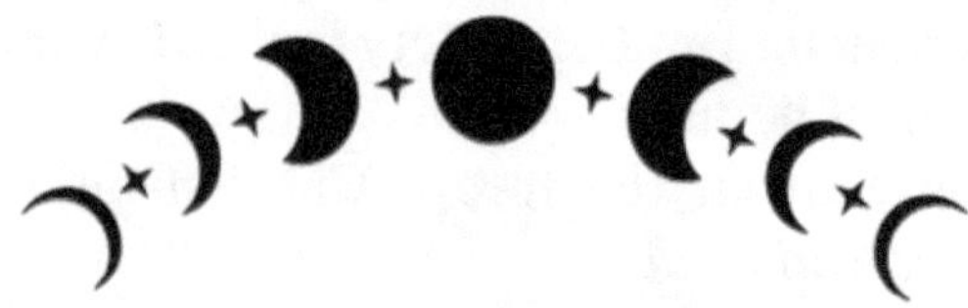

Back at the Seelie Court we enter the throne room and find Wisteria standing nervously, holding Aneira's crown between her hands. With the crown returned to the court the air feels steadier, the earth not subjected to the frequent quakes that have been rocking it for days.

She breathes a sigh of relief as the three of us enter. Wisteria crosses the space, her coppery curls bouncing, and she practically tosses the crown into my hands.

"That was the worst experience of my life. Do you know how close I was to getting squished by that rock faerie? I mean honestly, if I hadn't stolen his magic temporarily, I would have been *fucked*."

"I'm sorry. If it makes you feel any better, I killed him."

She's silent for a moment, then huffs. "It does actually, thank you."

I laugh but sober quicky. I'm holding the Seelie Court crown in my hands. Between my fingers is the very thing that lets the monarchy pass to the new ruler. All the magic in the realm controlled by this very object.

Breathing deeply, I find Maelona, anticipation rolling off her in palpable waves.

"Are you ready?" I ask carefully.

Maelona nods shakily. "I am."

"Then kneel."

Maelona does as commanded and I approach her. Wisteria and Emrys look on in silence. Anticipation makes the Lady's hair transform into a riot of iridescent color, every emotion flooding through her. I hold the crown above her head.

"I, Lady Evelyn Corianne Vanora of the Light Court, herby crown you, Lady Maelona Eidolon, in a private ceremony as Queen of the Seelie Court."

Then I place the crown on Maelona's head.

I draw in breath, waiting for the transformation.

Nothing happens.

We wait a breath more, all of us holding our lungs.

But still nothing happens.

Maelona rises and fury skims every inch of her body. She tears the crown from her head and glares at it with wrath.

It should have worked. The realm settled. So, why didn't the crown change for her? It didn't change for me either, which means Maelona's earlier anxieties were for naught because I am not heir apparent. But evidently, neither is she.

"It must be one of the replicas! All that for nothing!" Maelona shouts and tosses the crown across the room. It tumbles and spins, the metallic ting of the spires alarmingly loud. It stops at the edge of the dais that holds the empty Seelie Court throne, pitched on its side. Mocking. "We've failed!"

Lady Maelona sinks to the ground in her beautiful bronze dress and black diamond corset, and gives up.

"No, that can't be it," Emrys says, frowning. "There must be something we're missing. Is there an official ceremony we have to perform?"

Maelona shoots to her feet and stalks to the crown. "Here! You figure it out!" And then she flings the crown at Emrys.

Emrys instinctively catches the crown and inhales sharply.

It transforms in his hands.

The fleur-de-lis melt away, the rubies morph into black diamonds. The gold stretches and grows, twining with black iron into two dragonesque horns like those Aneira once possessed. Gilded branches wrap the base, and vicious-looking flowers wind through it. A crescent moon marks the very center before it comes up into two large horns.

I stare at my husband, all the pieces coming together. Taking in the features I overlooked. And in the stunned silence I whisper:

"You're Aneira's son."

My soulmate meets my eyes with abject horror. "I am."

CHAPTER 37

Aneira never claimed a successor. All these years, all this time, there has never been an heir apparent. All this time Maelona thought she was destined for the crown, anxious about the guilt and desire for it at the expense of the female who took her in. All of it was for naught because Emrys is Aneira's closest blood relative—her *son*.

It makes sense now. The hatred he had for my queen. The dark glares. The jabs. It was all because she abandoned him, handing him off to Caethes like he was an inconvenience better pawned. *Fuck*, it all makes sense. How did I not see it?

They have—they had—the same teeth, the same mouth, her jawline was just as severe as his. *How* did I never see it?

I suddenly recall the conversation Maelona and I had weeks ago about the crown's succession over the rim of a spiked teacup.

If Aneira had a child it would go to them, but as she doesn't become intimate with men, she never had children, so it would likely go to a distant cousin.

And Maelona's correction.

That's not entirely true, she did try a man once just to see what the fuss is about.

Once. Once was all it had taken for her to become pregnant with Emrys.

And then I remember Emrys telling me his mother was mended back to health by a witch after her wings were severed.

I cup a hand over my mouth, realizations flooding over me. Aneira lost her wings. Aneira is Emrys's mother. Emrys is half witch. Emrys was sent to kill Corvina. *Aneira is Emrys's mother.* Emrys is my *soulmate.* My soulmate killed my sister.

My entire world is thrown to the stars, leaving me to float through space, untethered. My head spins and I take a step, and place my hand on a golden column to steady myself.

We're all looking at Emrys, painted in similar shades of shock. Emrys looks horrified, staring at the crown that just finished growing in his hands.

"*What the fuck,*" Wisteria breathes, finally breaking the silence.

I stare at the new King of the Seelie Court. This doesn't make sense. Aside from Emrys being Aneira's son, how was she so unprepared that she never named an heir? That's never been her. The former queen always had plans, she was always organized, never one to leave something this important to chance.

Then it hits me.

There *was* an heir.

"It was Corvina," I whisper beneath my hand. Everyone's eyes snap to me. Tears leak over my fingers. "Corvina was her heir."

Understanding dawns on Maelona's face, the blow sitting her on the floor.

It would have made sense. Corvina as queen and me—the Harbinger—as her protector. It would have been perfect. The gentle, kind-hearted, generous Corvina ruling; with brash, unlikable, vicious, Evelyn, as her guardian. It would have been the ideal arrangement. Each of her daughters given a blessing of importance. Yet insidious thoughts seep in when I question about her son.

Corvina's death threatens to swallow me whole and I stare at her murderer—my husband, my soulmate, my king. I'm suffocating, drowning in the sensation, feeling the waves close over my head. It decimates me.

"I need to speak to my husband alone for a moment."

Maelona doesn't question me, she simply strides over to Wisteria. The Lady takes the witch's arm and steers her from the throne room. Through the deluge of my pain, Wisteria whispers, "Is she going to be queen now?"

They leave us before the throne—his throne. He stands and stares, pained and sore. There are words in his eyes that he has not yet said. He thinks he's lost me as soon as he got me back.

Emrys casts a King's Glamour over us, hiding us from all perception. We are invisible, silent even if we scream. He stretches it to form barriers against all the entrances and exits as impenetrable as diamond or iron. We are untouchable.

I don't even know where to start.

"How long have you known?"

Hurt flickers across Emrys's face as he glances down. "Always."

Astonishment flashes through me. All this time. "And you never thought to tell me?"

"I could not." Ah, so convenient, these oaths.

"So, you knew when you touched that crown there was a chance it would accept you."

"I didn't think about that when I caught it."

"What *were* you thinking, then?"

"I was thinking an object was flying at me and I needed to catch it. That we shouldn't throw away the crown because it didn't accept Maelona. I knew as well as you did that this was the right one. You felt it when we returned to the court, just as I did. I never imagined that Aneira wouldn't have a named heir."

I cannot deny his words.

"And Corvina?"

"I didn't kill her."

Relief, like poison scours through me. It is an acidic balm on my soul, scraping away the walls I had begun to build in my heart. The heart in question hammers against my ribcage, needing my husband.

"But you were sent to."

He nods. "We fought and she was a force to be reckoned with. She knew there was someone in the territory interrogating and killing Unseelies and when she saw me, she put it together. She didn't give me a chance to explain and instead started her own interrogation.

"She was demanding to know what I knew of the Harbinger, where I could find—well you—and she only stopped when I said I was looking for *her,* too. It was my use of 'her' that made her pause." He shakes his head, a sad smile drawing across his face. "She looked so much like you Vanna, and for a breath when I saw her, I thought she *was* you, that maybe you dyed your hair. But my heart knew it wasn't."

I'm silent, waiting for him to continue, not trusting my own voice.

"She said *'you know who she is?'* and I told her I knew the Harbinger was her sister." He chuckles. "Your sister was smart, love. She figured out immediately who *I* was and I suppose being around her, so close to someone who is a part of you, I lowered my defenses and she…she knew I was in love with you. We agreed to work together. Evidently her and Maelona never spoke of me because she had no idea we'd also teamed up and were searching for you."

"Then how did she die?" my voice breaks.

This time guilt flashes across my husband's face. "It was my fault. We were—" he mulls a word over in his mouth—"torturing a faerie for information, we pulled out their teeth and nails, burned them with iron. They didn't know where the Harbinger was but they were stalking a human girl, which I realize was probably you. It was only a few kilometers from your cabin."

I recall the exact faerie he's talking about. Jagged iridescent wings.

"After we'd killed them, Ransom and Lamia with her beast came upon us." He swallows and looks away. My anxiety ratchets. "They thought Corvina was the one going around killing Unseelies and she wouldn't let me tell them otherwise. She was determined to keep the suspicion off me."

I remember the faeries. The lilac-haired and cloven-hooved Lamia. The sickly pale, once-Seelie, Ransom. The hairless beast. They'd killed Callahan. And I'd killed them.

"So, she attacked me."

My eyes close. I don't need to hear the rest to know what happened but I do anyway. Hearing the post-mortem names is like a sick sense of irony. My sister's murderers are already dead, avenged in the wrong name.

I feel empty.

"They were on her in an instant and I could do nothing, Vanna. Lamia sicced her fae beast on her. It chased her and before she could get to an inbetween it caught her and they injected her with faebane."

Faebane. My heart stutters. A rare and potent poison that blocks all fae magic in our blood from being accessed. Everything from casting glamours to accessing the Roads and our increased healing abilities, as well as conciousness. It's a terrible concoction, one that took Emrys and I five years to become immune to. Ordinarily it takes days for a single dose to burn from a person's system, but more could be weeks.

Long enough for Corvina to stumble upon the cabin and promptly die at my feet.

"Ransom thought I was in danger and summoned Arawn. I didn't even have a chance to fight them before I was brought to Caethes. I think that's when she began to be suspicious of me.

"I'm so sorry. So deeply sorry, Vanna. I tried to find her. I swear I did. But Caethes kept such a short leash on me after that. I didn't know what to do and I knew time was running out—" he catches himself and cuts off the next words.

This revives me.

"Because Lady Chaos put a time limit on the bargain," I finish the sentence he refuses to, stepping forward. "Because you were going to die on the last day of this July if I did not fulfil the requirements."

Emrys looks away. "Yes."

I step forward again. Trying to compartmentalize my emotions, everything I'm feeling and thinking. I list what I'm sure about and begin speaking.

"For your part in Corvina's death, I forgive you."

Emrys's shoulders drop. He turns to face me and a tear slips from his eye. I approach him and softly cup his cheek, wiping away the salt track. He hitches a breath, letting go of the terror of losing me.

"I am not angry you kept your parentage a secret. I am just sad that I did not know Aneira as well as I thought I did." The grief eases a little as I explain.

"I'm sorry, Vanna. I know you loved her."

"I did. And you knew I had to love and lose for the bargain. You had to hope for it, and dread it simultaneously."

"Yes, that's what you traded for my life."

"I'm sorry."

"Don't be." He twists the crown in his hands, wanting to touch me yet not sure if he can. If he should. "In the end you chose me." He pauses. "Unless I misunderstand and you do not choose me."

I put a hand to his chest and slowly but surely, I push him, backwards, steadily up the dais steps. I punctuate each step with my words. "I choose you, Emrys Gorlassar, the Revenant, my king, my husband." I pause on the final stair. "My soulmate."

Emrys startles, golden eyes wide. "Soulmate?"

Slowly, I slide my hands up his chest. "Before she brought you back, Lady Fate told me she had destined us for each other, bonding us with her red thread." I bite my lip, holding his eyes. "We are fated mates, Emrys. Soulmates, mates, whatever word you want to call us—we are meant to be. I am meant for no one else, but you."

A gasp catches in his throat. I keep one hand on his chest, the other going to my own.

"I love you," I tell him without hesitation. My voice is ardent and unflinching with commitment. "You are my reason for living. Everything I am, everything I want to be, everything I ever will be, is yours. You are the other half of my heart, my soul, my very essence. And I am so desperately sorry that the price we paid to get here was so heavy."

"I'm not," he says with adoration, brushing a lock of silver white hair behind my pointed ear. "Because I was able to watch you begin to fall in love with me all over again. I was too stubborn to see it the first time and I am so honored that I was worthy of being someone you fell for twice." Emrys's eyes water as he takes me in. "I love you, too."

And then his mouth is on mine.

CHAPTER 38

The crown dangles from Emrys's hand as he wraps his arms around me, crushing my lips with his. I open my mouth on a moan, letting his tongue claim me, learning every shape of me. Our mouths dance together in perfect harmony, perfect rhythm. Perfection incarnate.

Wordlessly, I pull the hem of his shirt from his waistband. Pushing it off his shoulders, I let my hands coast over the firm lines of his body, skating my palms over his muscles, his nipples, the scar. Dipping lower, I free the buttons on his pants just as he takes one hand into the open back of my shirt and tears it off me.

I gasp as cool air encounters my breasts, the mixture of the chill and arousal has them hardened to tightened points. Emrys's mouth wastes no time slipping down my jaw, my throat, lower to take a nipple into his mouth. He sucks and bites, flicking his tongue against it causing me to arch into his touch. Liquid blooms at the apex of my thighs. Meanwhile, that dastardly and talented hand slips the laces from my pants.

As impressed as I am by his one-handed maneuvers, I reach down. Sliding my fingers against his muscled forearm, I briefly trace his veins before meeting his hand on the crown. I pluck the newly transformed crown from his grasp and place it atop his head.

He smiles against my breast. "Thank you," he murmurs, the vibrations sending tingles between my legs. "I didn't know what to do with that yet."

In a teasing voice I announce, "I, Evelyn Corianne Vanora, of the Light Court, crown you, Emrys Gorlassar, as King of the Seelie Court in an intimate ceremony."

He chuckles. "We'll have to discuss last names later."

"Names?"

"Ours."

"Later," I say on a smile.

I clutch him as he does something absolutely fantastic with his tongue, applying suction and a light scrape of his sharpened canines. Goddess, I could come from that alone.

I return my efforts to his pants while he—once again two-handed—yanks the laces from my leathers. He's pushing them down my hips, my thighs, skimming his fingers against my skin, sending electricity through my knees. He helps me out of my boots and socks and pants, tossing them across the dais.

He stands once again. I've managed to get his three buttons undone and eagerly shove down his leather pants, his cock freeing from the constraints while he groans. I sink to my knees and remove his clothing as he'd done for me, but instead of rising as he had done, I stay where I am and take his dick in my hand.

"*Fuck*, Evelyn."

My fingers skim the proud length of him, caressing the veins that throb against his silky flesh. The steady pulse looks nearly painful. Wrapping a hand at the base of his cock, I look up at him and take him in my mouth.

Emrys's moan could be heard for eons if not for his King's Glamour.

It's the first time I see him fully crowned as the new king. While he looks splendid in Unseelie silver, he was meant for Seelie gold. The horns reach high above him, a direct nod to the queen, leaving no question to his parentage.

He may be our new king, but he's all mine. And I'm kneeling before his throne, giving him the reverence he deserves.

I bob my head up and down his shaft, pulling him out nearly entirely and swirl my tongue over the head of him. A salty pearl of arousal beads from the tip and my eyes do not leave him as I lick it away. His cock jumps and I return him back to my warm, wet heat. I take him as far back as I can manage, suppressing my gag reflex, compensating with my hand. I pump him in tandem, my free hand going to his firm backside, nails digging into the cheek.

One of his beautiful beringed hands go to the nape of my neck, wrapping my hair around his fist while he gazes down at me like I am his world. But I look back up at him like he is my sun. Then I watch as he takes his crown and places it on my head. It feels heavy but right, just like he does in my mouth.

"It looks so good on you, wife. Almost as good as your mouth around my cock."

I take him deeper, challenging the limits of my subpar gag reflex. A reward for such high praises. Tears prick at my eyes, but I continue taking him. The hand on his ass traces the seam of his backside, prompting a thrill through both of us.

"Goddess, Vanna. You feel so good. Look how well you take me."

I feel his cock tighten and flex, and I know he's close. I keep up my ministrations and suddenly he groans, pulling my hair as he comes. He pulses across my tongue and I swallow his release, letting it slide down my throat before I lick the last drops of cum from the small slit.

Before I have a chance to do anything else, Emrys draws me up, and with firm, direct hands he pushes me slowly. He seats me, naked, on the Seelie Court throne, eyes watching me hotly as he sinks between my knees and parts my thighs.

There, wearing the Seelie Court's crown, sprawled on the Seelie Court throne, I spread my legs while the king kneels between them. Before his own throne.

The first plunge of his tongue is passion, plundering me and laving me with love and desire and owning. My hands thrust into his hair, shoving him against my core as I buck my hips on a thready moan. His arms curl beneath my thighs to drape them over his shoulders, splaying me out as much as the throne allows. His hands are on my ass, kneading to bruising, but it is exquisite. He growls against my sex and then drags that expert tongue up through the very center of me and focuses his attentions on my clit.

Emrys has always been good at eating pussy, but there's something so feral about him in this moment. The possessiveness has me so wet and aching. It's a claiming and a devouring. A husband claiming his wife. A king claiming his queen. A soulmate claiming his other half.

His tongue flicks perfectly against that bundle of nerves, his mouth greedy on me as he suckles my clit into his mouth. I moan shrilly as my orgasm threatens to take me already. It builds low in my belly, coiling outward, reaching my toes. It tingles in my breasts and I reach down to tweak a nipple, the sensation heightening.

"That's right love, touch yourself. Get you where we want you," Emrys whispers on my clit. "Such a good girl."

He returns his tongue to that nub he so loves and I come hard. My orgasm slams into me with blinding force and I shriek as I thrust against his mouth. He eases me through the waves as I see stars, the pleasure incandescent. I ride the high of the climax, feeling myself turn languid and loose on the Light's seat of power.

Emrys just tongue-fucked me on the Seelie Court's throne while wearing his crown.

Suddenly, I'm being lifted from the throne and Emrys wraps my legs around his waist. I tighten my hold on him, feeling him hard again already. I gasp and wrap my arms around him, mouth meeting his. We melt into a waltz of kissing, tasting each other's essences on the other's tongue, lips tasting of salt and sweet.

He turns us around and seats himself on the throne. He repositions my legs and his intentions are clear. I pull back from the kiss and meet his mischievous, lust-dazed eyes.

"Ride me on my throne, wife. Wear my crown and fuck me. Claim this court as our own." He fists his hand in my hair, sinking his teeth against my throat. "We'll turn this world into ours."

It's so reminiscent of what he said so many weeks ago.

We could join forces, we could destroy and remake this world if we wanted to.

In answer, I sink down onto his cock, impaling myself to the hilt. I throw my head back in pleasure and begin riding him. My hips roll as I rise up and down on him, the hand not in my hair coasting over my hips, ribs, breasts. His mouth drops to pull a nipple into his mouth, nipping it and suckling at it, coaxing out legions more pleasure as I grind my clit against him.

Emrys clutches me to him as I feel him draw close to another orgasm. I speed up my pace to punishing, my greedy clit so close to giving me what I want, what I need. I fuck my husband harder, his teeth scraping against my nipple, his hand pulling my hair. The combination has me coming, my inner walls contracting around him, pumping him for his release. I scream my pleasure and he comes at the tail end of my orgasm. His groan into the juncture of my throat shatters me further as I feel his warm release fill me.

He has no words but he captures my mouth in a savage kiss, possessively holding me astride him. The kiss slows into something gentle and I meet him for every stroke of his tongue and every press of his lips.

"I love you," he murmurs against my mouth.

"I love you, too."

We disentangle and find ourselves lounging at the foot of the throne, sprawled in each other's arms, tracing meandering shapes on skin and imprinting kisses on tantalizing flesh.

"Ryss," I start, my words turning up in a question, "do you *want* to be king?"

Emrys sighs, pulling me closer and dropping a kiss to my shoulder. "I'm a warrior. I've always known I was a warrior. It's what I trained to be for my entire life. I don't know how to be a ruler, but I'm not sure that means I shouldn't."

I place a kiss on his chest. "Whatever you choose, I stand by you."

For a moment there is silence.

"If you decide not to accept this, who would you abdicate for?" I inquire gently.

"Maelona. But I feel oddly territorial about it now. I truly don't know if I'll abdicate at all."

I smile softly. "Territorial for everyone but your wife."

His tongue plays with the inside of his cheek while he observes me wearing his crown. "I'm incredibly territorial about you, but I will share it all with you. Whatever is mine is yours."

"And all that is mine, we share."

Emrys chuckles and kisses me ardently. His hand cups my cheek and he gazes down at me. "I think I want to do it. I think I want to be king."

"Then I suppose we have a coronation to plan."

Despite the immortal long lives of the fae, we are known for being notoriously impulsive. Faeries like to do things quickly and heedlessly, to hell with the consequences. We are often driven by passions and wants and desires. The coronation will be the same.

"I suppose we need to fit you for a crown then," Emrys tells me idly.

"What?" I ask stiffening in surprise. "No, wouldn't I just be a consort?"

Emrys pulls me over him so I'm looking down on him. His hands stroke my thighs, his face open and earnest. "You are my wife. You are my equal. And I want you to be my queen."

I smile, glowing from the inside out and still wearing Emrys's flowered and horned crown. "Then I'll be your queen."

"In that case, let us consummate this decision." Emrys rolls so I'm beneath him. "And in the meantime, perhaps we could think of the surname we'd like to adopt."

Carefully, he parts my thighs and I crown him once again as the head of his cock nudges against me. "I'm not sure I'll be doing much thinking, I think I'll be quite distract—" I cut off on a moan as Emrys slides into me, indulgingly smooth.

He rolls his hips exquisitely, grinding up onto my clit with every slow thrust. His hand hitches my leg higher onto his hip as he slowly makes love to me, savoring me. Savoring us. His movements are measured and I can feel the adoration pouring into me.

Emotion surges in me and I take his mouth in mine, kissing him leisurely, decadently. Our tongues caressing, breaths mingling. I meet his hips stroke for stroke, surging in a sensual rhythm.

This moment is so intimate, so sweet. He's mine and I am his.

Suddenly, I feel something in me wake and with an unravelling I sense that thing reach beyond me and touch Emrys. I gasp as I feel a bond grow into existence, tethering between our hearts. Diving beneath that scar. I blink and I can see a red thread linking between us, and all at once I feel all of him. All his devotion. All his love. Everything sweeps into me with the force of a tidal wave and I can see both in his eyes and from the bond the same experience is overtaking him, too.

Our climaxes claim us at the same time, a slow sprawl building in my belly and expanding outward. The waves of ecstasy are easy bliss and mind-numbing pleasure. I let out a breathless mewl as he groans against my throat, his own orgasm throbbing into me as my pussy trembles around his cock.

    The red thread of fate has linked us.

    I look into my soulmate's eyes and I see my forever.

CHAPTER 39

As per fae law we must invite the Unseelie Court to the coronation. It is a blessing and a curse. A blessing as we know exactly where they'll be during the event—wherein an ancient law dictates there is to be no violence between the courts during the celebration—and a curse as we'll have to show our hand and reveal Emrys as the king.

The next day we begin by telling those closest to us and the crown in addition to a few necessary bodies.

I've gathered Maelona, Wisteria, Julia, Violante, Drysi, Bleddyn, Rachel and Lorelai—the sisters from Aberth—in one of the smallest council rooms, my back nearly against a side door. At Drysi's suggestion, Commander Baphet—a ram horned faerie—and Aveda—also known as the Admiral for her namesake butterfly wings—are also invited. Aveda is the only faerie I know of that can use the karma gift, so I consider her an asset despite my personal reservations, but I'm taking a chance on Drysi's suggestions—and the brunette sisters—and I pray it doesn't backfire. Though I can't help it, I balk as I realize how limited our trusted ones are and how vulnerable Emrys will be. I internally determine to rectify that and begin trials to replace Aneira's decimated Queensguard.

Staring up at the writhing golden ceiling, appeased since the crown has returned to the court, I drag in a breath. Sprawling my hands on the large, raw edged table before me, I push away papers and dossiers, meeting the eyes of those assembled.

"I have not been entirely truthful about many things. Much has transpired since Aneira's death." I lick my lips and prepare myself. "First, I must swear you all to secrecy. Those of you who are not fae, please consider this a trial in testing your loyalty."

Everyone swears without question.

Suddenly, I am overcome by the enormity of the situation and everything about to be revealed. I clench my jaw, staring at the heavy paperweight in the center of the table, the object in the shape of the Seelie Court sigil.

Emrys strokes reassuringly against our thread and my fears ease incrementally. It had taken us some time last night, but we'd figured out how to quiet the influx of emotion that was all too determined to flow between the bond. Now, it settles within me comfortably; within reach. It feels like it's always been there.

Like it always should have been.

"As you all know during Aneira's assassination the crown was stolen." The words taste like acid on my tongue and I move on, prompted by the listening sounds of assent. "And as you can surely tell the court has been quelled. Recently, myself and others took it upon ourselves to retrieve the crown from the Winter Carnaval. We were successful."

A couple gasps pepper the room and I catch Drysi's eye, a dark brow quirked upward.

"Upon our return we discovered to our dismay that Aneira had not named Maelona as heir." Even more sounds of surprise go up, but I continue. "We realized she had named an heir, but…" I trail off, my eyes glancing at Drysi. "Corvina is no longer with us."

Drysi's face blanches and Bleddyn swears below his breath.

"So, who has succession gone to?" Baphet inquires, confusion written across his face.

I steel myself, twisting my wedding ring. "Aneira's son."

Shock explodes in the room, my biological mother's eyes wide. The humans are as equally surprised while Violante watches with quiet determination. Maelona and Wisteria already know the rest.

In addition to our bond snapping into place last night, our love making and acceptance of the title of king was enough of an act to convert him into a Seelie. *Back* to a Seelie, as he was at birth.

"Aneira had a child?" Drysi whispers in astonishment.

"Yes." I pause. "He is also my husband."

I should be used to the shock by now. It should be comical. But still, I am twisted in anxious knots, my stomach roiling, the nausea choking me.

"Who?"

Now, I send through the fated thread.

Leaning, I place my hands behind my back and find the knobs of the double-doors. "Emrys Gwyndolyn-Vanora." And then I swing the doors open.

Emrys steps through the threshold. Garbed in his traditional black blouse and leather pants, but in addition to this he wears gold chains, gold earrings, and that newly transformed gold and ebony crown.

He inclines his head and a muscle feathers in his cheek. His golden eyes are bright and I am the only one the wiser to know it is from fear. Emrys has no training to be a king, but he wants to see the change and he's willing to be it.

"That's one of the Unseelie Queen guards!" Rachel hisses, stumbling back and plastering herself against the wall.

I shake my head. "Not any longer."

Emrys reaches out and we link hands. He is warm, comforting, but I can feel the shake in his fingers. I squeeze his hand and send a similar sensation through our connection.

"I am no longer a member of the Unseelie Court," he announces firmly to the gathered. "I defected weeks ago and only now have I properly earned my position."

"As king," Bleddyn says flatly.

Emrys nods. "Yes, and tonight I will be formally crowned with my wife taking the mantle of queen beside me."

A roar of silence falls upon us.

And then it is anything but silent.

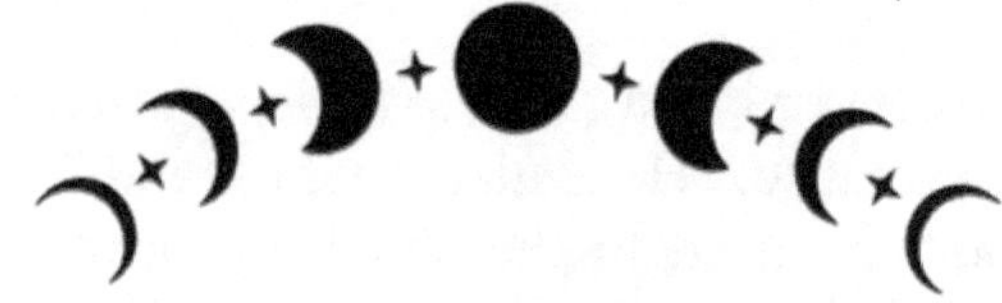

We manage to eventually calm everyone, treating them gently from the emotional whiplash of so many revelations. After a time, we delegate tasks to everyone from a quick assembly of decorations, to enlisting guards for tonight—which will then evolve into training a new Kingsguard—as well as sending out invitations.

We rush the coronation to stay ahead of the news. As per tradition, coronations take place upon a late hour free of a full or new moon. During the ceremony, pacifism is promised by fae law until the stroke of midnight, which is when challenge may occur.

The invitations are deliberately vague, inviting to witness the crowning of a new Seelie monarch. No names, no hints towards identity. Hours later we receive every single one of them back with confirmations of attendance.

Caethes's comes with a note:

My salutations to the new Seelie monarch. I was under the impression that the crown had disappeared, but it seems with this coronation moving forward it has been retrieved. I'll be sure to reach out to the Carnaval discover who was at fault for this transgression.

I am eager to learn who will be bestowed the crown.
With Regards,
Queen Caethes of the Unseelie Court

I can feel the venom dripping off every word through the ink. She is furious and she is curious, and she hates that she is both. I grin.

Everything comes together, including the seamstress that tailors mine and Emrys's clothing for the coronation. We are dressed and draped in black and gold and emerald, silk and leather and velvet.

We are given virtually no time to ourselves; everything is the hustle of preparation and questions. And there are many of the latter. Despite the fact information about our marriage has begun to make its rounds from Prague and the Winter Carnaval, more questions come from it. How long have we been together? How did we end up together considering we're from rival courts? Is it political? Did we plan to take out Aneira so we could usurp the crown?

The last one swiftly earned bloody teeth.

On our pedestals we get measured and during such time Drysi intercepts us.

"I have a list of possible candidates to be part of tonight's Kingsguard," Drysi says holding loose sheets of paper. "Would you like to look them over before I make the final decision?"

I motion to the tailor and they back off as I step down. Crossing over to Drysi, I extend my hand and she gives me the papers. I peruse them succinctly.

"Not Afan," I tell her, handing over the documents. "The rest are competent."

"As you wish." She makes a motion to leave but then stops herself. "Evelyn...I—"

"Yes?" I press.

"It probably doesn't matter now, but Aneira called off the assassination on Gideon before she passed."

"You're right, it doesn't matter now."

Drysi bites her lip, looking truly uncomfortable—an expression I rarely see on her. Her eyes flicker to my husband over my shoulder, clearly wanting to ask. "How long have you been...?"

"Nearly seven years."

"And was it for love...?"

"It was for love." Through the thread I can sense Emrys watching this exchange, glowing from my words.

She nods her head and looks away, discomfited. "How?"

"It is quite a long story."

"I would like to hear it one day," she says tentatively.

A small and warm thing stirs in my heart, completely unexpected but not wholly unwelcome. Drysi and I have never been close, never been able, due to her absence and my ability to hold a grudge. The litany of abandonment echoes in my head but I bite it down, Surely, she's not just this cruel. Surely, she had her reasons. But she is fae. As am I.

I let a genuine smile spread across my mouth. "We'll set a date."

"I'd like that."

Drysi begins walking away again, then pauses. "Evelyn?"

I turn, expression open.

"I am happy for you. Congratulations."

"Thank you."

My biological mother nods again, then vacates the room.

Suddenly, a foreboding urge grasps me and I chase after Drysi. My footsteps are loud and I don't even need to call her before she turns. Her black hair whirls like a spray of ink.

"Did you know my father was a witch?"

Drysi's eyes widen and she glances about the hallway, looking for eavesdroppers. "How did you find out about that?"

"I inherited some of his gifts."

Panic floods through Drysi's features and she rushes me, covering my mouth. "Please tell me you haven't told anyone of this."

I'm so surprised I don't move away from her muting of me. I do, however, peel her hand off my mouth. "No, I have not told anyone, but some have figured it out."

Emrys senses my emotional distress and peers down the bond. I let him in and allow him to observe.

"Who?"

I hesitate. "People I trust."

Fear drains her face and she clutches my hand—when did she drop the papers? "Do not tell another soul. Please."

"Why?"

Her eyes flicker from side to side before she drags me into an alcove, leaving the papers strewn on the floor. "The King of Vampires has taken a keen interest in any supernaturals who are the product of more than one supernatural type. There have been whispers of experimentation and torture for decades. He frequents the Winter Carnaval searching for new '*discoveries*' as he calls them."

Images of Joseph Harrow possessively clutching Annabelle Laroche rush through my mind and my blood turns cold. Drysi reads me like a book.

"You saw him there, didn't you?" I nod and she quickly continues. "Stay away from him and if he propositions you, I do not care what he threatens or offers, do *not* accept. Those who go to his court do not return."

I swallow. "We already turned him down."

"Good. Stay away from him and whatever you do, do not bleed around him. He has an unparalleled sense of smell and through an open wound he'll be able to detect your witch blood even through our very potent fae blood."

"Why did you even have us if you knew about this danger? Why not terminate us?" I say it so bitterly that the words take me aback.

Drysi's eyes—my eyes—soften. "Because we wanted you so desperately."

I blink back the astonishment. "Then why did you leave us?"

Drysi's lips press in a line and silver edges her eyes. "Because Joseph became aware of the possibility of your existence. Your father left to protect us, to throw him off the trail, but he made a mistake." Her voice wavers. "He sought solace with his mother's coven and they turned on him, selling him out to the king. He refused to give us up—all of us—and he died for it." Drysi swallows and her mercury eyes bleed down her face, the tears shimmering on her pale skin. "When news reached me of his death, I changed my name and swore vengeance. I was bound to my word until I'd killed every last one of those witches. I just didn't know how long it would take." She raises her pained gaze to mine. "It was sixteen years, Evelyn."

I feel like shattering glass. The delicate crack and ping. It all makes sense and all my preconceived notions about Drysi's selfishness come crashing down. She didn't abandon me because she didn't want me. She left us in the care of the queen she trusted while she found revenge. She was bound to her word. But she did it out of love.

Emrys senses my emotional spiral and soothes me, sending love through that red thread of fate.

"I never knew."

"I was ashamed of myself. And you hated me so fiercely when I came back. I didn't even know how to begin."

I take her hand. "We have the rest of our lives now."

Drysi nods, salt tracks dripping from her chin. "I'm so sorry, baby."

The words are a blade directly to my heart. That lost and abandoned child in me screaming out, having begged for more than two decades to hear those words.

"I wish Corvina were here."

She nods fitfully, tears dripping freely. "Me too, baby. Me too."

"What was his name? My father?"

"Rhodes. Rhodes Whitecrest."

The sudden revelation of my father's name hits me like a punch to the throat. I can't breathe, I can't bring in any air.

All my life, the twenty-three here and the one hundred during Century Training, I never knew. But here it is. Rhodes Whitecrest.

For a moment I don't know what to say or do, but I nod and let Drysi go. "I need to get back to get my dress finished."

"Right, right. Yes, of course." Drysi quickly wipes her eyes with the back of her hand. "I'll let you get to it and I'll get these warriors briefed for tonight."

"Thank you, mom."

Drysi sucks in a tight breath and new tears shimmer in her eyes, a terrified but hopeful smile spreading across her face.

"I'll see you tonight. You will make a stunning queen."

Without another word, Drysi leaves me and proceeds to pick up the dropped papers with lightning speed before taking off down a hall.

I stand in the alcove for a minute more before I return to the seamstress. I retake my place on the gold pedestal and Emrys extends his hand. I take it.

He squeezes.

I squeeze back.

CHAPTER 40

The coronation is beautiful. The golden sky ceiling undulates above us, content and relaxed. Green and gilded ivy march along, and white chrysanthemums in elaborate floral arrangements spot throughout. Between ivy-wrapped golden pillars are heavy benches like church pews, and an emerald runner spans the aisle.

Courtiers, dressed in their best finery, who have been milling for the past hour are beginning to get to their seats. Their anticipation is thrumming through the room with a wild energy. Guards line every wall of the space, like rows of golden nutcrackers, holding bright swords and helmed in the same auric metal. Their nervous energy is also palpable.

The dais where Emrys and I had done all manner of fucking is scrubbed to a near-blinding shine, with a wide, green velvet pillow sitting before the massive throne of trees we'd also defiled. The golden light pulses through it, the Seelie sigil in the center glowing with the strength and vivacity of the new monarch.

Emrys and I watch all of this through a spyhole in an adjoining council room.

Like a tremor that the court has only recently dispelled, an ominous air enters the space and I watch Caethes enter the throne room. She wears a heavy black gown with silver embroidery that runs down her bodice like wilting flowers. The neckline is low, a gentle curve to the drop shoulders of the train grazing sleeves with a slit up the center of the gown that opens to an A-line. The supple swath of her moon white skin is displayed, graced with silver tattoos of moon cycles down each leg all the way to the diamond studded heels she regally struts on. She is furious and she wears her wrath like she wears that diadem perched between her antlers; like a queen. The diamond dangling between her brows trembles as if it too fears her anger.

She is surrounded by six guards—I recognize Cariad and Tegwyn—with Gideon in tow.

My heart pangs with loss, but not longing. There is nothing left of the desires I once held for him. No longer do I feel like I'll spiral without him. Nothing about me loves him any longer, but there's a small fissure in my heart where his betrayal lies. It is a blackened, necrotic thing, and one day it will fall away.

Beside me, Emrys catches my hand wordlessly, saying everything he needs to through the bond. In the room with us is Maelona, Drysi, Bleddyn and the Kingsguard's temporary replacements. They are all dressed in golden armor, save for Maelona. She wears a gown that looks painted on, all green silk and gold chains. A spiked headdress like the aurora of the sun atop her head complements the sunburst earrings that curve up her ear and dangle from the lobes.

Through the spyhole, I see Ghislain, the auburn-haired, green-eyed fae, with magic in his veins, mount the stairs and stand before the velvet pillow. The magic that writhes under his ochre skin is the gold of the false sky, pumping to the rhythm of his heart. I'd always assumed it was secular but with new knowledge it's clear that Lady Karma may have been the one to favor him. So, perhaps not secular at all. Perhaps elusive and directly blessed.

A few moments pass and I realize it's time.

I drag in a long breath as Maelona takes up a velvet pillow, tassels hanging from each corner. Emrys's crown, transformed, sits upon the plush surface like an omen. Like a memory of the dead.

We watch together as the crowd turns, breaths held as the Lady Maelona enters. Surprise flickers on more than one face as they realize that while the Lady may be carrying the newly transformed crown, it is not hers. Maelona holds her head proudly and not even her hair betrays her emotions as she walks down the aisle. She ascends the stairs and then comes to a stop beside Ghislain, holding it in steady hands.

Surrounded by her guards, Caethes's eyes narrow as she takes in Maelona—she, being one of the many who'd believed Mae to be the heir apparent. She views the Lady with highly critical airs and turns her nose up at her. Maelona does not react.

"It's time," Emrys whispers to me.

My breath catches as we get into position. The Kingsguard flanks us, Bleddyn and Drysi directly behind. Their wings are spread, like a reminder of the very ones we lost. That were taken from us.

The doors open once again and with our hands aloft, we step forward.

The moment we cross the threshold, the atmosphere of the room changes. It charges. It fills with everything from shock to horror to dismay to downright fury. Titters and whispers fill the room as Emrys and I make our debut together. For the first time in a public and formal space we are announcing that we are together. That we are the future of the Seelie Court.

If I thought Caethes was furious before, I was wrong. She is absolutely and completely full of vicious, vengeful *rage*. Her face burns crimson and I can feel the energy of chaos crackle, her nails turning to claws.

If she could decimate us in this moment, she would.

The Unseelie Queen stares at her turncoat Revenant and his warrior bride who has been a thorn in her every side. The betrayal on her face is the most delicious thing I've ever seen. It gives me a sick thrill of pride, to bring this queen down so low when I've yet to receive my crown.

We proceed down the aisle while Caethes's gaze burns. A hooded faerie near the back cackles and the sound sends a shiver down my spine. Afan, the faerie I did not select for tonight's guarding duties stares gape-jawed at us, the gears turning in his head. Then, three rows from the front, I catch sight of an amber gaze.

My breath hitches in my throat as we make eye contact. The gulf between us stretches, the absence and distance of everything between us yawning despite the steps that draw me closer. Nothing in my life is built for Gideon. There is no place for him anywhere I live and reside. My heart does not call for him. My soul does not yearn towards him. My mind does not despair over him. He has betrayed me in so many ways and in so many ways I have betrayed him. We are toxic for each other. Our love was borne of survival and proximity, but anything that was or could have been between us is well and truly over.

I try to portray this as clearly as I can through my eyes while I leave the fated thread wide open between me and my soulmate, allowing Emrys to be privy to every belief and feeling—or lack thereof—in regards to Gideon.

We ascend the dais together; the long velvet cape Emrys wears trails down the stairs like my train. His cape is deep emerald with gold stenciling of the Seelie Court crest and words of the ancient fae. He wears a black jacket over one of his black blouses, the buttons and threads all ostentatious gold. His pants are tailored to his body, black with golden crescent moons on the knees, matching the epaulets that attach to the cloak and his shining black boots are elaborately done with even more gilded buckles.

Next to him, I drip emeralds and gold molds to me. The velvet gown is sculpted to my body with a sweetheart neckline and thigh slits allowing ease of access to the knives sheathed on my thighs. My back is bare and my hair is half pulled up, but the silvery sheet does little to hide the map of scars that mar my flesh. But I care not one whit for anyone's thoughts.

At the top we turn, our backs to the throne as Emrys guides us before the pillow.

"Please kneel," Ghislain says.

Emrys takes a knee and stares out at the sea of faces beyond.

Caethes is positively cataclysmic in her seat.

"Tonight, we officially crown the new monarch of the Seelie Court," Ghislain begins, voice amplified by a spell, courtesy of Wisteria. "Tonight, loyal denizens, nosy creatures, treacherous enemies, we gather for a new era. For tonight, I, Ghislain Ellorian of the Light Court, crown Emrys Gwyndolyn-Vanora as King of the Seelie Court." He directs his words to Emrys now. "Do you swear to be protector of the realm and the sword that guides the lives of the Light Court?"

"I do."

"And do you swear to uphold the virtues of the Seelie Court and rule it for as long as you feel fit to reign?"

"I do."

Ghislain turns to Maelona and takes up the horned and flowered crown, hovering it over Emrys's head. "I hereby name you *king*. May Lady Fate bless your rule."

Emrys rises with the crown atop his crimson waves, his golden eyes vibrant in his flushed face. He stares out at his court, at his enemies, at those who simply want to know. He takes them all in and then he turns to me.

"Kneel, my love."

I do as he says, staring up at him and a vision of me on my knees before this very throne only hours before flashes through the bond. I can feel the arousal threatening to show on him. I smile mischievously.

Suddenly, Emrys takes the crown from atop his head and holds the base in one hand and the root of the horns in the other. More than just my confusion takes the room and I watch him in curiosity. And then I see what he's planning to do from the open connection through our bond.

By sheer force of will Emrys halves the crown. Ripping the branches and flowers from the horns to form a new circlet.

I watch in shock as both the crowns transform, the great horned one forming new branches and flowers and chains while the circlet weaves together to form a smaller shape. From the roses on the crown bloom thorns, and on those thorns, grow long black spikes—seven in all.

The horns reflect his parentage, and the roses and thorns reflect mine.

My mouth is open in a small O as Emrys replaces his crown once again and holds mine between his hands.

"I, Emrys Gwyndolyn-Vanora, King of the Seelie Court, crown you, Evelyn Corianne Gwyndolyn-Vanora, my wife, Queen of the Light Court."

Emrys sets the newly manifested crown atop my head and the weight is uncompromisingly *right*. As soon as it settles atop my silver locks, there is a significant ripple in the air as the Seelie Court accepts me. The golden magic of the Light Court glows, the false sky brightening for a fraction before returning to its normal stately waves. I feel the change yet nothing could have prepared me for the sudden rush of power this object instills in me—both tangibly and intangibly.

My husband grins at me and offers a hand to stand. I take it. Overcome with emotion, I cup his face and draw him close, kissing with all the devotion I can pour into the bond. With this kiss, as our lips slide against each other, I am claiming him as mine in front of the court. In front of our enemies. In front of all. Gasps and cheers and scoffs go up and I gently nip his lower lip before pulling away.

Suddenly, screams erupt from the back of the room and I watch bodies scramble and shadowy figures infiltrate the space.

The entries and exits are locked until midnight, which is still fifteen minutes off, and all those living are trapped in the throne room until the law lets the court free. It's pandemonium as everything from fae to humans scatter to the walls, plastering themselves away from the beings as they advance on them with flickering maniac smiles. Weapons of smoke and shadow undulate on an unseen breeze, while those few brave souls among the living swipe uselessly with weapons they'd sneaked into the coronation.

Horror spikes with the appearance the Wild Hunt's smoky shapes. I shed the Kings Glamour obscuring Oath-Sworn from view as I draw it from my back. I wield the Harbinger sword knowing it and the Revenant's mirror blade, Heart's-Desire, are the only two weapons that can harm the Hunt in this form.

Like they're herding, a horribly familiar figure strides down the aisle, russet hair faded to gray, his pallor just as deceased with dulled, dark depths for eyes. He's wreathed in smoke and shadow but I can still see the fatal wound I'd dealt him all those weeks ago.

Caethes is smiling.

Stepping in front of Emrys, I hold the sword before me and level it as the shadowy-dead apparition of Arawn strides through the crowd.

"*Fear not, New Half-Queen,*" Arawn murmurs, his voice muddled like speaking through a film of water. "*The Hunt cannot touch save for full moon nights. Our ability grows closer to the lunar moment, but we are intangible until then.*"

"I think this sword can still destroy you in this form, can't it?" I hiss, taking a step forward, aiming for Arawn's breastbone.

Arawn's lips thin, unable to lie even now.

"So, why are you here?" I demand, fury burning me, the rage threatening to turn me shaky. But I did not train, holding a goddess-damned sword for hours, to let my emotions be the cause of a tremble now.

"*I do not care for the Light Court,*" Arawn says blandly, pacing before the dais steps. I watch him like a hawk, sword following. "*I wish to see it decimated.*"

"You've made that abundantly clear."

"*Laws and oaths bind the courts; even war has its difficulties circumventing these. But the Hunt is* other, *it does not fall prey to the game of kings and queens, and thrones and crowns. As other, I am able to act in my own interests on behalf of another without consequences from the goddess.*"

"You are talking too much to be saying so little."

Arawn chuckles and spears me with his eerie void eyes. "*I am saying I am not constrained, Half-Queen.*" A wicked gleam enters his eyes and he turns to the awaiting crowd, bracketed by members of the Wild Hunt. "*Hear me!*" Arawn booms in that echoey voice. "*Without oaths I can reveal to you the true identities of your new king and queen!*"

No.

Blood drains from my face, my jaw slackening as I begin to descend the steps, and from the rustle of armor, I know Drysi is following. But it occurs as if in slow motion. Like my footsteps are dredging through cold molasses, my muscles restrained. Too slow.

"*Behold! The Revenant and the Harbinger, your new King and Queen of the Seelie Court!*"

I slash at his form with my sword, but he dissipates with a cruel laugh before the strike lands. His spirited form rises and reforms again down the aisle and directly beside him I find Gideon, his amber gaze widened with surprise.

Failure. Failure. Failure.

I glance at Caethes and see confusion and cold, vicious fury on the Unseelie Queen. Then realization dawns on her like a dramatic curtain call, the red velvet lifted and all revealed beneath the spotlights.

Every possible emotion stares back at me over at the assembled crowd, every possible degree of wrath and excitement and betrayal and loss growing across every face.

Memories of those I'd taken from them flickering behind their eyes, their hands itching to exact revenge.

Gideon's astonishment is dimmed, but his mouth is pressed into a thin line and I find myself in shock.

Gideon never told Caethes my identity.

He couldn't have, not with the shocked blow Caethes let play across her face like a theatrical show. Through it all Gideon maintained my secret. Under the pressure of torture and blackmail, against it all he held my identity in confidence. But why? After all the betrayals, after using the command on me, what was stopping him from playing this card? Was it a last resort? His final bargaining chip? Surely, he was questioned about the Harbinger during his captivity so why did he withhold or lie?

If Gideon has always been one thing, it's a liar, but this is the first time I've ever been truly grateful for it.

I have some explanations for why Gideon never said anything, but I have no answer for why Arawn never did. Power? Bargaining?

Caethes's fists rise and I can feel her funneling chaos into her body, the air crackling with the rush of magic. The energy changes and I know for at least another few minutes she cannot use it, but the fact that she is building and preparing it is wholly terrifying.

Unseelies grow antsy, half wanting to leave and half wanting to fight. Terror strikes me as I realize how defenseless the humans we have at the coronation are.

Not looking, I call behind me. "Drysi, gather the humans and direct them to an interior exit, be prepared to instruct them to run and find safety.

Arawn, reformed, still in the aisle chuckles and pretends to check his non-existent watch. "*It is time I depart, Harbinger, but soon your present will arrive. I hope you enjoy.*" And with that Arawn and the rest of the Hunt evaporate, shadows flying through the blocked exits, unencumbered by the state of living.

A clock tolls midnight and then mayhem ensues.

Caethes erupts with the force of her assembled chaos, but before it can strike either myself or Emrys, Wisteria leaps in front of us with a veritable shield of her own chaos. The Unseelie Queen's magic slams into the invisible force of Wisteria's.

The witch and the queen begin battling it out, chaos magic against chaos magic. The borrowed fights the owned, snaps and booms colliding with every wave and missile of magic. Their arms begin moving so fast, hands pushing and holding, faces gritted.

Half of the Unseelie faeries abandoned the ceremony, the other half duel against Seelie forces, steel ringing out and cries going up. Gideon is fighting for the Dark Court.

The battle is not unprecedented, but I'd hoped it wouldn't come to this.

Emrys and I are pushed back towards the throne like helpless children by Bleddyn and our other temporary guards, calls of *"protect the king and queen"* going around. Sequestered into a role of protected has me lashing at the proverbial restraints. I am a warrior, a goddess-damned Centurion, and I will *fight*.

Emrys, reading me through the bond nods and tears off his cloak while I rip my train, and the two of us throw ourselves into the fray, heedless of our guards. We battle with our legendary prowess, taking on Unseelie after Unseelie while Wisteria continues to fight against Caethes.

"Help Wisteria!" I scream to our Kingsguard. They take off without question knowing their duty to us is to follow orders, we don't need protecting.

New screams erupt and vampires descend.

Black-clad and crimson-eyed, they take hostages among the bedlam. People are dragged to the sidelines, just as they were herded by the Wild Hunt. Only this time, they sink their fangs into their throats and force them to become thrall to the mayhem by their near drugging saliva.

Emrys and I cut through them too, my husband with two long blades, myself with Oath-Sworn.

A hooded faerie twists against a male vampire's hold and the figure snaps his arm with an audible crack. The vampire howls and as we cut through the swaths of bodies, the hooded figure then withdraws a familiar blade and slides it through the chest of the vampire. He chokes before the slick noise of the exiting blade has him falling to the floor with the rest of the ended.

Apprehension fills Emrys and I as we continue cutting through, now aiming to the hooded figure; curiosity and a strange sense of hope arrowing us. And the figure drives towards us. They're making their way through the carnage, intent on us. It is not a predatory air, it is one of determination and a goal.

I recognize it.

Enydd pulls back the hood of the cloak as she reaches us, her plum eyes filled with mirth. Her mouth curves into an amused smile. "Well, you two have come a long way, haven't you?"

She looks the same. Same dark skin, same cinnamon freckles, same violet braids. Same emerald and gossamer wings.

"How are you here?" I question, struggling to form words.

Behind me, Emrys effortlessly battles away a lunging vampire, returning his attentions to us. I raise one of my sheathed thigh daggers and drive it into the center of an Unseelie's skull.

"That is a very long story, fit for another time," Enydd informs us baldly. "But I figured you might need this." And with that she extends Emrys's lost Revenant's blade, blood still dripping from its edge.

Heart's-Desire is untarnished. Silver, spiked above the hilt, sharp, a skull wrought into the pommel, wings like the ones he lost flaring at the hilt.

Amongst the massacre the Wild Hunt and Unseelie Court has elicited, Emrys reaches out and takes his sword. Once again reunited with the blade he'd wielded before he died. The one he had when we cut down the oath-bound mentors.

The one he used to battle the Wild Hunt. The one I used to finally kill Osian. The one Lady Chaos stole.

"How—"

"We'll speak later, young ones. In the meantime, let's secure your court."

Enydd unwraps her urumi from her waist and we immediately give her a wide berth. Her use of the multi-bladed whip has always been terrifyingly lethal and despite Emrys and I knowing how to use it, we never favored the flail style of battle. Immediately she dives in with a new vengeance, and Emrys and I revitalize our efforts.

A vampire I recognize as Maelona's former lover strides towards us, a wicked smile on her fanged mouth. She reaches us just as Drysi returns from getting the humans to safety. Seemingly without thought, my mother launches herself at the vampire, wings pinned to arrow her body into form. The two tumble together and three more vampires surge to contain Drysi, two capturing her wings, one with their arm around her neck.

Fear spikes through me as I watch the vampire look down at Drysi. Drysi shrieks against the iron rings that adorn every one of the vampires' fingers. Smoke and sizzling rises from their caging hold. For one of the first times in my life, I lose composure during battle and Emrys has to bat away a blow that would have landed against my ribs.

"Come any closer and we cut her throat."

I freeze, Oath-Sworn at my side.

"So, the little pest wanted by the Unseelie Queen is also the *Ceidwad Cudd* and the Harbinger?" Maelona's ex-vampire-lover cackles, holding Drysi's jaw in a steel grip. "Oh, this is too good. Tell me, little warrior; are all those titles worth your *precious mommy*?" Her voice simpers into baby talk as she brushes a midnight lock of hair back from Drysi's face, a red mark of burning growing on her cheekbone in the exact shape of the vampire's rings.

"Do not trade anything for me," Drysi hisses through her teeth and the vampire clamps a ringed hand over my mother's mouth. Drysi's eyes widen in pain as I watch smoke coil from between the vampire's fingers.

"I wasn't speaking to you," the vampire returns to my mother, mouth level with her ear. "Does this bring back any nostalgia, Evelyn? Does this make you think of when you lost your precious Aneira?"

Terror and anger clash within me, my grief rising to the surface.

The vampire isn't wrong, this is too much like Arawn baiting me. Forcing me to choose Maelona and the others or Aneira. Only now the choice is me or Drysi. The parallel is horribly ironic.

"Do not speak of her," I whisper viciously. But I know from her enhanced hearing she heard, just as I know from the vampires' enhanced strength that Drysi won't be breaking free of their hold. Not now, not when they have her pinned as they do. She is utterly at their mercy.

The vampire woman pouts mockingly. "Aw, was she your mommy too? Do you even care about this one? Or should we just toss her out?"

One of the vampires holding Drysi laughs with the vampire woman and my eyes, in panic fly to my mother. I'm losing ground. I can feel Drysi's life slipping through my fingers.

"Let her go."

"No, I don't think I will."

Emrys and I could take them, but we couldn't before they kill Drysi. I'm out of options.

"If you hurt her, I *will* kill you." I step forward. More vampires circle us.

Drysi bites down hard on the vampire woman's fingers and she squawks in surprise and pain.

"Emrys, don't let her do this!" Drysi yells. "Please!"

In that moment I realize several things simultaneously and time stops.

In this moment Drysi is sacrificing herself. She is commanding the king, begging my husband to be the villain, begging my soulmate to save my life.

Emrys does not hesitate and I feel his desperate pleas for forgiveness as his arms band around my body. I'm forced to watch as Maelona's former lover snaps my mother's neck.

I scream as incandescent rage fills me. I buck against my husband and Emrys's grief pours through the bond, mixing with mine in a new noxious substance. I feel our shared anger brew, and as the light disappears from Drysi's eyes, we act.

There are no thoughts as I brutalize these vampires. In seconds Emrys and I have butchered them beyond comprehension, the lives of four snuffed out because they took one. We are coated in blood, our blades bleeding with it and none of it makes me feel better.

The circling vampires scatter.

I was just making strides to better my relationship with Drysi and now she is gone. Just when I was beginning to understand her. I am alone. My family—my *entire* family is dead. So many of those chosen and all of those of blood. I confront the fact that I am the only one of my blood left, because Rhodes, Corvina, and Drysi…all of them are *gone*. Only Emrys is left.

Fury propels me and I seek out Caethes. This is all her fault. This is all her doing. Caethes is the crux of the issue. She is why I was taken by Jacob Dugal. She is why he severed my wings. She is why I was isolated and surviving for two years. She is the reason that Corvina and so many others are dead.

She needs to pay.

With single-minded determination, I grit my teeth and dart directly for the queen. With Emrys beside me, we cross the carnage-filled throne room together. Bodies fall in our wake as my goal draws closer. Her and Wisteria are still battling it out with their chaos, distanced from everyone else. They have built a bubble of containment between the two of them where no other can touch. They are singular players in a game of chess, one of silver, the other clad in gold.

Hoping Oath-Sworn is the key, I slice through the barrier just as I once cut through the Wild Hunt, and step past the bubble of chaos.

As I step through, Gideon attacks Emrys and I hold my breath as my husband shoves my former lover back. They begin battling and I can feel through our fated thread that Emrys has no intentions of killing Gideon for fear of it hurting me. I seethe and give him permission, but he still refuses.

Turning to the queen, within what *was* a protective bubble, her eyes widen. Caethes's heavy black gown is scorched in places. The Unseelie Queen steps back on shaky legs and I realize her magic—though chaos saturates the air— is spent, her reserves burnt out and she has no formal weapons training.

I snarl at the Unseelie Queen, my face bloodied. The sounds of battle and death, blades ringing and shouts go up around us. I hear Emrys and Gideon fighting outside and the heaving breaths from Wisteria. All I can smell is blood.

Wisteria is leaning against the opposite wall, her energy clearly flagging. Her limbs tremble and her eyes, currently possessed by the magic of Caethes, are glazed. The witch is near depleted and I don't know how much time we'll have contained here.

I nod once to Wisteria and she nods back weakly before I turn my attention to Caethes.

"You have taken almost everything from me and I refuse to let you take anything more," I growl, striding toward her. Queen to queen. "It is time I take everything from you."

Caethes hisses at me like a cornered animal, backing against the furthest edge of the bubble where Tegwyn and Cariad swing swords at Seelie warriors. She is trapped and though her magic has let the dome go, Wisteria's hasn't.

"You've taken my Arawn, you've taken my Revenant. What more do you want?"

I raise my sword, speaking through my bared teeth. "No. The Revenant was never yours. He's always been *mine*."

Caethes's lips pull back over her teeth. "You silly little girl. You think he'll forsake his queen just for that slit between your legs? Wait until he tires of you and returns to me."

I laugh and it is a mean sound. "Let me put this simply for you; Emrys is my husband, my soulmate, and my king. He will never belong to you."

"He is Unseelie!"

"No. He is not. He is born and once again Seelie, and he has always hated you."

"You vicious little bitch," Caethes seethes.

"Odd choice for last words, Your Majesty."

With that, I rush Caethes, heels eating up the distance between us.

With the barest reserves of chaos magic, Caethes sends a small burst at Oath-Sworn and the blade goes flying out of my hand. I hiss with the pain of the reverberation but continue forward, launching myself at the queen. I tackle her against the false chaos wall, grasp her by her antlers and attempt to sever her spine. She grasps me by the throat and a ripple of chaos restricts my muscles. In response, I slam the back of her head against the wall, repeatedly.

She's cutting off my airflow, but I know how much time I have before it becomes debilitating so I continue smashing her skull despite her magically restricting me. I can feel the cage of the magic centering on my wrists, disabling me from twisting. Even so, I keep trying to get the leverage to snap her neck.

The Unseelie Queen is dazed, but she claws my arm with her free hand, shredding the drop sleeves of my gown and drawing blood. It stings but it is nothing compared to the burn of wrath in my veins. She swats against me almost uselessly, and knocks my crown from my head.

"You don't deserve the title," Caethes hisses, her magic waning as her hand goes to one of my wrists and wrapping, pulling it away from her antler.

I let go of the opposite antler and Caethes releases me in surprise and defense. "And neither do you," I hiss as I wrench her diadem from her head.

I scream as I feel the Unseelie crown burn me.

CHAPTER 42

I stare at the Unseelie Court crest branded into my palm with uncomprehending disbelief.

The Unseelie Queen has not named an heir for her throne.

So, her heir is her closest blood relative.

And the heir is the only one who can be burned by the crown.

The brand is stark against my left hand and I look up from it and into Caethes's terrified eyes.

Somehow, somewhere we are related and I am her closest blood relation. But I am only the closest relation because both Corvina and Drysi are dead. Drysi's life was the only reason why the diadem never burned me before.

I am the heir to the Unseelie Court.

With that realization comes a voice inside my head, carrying a tune. I recognize the voice in a terrible and distant way. I've only heard it once and it was monumental to the worst moment of my life. The melodic voice turns into words.

> *Rooks are crown and scorn,*
> *She is deceit, hers was apart*
> *Knights are murder and mourn,*
> *She is failure, her grief is heart*
> *Bishops are sacrifice and cost,*
> *She is three, his was death*
> *Royals are found and lost,*
> *She is true, his lies are breath*
> *Pawns are bait and invention,*
> *They will die, they will define*
> *Herby states the play of ascension,*
> *A Game of Lady Fate's design.*

Reality slams into me as the melody fades out.

I was wrong. My life isn't The Game. It's a key player in The Game. The Game is of crowns and thrones and Lady Fate's lullaby outlines the players and moves until the queens and kings take their rightful place. The lullaby is the tipping of the hourglass when it's time for new rulership to come to pass.

But why now? Why did Lady Fate punish Bambalina when she tried to speak it into existence before? What changed? Was the moment wrong? Did I have to know my place? What is the difference?

It's not until I look around at the shattered bubble and stare at the bloodied faeries and vampires that it's made known that Lady Fate did not speak to me alone. She spoke to everyone gathered in this coronation. She made her presence known because the era of the fae is changing.

Caethes and I stare at each other across the expanse of the ruined bubble. Heirs cannot kill monarchs and monarchs cannot kill heirs. We are at a stalemate. As if we are two kings in check, we hold each other through the silence. But while I cannot kill her, Wisteria can, and I feel the prick in the air as the witch starts to gather magic into her.

Suddenly, the Unseelie Queen funnels the very last of her gathered chaos and *shoves*. The chaos hits me square in the chest and as the breath is knocked out of me, I go flying back, crashing into Wisteria.

The two of us tumble across the bloodied floor and I scramble to my feet, eager to return the attack. Before I can, Wisteria grasps my arm and tugs me away as Cariad and Tegwyn carry Caethes on the flow of their movements.

"You will *never* take my throne," Caethes growls through the growing distance. The rest of her guards and Unseelie courtiers surround her and immediately depart to the Roads.

Caethes retreats as she always does, knowing when to flee and forgo her pride. She is many things, but she is not an idiot. She came here to cause mayhem and mayhem ensued. My death would have been a bonus, but I realize that was not her goal. It was to cause pain.

I survey the room and as Enydd decapitates the final vampire with her urumi. The body falls to the floor while his head rolls in the opposite direction. Bleddyn is sobbing over Drysi's corpse. Emrys has Gideon in a chokehold, yet he isn't even looking at my former lover, he's watching me.

I stare across the floor at the body of the faerie who gave me life. Of the female I never got to know. My heart cracks and my eyes glaze, everything surrounding us turning to fog and mist. The grief Bleddyn portrays is a mirror of my own.

I tear my gaze and thoughts from the weeping, casting over to Emrys and Gideon. As if summoned, Maelona appears, bloodied, beside them.

"What would you like me to do with him, My Queen?" Emrys inquires.

I step towards them, pick up my crown and place it once again on my head, looking at the fear that fills Gideon's eyes. I glance around at those still living.

"Take him to the council chamber. Maelona, you are in charge in our absence."

Emrys drags him through the double doors and I follow, the heavy, oak doors slamming behind me.

The great table in the center is a flat replica of the throne, the three trunks twisting, gold magic writhing through the center of it. The chandelier above is a bare tree, hanging upside down, tiny fae lights replacing what would be leaves. A rug is Seelie emerald, matching the tapestries embroidered with the court crest and profiles of Aneira.

I turn away from Aneira's likeness and find my attention trained on Emrys and Gideon, still locked together. My husband's ringed hand wraps Gideon's throat, applying enough pressure to threaten force, but not enough to cut off his airway.

"Evelyn, please don't let him kill me," Gideon begs and the horrible terror in his voice has me off kilter. I do not show it, but Emrys feels it.

I cock my head to the side. "So, does that mean you'd prefer it if *I* killed you?"

"No," Gideon chokes. "I just want to help my dad."

My heart pangs for him. What wouldn't I do to get Aneira back? What I wouldn't sacrifice to save Corvina? What

I wouldn't give to have more time with Drysi? What I wouldn't trade to meet Rhodes?

Gideon is many things; a betrayer and a liar among two of them, but he is a devoted son and I can admire that. I do not have to forgive him for what he did to me, nor for the things he said, or how he commanded me, but I can understand the motivation behind it all. If Caethes is the only one that can give him the treatment his father needs, I'm not sure I wouldn't hurt anyone that stood in the way of that either.

I incline my chin. "What did Caethes originally offer that made you do all this?"

Gideon's face turns pleading, but I stay concrete.

"She said she could restore his health and extend his life if I helped her take down the Seelie Court and eliminate you in the process."

I sigh. "Gideon, we could offer the same thing. It's called vampirism. You should know that better than anyone else."

"No. I vetoed that. It was something else."

"There *is* nothing else. Fairwalker witches are restricted to new injuries and aside from that, anything neurological is nearly impossible to begin with." I remember Gideon telling me his father had a stroke several Christmas Eve's ago. "I'm sorry, but—"

"*No.* She said there was something else." There's denial in his voice. Desperate hope. He knows what I'm saying is true but he can't help but hinge everything on the chance. "She said she had the power to make it happen."

I roll my lips between my teeth and glance at Emrys. "Put him down, love."

Emrys does and pushes him away, coming to stand beside me. He caresses my jaw and gazes down on me. "You're all right, wife?"

I clasp his hand over my cheek, my fragile mental state quivering. "I am okay for now, husband."

I once again face Gideon.

"There is only one other option I can think of, but I doubt it can be done."

That desperate light in Gideon's eyes brightens and he charges me, reaching for my hand. "*Tell me*. I'll do anything."

Emrys protectively shoves Gideon and he launches back, erasing the distance between him and the table as he crashes, spine first, onto it. The crack is hair-raisingly loud, but I see the fissure running through one of the trunks and am reassured it wasn't Gideon's back.

As soon as the crack in the table appears, golden light spills into it, filling it like the Japanese art of *Kintsugi*—golden repair.

With a groan, Gideon pushes himself up onto his elbows and stares across at us, painfully lounging. He sends Emrys a vicious glare and me one of desperation. "I just can't lose him. His situation is getting worse, Evelyn. And if he's gone, Caethes has nothing to keep me in line."

An idea strikes me, a plan unravelling in my mind and I feel Emrys's presence as he tracks my mental progress. He follows the plan and I can feel his pleased surprise rise. I come to a conclusion and smile.

"If you agree to be a double agent for us—if you agree to sell Caethes's secrets and plans—we can arrange something."

"Can you promise that?"

"I can promise you that I will do everything in my power to make it happen but that is no oath that it *will* happen." I cross the space between us and halt before his legs hanging over the edge. "You must understand that this alone is me going out on a limb and trusting you. I have no assurances that your word is law, and all you've shown of *your* word is that your lies are breath."

Gideon's eyes widen. "That's my place in The Game."

"I heard half of the lullaby before. Your role was easy to guess."

Gideon's face flushes with shame and embarrassment. Glancing to the side I watch his jaw work, briefly reminded of thoughts I'd once had about that jawline. Intrusive thoughts about once touching it, kissing it, other things. I banish them immediately, feeling Emrys retreat from my thoughts, not having seen the mental images, but sensing them nonetheless.

"How can you be sure I'm not lying when I inform you?"

"I can't, but the Unseelie Court has Seelie spies just as the Seelie Court has Unseelie spies. I suggest you tread carefully. We will set you up with a contact and you are only to relay information to that person. The only exceptions will be myself or Emrys."

"Not Maelona?"

"She's too visible. It will be someone else.

"Now go. Repair what you can of this clusterfuck and make Caethes trust you again. Fuck her brains out if you have to, but I don't want to hear about it."

That color darkens on Gideon's cheeks as he slips off the table, standing directly before me, at my eye level. I'd forgotten we're the same height.

"Why are you even doing this? I have commands over you that I can still use."

I grit my jaw, staring at him. "Because Lady Fate has deemed you a place on my side of the board. You are doing atrocious deeds for acts of love. I cannot shame you because I would do worse. But if you ever attempt to control me again, I will ensure you live to regret it."

"I'm sor—"

I hold up a hand. "I do not want to hear apologies. They will ring false even if you mean them. So, for now, save those hollow words and replace them with actions."

Gideon hesitates, eyes flickering over my shoulder to Emrys.

"Was everything fake?"

I shake my head. "It was all real, but so much of it was hidden from me."

Gideon nods, his black hair swinging with the motion. "I'll hear from you soon?"

"Soon," I confirm.

"Thank you for trusting me."

"I am giving you the benefit of the doubt. Don't make me regret it or I'll string your organs about the court like garland."

He blanches but quirks a wry smile. "No threatening to cut my tongue or fingers this time?"

"Don't tempt me."

Gideon crosses the room with a backwards look, hand on the door when Emrys calls.

"If you double-cross us," Emrys begins, voice low and lethal. "I will kill you if Vanna doesn't first. I don't care whatever lay between you two once—you hurt her again and you are *dead*."

Gideon's face goes blank in a crafted façade, but he swallows. "Understood."

The door creaks as Gideon leaves and I deflate against the table's edge, Emrys cupping my face.

"I trust your judgement and I see the plan, but do you worry too much is being left to chance?"

"I wouldn't trust my judgement if I were you," I laugh dryly. "Leaving this in Gideon's hands is probably very stupid, but Lady Fate has deemed him one of our pieces in this Game of Crowns and Thrones."

"And Lady Fate? You really think you can summon her again?"

I bite my lip. "I don't know. But I did it once. It's not impossible to do it again."

Emrys is silent and then I feel my soulmate's love envelop me as he leans down, wrapping his arms about my waist, and presses a kiss against my lips.

"I know you're not okay and if you need to take this moment to break, you can. I will be here to put you back together."

His words unlock something and suddenly my emotions shatter against my soul and I sob. I turn boneless against him. I let out great tearing sobs that wrench my heart from its cage, feeling the sad battered thing fall on the floor. Every loss hits me, the memory of so many lives taken, so much love stolen, so much agony I've endured. I don't know how I remain standing.

Tears cascade down my face, cutting hot salty lines through the blood that freckles me. My eyes burn from holding them back for so long. They soak into Emrys's ornate black jacket as he strokes my hair and I cry harder.

"I'm ruining your coat."

Emrys laughs in astonishment. "Love, my coat was ruined before a couple tears landed on it. Do not worry about it, let your grief out and let me help you carry it."

The tears and sobs return in earnest, eventually turning into hiccups and soft whimpers.

Some time passes and the emotional distress fades. As I pull away from Emrys, blotting my cheeks, tears finished but redness betraying their presence, a knock sounds at the door.

Emrys and I both narrow our eyes, picking up on a fae signature with a hint of *other*. We both call to enter.

Enydd steps through the door, bloody urumi coiled about her waist, scarlet flecking her face and a rough homespun cloak hanging on her shoulders. She inclines her head and clasps her hands before she opens her mouth.

"We should speak."

CHAPTER 43

The three of us take seats around the table that Gideon cracked, Emrys and I sitting side by side, holding hands in unity. Enydd is on the opposite side, hands splayed over the golden lines.

There are so many emotions churning through the bond; nostalgia, uncertainty, curiosity, among other things, though we do not show our former mentor any of it.

"How are you here?" Emrys queries, point blank. "All these years we thought Osian killed you."

Enydd barks a short, sharp laugh. "He very nearly did. I languished in that realm, waiting for death. But it never came for me and no one else did either. I was on that floor for years, half dead, the realm not letting me go, until Lady Fate approached me." Her eyes flicker between us. "She knew what I had done for the two of you, the part I played in your union and reunion. She informed me of the bargain you struck and her sister's interference."

"Why tell you?" I press.

"Because she is Lady Fate and she not only told me of the deal, but of your fates. Of the fates that were derailed by one choice she did not anticipate."

My fingers tighten on my husband's, apprehension brimming. "You sound cryptic and I do not like it."

Enydd sighs softly, gathering her resolve. "Your fate was never meant to take you to the Yukon, Evelyn. That was your sister's destiny."

My heart stops. My breath stops. It all stops.

"What?"

"Lady Chaos interfered again. Jacob Dugal was never onto your identity as the Harbinger. He knew you were the *Ceidwad Cudd* and did not question further than that. His determination was that your sister was the warrior he sought. He thought he could sell her to Caethes with the open bounty she kept on the Harbinger and then force you to buy her back with your *Ceidwad Cudd* secrets.

"He was devious and shady, but he truly intended to take his money and run. But Lady Chaos whispered in his ear that the Harbinger was even closer than he anticipated and this stoked the rage of Lady Karma.

"Lady Karma crashed your plane, Evelyn. All these goddesses had hands directly on your life, vying for the attention and power you brought."

"But why did Lady Fate want Corvina to be the one trapped in the Unseelie Court territory? Why did it have to be either of us?"

Enydd sets a grim smile on her face as she glances down at the table. "Because it was a major play in The Game. Corvina was supposed to be the one to meet Gideon. Corvina was the one meant to fall in love with him. Not you."

My heart races, shame coiling within me. "But why?" I whisper even though a theory begins burning in the back of my mind.

"I think you know why."

"Tell me," I demand, unable to voice it.

"Corvina was Gideon's soulmate and she was meant to be Queen of the Unseelie Court."

Everything in me shatters at the reveal, crystalizing and coming back together. I see everything through a glass, fractures and pieces matching up as I see the new truth for what it is.

Gideon was never mine. He was my sister's. But like two ships passing in the night, they missed their opportunity. They met once upon her deathbed, never having learned what could have been. I feel like the cuckoo that has laid its eggs in another's nest, that I have cuckolded my sister's life, her love, her future.

I swallow. "Was I meant to die then?"

Emrys's grip tightens. "*No,*" he says adamantly.

Enydd shakes her head. "No, you were meant to rule beside Emrys as you are now. Gideon was meant to be Corvina's consort as the Unseelie Court is less open to the progressive ideals of equal monarchs. His halfling status was also meant to bridge the gap between the Vampire Court and Fae Courts."

"But that future is gone," I deadpan.

"That future is gone," Enydd echoes.

I roll my lips between my teeth, eyes skyward as I process this influx of fate.

"What did you trade the goddess for this information?" Emrys interrupts my reverie. His eyes are trained upon our former mentor. "How were you released from your oaths?"

"The oaths to Osian lifted with his death. Those that bound me to the realm were lifted by Lady Fate when I pledged my allegiance to her, swearing I would do everything in my power to see the end of The Game through."

Emrys narrows his eyes. "So, you became a piece."

"I became the final piece in the board. I am your last pawn and I am destined to fall."

"So, no matter what we do, you die?"

"That is what I traded to be freed from that pocket realm. You have already lost three of your Pawns and your Queen, but that does not mean the rest of them are doomed."

The reality hits me like a train. "Corvina was the Queen."

Royals are found and lost,
She is true, his lies are breath
Corvina and Gideon were in the same fucking line.
Fucking soulmates.

He is our King piece. We lose him and it is all over. But how? None of that makes any sense. Shouldn't Emrys be our King piece? If not him, then at least me? Gideon's life or death should not be the one to signify the end of The Game.

But of course, he was meant to be Corvina's consort. He was meant to take on the Unseelie Court with him at her side.

Suddenly, I grieve the future that could have been.

My twin. Her and I would have been queens. For the first time we would have united the courts, forced them to play nice. And we would have had our soulmates at our side as we did so. It would have been a revolution for the ages.

Tears, that I thought I wasn't capable of any longer fall down my face. It awakens the scent of blood in the air and it feels like my mouth is full of pennies.

"She was," Enydd confirms despite not needing to. "This prophecy was never meant for you. It was for her."

It makes sense now. Why I wasn't meant to learn the lullaby. Lady Fate was angry, furious even. Her plans were ruined with the death of my twin. I was the usurper that suddenly had to fill the place. Because, while I am a Bishop on the board, I am also now the inheritor of the Unseelie Court. I am fated to be queen two times over.

How can that be? How can I possibly possess two crowns at once?

The nails of my free hand dig into my blood-stained thigh and I use the pain to focus on my breathing.

It doesn't matter whatever fancy fucking title we slap on ourselves; of Bishop, Queen, King, none of it. We're all fucking pawns in this cosmic game fought by petulant and recalcitrant goddesses, sniping at each other. One upping. Like we're just fucking *things*. Fucking *objects*.

"After I made the trade to enter the board, that realm became abandoned. There will never be any more Centurions. You two are the last."

The blow lands on us, heavy. It takes a moment for the impact to absorb, but it does and despite the revelation settling, I am still rattled. I think I need a year to wrap my head around it all.

"What about the Dark Court's lullaby?" I ask abruptly.

Enydd shakes her head. "You'll have to interrogate an Unseelie, whoever was here tonight heard the Dark Court's verse."

"Lady Fate did not give you a hint?"

"No, and then once she finished them her sisters took the lullabies and set the wheels of the Game into motion. It has been hundreds of years since the reign of the queens has changed."

"Does that mean Lady Karma is our champion?"

"No," Enydd says, her voice full of weight and depth. "Lady Karma chose Aneira. Lady Fate chose you and Corvina." Enydd pauses, taking in my reaction. It is one close to paralyzing. "You now play a precarious role on the board, you have become the most valuable piece and due to that amusement, she has championed you. But do not think it means you are safe. She is a goddess after all. She allowed Arawn to be reborn."

"Do you know why he didn't reveal me as the Harbinger before tonight? He's been in contact with Caethes for weeks and clearly she didn't know."

"It was a stipulation of his resurrection. Your goddess-given identity could not be revealed until she deemed it so." Enydd shrugs. "It all has to do with her own timing."

Right. Because it's just a game to them.

Like fucking mice in a maze.

"So how does all this end? When Caethes dies? Or when the next Unseelie monarch takes the crown?"

"Are the two not synonymous?" Enydd raises a brow.

"No, because Caethes could abdicate."

Enydd tosses her head on a dark laugh. "You and I both know she will never do that. We'll be prying the crown from her cold, dead hands."

"It's unlikely that will be me," I grumble. "I can't kill her." Fucking heir and monarch laws.

"You have a husband and other trusted companions that can surely deliver that blow."

"I don't want to risk them getting that close to her."

"Have you asked? I'm certain your witch-friend seeks revenge. Surely, she'd do it. Or Lady Maelona? She has a grudge to bear against the queen. What about all those human warriors you've been training? The Crows?" Enydd tsks. "You are not the only ones who despise the Dark Queen."

Enydd inhales, shutters her eyes and then exhales slowly. "I will give you time to mull this over. I know I have delivered very heavy news tonight. We will speak more on the morrow."

"We appreciate that, thank you," Emrys announces, a slight regal lilt to his words. "It's good to see you again, Enydd."

I echo the sentiment, voice somewhat distant.

Enydd gets to her feet, her eyes holding the weight of Atlas. "It *is* good to see you two, well and together. You achieved more than I could've ever dreamed of and I am proud to have been your mentor."

With that Enydd departs and Emrys and I are once again left in the council chamber.

EPILOGUE

The throne room is utter despair. Blood paints the gold in garish streaks and stains the earthen floor with shades of maroon. Bodies litter the floor despite servants and guards removing them. They're carried into the same courtyard we'd held Aneira's funeral and the memory knocks against my heart. Emrys is at my side, internally reassuring me as we move through the masses.

Maelona and Wisteria are near the dais, directing individuals to specific duties. The warrior princess is nonchalantly checking the witch's vitals while the witch herself weaves spells to scour the blood from the walls.

"Vampires to the left, the sun will reach them first and will take care of their corpses for us," Maelona calls over the din. "Separate the Seelies to the furthest right and then keep Unseelies to the left-middle. I want identifications and roles immediately."

"You command them well," I say.

Maelona's eyes reach me and there is drive in them. "You gave me a duty, My Queen."

"Please don't call me that," I whisper, cringing. "I'll always be Ev to you."

Maelona smiles. "I'll do it only to piss you off, then."

"That sounds more like it."

Maelona gives me a glowing smile and I'm hit with it like a blow to the chest. I hadn't realized how much I was worrying about my new status effecting our friendship, but it seems the Lady has taken it all in stride. I resolve to find her a role where her intelligence and power are acknowledged to their full potential.

Wisteria interrupts suddenly, still casting, "So, you can't kill the Unseelie Queen, huh? That's unfortunate."

"Ever the perceptive one."

Wisteria smiles. "Does that mean I get to do it?" A dark look crosses her teak eyes. "I want her to pay for Elliot."

The tone of her voice is so low and calm, but utterly lethal. She still casts while she holds my eyes and I can't imagine how horribly drained she must be. Is rage keeping her on her feet? Is the possibility of being the one to kill Caethes keeping her afloat?

"You'll get your revenge," I answer, careful to skirt any definitive words. "Have you seen Julia?"

"She's tending to the wounded."

Emrys and I make our way over to the makeshift infirmary, utilizing an empty council room. The actual infirmary is too far away for the amount that require help and all hands are on deck.

Moans and cries of the wounded reach our ears before we even cross the threshold of the council room. Upon blankets are injured fae and humans, some missing limbs, some writhing from withdrawal symptoms of vampire saliva, others clutching gashes or punctures. White bandages are turning crimson and hands reach for us as we pass. We give soft words of reassurance and thanks, touching hands and holding them.

We find Julia quickly and call her over. She looks up, surprise in her peculiar gold-blue eyes but hurries over. Her black bodysuit is slashed in places and she walks with a limp but appears to be in surprisingly high spirits all things considered.

"What can I do for you, Your Majesties?" Julia inquires surveying us as she pulls her long dark hair into a messy bun.

"That's going to take some getting used to," Emrys mutters in my ear.

I don't disagree.

"We need to speak to you about something very sensitive," I tell her lowly.

Her eyes flare but she nods and we lead her to the council chamber we'd recently vacated after our meetings with Gideon and Enydd. The door closes with a squeal of hinges and Julia's eyes dance warily.

"What is this about?"

"We need you to be a contact for a spy in the Unseelie Court," I tell her carefully.

"Why me? And who to?"

"Because you can operate unseen, you are human and they will dismiss you. And you can lie. We also trust you." I hesitate before continuing. "You'll be receiving intel from Gideon."

Her brows shoot into her hairline. "Gideon? Like, your ex, Gideon? The guy who literally just fought for the opposite side tonight and can command you against your will?"

"I do not expect you to understand my motivations, but yes."

"You're right, I don't understand. But I did hear the prophecy like every other ally of the Seelie Court tonight. Are you saying he's one of our pieces?"

"Yes," I say, point-bank. "And so are you."

"I am?" she asks, excitement and surprise mingling in her voice. "What am I?"

"You are a Knight."

"That's so fucking cool."

I raise a brow. "You're excited an infinite goddess has chosen you to be one of her toys?"

Julia shrugs. "It means I have a purpose. That I'm important and whatever I'm doing is what the universe was hoping for. What more commendation could I ask for?"

"I'm glad you see it that way."

"Is that all you need from me?"

"Yes," Emrys responds. "We will bring you more information such as meeting points and times when we receive it. Thank you for all you've done for the court."

Julia dips, almost like a curtsey and then slips out the door, leaving us one again alone in this chamber with the glowing table.

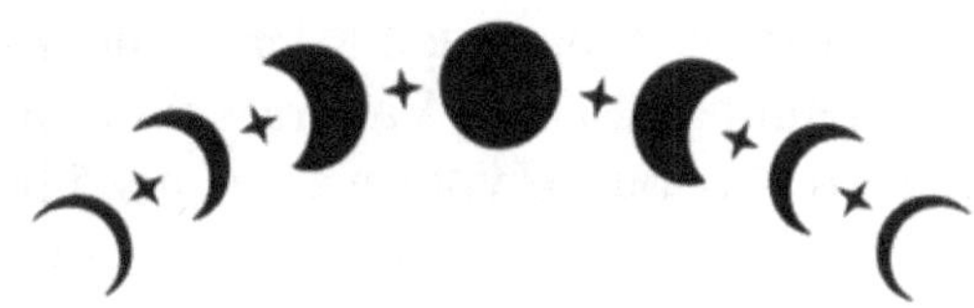

There's an adjoining door from the council chamber to a balcony that overlooks the field the Seelie Court sits in the middle of. Emrys and I both take to this balcony together, letting the cool night air wash over us.

I breathe in deeply, scenting pine and wet earth on the wind. Beside me, I catch the notes of vetiver, leather, and lemon mixed with the coppery smell of blood.

The railing is wrought in gold and waist high. We're upon one of the few balconies imbedded into the hill the court resides in, this one rising on an outcropping. There are towers and suites and wings that protrude out of the earth like a titan's reaching fingers, each one spearing towards the starry sky. Most of the Seelie Court is underground, but some—like my chambers—reside on the surface with a convenient ladder of ivy leading towards the stained glass panes of my windows.

It's been hours since the battle, hours still where our people clean the mess we brought on. After Julia left, we were inundated with meetings after meetings, edicts to sort out, directives to sign. Funeral arrangements.

Bleddyn had been one of our meeting seekers. He'd come to us, shrouded in grief and my unspoken theories were confirmed. He was involved with Drysi, and now he has lost her. He twists his hands before him, his ruby wings drooping with devastation.

"Your Majesty—" he began but I stopped him with a raised hand.

"Just Evelyn, please. You've known me too long to call me that." That and I could not bear the honorifics.

"Evelyn. If it isn't too much to presume, I'd like to be involved in the planning of Drysi Vanora's funeral. I'll do all I can to help and I'll stay out of your way, if need be. I just—"

"Consider it done," I told him, tears pricking my eyes. "I think she would appreciate knowing you wanted to do this with me."

He nodded, his ebony waves hanging about his face. "Thank you, Evelyn."

He'd left with that, and I was left with a hole in my heart. Right where the love for my mother had begun to grow. Now, it is a blackened crater and the only balm is time.

The court is eerily silent. Like the calm after a storm, only this storm is the beginning of our reign. The beginning of our rule was rung in by so much bloodshed and loss. So much *needless* loss. So much of this war has been a battle of paper on wills and arguments and semantics. Now it has become all too real and the gravity of the situation strikes me like a cudgel to the chest.

I stand beside Emrys, taking in our court and the diamond-studded sky as the carnage behind us sinks its hooks into history. This was the first battle of the Gwyndolyn-Vanora reign and it won't be the last.

Emrys takes my hand in his, pressing me flush to his chest so we are heart to heart, hips to hips. We are both covered in blood but neither of us acknowledge it. We both wear crowns but neither of those matter. What matters is this male holding me in his embrace, his fierce golden eyes locked onto mine.

"I feel like my world is falling apart," I admit to him, sensing the question through the bond. "I feel cheated out of my life and choices. We're all just tools for goddesses."

"We still have free will, love. And despite it all, with the other goddesses interfering, you and I still made it back to each other. No one, not even Fate, Chaos, or Karma can stand between us and I think it's because we chose each other."

I laugh softly. "Don't you mean Lady Fate chose us?"

"No, I think we're able to reject it if we want to." Emrys reaches down and cups my chin in his beringed hand. "You are my best friend, Vanna. You are truly my other half and I knew it even before we learned we were soulmates. Even when I hated you, I felt like half of my very existence was missing. I love you to the very ends of the earth and beyond every star in the sky. Nothing—and I truly mean nothing—will keep me from you. Not even death."

My eyes water as stars begin winking out around us but I nod. "And the crown will not change how you feel about me?"

"If you had wanted me to forsake the crown I would have. If you wanted me to abdicate right now, I would. Just say the word."

"We've just invoked so much violence. Our reign—"

"Our coronation is not the fault of all this death. That was Caethes's manipulations."

"And I cannot even kill her in return because I am her heir." The silent question follows about our possible relation and Emrys's silent answer is an *I don't know*.

"Not you specifically, but I can. And we can adopt her means or turn to our allies," he answers my spoken words.

"That is not a fair call to make," I argue softly, emotions surging.

"Wisteria seems all too willing. We are the king and queen now, Vanna. We have to make the hard choices." He brushes my hair behind my ear, tucking the loose locks, wiping some stippled blood. "It's not too late. You know I choose you over anything—anyone—else."

Shaking my head, I clutch him tightly. "We have a duty to this court, to the people. We have to see this through—Lady Fate and all."

"We will see it through, then. And I will remain at your side."

Emrys dips down, his lips descending on mine and I meet him halfway, parting my lips. Our mouths touch and a soft sigh slips from me and he returns with a rumbling growl. Our mouths slide over each other, tasting and pressing. I pull his lower lip between my teeth and gently suck the plushness of it. One of his hands fists at the back of my ruined gold gown, the other tangling in at the nape of my neck. I hold him just as fiercely, a hand burrowing between the layers of finery to find his chest, the other tangled at his crown, pulling him down. Tongues slip and dance and despite the tang of blood, all I can taste is Emrys. My husband. My soulmate. Lemon and vetiver and leather.

I pull from him. "I love you."

"I love you, too," he whispers against my mouth. "And we will make Caethes rue the day she ever chose to make enemies of us."

"You swear?"

"I swear," he promises, sealing it with a kiss upon my hand.

And so, we enter the first dawn of our rule—the Gwyndolyn-Vanora reign marked by a bloody sunrise and the remnants of its first battle with the carnage of goddess-chosen royals playing The Game of Crowns, Thrones, and Fate.

THE
END

PRONUNCIATION GUIDE

CHARACTERS

Evelyn: EVAH-LINN
Gideon: GID-EE-UN
Maelona: MAE-LOW-NA
Aneira: AH-NAY-YA
Caethes: KI-THES
Violante: VEE-OH-LAN-TAY
Enydd: EN-NED
Urian: YUR-EE-AN
Desmond: DES-MON
Cariad: CARE-EE-AD

Emrys: EM-RISS
Tegwyn: TEGG-WIN
Tadhg: TAIG
Róisín: RO-SHEEN
Arawn: AIR-RAWN
Osian: OH-SHAN
Cothi: COTH-EE
Una: OONA
Reagan: RAY-GAN
Carrick: CARE-RICK

OTHER

Ceidwad Cudd: KAI-YD-WAH COO
Aberth: AH-BEH-TH

ACKNOWLEDGEMENTS

These Ruined Dreams was the fastest book I've ever written, but painful to edit. There are moments in this book that I've been desperate to write for years and I'm beyond thrilled for them to exist now and that I'm sharing them with you. This is possibly my favorite book I've written so far.

Thank you, again, to my husband, Michael. You have been there for me every step of the way, through every breakdown and hiccup. I couldn't ask for a better partner in this life and I love you so much.

Thank you to Rebecca F. Kenney, for going over some rough chapters for me. Your advice really made me kill my darlings, but it was very much needed.

(2025 ADDITION: To Bookish Averil, THANK YOU. You all cannot tell me you're not obsessed with Emrys on the cover. She knocked it out of the park. Thank you always and forever.)

To my writers group (Karissa, Maddie, Julie, KP, Sydney, Jae, and Selbe), thank you times one million. I feel so honored to have been able to join this amazing, supportive group and I am grateful every day for our absolutely insane conversations, especially when our trigger word is spoken. You guys have been there for me throughout the ups and downs of this pregnancy, the hurdles of this book, and the absolute gong show my life has turned into these past few weeks. I love you all.

Ali, thank you for the incessant roasting of edits, especially the first draft of chapter six—that thing was a dumpster fire. Thank you for all the Emrys thirst and your hilarious comments. I swear I'll do better when it comes to stained glass.

Thank you to everyone who showed an interest in my little fae trilogy, shared any posts, or liked my terrible TikToks.

And finally, thank YOU Lovely Reader, for picking up this book. I hope you stick around for the next one and find out how Evelyn's story ends...for now.

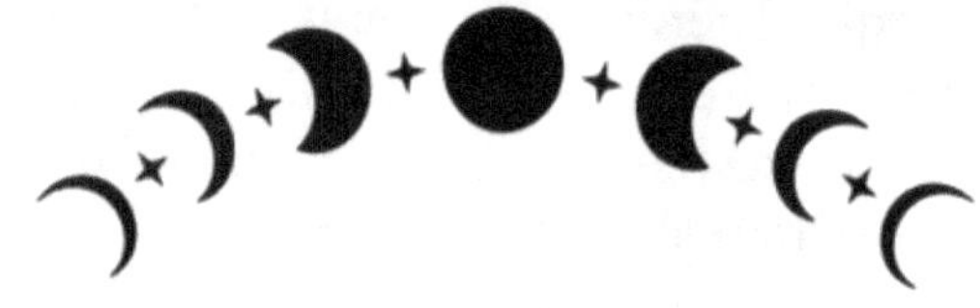

ABOUT THE AUTHOR

Kayla McGrath has been writing since the age of thirteen out of spite, having read a book with a love triangle that didn't go her way. After that, it became a passion. If she's not writing, then she's reading, or drinking endless cups of chai. Kayla lives on Vancouver Island with her husband, daughter, and two boxers.

These Ruined Dreams is her second book.

You can find her on TikTok (@kaylamcgrath_), and on Instagram (@kaylamcgrathbooks).

OTHER BOOKS BY KAYLA MCGRATH

COLD AS IRON
This Broken Memory
These Ruined Dreams
Our Shattered Fates

A DEATHLESS EMPIRE
A Deathless Empire
AUQ {Coming 2026!}

INFERNAL CURSES
The Nightmare Curse
The Hallow Curse

LOVE AND OTHER TROPES
Love & Other Tropes (Emmett & Illiana)
Romance Thy Enemy (Mina & Graham)
JTW (Nate & Sloane) {Coming 2026!}

www.ingramcontent.com/pod-product-compliance
Lightning Source LLC
Chambersburg PA
CBHW061544190726

48289CB00004B/1157